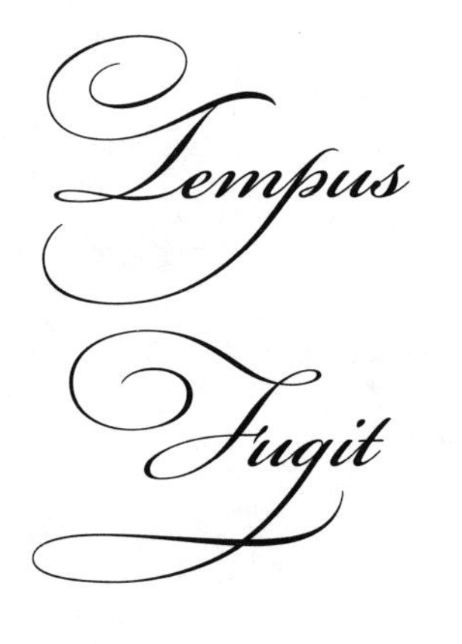
Tempus
Fugit

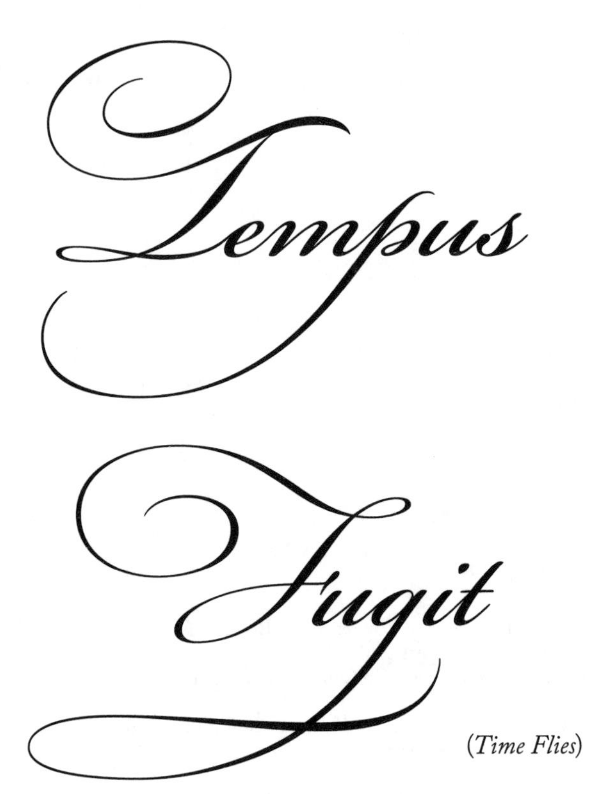

(*Time Flies*)

A Novel

Lawrence Lee Rowe Jr.

Tempus Fugit may be purchased at reduced rates for educational or promotional use. For information, e-mail: llrowejr@lawrencerowe.com.

First Edition published in 2005 by Lawrence Lee Rowe Jr.

Cover painted by Sandra Clay, www.sandraclay@sbcglobal.com.

Book design by Cox-King Multimedia, www.ckmm.com.

ISBN 0-9767668-0-9

Library of Congress Control Number: 2005906553

01 02 03 04 05 06 07 08 09 10 11 12 13 14 15 16 17 18 19 20 21 22 23 24 25

For my mother, Janeth N. Rowe.

~

And our founders, for a *Constitution* and government
that is the greatest gift ever bequeathed to a people.

Acknowledgements

FOR HELPING ME at various times and in myriad ways, I would like to thank:

Cody Kramer.

The Newmans. Bob. Meredith. Stacey. Kelly. Jenny. Peggy. Andrew.

The Lennons. Bill. Mrs L. Mike. Joe. Bob. Emily.

Steve Romslo. Paul Romslo. Paul Kubesh. Kyle Snyker. Duane Gray. Lisa Romslo. Gina Romslo. Mrs. Kubesh.

Toby Moleski and his family.

Bryan Gahan. Paul Armstrong. Eric Seifferlein. Craig Blomker. Sean Kolodge. Hans Johannes. Rob Busby. Brad Rickert. Jason Mack. Jon Brandt. Matt Vaupel. Michael Martin. Dan Sinnott. Dustin Kolodge. Dave Brandt. Tim Taylor. Scott Doyle. Keith Bierd. Daryn Oxe. Steve Hartsock. Ian McKay. Chad Northington. Craig Pelletier. Rick Leslie.

Ross Waterfield. Chris Lovering. Tuckie.

Jerry Beeney. Brian Malek. The Schmidt brothers.

Keri Bachelder. Michelle Sterret.

Stephanie Williams. Catherine Rinaldo.

Kevin Giroux. Billy Clark. Rocco Levo.

Terry Cockream. Rudge Wynn. Keith Hawkins.

Lou Beard.

Josh Folcik.

D. Smith for meticulous copyediting, Sandra Clay for a fine cover, and Charles King for a superb layout. Staff members at Mount Vernon, Monticello, The Franklin Institute, University of Virginia, and the Library of Congress. Their help was invaluable, though this acknowledgement should not be construed as their endorsement of this work.

I haven't kept track of those who helped me as much as I should. My apologies. Any omissions are a slip of the mind, not the heart.

Benjamin Franklin (1706–1790) Printer, Writer, Scientist, Inventor, Clerk for the Pennsylvania Assembly (1736–51), Member of Pennsylvania Assembly (1751–76), Penned and published *Poor Richard's Almanack* (1751–64), Performed famous kite experiment that proved the electrical nature of lightning (1752), Deputy Postmaster General to the American Colonies (1753–74), Pennsylvania Minister to Britain (1757–62), American Minister to Britain (1764–75), Pennsylvania Delegate to the Continental Congress (1775–76), United States Minister Plenipotentiary to France (1776–85), President of the Executive Council of Philadelphia (1785–88), Pennsylvania Delegate to the Constitutional Convention (1787).

~

George Washington (1732–1799) Surveyor, Farmer, Virginia Militia Officer and British Aide-De-Camp (1753–58), Member of Virginia House of Burgesses (1758–74), Virginia Delegate to the Continental Congress (1774–75), Commander in Chief of the Continental Armies (1775–83), President of the Constitutional Convention (1787), First President of the United States (1789–97).

~

Thomas Jefferson (1743–1826) Farmer, Lawyer, Member of Virginia House of Burgesses (1769–74), Virginia Delegate to the Continental Congress (1775–76), Drafted *The Declaration of Independence* (1776), Member of Virginia House of Delegates (1776–79), Governor of Virginia (1779–81), Virginia Delegate to the Continental Congress (1783–84), United States Ambassador to France (1784–89), First Secretary of State of the United States (1789–93), Founded Democratic-Republican Party (1793), Second Vice President of the United States (1797–1801), Third President of the United States (1801–09), Founded the University of Virginia (1825).

The preservation of the sacred fire of liberty, and the destiny of the republican model of government, are justly considered as deeply, perhaps as finally staked, on the experiment entrusted to the hands of the American people.

George Washington

A republic, if you can keep it.

Benjamin Franklin

I tremble for my country when I reflect that God is just.

Thomas Jefferson

George Washington peered at Ben Franklin and paled. "By Providence! Ben!" His brow scrunched in disbelief. "Ben?"

"In the flesh," Franklin said.

Thinking he must be a ghost or mirage, Washington poked Franklin, who chuckled as he backed up to escape the prods. "I said in the flesh."

Washington grew paler. "You died seven years ago!"

"That's good to know."

"Unflappable as ever."

Franklin smiled. "Even in death."

Washington thought of Franklin's protracted expiration, and frowned at the ignorant sarcasm. "My hair stood, then there was a flash."

"A blue flash," Franklin said. "And here we are?"

Washington surveyed the surrounding forest. "Where is 'here'?"

Franklin shrugged. "You look older."

"Seven years older?" Washington asked.

Franklin smiled again. "Perceptive question."

Spruce shadows cloaked Thomas Jefferson, obscuring his facial features as he entered the clearing. "George? Ben? Is that you?"

"Yea," Washington and Franklin said in unison.

"But how, for Providence's sake? How could you both be alive?"

"I was about to ask Ben the same ques—" As Jefferson stepped into the light, Washington's reply died and he froze.

"You're an old man!" Franklin gasped.

Jefferson smiled wistfully. "Yes I am."

Franklin was as intrigued as he was surprised. He was born in 1706, Washington in 1732, and Jefferson in 1743. The Thomas Jefferson he knew was thirty-seven years his junior, and middle-aged.

"There was a bluish-green flash, and th—" Jefferson saw the recognition on his friends' faces and left the thought unfinished. "I may be older, but you've both been dead for decades!"

"I don't remember dying," Franklin said.

"Nor I," Washington replied.

Shock saturated all three founders as they faced the supernatural implications of their situation.

"I must be ripe for Bedlam[1]!" Jefferson said. Mental degradation had always frightened him more than physical, and he was gripped by fear as he thought of his retarded younger sister Elizabeth, his daughter's suicidal husband Thomas Randolph, and his delusional Vice President, Aaron Burr.

"If you are ripe, then I am rotten," Franklin replied. "Though I think both situations improbable. I have never heard of a case of collective lunacy. Let us meet crisis with calm and consider mundane, rational explanations first."

Jefferson chuckled nervously. "This situation seems to offer little that is mundane or rational."

"True. True." Washington peered at Franklin suspiciously. "When did we first meet?"

"1755. Braddock's French & Indian War campaign."

"Our first correspondence?"

"1756. About a post route between Winchester and Philadelphia."

"My first action when I arrived in Philadelphia for the Constitutional Convention?"

Franklin smiled. "You called on me. We had not met in over a decade, since 1776, and you wished to renew our friendship."

"You hosted a dinner for the Convention delegates. What spirits were served?"

"A cask of porter an English friend had sent."

"It was marginal, as I recall."

"Nay. The company agreed unanimously that it was the best porter they had ever tasted." Franklin chuckled. "I feel like I'm in the Cockpit again."

Washington ignored the quip. "The Weissenstein letter?"

"A Crown attempt to subvert our revolution by offering titles and lifetime pensions to America's leaders."

"My pension amount?"

"The monetary amounts next to our names were left blank. Presumably, we were to determine the price of our principles and return the letter."

"My title?"

"If you abandoned the American cause, you were to be immediately made a British Lieutenant General."

---

1 Ripe for Bedlam. Insane. The Priory of St. Mary of Bethlehem, or The Bethlehem Royal Hospital, was the first insane asylum in England. Bedlem or Bedlam were short slang abbreviations for Bethlehem, and came to be used as a generic descriptor for all insane asylums.

"My observation when we spoke of it privately years later?"

"Irony. You noted that one of your childhood dreams was a British Generalship, but you never imagined it would be offered in such a contemptible manner."

Washington nodded. "Who was Charles de Weissenstein?"

"A pseudonym. His letter arrived anonymously at my doorstep in June 1778. French magistrates never determined his identity, but certain phrasing mannerisms led me to believe the letter was drawn by King George himself. Is the inquisition complete, George? Do you believe I am myself yet? Or shall you construct a rack and make inquiries at your leisure?"

As Washington smiled at Franklin's characteristic wit, his last remnants of suspicion drained away. He repeated the process with Jefferson, who also answered all questions accurately. "Neither of you wishes to question me?" he concluded.

"Your appearance, knowledge, and characteristic caution are proof enough," Jefferson said.

"Which aristocrat's daughter was the first wench I seduced?" Franklin replied. "Where did I attend grammar school? What General inspired my second ballad? When did we encounter Mrs. Silence Dogood?"

While Washington rolled his eyes, Jefferson chuckled. Franklin's early encounters were with low women, he had been too poor to afford a grammar school, the poem he published at age twelve was about Blackbeard the Pirate, and Mrs. Silence Dogood was his first nom de plume.

Washington endured a few more of Franklin's sarcastic questions, but eventually rebelled. "Are we in heaven?" he interjected.

"If we don't remember dying, heaven seems an illogical assumption," Franklin replied.

"You assume a person would remember their passing," Washington said.

"I will adhere to that assumption until I am fortunate enough to converse with someone dead."

"Perhaps you're doing so right now," Washington suggested.

" 'Perhaps' isn't proof."

"True," Jefferson conceded. "But how else could you both be alive?"

"If we haven't died yet, the mere act of existing isn't as impressive as you make it sound."

"Easily spoken, Ben," Jefferson replied. "You didn't see me die."

Franklin wanted to ask about his "death," but knew the issue was secondary for the moment.

"If this isn't heaven we are vulnerable," Washington said.

"I am unarmed," Jefferson replied.

"I feel safer already," Franklin joked.

"Ben's wit won't save us if savages are nearby." As Washington scrutinized the surrounding forest, his underbite jutted and his jaw set itself in a rigid line.

To colonials in uncharted wilderness, savages were the paramount concern. Every revolutionary-era American knew of their atrocities: They butchered pregnant women, brained children, and defiled corpses with their infamous scalping.

All three founders had associated with savages in peaceful settings, but only Washington had faced them in combat. Savage prowess in warfare was unforgettable, and even now, decades later, his memories were still vivid. Animalesque war whoops that pierced a soldier's heart as easily as the air. Savages sprinting effortlessly through the woods, ducking trees and other obstacles without slowing, as if they were forest appendages rather than men. Throats cut in a blink, chest cavities hatcheted like firewood, oftentimes without savages breaking stride.

Washington reviewed this mental collage in an instant, and then shook his head fractionally. "No sword, no musket, no pistol, not even a bodkin."

With the trained eye of a naturalist, Jefferson noted the sparsely spaced spruce trees that surrounded them. None of Virginia's dense hardwoods could be seen. "These are not the forests of our country[2]. Or the East."

Washington nodded agreement. "Where are we then?"

Jefferson shielded his eyes with his hand and peered at the sky. "The sun is further east and brighter than it was at Monticello. For me, morning has instantaneously become afternoon."

"I need not hazard sidereal estimates," Franklin replied. "My Philadelphia night is now day."

"Unless my latitude has changed, the spring I left is now fall," Washington said. "Though we have greater worries than the climate. The blue flashes we all seem to have experienced may attract savages. We must depart this region."

"Could other acquaintances be arriving?" Franklin asked. "Should we wait for them?"

"We will search as we leave," Washington answered. "But we must leave. Now."

Franklin and Jefferson obeyed without question. Military matters were Washington's purview.

"We must be wary of ambuscades of Indians," Franklin said. "From constant practice, they are dextrous in laying and executing them."

---

2 Country. Virginia. Country was a term some colonials used to denote their home state.

"St. Clair," Jefferson whispered.

"Doctor St. Clair?" Franklin asked. "The physician?"

Washington nodded. "Though he'll always be General St. Clair to me. During my Presidency I appointed him commander of an expedition that established a road and chain of military posts through the Northwest Territory. I cautioned him to be wary, but 900 of his 1400 men were nonetheless decimated in a pre-dawn savage ambuscade."

"Your Presidency." Franklin smiled.

"St. Clair's rout was the worst America ever suffered to savages," Jefferson added.

Washington nodded again. "The loss of life was vexing enough, but Congress' formal inquiry exacerbated the fiasco. I have given ambuscade warnings to every officer under my command in the wilderness, and shall now heed my own advice. Stay together. We all have questions, but no talking. Point if you spot an attacker. And remain vigilant. An instant of distraction could cost us our lives."

"Wouldn't want to die twice," Franklin said.

Or assume savages might be peaceful, Jefferson thought. *As they were to my father, and me as a child, and Meriwether and William*[3].

As they crept toward the forest, and the unknown, the founders' thoughts became uniform. Unarmed, in garb that made them stand out like redcoats, they would be fodder for aggressive heathens if any were nearby. Franklin was sedentary, Jefferson an old man, and Washington was no match for even a small scouting party.

Yet Franklin and Jefferson were comforted by Washington's presence. They knew he would face even the direst situations with steadfast valor, and the certain knowledge he was immune to fear helped them quell theirs.

Washington paused momentarily at the clearing edge and gave his civilian compatriots a severe look. "If combat ensues, expect no mercy. Warring savages have nothing human about them except the shape."

THE FOUNDERS WALKED a short distance in silence, then exited a break in the woods. A mountain sculpture containing four enormous faces was visible in the distance.

"That's you!" Franklin gasped, while Washington and Jefferson gaped at their granite reflections. "Both of you! Even a purblind old fool like me can see sculptures that big!"

---

3 Meriwether and William. Meriwether Lewis and William Clark, leaders of the famous transcontinental expedition.

Neither man responded.

The hilltop remained silent and still, save the shrill whistling of the wind.

Eventually Washington looked back and forth between Jefferson and his sculpture. Jefferson did the same to Washington. Neither man acknowledged the other's glances.

After the comparisons concluded, the silence persisted. Washington and Jefferson remained transfixed by the mountain mirror.

Franklin's exclusion enabled him to juxtapose both faces with their sculptures, but this was a small consolation. He realized he was probably viewing a monument, and though he felt stung by the slight of omission, he was too benevolent to feel resentment or envy toward men of Washington and Jefferson's caliber in anything but twinges.

His interest in the sculptures waned before his companions' did, but Franklin did not speak. Doing so seemed sacrilegious. Washington or Jefferson should break the silence.

Franklin watched his two friends. He wondered what they were thinking, what they would say. He wondered what he would have thought or said, and strangely, had no idea.

As the wind abated, Jefferson turned his head, faced Washington, waited for him to make eye contact, and in an unusually soft voice said, "We are now Sphinxes."

You've always been a Sphinx, Washington thought.

The two men savored a moment and a bond that required no enunciation, and was beyond words even if it did.

Like all leaders, the founders wanted to be remembered. For they knew that history forgets men, even great ones. Bloated by the inexorable accumulation of events, it distills, then prunes, and finally amputates. Jesus, Buddha. Socrates, Confucius. Alexander, Caesar. Out of the myriad annals of antiquity, only a handful of names had survived and remained in the collective human psyche. Looking at their sculptures, Jefferson and Washington realized they were a part of this junto, and would stand as an almost permanent part of history. Long after their identities and accomplishments were forgotten, their visages would endure.

"More than I might have hoped," Washington said.

Jefferson nodded. "Yea. Much more. We are as close to being immortal as any human can ask to be."

"Congratulations!" Franklin said. His smile was honest, his joy for his friends sincere.

Jefferson thanked Franklin and put a consoling hand on his shoulder. "You should also be sculpted."

Franklin's grin broadened, and he waved a hand dismissively.

"I suspect the answer to this question," Washington said to Jefferson. "But I must still ask it. Were these sculptures begun during your lifetime? After our deaths?"

"Sculpting a mountain? The America I left could not create such a wonder. Not with ten-thousand slaves or a hundred Houdons[4]."

"I didn't think so." As Washington scanned the forest behind them, he seemed more nervous than before.

"Who are the other two sculptures?" Franklin asked.

Silence again.

"Where are we?" Washington asked.

Yet another silence, the longest yet. And a chilling, ghastly calm. Even the air seemed still.

Franklin peered at Washington and Jefferson simultaneously, then said, "*When* are we?"

Washington's close-mouthed exhalation was more of a grunt. As his nods accelerated, his eyes grew distant.

"We can't be. It can't be. This just can't be!" Jefferson's denials were a subconscious acclimatization mechanism, and he didn't seem to believe them. "This is a prank. A dream. A metaphor? Perhaps a hallucination?"

"Are you ripe for Bedlam now?" Franklin asked.

Washington chuckled. Jefferson and Franklin joined him, but the levity was fleeting. Nervous glances were soon exchanged. The severity of their predicament became apparent, and as realization seeped into them, memories pierced the founders, flooding their psyches. Memories they hadn't known were memories until this moment.

Jefferson saw Monticello, his daughter Martha and his grandchildren. Franklin pictured Madam Helvetius, his late-life love, who he'd left in Paris and always dreamt of seeing again; also his house in Philadelphia, his large circle of scholar friends, and his flock of grandchildren. Washington thought of his wife Martha and Mount Vernon.

The nostalgic trance lasted but a moment, and was followed by fanciful denials that were more heartfelt than Jefferson's.

No one gave them voice.

"The people and homes we loved are probably gone," Jefferson said.

Washington nodded. "All gone."

"What else is gone?" Franklin asked.

---

4 Houdon. Jean-Antoine Houdon. The most renowned sculptor of the colonial era. He sculpted Washington, Jefferson and Franklin, and other icons including Catherine the Great, Frederick the Great and Voltaire.

Yet another silence.

A despondent silence.

A consuming silence.

The founders realized there were more optimistic potentials, but the symmetry inherent in the Sphinx metaphor was alluring. Not desirable, but alluring. The Sphinx had outlived Egypt. Had this mountain sculpture outlived the United States?

Contemplation of the American death was sobering. Franklin, Washington, and Jefferson had hoped their creation might endure, ushering in a transcendent Renaissance that would spread freedom, enlightenment and prosperity across the globe. Had a golden age come at all? Come and gone?

The silence expanded, and might have become an engulfing chasm, had it not been interrupted by a child's gleeful shriek.

"HEY UP THERE!" The voice was squeaky and prepubescent, but unmistakably male. "You guys! Hey!"

The founders glanced down the hill they stood atop, and saw a child jumping up and down waving his arms. Two adults stood behind him, but their reactions could not be gauged.

"Shall we treat?" Franklin asked.

Washington nodded.

"Hey up there!" the child said again.

"Hey down there!" Franklin responded.

This was all the encouragement the boy needed. Immune to the grade of the hill, he sprinted toward his quarry.

"The father appears unarmed," Washington said.

"Appears," Franklin replied.

Washington smiled. His painful dentures made the gesture seem forced and unnatural.

"Look at his garments!" Jefferson whispered.

"I've never seen anything like them!" Franklin gasped.

"Great costumes!" the boy said, as he barreled up and skidded to a stop. "Man oh man. What realistic . . . costumes!" His lungs heaved and he spoke in gasps. "They don't look . . . bran freakin' . . . new like . . . those cheesy ones . . . you always see . . . in parades." He spat, then peered up at Washington, whose towering physical presence commanded his attention first.

Standing 6'3" tall, fit and straight-backed even in old age, Washington had the natural grace of an athlete and a magnetic stature. He exuded strength. Washington was thick-boned, with unusually long arms and legs, monstrous hands, and a rugged frame that rippled with muscle. His face seemed engineered for anger; a pugnacious, mountain of a nose rose from the center of its landmass, pockmarks and sunlines formed valleys, and his hairline receded appreciably atop the continental shelf. Washington's underbite was pronounced, his pursed lips suggested impatience or irritation, and his jaw and lower cheeks seemed puffy, almost swollen. But as most everyone who met him observed, his most striking feature was his eyes. Pitiless blue orbs that measured men and events harshly, without emotion. They were the eyes of a predator.

The boy gaped while he looked back and forth between Washington and Rushmore. "You look just like him!" he gasped.

The founders exchanged guarded smiles while the child repeated the process with Jefferson. "Man!" he said with awe. "Man oh man! You look just like Jefferson, too! Except maybe older. Man, what great costumes!"

The parents seemed accustomed to their son's hyperactivity, and didn't hurry to catch up. "I can see why Washington, Jefferson, and Lincoln are on the mountain," the husband said, as they approached. "But why include Roosevelt?"

The founders were familiar with the Roosevelt and Lincoln names; American sugar magnate Isaac Roosevelt had donated huge sums to the revolutionary cause, Major General Benjamin Lincoln was one of Washington's more esteemed officers, and Levi Lincoln was Jefferson's attorney general during his Presidency.

"Who would you replace Roosevelt with?" the wife asked. "And if you say Nixon again, I swear to God I'll scream."

The founders also knew the Nixon name. Brigadier General John Nixon was a hero of the American victory at Bunker Hill.

The parents quieted as they neared the founders. Greetings were exchanged. Like their son, they noticed Washington first, compared him to the mountain, and then focused on Jefferson.

At 6'2", Jefferson was only an inch shorter than the muscled Washington, but lankiness of body and face made him seem slighter. His large hands, gangly limbs, and jutting neck conveyed awkwardness. Though still good-postured, he had bent slightly with age, and his stature seemed more aristocratic than athletic. His serene face was angular; its most prominent features were a long, thin nose that was decidedly large and triangular when viewed from the side, and freckles that confettied his pale skin. Jefferson's introspective, almost feminine lips conveyed kindness and mirth with subtlety, and his bushy eyebrows stood ready to accentuate expressions of skepticism or scorn. His unusually fine hair had once been red, but was now gray, and he still wore it longer so that it covered his ears and neck. Wistful, engaging hazel eyes hinted at enormous intensity, complexity, and intelligence.

"The resemblance is uncanny!" the father said, as he stared at Jefferson and the mountain. He seemed unnerved.

While the family examined the founders, the founders examined them. The father was a frizzy-froed intellectual whose plain-jane wife was unusually thin. He looked the stereotypical professor, she the librarian. Both parents seemed intelligent, and the trait appeared to have been magnified in their curious son, who had his mother's body and his father's hair.

"You're Ben Franklin," the boy said to Ben Franklin.

This was hardly a stupefying deduction. Franklin was wearing his famous undersized spectacles, tricorne[5], knee-length coat, knickers, stockings, and square-buckled shoes. "I'm me," he said.

"We've been reading about you guys in history class."

History class. The founders were careful to keep neutral expressions.

"Can I see your bifocals?" They contained four glass half-circles, and their archaic appearance intrigued the child.

"I'm sorry," Franklin said. "I need them to see."

"I won't break them."

But if you did, I would be right diddled. "I'm sorry. But I can't see *anything* without my spectacles."

"The kite experiment was cool!" the boy said.

Franklin smiled. "The electric fluid is fascinating. I was never before engaged in any study that so totally engrossed my attention and my time. Though I am chagrined we have been unable to produce anything of use to mankin—"

The father smiled at Franklin's puzzled expression. It seemed so genuine! Perhaps the peculiar modus operandi had been selected to achieve greater suspension of disbelief; rather than having actors give speeches on a stage, they would roam the park, and tourists would bump into them matter-of-factly, like normal people.

"Did you really touch the kite key with your finger?" the boy asked.

"My knuckle actually," Franklin said. "But yea."

"Yay? You mean yes?"

"Yea. Yes."

"And the key shocked you?"

Franklin nodded quickly. "I felt the electric fire."

"Weren't you afraid of getting electrocuted?"

"No."

This fearlessness was the result of ignorance, not bravery, but the boy didn't know this, and was impressed. He smiled at Franklin with admiration, and

5 Tricorne. A triangular colonial hat.

examined him as he had Washington and Jefferson.

The 5'10" Franklin was an amorphous man whose physique hinted at long-abandoned fitness. His gut was a globe, his fingers and calves pudgy, and his breech-stretching buttocks resembled ham halves. Drapes of chin fat hunched above his shirt collar. Franklin's enormous, elongated cranium was a fitting capstone to his body. His large eyes seemed sad and docile even though he was not, and in general, his facial expressions and body language revealed little. As was his habit, Franklin pursed his lips somewhat peculiarly, creating an expression that hinted at amusement and seemed to perpetually foreshadow a smile. His flat-ridged nose and stubborn, somewhat-pointy chin were also prominent. Unlike Washington and Jefferson, who conveyed a sense of greatness and looked the part so to speak, Franklin was physically uninspiring.

"Where's Lincoln?" the father asked. "And Roosevelt?"

Good question, Franklin thought, as he glanced at the mountain. *Very good question. And which is Lincoln? The fellow with the mustache or the beard? The mustached seems to vaguely resemble Isaac.* "I think Lincoln had too many ales last night. He is frequently tardy."

"And Roosevelt?"

"We do not know where he is," Jefferson said. *Or who he is.*

"Why are you here?" the mother asked. "Do you work for the park?"

Another excellent question. Franklin glanced at the sculptures again. *Another very excellent question. Why are we here?*

"Yes," Washington replied. "We work for the park."

"Did you ever tell a lie?" the boy asked.

"Yes."

"How many?"

"Not many."

"Give me an example," the boy said.

"I must graciously decline your offer."

"You won't get mad if I ask something personal, will you?"

"No."

"You aren't lying, are you?"

"No," Washington growled.

"Just checking." The child extended his palms outward and backed up. Once he was sure Washington wasn't angry, he said, "Why is your face scarred?"

"Smallpox. When I was nineteen, I went to Barbados with my brother Lawrence, where I contracted the disease. He had tuberculosis and the warm climate was viewed as beneficial."

"What's smallpox?" the boy asked. "Is it like chicken pox?"

Washington, Franklin and Jefferson resisted the urge to exchange a glance. Smallpox was the colonial world's most feared disease; its epidemics had killed and maimed millions, and every member of their civilization knew what it was.

"Smallpox is like fowl pox," Franklin said to the boy. "Except it can kill you."

Washington nodded grimly as he remembered the three agonizing weeks he had spent in bed recovering from the disease. He had barely survived.

The child seemed disinterested. To him, like most moderners, smallpox was an irrelevant abstraction. "What about that scar on your left cheek. That wasn't caused by pox, was it?"

Washington shook his head. "An incision was made to treat an abscessed tooth."

The boy's jaw dropped. "They cut you open like *that* just to get at a tooth?"

Washington nodded nonchalantly.

"That scar looks so real," the husband whispered. "I could see how they found an actor with severe acne or pockmarks. But a knife scar too?"

The wife nodded. "He could be wearing make-up. That might also explain why his complexion is so sallow and his cheeks seem sunken."

"So would cirrhosis from daily drinking binges with Lincoln and Franklin."

"Paintings of you don't show the scars," the child said.

"Artists can be sycophants," Washington replied.

Franklin rolled his eyes. "And sometimes their subjects don't mind a little flattery. My moles were rarely painted."

The child stared overtly, the parents discreetly. With a clinical manner, Franklin pointed out the moles on his left cheek and lower lip.

"Why aren't you wearing a military uniform?" the child asked Washington.

"I resigned my commission long ago. I'm a planter now, not a General or President." Washington smiled serenely.

Jefferson noted that Washington was wearing one of the dark suits he preferred as President, and for formal occasions. Unlike many colonials, he did not wear a dress wig, but his hair was powdered. When had he come from?

"Do you have a musket or a sword?" the boy asked.

"No," Washington replied. "Unfortunately."

"Maybe they sell them at the gift shop."

"Hopefully." Washington made momentary eye contact with Jefferson and Franklin. "And thank you, lad."

"You're welcome. Say, who do you guys think was the greatest President?"

"Do we have to pick one of the Presidents on the mountain?" Franklin asked.

"No," the boy said. "You can pick any of them. Except Nixon or Clinton."

The founders also knew the Clinton name. There were several colonial Clintons, the most famous being George Clinton, Brigadier General during the revolution and Vice President under Jefferson.

"Why are Nixon and Clinton excluded?" Franklin asked.

"'Cause they're like the worst Presidents we've ever had. Duh. Even my parents agree about that."

"Maybe not the worst Presidents," the mother said.

"Top five for sure," the father replied.

"Clinton wasn't that bad."

"He was only the third President ever impeached."

"Starr's investigation was a charade!"

"If Clinton had a sense of decency he would have resigned and spared the nation the mudslinging."

The parents continued their conversation and the founders listened. During a brief moment when no one was watching them, they exchanged another look of amazement.

"I want to know what the founding fathers think!" the boy whined.

The parents quieted.

"Well," the boy said. "Who was the best President?"

"Washington," Jefferson replied.

"Jefferson," Washington answered, somewhat dourly.

"And you?" the boy asked Franklin.

Franklin feigned deliberation, then said, "Lincoln."

"Lincoln's my Dad's choice too."

"He did win the Civil War and reunify the union," the father said.

"Don't you mean reunionfy?" Franklin asked.

While the parents laughed, the founders once again exchanged concerned glances. *A Civil War? Reunify the union?*

"Why'd you choose Lincoln?" the father asked Franklin.

"The same reasons you did. Besides, Washington and Jefferson aren't as great as everyone thinks."

"I agree about Jefferson," the wife said. "He was too much of a hypocrite to be considered one of the greatest Presidents."

Jefferson bristled ever so slightly.

"Thomas Jefferson belongs on Rushmore," the father said. "I agree about the moral flaws, but don't forget *The Declaration of Independence*, Lewis and Clark expedition, and Loui—"

"I know what he did." The wife spoke more softly, so her son wouldn't hear. "And who."

Jefferson prided himself on his enormous self control, and rightly so. To the family, he seemed only mildly annoyed, but Washington and Franklin realized the subtle tenseness of his posture indicated a high degree of agitation.

"So Clinton was maligned unfairly," the husband said. "But Jefferson is too much of a hypocrite to be considered a great President?"

The wife rolled her eyes. The husband laughed.

Maria Cosway? Franklin wondered. Cosway was the beguiling but tragic painter Jefferson fell in love with while American Minister to France. Franklin knew of no one else embarrassing. Jefferson was hardly a libertine[6].

But Cosway didn't fit. Though she was married, Jefferson was single, and they had been in France, where adultery and whoring were as ubiquitous as wine. Even if one made the optimistic assumption that the chaste Jefferson rogered Cosway, this was hardly a ruinous scandal. Unless morals had grown much more rigid.

While his parents resumed their conversation with what seemed like typical vigor, the boy approached Jefferson. "Would you sign *The Declaration of Independence* for me?" He produced a copy and unrolled it ceremoniously.

Jefferson examined the tiny reproduction and smiled. *The Declaration* had survived! He felt triumphant, and wanted to show excitement, but did not. "Do you have a quill?" he asked.

The father handed him a pen, and Jefferson held it gingerly. He dabbed his fingertip, but no ink flowed.

"You have to click it," the boy said.

Jefferson handed the pen to the child, who clicked the top and handed it back. Jefferson mimicked him, and clicked the pen several times while observing it. *Pounce*[7] *must be obsolete,* he thought.

An instant before drawing, Jefferson paused. When he'd first signed *The Declaration of Independence*, exuberance was tempered by fear, for the document was a royal death warrant as well as a proclamation of freedom. Now, as he drew a new signature next to his old, as he recalled the prolific patriots whose autographs surrounded his and pondered his current situation, exuberance was once again tempered by fear.

"Wow!" the child said. His eyes bulged. "Your signature looks just like the real one!" He showed the parchment to his parents, who agreed and smiled at each other. These actors were a regular Cirque Du Soleil, all right!

"Shall I sign *The Declaration*?" Franklin asked.

---

6 Libertine. A person who leads an unrestrained, sexually immoral life.

7 Pounce. A fine powder formerly used to prevent ink from spreading and to prepare parchment to take writing.

"Who wants Ben Franklin's signature?" the boy replied. "Maybe if I had a kite or something."

"I helped draw *The Declaration.*"

"So what? Jefferson did all the real work. Everybody knows that. Franklin and Adams just proofread. They were like secretaries. Would you sign *The Declaration*, Mr. Washington?"

Mister. Not General or Your Excellency. How peculiar. "I never signed originally, lad."

The boy checked *The Declaration*. "Why not?"

"I was already commanding the Continental armies."

"Did you sign *The Constitution*?"

"Yes."

"He chaired the Constitutional Convention," Franklin said.

"Geez," the boy said. "They put you in charge of everything."

Washington nodded somewhat glumly.

"Well I've got *The Constitution*, too. You can all sign that."

"I did not sign *The Constitution*," Jefferson replied. "I was in France serving as American Minister when it was drafted."

"I will only sign if Franklin may," Washington said.

The child accepted Washington's deal. As it had Jefferson, a peculiar déjà vu affected the cosigners. Especially Franklin.

Though the child was once again awed by the likeness of the signatures, he favored *The Declaration of Independence*. "Can you read it for me?" he asked Jefferson.

"I don't need the parchment, lad. I could never forget the words." Jefferson smiled as his eyes grew distant. "When in the course of human events, it becomes necessary for one people to dissolve the political bands which have connected them with another . . ."

The parents stood behind their child. The founding fathers were in their foreground, Mount Rushmore the back.

"And to assume among the powers of the Earth, the separate and equal station to which the laws of nature and of nature's God entitle them . . ."

They boy followed along in his text.

"A decent respect to the opinions of mankind requires that they should declare the causes which impel them to the separation."

Jefferson's voice was unusually soft and quiet, and though he accentuated certain syllables and paused to allow a dramatic moment of reflection between each clause, his was hardly a roaring oratory.

It didn't have to be. The words themselves were rousing enough. Especially the preeminent and most immortal portion of the preamble, which resonated like a thunderclap, causing everyone but the child to tingle:

"We hold these truths to be self-evident, that all men are created equal, that they are endowed by their creator with inherent and inalienable rights, that am—"

"Wait a sec," the child interrupted. "This says certain unalienable rights."

"Sorry. I made many revisions. As did Congress." This last comment was acidic, but Jefferson remained pleasant, and smiled at the boy. "And I'm getting old."

"Too bad Lincoln's not here," the father whispered to the mother. "I'd love to see him recite the Gettysburg Address."

"We hold these truths to be self-evident," Jefferson said. "That all men are created equal, that they are endowed by their creator with certain unalienable rights, that among these are Life, Liberty, and the Pursuit of Happiness."

"What about your slaves?" the boy asked. "Were they created equal too?"

"Of course not. Nature, habit and opinion have drawn indelible lines of distinction between the two races."

"Why don't we talk about something else," the mother said.

"Yes," Jefferson replied. "Why don't we."

Jefferson didn't seem fun anymore, so the child returned to Washington. "Did you really chop down the cherry tree?"

"Yes. A few, in my lifetime." The relevance was not clear to Washington, and his expression reflected this confusion.

"Are your teeth wood?"

"Nay. I've never heard of such a thing. Why would anyone wear wooden teeth?"

"Nay? You mean no? But they're fake, right?"

"Yes. But made of hippopotamus ivory, not wood."

"Can you take them out?"

"I can, but I won't. Doing so causes me discomfort." *And makes me look feeble.*

"Unlike my students, they've done their homework," the father whispered. "Give them that much."

"What was Valley Forge like?" the child asked.

Washington's eyes grew somewhat vacant, and he stared past the boy into space. "Every idea you can form of our distresses will fall short of the reality."

The child asked other questions about the debacle, but Washington would say nothing more.

"Why don't I ask you a question?" Franklin said.

"Yeah!" the boy replied. "Heck yeah!"

"May I have that pamphlet?"

"Sure." He handed it over and Franklin thanked him. "Is that the only question you have?"

"Could you tell me the time and date?"

The child peered at his digital watch. "September 5th. 2:37 PM. Don't you have any cool questions?"

Franklin laughed. *What is the year?* "Who's your favorite President?"

The boy was suddenly sheepish. Franklin guessed the reason, and leaned in close. "You can tell me," he whispered.

"Man you stink!" the boy gasped. "All three of you. I couldn't say that in front of my mom cause she'd ball me out for being rude, but man oh man! When was the last time you guys took a shower?"

Franklin laughed hard. "I apologize for my malignance, and promise to shougher tonight, if possible. Your favorite President?"

"I don't wanna hurt anybody's feelings." The child looked at Washington with obvious fear. "Or make him mad."

Franklin winked at the parents as he and the boy walked several yards away. "I won't say a word."

"I used to think Washington or Jefferson were my favorite Presidents. But Washington's kind of boring and mean, and Jefferson seems racist."

Franklin laughed. "There's always Lincoln."

"Maybe Washington and Jefferson aren't as great as everyone thinks."

"They are not perfect, lad. No one is. But Washington and Jefferson are actually greater than everyone thinks."

"Are you sure?"

"Yes. I am sure of few things, but this is one of them."

The boy still seemed skeptical. "Are they greater than you?"

"Yes. Though that isn't difficult."

"Are you sure of that too?"

"Yes."

"Why weren't you ever President?"

Franklin smiled. "I was lucky."

"Are you kidding?"

"No."

"People want to be President. Don't they?"

"Not the ones that should be."

"Did Washington want to be President?"

"No. Most definitely not. Neither did Jefferson." As Franklin pressed the pamphlet into his jacket's interior pocket, his facial expression shifted slightly.

"What's in your pocket?"

"Your pamphlet."

"What else?"

"Washington's wooden teeth."

"How stupid do I look?"

"I know I could never deceive a lad as cunning as you. That's why I was completely honest."

The child was unconvinced, and continued to press. Franklin continued to tease, until the parents decided it was time to leave. Goodbyes were said and the family walked off, leaving unrealized remnants of their past alone in the present.

Two

Washington demanded silence until they returned to the safety and seclusion of the forest. As soon as he lifted the excommunication, Jefferson said, "We are in the future!"

"But when?" Franklin replied. "I wish the child had revealed the year."

"Speak softly!" Washington said. "We must not attract other strangers."

"The future," Jefferson whispered. "The future! It's good just to utter it. To accept it."

"Or try to anyway," Franklin said.

"Stating it explicitly is sobering," Washington agreed.

"How were we transported?" Jefferson wondered. "Is such travel common in this era, or is our situation unique? And are we marooned, or can we somehow return home to the present?"

"If time transport was common, the family wouldn't have assumed us actors," Washington said.

Franklin reached inside his jacket. He removed the pamphlet and a thick stack of money. "These may provide clues."

"Were those notes on your person when you arrived?" Washington asked.

"I believe so. I didn't discov—" Franklin froze when he saw his portrait, and handed each man a note[8].

"You don't seem shocked," Jefferson said.

"After the mountain?" Franklin shrugged. "Perhaps we should examine the pamphlet first. It intrigues me more."

"More than notes with your portrait?" Washington said.

"Notes won't tell us what to do next."

Washington thought of the eerie, handless watch that glowed like a firefly. "We should pocket them, then. Copious notes could provoke a theft."

Awash in mental imagery of criminals wielding futuristic weapons, Jefferson and Franklin complied.

The pamphlet was soaked with Franklin's sweat. It was unopened, but headings on the back said:

---

8 Note. Paper money.

Mount Rushmore National Memorial	National Park Service
South Dakota	U.S. Department of the Interior

"Dakota savages[9]?" Washington asked.

Jefferson nodded. "I lived to see America make peace with them. In 1815. We planned to cede them an enormous tract west of the Northwest Territory. It was already being called the Dakota Territory."

"An American monument on Dakota land?" Franklin said.

"Probably not," Jefferson replied. "We must have acquired it—through further negotiation, I hope. The region may have been split into a North Dakota the savages kept, and a South Dakota America owns. Or maybe we finally acquired Canada."

"Another item for our burgeoning research list," Franklin said.

"What of this Interior Department?" Washington asked.

"During my Presidency and lifetime there were still only four Federal Departments," Jefferson answered. "Foreign Affairs, Treasury, Post Office and War."

"Your Presidency." Franklin smiled. "A trivial little detail you might have mentioned forthwith."

"I was the third President," Jefferson said. "From 1801 to 1809. And sorry."

Franklin's eyes twinkled with amusement. "Did you know Tom had served when you told the boy he was your favorite President?" he asked Washington.

"Did you know who Lincoln was?" Washington replied.

Both men smiled.

"To me, the term 'interior' connotes internal civic improvements," Franklin said. "And the nomenclature seems to designate this National Park Service as a subdivision of said Department. Could there also be a National Road Service? A National Library Service? A National School Service?"

"Don't you mean *State* Road Services?" Jefferson corrected. "*State* Library Services? *State* School Services?"

"Am I to infer opposition to a National Church Service?"

Jefferson chuckled. "You're still a clever old rascal."

"And you're still the most devout Christian I know."

Jefferson shook his head.

Franklin laughed. "Logic and historical precedents like Rome make a modest expansion of government seem plausible. A mature republic would

9 Dakota savages. The Sioux Indian tribe.

allocate resources for public works. This would account for a Department of the Interior."

"For authority to apply the surplus of taxes to objects of improvement, an amendment of *The Constitution* would have been necessary," Jefferson noted.

"Yes," Franklin agreed. "Obviously. All powers assumed must be enumerated. It will be interesting to examine *The Constit*—you look worried, Tom."

Jefferson glared at Washington, but said nothing.

Franklin opened the pamphlet and examined it holistically with his trained printer's eye. "The paper is exceptionally high quality. And the images . . . *totally* real . . . Michelangelo and Da Vinci could work in tandem and not match them . . . they can't be paintings . . . actual scenes must have been captured somehow."

"An improved camera obscura[10] was being developed after you two died," Jefferson said.

"A camera obscura!" Franklin tapped his forehead with his hand. "Of course! A camera obscura containing a plate or parchment smeared with Schulze's salts[11] or some other light sensitive substances?"

Jefferson nodded.

"I should have deduced that."

"You just did. And inventive prognostication is difficult. Even for a natural philosopher[12]."

Franklin grunted, then resumed his browsing and read snippets of the pamphlet's most significant passages. " 'A Shrine in the Black Hills . . . Rushmore was no less than the formal rendering of the philosophy of our government into granite on a mountain peak.' Interesting, but we need dates. 'The preservation of the sacred fire of liberty, and the destiny of the republican model of govern—' "

"An excerpt from my first inaugural address," Washington said.

" 'We hold these truths to be self-evident . . .' Yes, yes, an excerpt from Tom's *Declaration*. Ah, here we are! This Lincoln . . ." Franklin held the pamphlet up, squinted, then frowned. "Is smeared."

"How can you sweat so much?" Washington asked. "We only hiked a few rods[13]."

---

10 Camera obscura. Latin. Camera, chamber. Obscura, dark. Camera obscuras were essentially modern cameras without film. They existed since antiquity, and were used to draw shapes exactly and view eclipses.

11 Schulze's salts. In 1727, the natural philosopher Johann Heinrich Schulze discovered that liquids containing salts such as silver chloride would darken when exposed to light.

12 Natural Philosopher. Scientist.

13 A few rods. A short distance. A rod was a unit of length equal to 5½ yards.

"Roosevelt," Franklin said. " 'We, here in America, hold in our hands the hopes of the world, the fate of the coming years, an—' " A sigh. "The rest of that is smeared too."

"I feel like Tantalus[14]," Jefferson said.

Franklin examined term dates listed below portraits of Rushmore's Presidents. "Lincoln served until 1865, Roosevelt until 1909 . . . The phrase 'Shrine of Democracy' was coined at the 1930 dedication of the Washington head."

"Did you say 'Shrine of Democracy'?" Jefferson asked.

"Yes," Franklin replied.

"Not 'Shrine of Republicanism'."

"No."

This was a significant distinction to the founders. Fearful of hotheaded mobs and tryannical majorities that could wreak havoc in a pure democracy, the delegates at the Constitutional Convention had strived to create a more diluted representative democracy, or republic. Thus the term "republican" was almost always used to denote free self-government in colonial America.

"Has diction merely changed?" Jefferson wondered. "Or have *The Constitution* and government?"

Shrugs. Dry portions of the pamphlet rustled as Franklin flipped it over. A large image showed suspended workers carving the face of Lincoln.

"Are they slaves?" Jefferson asked.

"It is difficult to tell," Franklin replied. "The figures are indistinct, cloaked in shadow, and we can only see their backs."

"It would seem foolish to risk a Houdon when one could simply use slaves," Jefferson said.

Washington and Franklin exchanged a glance, and a more civilized speculation. Their emancipation implication hung ambiguously in the air, but neither man commented.

" 'Dynamite' was used to 'blast' the rock," Franklin read.

"Dynamis is Greek for power," Jefferson said.

"Is dynamight futurity's gunpowder?" Washington wondered.

"A reasonable assumption." Franklin pointed out other advanced tools like an air-powered hammer, read a few more snippets from the construction summary, then focused on a map in a lower sidebar. " 'Mount Rushmore is 25 miles southwest of Rapid City . . .'," he began.

Too far to trek with these two, Washington thought.

---

14 Tantalus. Figure from Greek and Roman mythology condemned to exist near a lake and fruit tree that receded whenever he tried to drink or eat them. His desires were always in sight, but eternally elusive.

" 'And three miles from Keystone . . .' "

Washington felt palpable relief.

" 'Drive carefully on Black Hill roads . . . drivers and passengers must wear seatbelts . . .' "

"Drivers of what?" Jefferson asked.

Franklin shrugged. "Major airlines and bus rou—airlines?" He peered up at the sky. "Airlines?"

Washington and Jefferson also looked up.

"Any relevant new inventions after we died?" Franklin asked Jefferson.

"No."

"Improvements to the balloon?"

Flight was not a totally foreign concept to the founders. In 1783, while American Ambassador to France, Franklin had observed humanity's first manned ascension, a balloon ride over Paris. In 1794, during Washington's Presidency, he and Jefferson watched the first American balloon flight. The French military used anchored balloons to scout and observe battles that same year. Balloons were a colonial craze, and though postulated commercial and military applications stirred imaginations, flight as colonials knew it was a hazardous amusement rather than a harnessed technology.

"Stability and flight duration of balloons was enhanced," Jefferson answered. "But nothing revolutionary."

" 'Major airlines and bus routes serve Rapid City,' " Franklin read. He peered at the map. Rapid City was a large square, Keystone a small blip. "Rapid City is the largest settlement in the vicinity of Rushmore—a logical hub."

Silence as each man immersed himself in thought. Franklin envisioned fleets of balloons guided by tethers, or airlines, but knew this was probably a laughably primitive conception. Balloons were aimlessly roaming slaves of the wind; if used as airborne coaches, they would require an enhancement that counteracted air currents.

Washington and Jefferson encountered problems similar to Franklin's; they sensed they should be envisioning something fantastic, but had no idea what attributes to assign.

"The balloon may have cobbled the way to some discoveries in natural philosophy of which we at present have no conception," Franklin concluded.

Jefferson smiled. Unlike lesser natural philosophers who feigned knowledge, Franklin was humble enough to admit ignorance.

"Are we a thousand years in the future?" Washington asked. "Two?"

"Only a few nations have lasted that long," Jefferson replied. "And though scholars like Madison studied every civilization in history and learned from their mistakes when designing our government, a millennium seems presumptuous."

"How long then?"

Jefferson thought a moment. "I'd guess we're six, maybe seven hundred years in the future."

"Ben?"

Franklin answered immediately, with surprising confidence. "Five hundred years at the absolute most. Maybe centuries less."

Jefferson arched an eyebrow. "Your rationale?"

"My guess, like yours, is rooted in assessments of invention and natural philosophy. Evidence is scant, and we may have erred. But recall Ancient Greece and the Renaissance; when wisdom accrues, it does so in rapid spurts. If the freedoms we enumerated have endured—and the family, pamphlet, notes and mountain suggest they have in some form—then prospering republics may have cultivated a Renaissance spanning several centuries. Invention and natural philosophy may have advanced at a rate beyond our comprehension."

"May have," Washington replied.

"A republic plagued by a Civil War and impeachments may not have prospered consistently," Jefferson countered. "Even if America did, your predictions seem optimistic. Rome prospered for centuries and never developed anything like that boy's watch. Or an airline, whatever it is."

"Natural philosophy was an infant then," Franklin replied. "The Romans hadn't comprehended electric fire or built advances like printing presses which speed the dissemination of knowledge. In our time natural philosophy was building momentum, like an avalanche."

"I've been alive almost four decades since you died," Jefferson said. "Your avalanche hasn't hit yet."

"That doesn't mean it'll take six or seven centuries."

"I disagree," Jefferson replied. "But I'm not going to dispute America's most renowned natural philosopher."

Franklin laughed. "You just did. And rightness is more important than reputation."

"You have the reputation you do because you're often right."

"That's all the past," Franklin said, as he folded up the pamphlet. "In this era, the dimmest child probably understands more about the workings of nature than me. I know little."

"We know little," Washington amended.

"We know it is at least 1930," Jefferson said. "And we know our approximate location. That is a start."

"Speaking of starts, I'd like to know when you both came from."

"Excellent idea, Ben," Washington said. "Chronological order seems logical. After a brief respite, you narrate first."

"My trip was instantaneous," Franklin said. "My hair rose and a tingling I recognize from my electric experiments served as a kind of premonition. A blue flash followed immediately. I closed my eyes to avoid being blinded, and when I opened them, George was staring at me like a specimen."

Washington and Jefferson's experiences were the same as Franklin's. It was quickly determined that all three founders had arrived within seconds of each other.

"I am 81," Franklin said. "For me, it was September 18, 1787."

Washington's eyes catapulted. "The day after the Constitutional Convention?"

"You and I signed *The Constitution* yesterday."

"That was a decade ago for me."

Franklin smiled. "You do look a little older today."

"The Presidency has that effect," Jefferson interjected.

"*The Constitution* was the last politically significant act of your life," Washington said to Franklin. "You died roughly two and half years later."

"Of what?" Franklin asked.

"Starvation," Washington joked.

"I thought it was crapulence[15]," Jefferson added.

Franklin chuckled. "You can't tease a man about his death."

Jefferson outlined Franklin's last few years of crippling pain, which were consumed by his gout[16] and stone[17]. He had taken laudanum to ease his suffering, but was a bed-ridden skeleton when he finally passed.

"It seems I'm destined to lose weight after all," Franklin said with concern.

Washington nodded solemnly.

"Do I still have only two and half years left to live?" Franklin wondered.

"We'll return to that point later," Washington said.

"Just don't take two and half years."

"I am 67 and have just been relieved of the Presidency," Washington said. "It was March 5th, 1797 for me."

"Adams'[18] Presidential Inauguration?" Jefferson replied.

---

15 Crapulence. A hangover.

16 Gout. A disease characterized by painful calcifications in, and inflammation of, the joints.

17 Stone. Kidney stone. A urinary-tract precipitation which can obstruct the body's outflow of urine.

18 Adams. John Adams (1735–1826). Leader of Massachusetts protests against the Stamp Act (1765), Massachusetts Delegate to the Continental Congress (1774–1777), drafter of *The Declaration of Independence* (1776), author of the *Massachusetts Constitution* (1780), co-negotiator of the Treaty of Paris that ended the Revolutionary War (1782–1783), first American Minister to Britain (1785–88), first Vice President of the United States under George Washington (1789–97), and second President of the United States (1797–1801).

Washington nodded. "And yours. Both yesterday, for me."

"Adams was President?" Franklin was concerned rather than surprised. Adams was one of the most prominent revolutionary figures, and his ascension was hardly shocking. But he seemed a poor choice for the Executive.

"I was Vice President under Adams." Jefferson trudged the words, then confirmed Franklin's fears with a glance. "Your Presidency was the last politically significant act of your life," he said to Washington. "You opposed the Kentucky and Virginia Resolutions, and took command of the armies in case war with France broke out, but it never did."

War with France? Franklin thought. He was surprised, though given the historical fickleness of European alliances and their ceaseless conflicts, only mildly. France was America's only ally during its revolution. A decade later the two nations were on the verge of war?

"What are the Kentucky and Virginia Resolutions?" Washington asked.

"Are you jesting?" Jefferson replied.

Washington's blank expression was ample answer.

If you were plucked before Adams turned tyrant, it makes sense. "You don't know what the Alien and Sedition Acts are either, I suppose."

"No."

"They sound ominous," Franklin said. "Almost British."

Jefferson nodded. "George and I disagreed very strongly about these matt—" His expression grew vacant and his eyes darted around without focusing. "This is strange. Very strange."

Foreboding filled Jefferson. And Franklin. Both men were trying to tackle a ghost. Not inundated by time travel concepts like moderners, and forced to contemplate their nuances for the first time under less than leisurely circumstances, they had only a vague sense of the inherent paradoxes.

"My death?" Washington seemed almost disinterested.

"December, 1799," Jefferson replied. "A few weeks before Christmas. A throat ach complicated by swelling. You were bled repeatedly, and died the same day. The entire country mourned an—"

Washington raised a halting hand. "I apologize for interrupting, but extensive details of my passing are not relevant."

"One detail is," Franklin said. "Like me, you have roughly two and a half years to live."

Washington shrugged. "That doesn't help us at the tick."

"You don't find these parallels and paradoxes even a slight bit disturbing?" Franklin asked.

"What if I do?" Washington replied. "I can't change the situation, so it makes little difference."

"I am 82," Jefferson said. "For me, it was March 8th, 1825. The University of Virginia opened its doors yesterday and has been my primary focus."

A University of Virginia did not exist during Franklin or Washington's lifetime, but they had often heard Jefferson talk about founding a college when he retired. "Your creation?" Washington guessed.

"Yes. Though I suspect I didn't accomplish much more either. I wish Madison or Monroe would walk out of the forest and tell me how I died."

"But then we'd need someone to tell them how they died," Franklin said. "It's an infinite quandary."

"For now," Jefferson replied.

Franklin laughed. "There's always the future."

"And history books hopefully," Jefferson said.

"So we've been drawn from three separate times," Washington summarized. "Immediately after our final services to the republic were rendered. What does this suggest to you?"

"If we were taken from a single place or time an argument for chance might be made," Jefferson said. "But this seems more like a deliberate act."

"By whom?" Washington wondered.

Silence.

"Providence?" Washington asked.

More silence.

"The fact that we were taken after making our primary contributions to the republic suggests that whoever or whatever did so had foresight or hindsight as an advantage," Franklin reasoned. "Our old present may be their past."

"Our Puppeteer may be friendly to the American cause," Jefferson speculated. "It might have been easier to transport us when we were in one place together. Or at least paired. But doing so may have removed some of our 'future' contributions from history."

"Could our absence from the revolution have improved America?" Washington asked.

"Irrelevant question," Jefferson said. "It didn't happen."

"Tom's initial observation is the key one," Franklin replied. "We appear to have been assembled on purpose. With purpose. For a purpose."

"What purpose?" Washington asked.

"To show us the future?" Jefferson said. "As either a reward for past service, or to see our reactions? To meet us? To study us?"

"Trifling motivations for such an arduous trip," Washington said.

"Trifling motivations to us," Jefferson countered. "But perhaps not to the posterity of a republic we founded."

"The same may be said of time transport's arduousness," Franklin agreed. "The feat could be trivial to our Puppeteer."

"Do we exist in our own time anymore?" Washington asked.

"One can't duplicate living beings," Jefferson said.

"Before today I would've said one can't just send people to the future either," Franklin replied. "Intuitively, I would say a person moved to a new place doesn't exist in his original location anymore. But natural philosophy isn't always intuitive. Intuitively I'd say time transport isn't possible either."

"Why?" Washington asked.

"The same reasoning I applied to the concept of a person existing in two places at once. We live in an ever-changing present. The past may exist in memories and through the written word, but I don't believe it to be a tangible, physical place. At least, I thought it wasn't."

"If we vanished, our absence would have been noted," Jefferson said. "Especially you two. You were the two most famous men in the world."

"If George and I vanished you would already know," Franklin replied. "Both events would be part of your past."

"True," Jefferson said. His expression grew blank again.

"And even if you somehow managed to remain ignorant, our disappearances would have been an infamous historical mystery—one the family probably would have asked us about."

"A mystery only until a time transport device was invented," Jefferson said. "And hardly infamous if our experience was replicated and became widespread."

"The family probably would have mentioned such a mystery," Franklin replied. "Optimistically assuming they simply forgot to ask, we must still re-confront their assumption that we were actors in costume. This suggests they know nothing of a time transport device and that the phenomenon is not widespread."

"Reasonable suppositions," Jefferson said, "but something has to explain the facts. Or should I say the contradictions? How can I have visited you on your deathbed two years after you were brought here? How could George accept command of the American armies months after he vanished in a blue flash? I *lived* these events."

"Providence," Washington said. "Only Providence has such power."

Franklin and Jefferson preferred technical explanations to the mystical, but knew of no other rational interpretation.

"If I've vanished Martha must be concerned," Washington said.

"My Martha too," Jefferson replied. His wife Martha was long dead, and he was referring to his only living daughter.

"There's nothing to be done about it now," Washington said.

Franklin nodded as he pulled out the bundle of notes. "Or forever perhaps."

The founders were anxious to explore their new world, but they realized they had to arm themselves with all available information first. Thus, they turned to the money. A nation's currency was a telling barometer of its overall health.

Before retiring and beginning the life of natural-philosophic inquiry and public service that made him famous, Franklin spent thirty years as a printer. He produced paper currency for states during this time, and was the logical person to scrutinize the notes.

Franklin was hunched over a hundred-dollar bill, squinting at it through his tiny bifocals with such intensity that he appeared cross-eyed. He was the personification of scholarly focus.

"What do these notes tell you?" Washington asked.

"They question us before revealing anything," Franklin replied. "They ask us why they are here."

"And what are you telling them?" Washington asked.

"That they are further proof our presence here is intentional. That they are a gift from our Puppeteer."

"This is a large denomination and quantity of money," Jefferson said. "Either our Puppeteer bequeathed a fortune, or the notes have been depreciated[19] relentlessly."

Periods of rampant depreciation aside, a hundred dollars in colonial times represented the annual income of several middle-class citizens. The founders held a claim to the annual output of a small colonial city. In their past, anyway. What about now? Would their notes buy a colony, a city, a mansion, or merely supper?

This question would affect their standard of living, but it concerned the founders for far more practical reasons. They understood that honest money was a pillar of every prosperous nation in history, and that when its currency is corrupted, so is a republic.

"Depreciation!" Washington felt stark fear.

"We won't know if it has occurred until we determine the cost of wares," Franklin said. "Of course, under an honest medium, overall price levels would not rise significantly. Even over the course of centuries. And in an inventive society, they might even decline."

---

19 Depreciated. When additional notes are printed, each is worth less, and they have been depreciated.

"You never should have chartered the First Bank of the United States!" Jefferson said to Washington. "I warned you!"

"Time will tell," Washington replied.

"It already has," Franklin interjected. "If we're where we think."

"This isn't a time for old arguments," Washington said.

Franklin laughed. "They weren't old a few hours ago."

"Yes they were," Washington growled.

Franklin was intrigued. He had never seen Washington and Jefferson disagree so vehemently, especially on such a fundamental issue.

"Why do you suppose you are on the notes?" Washington asked.

"Because I'm handsome." Franklin's expression was earnest.

Washington and Jefferson laughed.

"Or maybe they ran out of mountain and felt guilty for the slight."

More laughter. "What else do you see?" Washington asked.

Franklin polished his spectacles, knelt with a grimace, laid several bills on the ground, and then examined them. "You'd expect currency to utilize a society's most advanced printing capabilities. Otherwise counterfeiting would be rampant."

Franklin pointed out the notes' cloth-like texture, embedded strips, three-dimensional lettering, life-like portraits, watermarks, and intricate border and background designs. He marveled at the clarity and precision of the printing, and the fact that every note was *exactly* alike.

Exactly alike except for the the cipher that varied note to note. This amazed Franklin most. If it was changed on every bill rather than on each printing run . . .

Franklin could only shake his head at the thought. For a colonial printer, this feature would have been a nightmare; the press would have had to be manually changed after each note, making large-scale production essentially impossible.

"That wouldn't be entirely bad," Jefferson said.

Franklin chuckled. "If you had to become a banker or a priest, which would you choose?"

"Neither."

"If I put a pistol to your head and demanded a decision?"

"I'd let you pull the trigger."

Franklin laughed. *Good ol' Jefferson.*

"This isn't your Philosophical Society[20]," Washington said. "We don't have time to converse at our leisure."

---

20 Philosophical Society. The American Philosophical Society. Founded by Franklin in 1743, it brought leading scholars together to promote the advancement of scientific knowledge and invention.

"The presses that created this currency must be incredibly advanced," Franklin continued. "Unfathomably advanced."

"You don't have to be a printer to make the most telling observation," Jefferson said. "Series 2001."

A pause.

Mild surprise.

Previous assessments were mentally revised.

"Our natural philosopher's predictions were accurate," Jefferson said.

Franklin accepted the compliment with a nod. " 'In God We Trust.' Some form of spiritualism persists."

"Hopefully a purer, unperverted form of Christianity," Jefferson said.

The back of the hundred dollar note showed Philadelphia's Independence Hall, where *The Declaration of Independence* and *Constitution* were deliberated and signed.

"The trees have changed," Franklin said.

"How can you remem—" Jefferson began. He caught himself. "You were there yesterday."

Franklin's squint grew severe as he scrutinized the image. "Figures are standing in front of the Hall."

"Us again?" Washington asked.

"Only an ant could tell," Franklin replied. "Though I'd have chosen chesty, au naturel demimondes[21]."

Jefferson and Washington chuckled.

"Could the figures be a counterfeit prevention?" Jefferson asked. "Like your leaves."

Franklin had noted that each leaf's vein patterns were unique, like snowflakes. He proposed putting a superficially identical leaf on all continental currency, but varying the vein pattern on each denomination.

"It seems possible," Franklin replied. "If they can put a different number on each note, why not a different person?"

Franklin examined the notes' fronts again. Words in a watermark said: "'Ment of 'he Treasury." Signatures above "Secretary of the Treasury" and "Treasurer of the United States" corroborated the assumption that the Department of the Treasury still existed in some form.

"Thank Providence for my bifocals," Franklin said. "This print is miniscule. 'Federal Reserve Note.' 'United States Federal Reserve System.' 'This note is legal tender for all debts, public and private.' " A pause. "This is federal money. Issued by a national bank?"

---

21 Demimonde. A promiscuous woman or prostitute.

"So it would seem," Jefferson said. "It does not say American Note or United States Note, but Federal Reserve Note."

"Was *The Constitution* amended to allow for a national bank?" Franklin asked.

"No," Jefferson answered. "Not in my lifetime."

"How could a national bank be constitutional then?"

Jefferson glared at Washington. "It is not. And a national bank is not necessarily a public bank."

Franklin's eyes filled with fear.

Jefferson sighed, well aware what he was thinking. In the hands of the corrupt, money was the ultimate instrument of tyranny. Ubiquitous, yet subtle, it could be manipulated in ways, and with consequences, that the common run rarely discerned.

Jefferson sighed again as he remembered the panic of 1819, the new republic's first nationally manufactured depreciation. It ruined hundreds of thousands of Americans, including him. He recalled his battles against the bankers, his consistent advocation of constitutional principles, and the madness that led to the former being embraced at the expense of the latter. Jefferson was certain he had fought for what was right, but this was a small consolation; he had stood alone against a horde, and been overrun by it, and thinking about it now made him feel tired and dejected.

"A private monopoly of the nation's money?" Franklin said. "What fool would have approved such madness? Adams?"

"I approved the bank," Washington said. "Though the issue is not as simple as Tom makes it seem."

Jefferson's eyes grew intense. "A private central bank issuing the public currency is a greater menace to the liberties of the people than a standing army."

"Had you braved combat, you might have a different view," Washington responded.

Jefferson shook his head. "I respect your courage, but nay."

"Banks can be dangerous," Washington said. "But you sound the lunatic when you speak so severely."

Jefferson held up a note and smiled somewhat sadly. "The two most significant observations remain unstated."

"Enlighten us." Franklin's tone was humble.

"First, that this is paper, not specie[22]. It has no inherent value as merchandise."

Franklin nodded. He had felt no need to state such a self-evident truth.

"The second, most telling detail is what isn't written on the note. A promise that it can be redeemed for specie, merchandise like tobacco, or something of real value."

---

22 Paper, paper money. Specie, coin money. In the colonial era, specie was gold or silver.

Franklin nodded again. A more penetrating observation, but still a rudimentary one.

"This money is not merchandise," Jefferson said. "Nor can it be exchanged for any, at least not at a fixed rate."

Franklin developed the impression Jefferson was talking to Washington, not him. Jefferson was not ranting, but he was aggressive. Or more properly, unusually aggressive, for pugnaciousness from him in any form was rare; Franklin had met philosophers the world over and knew a more peace-loving man was difficult to find.

Washington's eyes narrowed and his crow's feet became claws. He was insulted not by what was said, or how, but the fact that Jefferson felt a need to say it at all. Yet strangely, he did not interrupt; Franklin knew Washington would not hesitate to intervene if he felt mistreated.

It was all bizarre and disquieting, but Franklin felt sure undisclosed events that transpired after his death would make these uncharacteristic behaviors seem more sensible.

"These notes probably have value only by fiat[23]," Jefferson continued. "And as human nature is invariant, a prediction is hardly taxing."

"Poor choice of words," Franklin said.

Jefferson smiled, but only slightly. "If this is unfunded paper[24], it is probably abused, and will reap the same crop it has for all of history when sown: tyranny."

"Until we understand the whole system we can't be certain," Washington said. "Banking may have evolved just as surely as printing."

"I'm sure it has. Though I doubt the primary beneficiary of this advancement is the common run. I hope we have missed some obvious safeguard, and would be exultant if proven wrong, but I suspect this foreshadows oppression."

"Well then," Franklin said. "Now that Tom's lifted our spirits, how do we proceed?"

"Final assessments," Washington said.

"You don't want to listen to Tom a little longer?" Franklin asked.

Washington allowed a very slight, closed-lipped smile, but the trace of warmth it conveyed was eclipsed by the chill emanating from his eyes.

Franklin gathered his thoughts, then said, "We have observed individuals with foreign clothing and advanced inventions, who assumed us actors and referred to our era as history. Future dates are listed on pamphlets and notes whose sophistication suggests highly advanced printing technology. You two

---

23 Fiat. An arbitrary government edict.
24 Unfunded paper. Paper money not backed by a commodity.

are etched on a mountain with two American Presidents who must have succeeded us. At least six other Presidents were mentioned by the family or shown in our pamphlet. And I am portrayed on currency. To me, this evidence suggests one and only one conclusion. We are in the American future. At a time later than 1930, possibly 2001 or thereabouts. When the republic still exists and we are revered."

"I agree with this assessment," Washington said.

"As do I," Jefferson added.

"Then I believe our course of action is clear," Washington said. "We must explore this new America. To avoid continuous attention and suspicion, we must maintain anonymity and proceed like spies in an enemy territory. We must find indigenous clothing, and a way to leave the vicinity of this mountain as soon as possible. Its presence makes us much more identifiable. This is the plan I propose. Do either of you have amendments to offer, or grievances to voice?"

Franklin shook his head.

"The plan sounds prudent," Jefferson said.

"This Rushmore tourist center might be a logical destination," Franklin reasoned.

"We would be especially conspicuous there," Jefferson replied.

"The town?" Washington suggested.

"We have no horses," Franklin said. "Assuming horses are still used for transportation. 'Though with my gout and stone, I couldn't ride anyway."

"We have feet," Washington said.

"But you don't have a bladder stone. Or gout. I can't make a long hike and I'm not going to try. I'm just not."

"Not disciplined. You need to spend less time writing about the virtues and more time living them."

"All the discipline and virtue in the world won't cure my gout or my stone. Prior to their onset, I suffered wilderness expeditions without complaint."

Jefferson felt sympathy because he knew Franklin spoke the truth. At age 57, he traveled more than 1600 miles on horseback, and in 1776, when he was seventy, Congress dispatched him on a diplomatic mission to Montreal, which was sequestered deep within the virgin wilderness of the Canadian territories. To reach it Franklin embarked on a grueling cross-country journey that would have been arduous for a man half his age.

"I can no longer make such trips," Franklin continued. "You can leave me and come back, or we can travel to the tourist shop as a group."

"We must stay together," Jefferson said.

"I agree," Washington replied. "Unity is our strength, just as it is America's. Even if some of our colonies are weak."

Franklin chuckled. "I die in two and a half years and you're chiding me for not being able to make a forced march?"

"I die in two and a half years and I can make the march."

Franklin wasn't angered by Washington's intolerance, but he regarded it as somewhat absurd. It would have been almost funny, were it not for the lethal look in Washington's eyes. Against someone less principled, Franklin could have made a reasonable plea for lenience, but like all great leaders, Washington led by example. In telling him to hike and endure the pain, Franklin knew he was requesting something he could have, and would have, done himself.

There were many fabled examples of Washington's prowess, but Franklin knew veterans of the Battle of Monongahela, and their accounts came to mind whenever the topic of his toughness arose. Recovering from a hemorrhoidal fever prior to the battle, Washington was deemed too sick and weak to ride, and was left behind with doctors. Unwilling to sit out, he made his way to the front, tied pillows to his saddle, and joined his commander General Braddock in time to see their 1300-man force massacred by less than 300 Frenchmen and savages. Braddock relied on the 23 year-old Washington to lead an attempted assault, transport him from battle once he was critically wounded, and once defeat was imminent, to carry word to a separate force that would be needed to support a retreat. Having already been awake for 24 hours, and on horseback for more than twelve, many of those in the strains of battle, Washington was exhausted, but he mustered resolve, rode through the night, traversed forty miles of forest, and delivered the message late the next morning in a semi-conscious haze.

George definitely isn't a hypocrite, Franklin thought. He sighed as he gazed at the rolling hills that led to Rushmore and envisioned the agony hiking them would entail. His gout created a continual, nagging discomfort that turned to crippling pain when he exerted himself, and his stone made him unable to endure even a carriage ride. When the constellations aligned and both illnesses offered reprieves, he could sometimes walk the eighth mile from his house to "Independence Hall," but that was on flat ground, and the constellations weren't aligned. Washington knew all this, and none of it mattered to him.

Franklin began another objection.

"Don't treat me like some French Minister or wench," Washington interrupted. "You're not negotiating your way out of this."

Franklin looked to Jefferson for help, but he had slinked into the background. He avoided conflict whenever possible.

"You're fourteen years younger than me!" Franklin said.

"And forty years fitter," Washington chided. "Now enough of your whimpering. We'll approach the mountain circumspectly, scout, then determine an approach based upon what we observe."

Washington turned, and with his characteristically long, quick strides, blazed a trail into the forest. "Onward to the new United States! Let's see what sort of man our child has become!"

Three

WASHINGTON WAS an excellent woodsman, and had no problem guiding the party through the forest toward a destination they couldn't even see at times. The only difficulty was Franklin, who was soon winded and couldn't keep up. Washington slowed the pace. "Your swimming days are long past," he chided.

"I'm old," Franklin wheezed.

"And fat."

Franklin did not retort. He realized Washington had assumed the mantle of leadership, was concerned with group needs rather than individual egos, and had criticized his obesity because it was an impediment that hampered the party.

As Washington contemplated the group's welfare, he realized he had considered everything except his companions, and he now attended to this final variable. His immediate impression was that his situation could have been better, but it also could have been much, much worse. Though a liability in survival situations, Jefferson and Franklin were two of the smartest men to ever walk the Earth.

Things could indeed have been worse.

To Washington, his companions' intellect was the party's greatest asset. Although soldiers would be more useful than scholars until the party was literally and metaphorically out of the woods, Washington reconfronted the possibility that they were marooned and would live the rest of their lives in the future. If this was the case, and they avoided violence and integrated into society for the short term, Jefferson and Franklin's intellects would prove priceless over the long.

As he hiked, Washington scanned the horizon and surrounding trees regularly. Finding nothing alarming in his latest sweep, he turned his attention to Jefferson.

Tom had changed. Who didn't in twenty-eight years? Still, this was worrisome to Washington because it made the enigmatic sage even more of an unknown.

No string of superlatives could summarize the Jefferson conundrum with sufficient severity. He was puzzle piled upon paradox; men who had known him for decades remained baffled by him. Franklin was that rarity a "normal" genius, but Jefferson was very much the neurotic stereotype. His brilliance was turbulent, and he was riddled with contradictions he seemed unaware of. In him, the idealism of a child was juxtaposed with Machiavellian cunning.

Trying to harness this genius was a tricky task, and as Washington knew firsthand, often a scalding one, but people bothered for a reason: in its areas of greatest aptitude, Jefferson's intellect eclipsed that of every founder, even Franklin, Madison, Adams or Hamilton[25].

Washington sighed as he contemplated wooing Jefferson again. Time travel had made a difficult task even harder.

Franklin, by comparison, was pleasant to contemplate. There was inherent psychological toughness in him, and a lifetime of steady accomplishment that commanded respect. Born into middle-class obscurity without the advantages of wealth and station that Washington and Jefferson enjoyed, Franklin fled home at age sixteen, made his way alone in the world, and through persistent industry and frugality, amassed a fortune as an author and printer. A respected regional figure when he retired at 42, he spent six years experimenting with electricity and made the natural-philosophic discoveries that earned him international fame. Rather than rest on these laurels, Franklin spent the remainder of his life in tireless public service. His greatest civic contributions were made at an age when most men are fishing, drooling, or dead.

Franklin excelled at anything intellectual, was inherently wise and likable, and got along with almost everyone. His buoyant personality and natural philosophic genius seemed perfectly suited to futuristic survival, and though his weight and failing health were tremendous liabilities, Washington nonetheless felt lucky to have him.

Washington didn't contemplate Franklin long because his attention drifted back to Jefferson. He tried to stifle and condemn his curiosity, but could not. Like so many others, he was drawn to the Jefferson mystique.

What sort of Executive were you? Washington wondered. His intuitive answer was another question. *Peace or war? You could be an exceptional peacetime leader, but your propensity to avoid conflict at any cost might be a tremendous liability*

---

25 Hamilton. Alexander Hamilton (1757–1804). Lawyer and Revolutionary Pamphlet Writer (1774–1775), Militiaman in the Continental Army (1776), Artillery Captain in the Continental Army (1776–1777), Aide-de-Camp to General George Washington (1777–1781), New York Delegate to the Continental Congress (1782–1783), Founder of the Bank of New York (1784), Delegate to the Annapolis Convention (1786), New York Delegate to the Constitutional Convention (1787), Co-author of the Federalist Papers (1787–1788), first Secretary of the Treasury under George Washington (1789–1795), Author of Reports on Public Credit, A National Bank, Establishment of a Mint, and Manufactures (1790–1791).

during war. Aware that the Executive changes a person, Washington also asked the other logical question: *What sort of man are you now?*

Franklin smiled as he watched Washington peer at Jefferson. He had rarely seen him look so intrigued.

"How many terms did you serve, Tom?" Washington asked.

"Four," Jefferson replied.

Washington's eyes narrowed. Fearful that a perpetually re-elected Executive little different from a monarch would eventually arise, Jefferson had criticized the lack of Presidential term limits in *The Constitution.* His abuse of the loophole he condemned angered Washington greatly but surprised him only slightly. It seemed he was once again at odds with Jefferson and his hypocrisies.

"Just jesting, George," Jefferson said. "I followed your example of voluntary retirement after eight years, as did Madison and Monroe, who served after me. A few more precedents will oppose the obstacle of habit to anyone who might endeavor to extend his term."

"That seems overly optimistic," Franklin said.

"Perhaps. If so, abuses may beget a disposition to establish the limit by an amendment of *The Constitution.*"

"The Executive," Washington said. "Eight years that felt like a score."

Jefferson nodded emphatically. "I wouldn't serve again for all the spices in the Indies."

"Nor I," Washington said. "Two terms were enough."

Jefferson laughed. "One term was enough."

Washington noted Jefferson's bearing. The changes were subtle, but nonetheless observable, and overall, an impression was forming. Jefferson seemed tougher and more confident.

Washington reminded himself not to let these assessments make him lax. Caution had to remain the primary focus, for if a life-or-death situation arose, he was probably on his own with two defenseless intellectuals to protect.

When Washington halted briefly to check their bearing, Franklin practically fell over against a tree. Jefferson was slightly winded. Washington wasn't even breathing heavily.

"What I wouldn't give for some wine," Franklin moaned.

"Or some water," Washington said pointedly.

"I'd settle for ale," Franklin said.

Washington looked at Franklin and shook his head. "I'll grant you they were uphill. But we've only hiked a few rods and you're already panting like a dog in August."

Franklin was too tired to defend himself. He simply sat and slobbered.

Jefferson stopped walking suddenly and cupped a hand to his ear. "Do you hear music?" he asked.

"Yes," Washington replied. "Coming from the mountain."

"It sounds like an orchestra," Jefferson said.

"In the wilderness?" Franklin's brow furrowed. "But you are correct. It sounds like one."

Jefferson usually sang or hummed while strolling, and was pleased. "Music will make our hike more enjoyable."

"It will also mask noise you two create during our approach," Washington said. "Now keep moving."

"I hope there's an infirmary near the tavern," Franklin wheezed.

Washington responded with another freakishly long stride.

"We aren't all camelopards[26], George."

"Soldiers in my army shorter than you endured marches longer than this at more straining paces. On sparse rations. For weeks at a time."

"I doubt you had any 81-year-old infantrymen."

"You don't have to enlist. Just try the sparse rations."

"What needs sparsening is your comments. I don't march like a soldier, and I'm not embarrassed by the fact."

"It certainly looks like you're blushing. And if you aren't, maybe you should be."

"Stick to soldiering and leave the wit to the writers."

"I'm not sure about wit, but you've got the eating and complaining stitched up. Tom's 82, keeping up fine, and he's no soldier."

Though faring better than Ben, I'm hardly "keeping up fine," Jefferson thought. *I hope these vexsome crotch pains do not increase their frequency or intensity.*

"Tom has always been exceptionally healthy," Franklin said.

"Tom has always eaten sparingly and exercised daily," Washington countered.

"He's also taller than me."

"It's not a question of height."

"The war's over, George. Lobsters[27] aren't nipping at our heels."

"Luckily for you."

"We're hounds," Franklin said. "George is the fox."

"A fox you'll never catch."

Jefferson laughed. "Now we know how the British felt."

---

26 Camelopard. Giraffe.

27 Lobster. Derogatory colonial American term for British Redcoats.

A CAWING HAWK circled high in the air. Franklin paused to crane his head upward and peer at it.

"What now?" Washington asked.

"Something occurred to me," Franklin replied.

"Can't things occur to you while you're walking?"

In the midst of pamphlet and note revelations, there hadn't been time to ruminate on peripheral topics. Hiking freed the mind, even for the exhausted Franklin, and the founders contemplated many of the questions they'd tabled as they traveled.

Franklin's focus was flight. He had pondered it many times in the past, but to a natural philosopher, knowing something is possible rather than thinking it might be is a huge mental difference, and this iteration was much more pleasing.

"Nature," Franklin said. "Nature." His brow furled and he assumed an upright thinker's pose. He seemed almost like an athlete making a great exertion.

Washington was impatient, but he realized Franklin might make a revelation. Respectful of genius, he did not interrupt.

"If I were going to fly . . . to fly . . . don't think of materials or inventions we know . . . knew . . . airlines probably utilize principles and innovations we could never deduce. If I wanted to fly, and could build anything I could conceive, what would I do?" Franklin squinted at the hawk. "I'd study nature. Mimic nature. Mimic birds."

"Wings, you mean?" Washington asked. "A flapping machine?"

The hawk answered. Its wings were motionless and it was gliding, making lazy circles in the air.

"Could a craft shaped like a bird mimic the one above us?" Franklin wondered. "Does a bird not carry cargo? Its brains, its organs, a fish, a worm? Couldn't a human sit in a bird machine's head or claws, like a worm or fish or brain?"

Jefferson was skeptical, but kept quiet; Franklin had already proved him wrong once, and the airline he now envisioned, an enormous balloon that used a futuristic steam engine to oppose air currents, still seemed primitive.

Washington could create a rudimentary mental image of the artificial bird Franklin postulated, but on a more fundamental level, it was beyond his conception. This was a large leap in logic for a non-genius resident of a time that lacked not just trains, planes, and automobiles, but also electricity and plumbing. In the colonial world food was usually cooked in pots over fires, water was carried from wells, candles were the primary light sources, travel was by horse or sail, and all of life's necessities were still produced by hand.

"Are you going to fly us to a tavern?" Washington asked.

Franklin glared. Mockery of natural philosophy was one of the few things that annoyed him, and Washington knew it.

"If not, let's get moving," Washington said.

Before Franklin obeyed, he peered at the hawk with longing, and let out a hearty laugh. "It is mischievous of nature to deny us the advantages that she has wasted so profusely on all the little good for nothing birds and flies."

A BREAK IN the trees allowed a staggering glimpse of Rushmore. Afraid that Franklin might keel over, and figuring they might as well enjoy a view while they rested, Washington called another halt. Franklin once again collapsed against a tree.

Rushmore had changed. The mountain and its subjects now had identities to the founders. It now felt like something they knew rather than some foreign monolith. Rushmore was American. It was America. They were a part of it, and it was a part of them.

"I still can't believe posterity sculpted us into the side of a mountain!" Jefferson said.

"Gods must be paid tribute." Franklin smiled when he saw Jefferson's sunny expression dim slightly. "Perhaps other families we encounter will think you've come back like Christ."

"If I had venom or quills," Jefferson said.

"Your disciples will wear quills instead of crosses."

"I would prefer to never have lived, than become the deity of a religion."

"Lived the first time, or the second?"

Jefferson smiled as he shook his head. If Franklin had a defining attribute besides genius or wisdom, it was wit.

Franklin laughed. "If disciples of Jeffersonanity alter your *Declaration* the way Christians have the Bible, who knows what it might say in another century or two?"

"I'd rather wipe *The Declaration* from history than let it be defiled in such a way."

"Shrine of Democracy," Franklin said. "One could substitute Shrine of Jeffersonanity. I like the sound of that."

"I don't," Jefferson replied.

Franklin performed a mock rosary. "In nomine Thomas, et Jefferson, et spiritus Monticello."

Jefferson groaned.

"You're right. It was vulgar of me not to include George. In nomine Washington, et Jefferson, et spiritu—"

"Et spiritus Franklin," Washington said.

Franklin laughed. "I'll gladly be one of Tom's apostles."

"I hope the Trinity has been catalogued in its proper historical place with Greek and Roman mythology." Jefferson's grin returned. "And if that is the case, might you not be Zeus?"

"The American Zeus is most assuredly George."

Jefferson didn't argue. "Ben, Ben, Ben. It's too bad you're not on the mountain."

Yes, Franklin thought. *It is.*

"I would gladly let you have your face on this Rushmore," Washington said. "If I could socialize in England and France while you froze fighting wars and served as Executive."

"I was President," Franklin replied.

Washington rolled his eyes. "Of Pennsylvania's Executive Council."

Jefferson chuckled. Pennsylvania's executive branch was headed by a council rather than a single individual, and Franklin had been elected President of this body.

"You could etch my face in the constellations and I still wouldn't want to be America's President." Franklin stood with help from Jefferson, offered the most flourishing bow his creaky body could manage, then said, "I was only teasing, George. I hope you have your face on every mountain on the continent."

"I think one mountain is enough, Ben. But thank you all the same. And stay behind the tree line so we remain hidden."

The founders relaxed and once again gazed at Rushmore.

"I still wonder if Lincoln and Roosevelt are back near the clearing asking where you two are," Franklin said.

"Your presence argues against that," Jefferson replied.

"A Civil War," Washington sighed. "I warned the nation about unity of government in my Farewell Address."

"We may give advice," Franklin replied. "But we cannot give conduct."

"A Civil War is tragic, though hardly surprising. In the decades after your deaths, a breach became almost inevitable." Jefferson shook his head. "I can scarcely contemplate a more incalculable evil than the breaking of the Union into two or more parts. Who can say what would be the evils of a scission, and when and where they would end?"

"History can say," Franklin replied. "Take comfort in the fact that an American scission is now in your past instead of your future. It is tempting to ask where we went wrong, but our nation's survival means we went right to some degree."

"Things could be worse," Washington agreed. "*The Declaration*, *Constitution* and America could all be history."

The founders nodded in unison. The comments highlighted their most profound realization, which was still the date. They were not millenniums in the future, but centuries, and would study America not as antiquarians, but citizens.

"Seeing my sculpture again without the initial sense of shock, and with knowledge of when and where we are makes me feel . . ." Jefferson hesitated. "Uncomfortable. Rushmore seems almost . . ."

"Vulgar," Washington said.

Franklin laughed. "The creators would be happy to hear that!"

"I wasn't criticizing," Jefferson said. "But the mountain nonetheless . . ." His look of dismay grew more pronounced. As did Washington's.

"I doubt Rushmore's builders thought you would return to see it," Franklin said.

Washington shuddered, turned from Rushmore, and hurried into the forest. Jefferson followed with equal enthusiasm. Franklin pulled up the rear. *At last*, he thought, with unabated amusement, *something that unnerves the fearless General Washington.*

"I SEE A building!" Franklin said.

Thank Providence you were a diplomat and not a soldier, Washington thought. *I glimpsed it ticks ago.*

"What do you suppose it is?" Franklin asked.

"A building," Washington replied. "And keep moving. This is flat ground. You should be able to talk and walk."

"What type of building?" Franklin asked. "Can you tell?"

"Sure. From a thousand rods away I can even hear conversations. Can't you smell the mutton and pudding?"

"I can see why Conway mutinied," Franklin said.

Jefferson winced. *Crimine, Ben! Talk about heaving manure!*

As Commander in Chief during the Revolutionary War, Washington hadn't just fought perpetual enlistment, training, funding, and supply deficiencies, but also conspiracies from his most senior commanders. In 1777, he suffered embarrassing defeats at Brandywine Creek and Germantown, while General Horatio Gates commanded a major victory at Saratoga that was the largest in the war at that point. Some members of the Continental Congress and the military wanted to replace Washington with Gates, and while he was floundering at Valley Forge, a political cabal led by General Thomas Conway tried unsuccessfully to do just that.

Washington grimaced as he recalled the episode. "If our diplomats had secured funding and military support in a more timely manner, I wouldn't have faced a mutiny."

"The French Navy was there when you needed it."

"At Yorktown," Washington retorted. "We could have won months or years earlier if it had been available sooner."

At the time of the Revolutionary War, the coastal colonies had no navy, and Britain's was one of the world's most powerful. This absolute sea dominance allowed the Crown to decimate American cities with her ships' cannon and transport troops with blazing speed, outmaneuvering Washington no matter how fast his armies moved. On the rare occasions he achieved a tactical advantage and cornered a British force, her ships simply whisked it away to safety.

Washington correctly foresaw that victory was impossible unless British naval superiority was countered. France was the only nation with an ability and potential willingness to do so, and her support was the central strategic proposition of the war.

To secure it, the colonies dispatched their most skilled diplomat, greatest sage, and only international celebrity. These honors belonged not to several people, but one man—the First American, Benjamin Franklin.

Who now enjoyed the last laugh. "I'm not sure about strategy and leadership, but you've got the excuse making and complaining stitched up."

Washington turned suddenly and reached for Franklin. His eyes glowed with fury. Washington had a hair-trigger temper; through sheer discipline he had tamed the beast, but the most domesticated wildlife still goes berserk occasionally. Franklin knew Washington wouldn't hurt him, but this realization did little to lessen his terror.

Washington countered Franklin's parry easily, feigned a punch, and slapped him on the belly, leaving a handprint on his sweat stained shirt. Then he smiled. "The French chefs and wine were there when you needed them."

"And the wenches," Franklin replied, as he tried not to telegram the pain the blow caused his stone. "One can't forget the French wenches."

Washington turned around and continued hiking. So did Franklin, who smiled at Jefferson, wiped his brow with relief, and kept goading. "If you'd won a major victory sooner, I would have been able to negotiate naval support sooner."

"I wasn't on holiday," Washington said.

A Valley Forge pun occurred, but even Franklin's impropriety knew limits. "Nor was I. I worked diligently to massage the French ego."

Securing French support had not been easy. At the time of the War for Independence, France was the purest, most entrenched monarchy in Europe, with a peasant underclass that lived in abject poverty. French intellectuals supported Republican principles, and therefore the American Revolution, but they did not wield power; King Louis XVI did. He had no ideological sympathy for an uprising against a monarch, even an adversary, and was wary of the danger of such a precedent[28].

Though the contradiction inherent in French support of America was glaring, political pragmatism creates odd alliances. Britain had grown frightfully strong, and was the most powerful nation on Earth. A chance to strip the Crown of her most valuable possession was tempting to France.

But risky. If France sided with the rebels, and they reconciled or lost, a unified England would turn the full brunt of her might against her most hated enemy. France could not intervene unless America demonstrated considerable resolve, and an ability to obtain victory. George Washington eventually proved the former, and the Battle of Saratoga the latter, but even then, convincing France to risk the wrath of Britain was a tricky proposition.

As is the case with any abridged historical episode where enormous significance is ascribed to a handful of men, it is possible to identify other heroes, but the underlying philosophical principles aside, Franklin's efforts to obtain French support and Washington's struggle to hold on until it arrived were the essence of the Revolutionary War. Not strong enough to engage the Crown's larger, more-disciplined, better-equipped army in a decisive engagement without assistance, Washington had no choice but to mount harassive campaigns and wait. When and if Franklin convinced France to bring her navy and troops to bear, he would be ready to strike decisively, risk everything, and win his one great gambit.

Both men succeeded, and America was born. While Washington cornered the British at Yorktown, the French Navy bottled them, preventing the usual sea rescue and ending the war. Though Washington's victory is immortalized, it is often forgotten that the mere presence of France's Navy, and the French loans Franklin secured throughout the war, represent a diplomatic Yorktown that preceded the military.

"I can't imagine you working diligently on anything but a chop or a carafe," Washington said to Franklin. "But I will admit France was conducive to this theoretical industry. You had all the luxuries of a man on holiday. I didn't frequent brothels or four-star restaurants while commanding the armies."

"I wasn't aware you frequented brothels even as a civilian," Franklin said. "But the admission is enlightening."

Washington scowled. "One would presume a diplomat would have more tact. Correction, *some* tact. And I wasn't aware France had a brothel you didn't frequent."

---

28 Rightly so. He was later guillotined in the French Revolution, which was inspired by the American.

"I did miss a few," Franklin said. "To my great regret. But even a Minister Plenipotentiary[29] can't successfully conclude all negotiations. And one would presume a general would have more tact-ical knowledge. Correction, *some* tactical knowledge. But Monmouth proved that wrong."

Jefferson winced again. In June of 1778, in Monmouth County, New Jersey, an attack on a British supply line that was exhausted from long marches in hundred-degree heat failed not because of poor tactics, but because one of Washington's most senior officers, Major General Charles Lee, disobeyed orders and did not make the initial assault. Washington personally rallied his troops and salvaged a neutral outcome from defeat. A court martial later convicted Lee for his actions. Franklin knew all this, and was being purposely inaccurate to annoy Washington.

Jefferson chuckled as more salvos were exchanged. To a stranger, these biting barbs might seem like a serious argument.

Jefferson was no stranger. He had worked with Franklin on Congressional committees and had succeeded him as Minister to France. He had watched Franklin negotiate concessions using stupefying tact and eloquence, had benefited from his literary genius and sagely advice firsthand, and knew of his low intrigues with mistresses and parlor maids.

Jefferson and Washington were Virginia plantation owners who served as Burgesses[30] before the war, and Jefferson was Washington's Secretary of State. He had seen Washington prevent the American crib death by refusing its kingship, and watched with awe as he brought dignity, respectability and moral precedent to the young nation and the Presidency. Jefferson had also seen the aging Washington put the republic in mortal danger by failing to recognize the Federalist threat.

Others knew Franklin or Washington better, but excepting only John Adams, and maybe the Marquis de Lafayette, Jefferson could think of no one who knew both as well.

His war victory made Washington a demigod. He commanded such respect and was so widely revered that people rarely disagreed with him; doing so after the hard-fought revolution would have been like heckling Jesus at one of his sermons.

---

29 Minister Plenipotentiary. Franklin's official title as American emissary to France. In colonial times correspondence could take months, and a negotiator often had to speak for a nation without consulting heads of state, making policy on the fly. Lesser envoys with the rank of attaché or charge might be sent for remedial tasks, but a Minister Plenipotentiary, one given powers to treat with the full authority of a nation, was an individual of great prestige.

30 Burgess. A representative in The House of Burgesses, the colonial Virginia legislature. It was the first elective governing body in an overseas British possession.

Franklin was the only American with stature comparable to Washington's. Called "the Pythagoras[31] of the New World" and "wiser than Lycurgus[32]" by contemporaries, he was the most famous man on Earth prior to Washington's rise.

Jefferson knew Franklin's comments to Washington were spawned by the artist in him, the prankster who continuously conjured quips and loved to lampoon. Like Washington, Franklin had a private side that he shielded from the public. Among his closest friends, his legendary tact was usurped by a scathing wit. Franklin found much to mock in humans and humanity, and reveled in allowing his intellect to do so. With Washington, he felt like a big game hunter who'd stumbled upon a saber toothed tiger or wooly mammoth; he loved sniping not common fodder, but the undeniable icon of the American nation.

Washington didn't take kindly to even mild criticism, especially if deserved, but he seemed to enjoy barbs from the only man of his era who could reasonably be regarded as an equal.

"How many major battles did you win?" Franklin asked. "One out of seven, wasn't it?"

Jefferson was sure Franklin knew the proper answer.

"Two out of seven," Washington said.

"Impressive," Franklin replied. "They should make you a General."

"But I did manage one trifling victory. The war."

Jefferson chuckled, and continued to listen. The conversation stretched on, like the forest before them.

Franklin usually found Washington's physical prowess inspiring, but as he continued to hike like a metronome, it grew disheartening. "You need to slow down, George."

"I'm already hiking quarter speed," Washington replied.

"Well, make it eighth."

"I've been Executive for *eight* years. I'm in the worst condition of my life."

"I know. I should march like a sixteen-year-old corporal."

"I'd settle for a fifty-year-old amputee."

"What I wouldn't give for my crab-tree walking stick," Franklin whispered to himself. "I could walk a lot faster with one."

Jefferson smiled at the shrewd plea for mercy; Franklin had bequeathed this prized possession to Washington.

---

31 Pythagoras (569–500 BC). The "Father of Mathematics" was the first to study odd, even, prime, and square numbers, and appreciate their significance as a tool to facilitate systematic understanding of the world.

32 Lycurgus. A renowned, ancient-Greek statesman who instituted progressive political reforms.

Who refused to grant latitude by acknowledging the gift. Washington approached a tree, grabbed a branch, and yanked. His muscles slithered under his clothes, and he stood unbending, using the leverage his long limbs afforded effectively. Flesh battled wood, but Washington was sturdier. His foe's death throe was a loud crack.

Franklin looked at the staff that had appeared in his hand almost magically. "What I wouldn't give for a balloon carriage with a wench in it." Sans wench, this was a frequent fantasy Franklin embraced when plagued by the pains of travel.

"I wish I had a balloon," Washington replied. "Though it would have to be the size of the moon to lift a pachyderm like you, it's the only weight-loss method that would stand a chance. I'd imprison you above ground, and deny you vittles indefinitely."

"I would only trust Tom with the tether. Though if you rotated the wenches for a little variety in my rogering, and made sure they were buxom so I could suckle milk . . ."

Jefferson chuckled. Franklin had once again turned the tables on Washington.

"You could roger all you want," Washington said, as he once again began hiking. "Anything to speed up the weight loss."

Franklin placed the walking stick ahead of him and took a three-legged step. "Thank you for the staff, George."

"You can thank me by keeping up."

Conversation returned to natural philosophy, and as they hiked, Jefferson gave Washington and Franklin a quick overview of inventions promulgated after their deaths. These included the cotton gin, loom, ether refrigerator, spectroscope, stethoscope, and difference machine.

"When I contemplate the immense advances made during my life, I look forward with confidence to equal advances by future generations." Jefferson's eyes were large, and he seemed to laugh as much as speak. "The daily progression of natural philosophy will enable futurity to administer the commonwealth with increased wisdom. They will be as much wiser than us as we than our fathers were, and they than the burners of witches."

Franklin smiled. "Tom. Always the dreamer."

Washington frowned. *Tom. Always the dreamer.* "Tell me more about this electric lamp."

"It utilized an exotic, 2,000-cell Leyden jar[33] to produce electric fire between two pieces of charcoal[34]." Jefferson explained that electric lamps were too deli-

---

33 Leyden jar. A primitive capacitor, or storer of electric charge, invented by Pieter van Musschenbroek in 1745. Leyden jars were colonial scientists' primary source of electricity.

34 It was essentially a crude spark plug.

cate for widespread use, and noted that powering them was also impractical because batteries were exorbitant. He emphasized the fact that most devices he described had similar shortcomings; they were prototypes rather than perfected inventions, and represented what might be rather than what was.

"Artificial lightning." Franklin smiled. "A logical progression. The phenomenon I deduced the nature of, and a defense against, has been replicated and harnessed."

"Surely additional research was performed on something as promising as an electric candle," Washington said.

Jefferson nodded. "In 1820 Warren De la Rue enclosed a platinum coil in an evacuated tube and passed electric fire through it. The platinum gave off light. Though the metal's cost made the device unfeasible."

"If a suitable substitute for platinum could be found, man might no longer be a slave to sunlight!" Franklin felt consuming excitement, and wished he were in a lab so he could perform the experiments that were occurring in staccato bursts.

"Had these interchangeable parts been used for anything besides musket production?" Washington asked.

"Cannon production?" Franklin joked. "Sword production?"

No one laughed.

"Armies of guns that facilitate large wars." Franklin pursed his lips sardonically. "Just what humanity needs. Especially the Continent[35]."

"There was talk of producing watches with interchangeable parts," Jefferson said. "Though it seemed inevitable that in time the concept would be applied to all manufactures."

Pervasive mass production was another portentous yet enigmatic concept to Washington. It was difficult for him to picture muskets that were all exactly identical, much less a world overflowing with cloned wares. In general, he was having difficulty jettisoning his colonial mindset, and the ease with which Jefferson and Franklin seemed to grasp futuristic concepts only served to heighten his sense of impotence.

"Tell us more about the steamship!" Washington said.

Jefferson smiled. "You are still enthralled by the creation."

Washington nodded. In 1784, while touring western lands they owned, he and Dr. James Craik stopped in the town of Bath, Virginia and encountered resident James Rumsey, who described his invention and demonstrated a model. "The miniature was amazing! To say nothing of the actual ship!" *And it is an innovation I actually comprehend.*

"My gout and stone kept me from attending the demonstration Fitch provided the Constitutional Convention."

35 The Continent. Europe.

Washington smiled as he recalled the 45-foot prototype that stupefied the delegates. It was built by inventor John Fitch, an adversary of Ramsey.

"The steamship seemed to promise being useful when the machinery was simplified and the expense reduced," Franklin continued.

"Rumsey devoted his existence to refinement of the creation," Washington testified. "A year before your death you and twenty others raised a thousand pounds to support the Rumseyan Society which financed him. Unfortunately, he died before completing his second craft."

"A thousand pounds!" Franklin whistled, then his expression grew perplexed. "If only I remembered this magnanimity."

"A pioneering inventor named Robert Fulton simplified the steamship and reduced the expense," Jefferson said. "In 1814 steamships began service up and down the southern Mississippi. There were less than a score at first, but in little more than a decade the quantity swelled to almost a thousand."

Jefferson described the riverboat revolution in more detail. Washington asked about the boats' speeds.

"They are quite fast," Jefferson replied. "They often travel ten miles per hour downstream, and half as fast up."

"No match for a ship of the line[36]," Washington noted.

"Not yet," Jefferson responded. "But a ship of the line can't be covered with metal that deflects cannonballs. Steamships have been. And as they create their own impetus, and do not need wind, they can move continually."

"Might they cross oceans?" Franklin asked.

Jefferson nodded. "Though such a craft would probably dwarf a ship of the line."

"Dwarf a ship of the line?" Washington shook his head with amazement.

"If a Watt engine[37] could propel a boat, why not a wagon?" Franklin said. "Why not machines on a plantation or in a home?"

"A steam wagon was proposed by Rumsey and others," Washington replied.

"And constructed," Jefferson added. He explained iron horses and the rail roads that would support and guide them. "The first iron horses were so heavy they collapsed the rails. Work continues, though admittedly, this is another device that needs refinement."

"Or perhaps needed refinement," Franklin said. He envisioned an agile iron horse with a compact Watt engine and a flexible body or impact absorbing

---

36 Ship of the line. A ship large enough to have a place in the line of battle. In colonial naval engagements, opposing lines of ships fired at each other broadside. Such battles were usually won by the heaviest ships carrying the most powerful guns. Ships of the line were the largest vessels in the colonial world.

37 Watt engine. Steam engine. Throughout the mid-to-late 1700s, Inventor James Watt improved crude steam-engine prototypes, making the invention practical for widespread use.

mechanism that would allow it to move anywhere it wanted without rails. Yet even this conception might be primitive. Might iron horses be extinct? Roads obsolete? In a truly advanced society wouldn't everyone have an artificial bird or airline? Was an airline a blue flash that instantaneously transported people to different places instead of different times? Could it be the precursor to the time transport device?

Franklin's brain churned like a cyclone as conversation continued, and he listened with frustration, able to join in only occasionally because he still lacked the wind to speak and hike simultaneously.

ANOTHER BRIEF STOP while Washington took a bearing.

Bloody gout! Franklin thought. He made sure Washington wasn't looking, then bent and rubbed the calcifications in his knees. The motion irritated his stone and pain knifed his abdomen. Franklin stood motionless for several seconds while he fought off dizziness, then straightened slowly. *Bloody stone!*

"Are you okay?" Jefferson mouthed.

Franklin nodded quickly and placed his forefinger perpendicular to his lips.

Washington telegrammed the fact that he was going to turn around, giving Franklin time to hide his pain.

Few people could provoke such vanity in him, and Franklin was aware that his behavior was childish, perhaps even foolish. Though Washington's approval in intellectual affairs was inconsequential to Franklin, his esteem in a military survival situation was important for some reason.

Jefferson smiled, breathed in deeply, and enjoyed the beauty of the forest and wildlife.

Washington did not admire the scenery, and would not have even if the journey was mundane and leisurely. *We're moving slower than bloody Braddock*, he thought with irritation. A hike that should have been a quick sprint had become a pilgrimage, but it was clear to him that Franklin could not proceed any faster. Washington fought the urge to lash out at Franklin for his obesity, for requiring others to pay the price for his gluttony. He reined his temper, and after a prolonged sigh, once again began hiking.

WASHINGTON LET FRANKLIN lead and set a pace that would not kill him. This gave him a view of, and invariably the ability to mock, Franklin's physical struggles. "Your well of wit seems dry," he said. "Unlike your shirt."

Franklin was now too tired for even occasional responses, and had to stand like some dueler and receive fire.

"You march at the same rate you procured my French ships."

All Franklin could muster was a derogatory grunt.

"What I would've given for a regiment of Franklins during the war. I would've made you my elite guard."

Franklin hacked phlegm and spat into the woods.

"Of everything but the food and spirits of course."

Franklin joined his index and middle finger and jabbed them upward, flicking Washington off.

"What do you suppose America would be if my whole army had been Franklins? An army of Franklins. We'd be a British colony still."

"Subtle as always," Franklin managed.

"Though the war would've been shorter. The British could have set up a buffet and I would have had to agree to terms."

WITH FRANKLIN LEADING, the pace slowed to a plod. Jefferson gradually lost himself in the labyrinth of his thoughts. Foremost in his mind was the age incongruity time travel had created. He realized the present marching order was a kind of family tree for the American Revolution: Franklin the grandfather, Washington the father, and himself the son. His position at the rear seemed symbolic.

Despite his innate intelligence and formal schooling, Jefferson knew in his youth that Washington and Franklin were wiser. Men he deferred to. Quite literally, his elders.

Yet here they were together, in the twilight of their lives. Time travel had changed their old dynamic irrevocably. Having served five years as French Ambassador, three years as Secretary of State, four years as Vice President, and eight years as President, Jefferson now considered himself an equal to Washington and Franklin. He nonetheless felt uneasy; it was disturbing to suddenly be older than one's elders.

WHEN FRANKLIN STARTED coughing up greenish globules of phlegm and complained of dizziness, Washington called a short rest break. Franklin asked for more time, but Washington refused. For the first time, there was kindness in his manner rather than brusqueness. "I know you're exhausted, Ben. But I need you to dig deep and find strength."

"I don't have any left," Franklin said. "I feel like I'm going to die."

Washington smiled at his friend. "I don't think our Puppeteer brought you here to expire hiking."

Franklin laughed. "The irony would be appreciable though."

"Though not appreciated," Jefferson said.

"The sun is falling," Washington said. "We are unarmed, have no warm clothes, and can't risk a fire. Not the ideal circumstances for our first night in an unfamiliar future. If we are going to secure lodging before dark, we must make haste."

Franklin's gout and stone made even plush beds painful, and he knew the ground would be right murderous. Motivated by this fear, he found new resolve and pressed on at a faster pace.

As THE FOUNDERS finally approached Mount Rushmore, it hid behind hills and tree lines, eventually fading completely from view. Washington nonetheless knew its location, and when he felt they were close he called a halt and scanned the steep hill directly in front of them.

Franklin once again collapsed near a tree, sponged his perspiration, and tried to catch his breath. "I feel like we just hiked Revere's ride," he gasped.

Washington surveyed Franklin's soaked form disdainfully, but for once said nothing disparaging. He was callous, but always ruthlessly fair, and treated each individual with respect proportionate to their measure. As Franklin had found during the hike, this could be a mixed blessing, but now that the ordeal was over, Washington gave credit where it was due. Franklin had taken his lumps goodnaturedly, and hadn't griped about his only legitimate excuse, the gout and stone. Even now, sliding down the side of a tree and grabbing his abdomen while wincing, he didn't offer a word of complaint.

"You did well, Ben," Washington said. "Very well."

"Thank you, George." Franklin smiled. His suffering now seemed worthwhile.

"What now?" Jefferson asked.

"Hopefully our last hike is to a tavern," Franklin said.

"You must procure new garments first," Washington replied.

"Don't you mean we?"

"I mean you. One costumed oddity is much less conspicuous than three, and since you are not sculpted, and are therefore less recognizable, you should make the journey. After I scout, that is."

Franklin was too tired to argue. "Take all the time you need."

"Wait here and remain *totally* quiet. I'll be back in a tick." George Washington crept up the hill, silent as a savage.

WASHINGTON WAS WARY when he returned. “Keep quiet,” he whispered. “There are people everywhere.”

“Why must we sneak around?” Franklin asked. “People will assume we are actors as the family did.”

“We already discussed this.”

“Like constitutions, plans must sometimes be amended,” Franklin replied.

Washington shook his head. “If Rushmore is government operated, it probably employs historians, guards or laborers who will know we aren’t affiliated with the mountain.”

“Then we tell them we’re patriots miming personas from history,” Franklin said. “I think we should explore Rushmore together, buy clothes, and talk to everyone we can. It’s the fastest way to answer some of our most pressing questions.”

“But not the safest,” Washington replied. “We will not approach the mountain as a group. I know you think my caution excessive, but remember this is the future. Problems may seem unlikely, but if calamity smites us, we have only each other.”

“What if calamity smites me while I’m alone?”

“An unavoidable risk.”

Franklin pursed his lips. “I know a way to avoid it.”

“Besides cowardice?”

“I’m not going alone.”

“Yes you are.”

“This is a democracy, not your army. Tom’s vote decides.”

“I agree with George,” Jefferson said. “We should avoid contact with indigenous peoples until we are less conspicuous.”

Franklin wasn’t pleased, but he obeyed the electorate.

“Let’s find you an embarkment point,” Washington said.

“I’m not a ship.”

“More like a continent. And about as easy to move.”

"Feel free to embark yourself then."

Before heading up the hill, Washington smirked and said, "You'll enjoy this."

"Enjoy what?" Jefferson asked.

The smirk became a smile. "Follow me. Step where I step, move quietly, and no matter what you see, don't say a word."

Mount Rushmore has two entrances, a paid-parking area directly in front of it, and an unpaid-parking area situated well below it to the right. Unpaid parking lies on an elongated hilltop that nuzzles the edge of a rock shelf. A cramped road with diagonal parking spaces on either side, it is accessed by a snaking pass from the left, and dead ends in a cul-de-sac on the right. The cul-de-sac's right flank is guarded by a trailer-of-a-building that was once a sculptor's workshop, and a wide rock stairway just above that leads up to Rushmore.

The steep hill below the lot is sparsely treed and devoid of cover; only a sniper or savage could hide in it. Washington realized this, and approached from the extreme right, behind the workshop, which shielded the party from the stairway and lot.

Mount Rushmore cannot be seen from unpaid parking, but this didn't concern the founders because dozens of parked automobiles were visible. "We need a spyglass!" Franklin said.

"Speaking of glass!" Jefferson gasped, "it's so clear! And the wagon hues are so bright!"

"This is almost what I expected," Franklin muttered. "What we discussed. These vehicles are not conceptually surprising. And yet . . ."

"They are still amazing!" Jefferson finished. "These devices make even a chariot and six[38] look niggardly! The work of savages by comparison!"

Washington smiled. He'd sat gaping like this for several ticks, hoping in vain to see an iron horse gallop, and for once he was less surprised than his companions.

"Look at the variety!" Franklin exclaimed.

"Keep your voices down," Washington warned. "And there is a limit to the variety." He pointed out pairs of Watt wagons that were identical except for their color. "Are they produced with interchangeable parts? Like muskets?"

"That seems logical," Franklin replied. "But the variety is counterintuitive."

"Very counterintuitive," Jefferson said. "One would expect Watt wagons produced en masse to be more uniform. But this gatherum[39]! The American civilization must be enormous!"

---

38 Chariot and six. An unusually ornate carriage pulled by six horses. It was a status symbol that only a planter or businessman of the highest station could afford.

39 Gatherum. Assortment.

"Or inefficient. The waste inherent in such variety seems staggering. This society appears to individualize complex manufactures the way we did swords and snuffboxes."

"Are these Watt wagons also airlines?" Jefferson wondered.

"This age's aprons[40] must be magicians!" Washington said.

"Or machines," Franklin replied.

"What of the thin metal protrusions that stretch skyward?" Washington asked. "Franklin rods[41]?"

Jefferson and Franklin couldn't formulate a guess, so Washington's stood by default.

"The wheels are the color of coal," Washington said. "But they have the texture of taffy, seemingly."

Franklin squinted, and had modest success focusing. "Some futuristic incarnation of Priestley's rubber perhaps?"

Elastic hevea tree excretions were discovered in 1735 by a Frenchman on a South American expedition, and the renowned chemist Joseph Priestley named the substance rubber in 1770 when he used it to rub out pencil marks.

"Priestley." Franklin smiled. "Priestley. My protégé."

"One of them," Jefferson said.

"We recognized rubber's useful properties," Franklin continued. "But it is most vexsome to form. Except when heated. Perhaps futurity developed some method of ref—"

The founders craned their heads in unison as a Watt wagon sped up the pass into the lot, accelerated recklessly down its straightaway, and then screeched into an opening. The driver exited, closed the door, aimed something in his hand at the vehicle, and pressed it with his thumb. Colored lights on the Watt wagon blinked and it let out two shrill beeps. The driver pocketed the device and he and his female companion ascended the stairway to Rushmore.

"No horse could keep up with that!" Washington gasped.

"I could barely see it move!" Jefferson said. "It was a blur! And what of the truncated bird chirps?"

"The device the man held communicated with the Watt wagon," Franklin deduced. "But how?" He recalled experiments he'd performed in which electric fire caused his hair to stand, deflected a compass needle, and was shot across a lake to a conductor on the other side. Did the Watt wagon contain a futuristic compass or conductor? Did electric fire produced by the man's device interact with it?

---

40 Aprons. Craftsmen.

41 Franklin rod. Lightning rod. Franklin invented it in 1749.

"Look at the road," Washington said.

"Ugly," Franklin muttered.

Jefferson nodded. "Designed for the taffy wheels, I'll wager."

"Are there any flesh horses left?" Washington seemed sullen. Riding was one of his great passions.

"Embrace the future," Franklin said. "Don't mire yourself in the past."

Washington chuckled. "I'm mired in the future, not the past."

Several more Watt wagons entered the lot. They didn't scream as they stopped, or chirp. Families exited the vehicles and ascended the stairway to Rushmore.

As they watched, the founders' discussion waned. But surprise endured stubbornly, and curiosity continued to crescendo.

Washington noted Franklin's intense expression. "What are you pondering, Ben?"

"Ships."

"Steamships? The way Watt engines were adapted to wagons?"

"Yea and nay. I was recalling my 1757 journey to England. Our captain of the packet[42] had boasted much, before we sailed, of the swiftness of his ship. Unfortunately, when we came to sea, she proved the dullest of the ninety-six sail, to his no small mortification. After many conjectures respecting the cause, he determined that she was loaded too much by the head. The casks of water had all been placed forward; these he ordered moved aft, on which the ship recovered her character and proved the best sailor in the fleet."

"I know your stories usually instruct," Washington said, "but this lesson eludes me."

"The episode demonstrated ignorance which seemed an allegory for ship construction. One man builds the hull, another rigs her, a third lades her and sails her. No one of these has the advantage of knowing all the ideas and experience of the others, and therefore cannot draw just conclusions from a combination of the whole."

"Ah," Washington said. "You think this kind of natural philosophic omniscience would be required to construct Watt wagons."

Franklin nodded. "And the lad's handless watch, and scores of inventions we have not seen. I picture an enormous new trade filled with Rumseys and Fitches who draw a just conclusion from a combination of the whole, applying diverse natural philosophic principles to build devices. Men who are half apron, half natural philosopher."

"Inventive philosophers," Washington muttered, "a fascinating conjecture."

---

42 Packet. A ship carrying mail and cargo on a regular schedule.

"Ingenerare philosophers may be a more accurate term," Jefferson suggested.

"Ingenerare?" Washington asked.

"To create," Jefferson answered.

Franklin chuckled. "Tom and his Latin. Why not use English? Or French?"

" 'Engine' philosophers?" Jefferson said. " 'Engignier' philosophers? 'Engine-er' philosophers?"

Washington didn't know the etymology, but engines were also military siege implements. Catapults and assault towers in the distant past, cannon in colonial times. Individuals who built and operated these "engines" were sometimes called engine-ers, or enginers.

Jefferson saw Washington's perplexed expression and shrugged. "It was just conjecture. Shall we examine the Watt wagons up close?"

"For that we need indigenous clothes." Washington looked at Franklin, who peered at the stairway and frowned.

That'll kill me, he thought. *Of course, if I refuse to climb it, so will George.* Franklin sighed as he stood.

"I'll ascend instead of Ben," Jefferson offered.

"We'd require teams of horses to transport your purchases," Washington replied.

"Iron horses?" Franklin said.

"As if you two are a couple of Republicans."

By Republican, Jefferson meant a frugal individual. Colonial monarchies spawned ultra-wealthy upper classes that maintained their life of luxury by impoverishing the masses. Many colonial philosophers viewed this as immoral, and favored a minimalist republican government that took from the people only that which was absolutely necessary. A leader that was a true "Republican" shunned pomp and opulence and lived a life of modest simplicity. It was fashionable in colonial philosophical circles to flaunt one's frugality somewhat, as a contrast to, and therefore as an indictment of, the sinful extravagance of European courts and monarchs.

"Ben and I are not Republicans," Washington conceded. "But we also don't spend like you. Regardless, Ben will ascend."

Franklin produced the notes, peeled off a few dozen, and gave the rest to Washington. "I have no concept of prices. But if this can't buy three sets of garments, then . . ."

"Then America is no longer free," Jefferson said.

Washington held out another eighth-inch stack of hundred dollar bills. "Assume the worst. I'd hate to make you ascend twice."

As usual, Washington was being exceedingly cautious, though not irrationally so. Clothes were exorbitant in the colonial world because all fabric was hand-made. The average person owned two or three outfits, which they usually patched and wore for at least a decade. A fine formal gown was comparable in value to a minivan, and a typical American spent more on clothing than they did housing.

Franklin accepted the eighth inch then cleaned himself up as best he could. "Should I wear my hat?" he asked.

"Whatever you prefer," Washington replied. "You'll probably stand out regardless."

Franklin donned his tricorne. "Anything else?"

Jefferson and Washington relayed their garment sizes. "Don't forget weapons," Washington said. "And don't take *any* unnecessary risks. I'll ascend and search for you if you don't return by dark."

"Relax," Franklin said, as he began to waddle across the hill. "I'm not a total rube. I just act it with you dandies."

"Good luck!" Jefferson said.

"Move faster!" Washington hissed. "Or we'll have grown cotton and sewn garments before you return!"

"You can sew?" Franklin quipped.

Washington cocked a fist. "I can punch."

"You and Tom picking cotton! I'd pay to see that. Your slaves would have too, I wager."

"I'll whip you like a slave if you don't get moving!"

Franklin slowed, looked around lazily and began whistling. Washington began to rise and Franklin sped up.

"If you're not back by dark I'll tan your hide!"

Franklin laughed. "If I'm not back by dark you are probably my most trifling concern."

WASHINGTON AND JEFFERSON stayed put and watched Franklin. He waited until the lot was deserted, walked past the Watt wagons slowly so he could examine them, and then began climbing. Franklin used the rail as a cane, and made excruciatingly slow progress. His brittle body motions made his pain obvious.

"I hope he doesn't expire," Jefferson said.

"He won't," Washington replied. "You and others coddle him far too much."

Jefferson chuckled. "I suppose you're here to rectify that?"

"Ben chose to grow fat and lazy. I doubt his gout or stone would be as vexing if he'd remained active and been less of a glutton. Should I increase the group's risk and send one of us or all of us because the journey is difficult for him?"

There was no arguing Washington's logic, but as Jefferson peered at Franklin's gradually shrinking form, he couldn't escape the conviction that making him climb was cruel.

FRANKLIN FELT LIKE he was hiking to heaven. His lungs burned, his joints grew stiffer by the tick and his stone seemed to be swelling. Each time he hobbled up another step he told himself the ascent was insanity, and fought the urge to descend.

Only fear of Washington kept him from doing so.

Washington, Franklin thought, with admiration and frustration. *He could've skipped up these stairs like a child.*

Franklin chuckled at his situation's myriad absurdities while he sang the next stanza of *The Old Man's Wish* in his mind. This was a famous colonial song whose verses included requests for things like a warm home, good friends, pudding on Sundays and a healthy horse. But now, in his old age, it was the reprise that appealed to Franklin:

> May I govern my passions with absolute sway,
> Grow wiser and better as my strength wears away,
> Without gout or stone, by a gentle decay.

I have sung that wishing song a thousand times when I was young, Franklin thought wistfully. *But I never really understood it until my gout and stone struck.*

As his knees flared with pain, Franklin nonetheless continued to smile somewhat. He had long ago realized that the "without gout or stone" clause was a dream, and now, with knowledge of his death provided by Jefferson and Washington, he knew that "a gentle decay" was also a fantasy.

It was tempting to hope that futurity's natural philosophers and physicians could perform miracles, but Franklin didn't want to delude himself. Until he saw conclusive evidence otherwise, he intended to assume the worst.

Franklin's smile nonetheless widened. *Ah, what a glorious challenge! What a sadistic struggle! What a grand adventure! This is life!*

And this was Franklin, the inherently optimistic philosopher that could find a nugget of wisdom and something to smile at in every experience, even a tortuous ascent or a death riddled with pain.

When Franklin vanished from view, Washington and Jefferson retreated to a less visible location. Once they were situated, Washington said, "It's affrightening to see you so much older."

Jefferson laughed. "It's affrightening to be so much older. Both in general, and than the General."

Washington smiled, then frowned suddenly. "I wish I could have said goodbye to Martha. Did you see her after my death?"

Jefferson nodded. "I called on her to pay my respects after you expired, but . . . as for later . . . when I contested Adams for the Presidency, Federalist papers manufactured fallacious charges. Like many Americans, Martha was swayed, and termed me 'one of the most detestable of mankind.' "

Washington smiled ever-so-slightly. "Tell me about your Presidency."

"I spent my first term fending off Alexander and his Federalists."

Washington grimaced glumly as his stomach flexed. Hamilton was his ablest and most trusted advisor, and Jefferson's ablest and most despised political enemy. "You probably blame me."

"Not more than the scoundrels themselves," Jefferson replied. "But partially. You and Adams. I warned you both."

Daily for almost four years while Secretary of State. "Hamilton wasn't a scoundrel. And only a strong national government could have survived, much less endured."

"If a republic's power grows too centralized it becomes an oligarchy. Large government and personal freedom are incompatible."

"Don't lecture me! The republic you envision would have succumbed to chaos."

"O praeclarum custodem ovium lupum.[43]," Jefferson said.

Washington did not speak Latin, but knew the quote because Jefferson had brandished it in the past. He recognized the fire in Jefferson's eyes for the same reason. Like some champion who immediately rises to defend his liege, the Sage of Monticello stood ready to rehash the defining political argument of his era, and most every era.

"This discussion is the past," Washington said.

"So you hope. There has never been an age where the power jobbers were vanquished. All power is eventually abused. That is why governments should be given the absolute minimum."

Thus American history's most ardent crusader for individual liberty stood with his Excalibur, his implicit belief in free people as the ultimate repository

---

43 O praeclarum custodem ovium lupum. Latin. "An excellent protector of sheep, the wolf." Attributed to Marcus Tullius Cicero, the Roman statesman who tried in vain to uphold republican principles during the final civil wars that destroyed the republic.

of a nation's power, drawn. Washington knew this core principle was as much a part of Jefferson as a limb or an organ; it was both heartfelt, and logically considered, and he would defend it anytime, anywhere, no matter how daunting the circumstances or odds.

Washington would never admit it, but he felt outmatched. His own education was minimal, and his philosophical inclinations were limited. Jefferson spoke French, Italian, Spanish and English, and had read thinkers like Cicero and Plato in their native Latin and Greek. Fifteen hours a day in his adolescence and early adulthood, with a fanaticism incomprehensible to a normal person, he had read rigorously, pursuing a systematic understanding of history, government, moral philosophy, natural philosophy, politics, architecture, and law. Jefferson's political beliefs were the result of a consuming quest for enlightenment; he had exposed himself to a huge portion of all the available data, and used an intellect only a few men in history have been granted to analyze it. Some could equal his acquired knowledge, and others his sheer genius, but few were a match for both.

Washington knew he was a match for neither. "Must our first discussion in this future be an argument?" he said.

"A reasonable request. And I'm sorry, George. About the Samson remark."

Washington stiffened and his eyes grew cold. "It is the past. Leave it there."

Jefferson obeyed. "If I was going to be stranded in the future with only one person, I'd want it to be you."

Washington thanked Jefferson, but didn't reciprocate the compliment.

The last step was the only one Franklin bounded, and he capped his celebration with a full-bodied sigh. Removing his tricorne, he wiped his brow on his coat forearm, then sat on a bench prudently placed near the stairway. Franklin basked in the breeze and caught his breath while he surveyed his surroundings.

The Rushmore Pavilion was built into a hill in front of the sculpture, and it resembled a theatre. Ascending rows of backless benches joined a small ground-level stage with two upper levels of buildings. Stairways enclosed the sides.

Like the mountain, the pavilion was rock. It blended with nature, and wasn't intrusive. Franklin realized lesser, more opulent architecture would have detracted from the sculpture.

Large panes of dark glass covered the lower building's rock façade, hybridizing past and present architecturally. Franklin saw trash cans, metal rails and other modern accoutrements, but none appeared structurally intrinsic.

Overall, the pavilion seemed like something a Roman might have built if columns and curves were outlawed, and it wasn't as futuristic as Franklin expected. This was comforting. It gave him the sense some creations might be timeless and immune to obsolescence.

As Franklin wondered what the architect Jefferson would think of the pavilion, a family walked by him, pointed, then whispered. He waved nonchalantly. As they waved back, Franklin noted their clothes, hairstyles, jewelry, postures, gestures and body language.

The most casual glance anywhere resulted in dozens of new observations and scores of questions. Franklin tried to stifle the latter and soak up as much as he could. The natural philosopher in him was now dominant, and Franklin had adopted an analytical mentality; he noted oddities like the towering poles that presumably contained lights and the mounted horns that produced music somehow, but no longer felt staggering surprise.

People came and went. Franklin studied them all. Most stared at him, none spoke to him.

Having recalled the boy's observation that their "costumes" didn't look new, and shrewdly considered the totality of his situation, Franklin realized that he was too dirty and disheveled to be mistaken for a park employee. Most moderners would think him eccentric and unsanitary. Curious, often judgmental glances bore this out, to Franklin's immense satisfaction. At least no one suspected the truth.

By noting rare individuals whose attire deviated from that of the essentially homogenous majority, Franklin developed the sense that functional clothing two or three steps removed from survival gear was the norm. Cultural inferences were more difficult, but some signs of profession and station like the sun worn face and calloused hands of a craftsman, and the bearing and comparably opulent dress of the wealthy, had persisted. In general, futurity's citizens seemed more clean, obese and pampered than colonials. Each new person Franklin saw strengthened this fundamental impression.

Non-whites and females also attracted his attention. Orientals were exceedingly rare in colonial America, and their prevalence was noteworthy, as was the *total* absence of Indians and the large increase in the number of Spaniards. Although the most glaring change was the liberated negroes and women, who conveyed independence in intangible yet conspicuous ways. Colonial America had favored rich, male caucasians, but a pervasive equality now seemed to reign. Franklin regarded this social evolvement as logical and inevitable, and found it pleasing. In the case of the negroes, anyway.

Franklin consulted signs and ascended to the uppermost level, where he saw a restaurant and the gift shop. They were situated on either side of a central walkway lined with square pillars. Flags atop the pillars whipped in the wind.

As Franklin swam through the stream of tourists that flowed into the pavilion nexus, and noted the armada of Watt wagons at the end of the flag-lined walkway, he felt glad he had ascended alone. It didn't take a prophetic imagination to envision Washington or Jefferson engulfed by a curious mob.

People still stared. Some pointed, and the daring few asked what he came to regard as the typical question. Why dress up as Benjamin Franklin at Mount Rushmore?

Franklin also endured what he came to view as the typical observations. His garb was amazingly authentic, and he looked *just like* Ben Franklin. A grungy Ben Franklin, but still Ben Franklin.

One mousy man wearing a bowtie and sports coat offered several rather snooty suggestions for improving the "costume."

Franklin looked at him with complete sincerity and said, "Do you really think I look like Benjamin Franklin?"

"Somewhat," the man replied. "Though I've seen closer resemblances."

"Really?" Franklin said.

The man nodded.

"Do you mind if I ask where?"

Hesitation.

Franklin pressed, but remained scrupulously polite. "How can you be certain?" he finally said, without a hint of sarcasm. "After all, you never met the real Benjamin Franklin."

This quieted the man, who squirmed away soon after. *No need to tell George about that*, Franklin thought with a chuckle.

The costume expert aside, Franklin found the questioners to be good natured, and responded in kind. But he didn't dally.

"What could Ben possibly be doing?" Washington asked. "You walk briskly up to the store, grab garments, pay and return."

"Ben doesn't walk briskly," Jefferson said. "Or shop briskly. He's very particular about his linen. Perhaps you should've sent me."

Washington gritted his dentures. *Jefferson the economist*[44] *or Franklin the hurrier. I haven't faced such futile decisions since the war.*

The flawless glass that covered the gift shop's facade engaged Franklin as he drew close. He could see *everything* inside *perfectly*! The walls were windows! The windows were walls!

---

44 Economist. A frugal individual.

Franklin followed the tourist herd through the entrance on the building's extreme left, and was immediately overwhelmed by the futuristic ambiance. The shop was bright, spacious and clean, and had palatial ceilings. Franklin contrasted his colonial store, a congested home that resembled a dim study, and was typical for his time.

There was nothing typical about this wonder!

As he peered at the electric candles in the ceiling, Franklin marveled at the abundant artificial light they provided. Even at night it would be as day in the store!

And the temperature! It was cooler inside than outside. Unnaturally cool. Artificially cool. Yet there were no fans.

And the oddly textured walls, not rock, yet also not plaster of Paris.

And . . .

Infinite ands.

As with the tourists, there was too much to analyze, and Franklin didn't try. Instead he stepped aside, let others pass, and struggled not to gawk while he took it all in.

Inventions Jefferson described were visible in their perfected forms, including tiny camera obscuras and a humming ether cooler that chilled bottles of water. Paper covered the unusually-thin bottles. Paper that contained writing of some sort.

Advertisements? Franklin wondered. *On each individual ware rather than newspapers, boards, or banners?* The concept was intriguing.

A United States map and flag were mounted on the shop's walls. Used to the sliver of East coast that was colonial America, Franklin was taken aback by its enormous descendant. The rectangular star pattern that had replaced the colonial flag's circular arrangement was also glaring.

Franklin wanted to examine these curiosities, and scores of others, but he realized doing so would take too long. With a sigh of resignation, he approached the clothing section near the entrance and began browsing. The sooner he made purchases and descended, the sooner he could rest his aching body in a tavern.

Every garment has George and Tom's faces on it! Franklin thought. Those that didn't stuck to the general theme of American patriotism, and were equally inappropriate for founding fathers trying to travel incognito.

Don't they have a "Long Live the British Monarchy!" shirt? Franklin thought sarcastically. He chuckled as he envisioned Washington's response to an "I'm not George Washington" shirt.

Franklin went through three more racks, found nothing, but remained patient. Long hours of natural philosophic experimentation had bred a tolerance for unexpected obstacles in him.

On a wall above the garments, images of America's 43 Presidents and their term years were displayed sequentially in a long row. Franklin had met the first six: Washington, John Adams, Jefferson, James Madison, James Monroe and John Quincy Adams. He recognized the 16th and 26th, Lincoln and Theodore Roosevelt, from Mount Rushmore. All others were unknown, though two stood out: James K. Polk, the 11th, because he was the first captured with a camera obscura rather than painted, and George W. Bush, the 43rd, because he was the most recent, having been elected in 2001.

Franklin checked shirt prices while he browsed, realized all were between $20 and $50, and felt mild relief. Unless comparative costs of other necessities like food and shelter had become skewed, the notes the Puppeteer had bequeathed represented an enormous amount of wealth.

New observations continued to assault Franklin. Simple things were very telling. Metal hangers, for instance. In Colonial America, metal was somewhat scarce, and simple utilitarian items like nails were expensive. Invention must have made mining and blacksmithing much easier. How else could the copious use of a precious resource for something as frivolous as hangers be explained?

Like the internally ticketed shirts, and most every other ware Franklin saw, the hangers were identical, and seemed to be produced en masse.

"Dressin' up like Franklin at Rushmore," Franklin heard someone whisper. "What a fuckin' dork."

He couldn't tell who made the remark, and didn't know what the words meant, but inflection made the general meaning clear. Franklin was grateful rather than insulted. Whatever a 'fuckin' dork' was, it was at least something familiar, and not terribly suspicious.

Franklin's haggard appearance continued to suggest indigence to many. One loud child asked his mother if the man in the costume was insane. Franklin simply chuckled. No matter how insulting the speculations became, any that weren't the truth remained fine with him.

"Can I help you, sir?" a female voice inquired.

Franklin turned and saw a young woman wearing one of the stars and stripes shirts he had considered purchasing. "Do you work here?" he asked.

"No. I'm just a good Samaritan."

"You look like one," Franklin said dryly. Returning her sarcasm seemed appropriate.

"So what are looking for, Mr. Franklin. A kite and a key?"

That's all anyone remembers me for. "I'm looking for a shirt. A plain shirt. No flags, no mountains, no bright hue, no portraits of Washington or Jefferson. Just a garden shirt."

"Garden? You mean like for gardening?"

"Nay. No. Ahh . . . generic . . . nondescript. Just a normal shirt."

"Let me guess," the Samaritan said, with especially thick sarcasm. "You don't want to look like a tourist."

"I have to get out of this costume. My other garments were pilfered and I reek."

She clearly agreed with the odor assessment, but was more polite now that an other-than-homeless-bum explanation had been offered.

"I need normal clothes," Franklin said. "These seem . . ."

She nodded. "Try a mall."

"Is there one nearby?"

"With 'garden' clothes?"

"Yes."

"25 miles. Rapid City."

"I need garments now."

"You'd probably have better luck buying the clothes off somebody's back, but I'll do what I can."

WASHINGTON GESTURED FOR silence as he and Jefferson re-approached the parking lot looking for Franklin. Aware that Jefferson possessed more stealth than Franklin, he risked a closer look that allowed eavesdropping.

A family exited their car while examining Rushmore brochures. Besides the parents, there were two boys, one teenaged and one that was perhaps ten.

"That's neat," the wife said. "They have flags for all fifty states near the pavilion."

"Fifty?" Washington gasped.

Jefferson was less surprised. "I haven't told you about the Louisiana Purchase," he whispered. "Or the Adams-Onis Treaty."

"I'd love to free climb Rushmore!" the teen said. "I'd lay a piton right up old George's nose."

"Could you really?" his younger brother asked.

"Are you kidding? Old George has got a schnoz the size of a teepee. It's big enough to wall camp in."

"It's too bad they didn't have plastic surgeons in colonial times," the wife said. "Washington's nose really is big."

The observation wasn't a revelation to Washington, who pondered his first love Sally Fairfax, and wondered if a better nose, teeth and complexion might have increased her interest. As Sally was the wife of his close friend and neighbor George William Fairfax, Washington knew this wouldn't have mattered, but he couldn't help fantasizing.

"Washington's nose isn't the point," the father said. "We are at a memorial that is a tribute to America, and my family isn't talking about history or politics or *The Constitution*, but nose jobs and rock climbing. It's disrespectful. These men risked everything to preserve the freedoms we take for granted."

"Come on, Dad!" the teen sighed. "No lectures. This is a vacation!"

"I wonder what the founders would say if they saw you treating their sacrifices with such flippancy and ingratitude?"

Washington raised an index finger, as people often do before speaking. He seemed ready to exit the woods and reply. Jefferson knew he would never do such a thing, and wasn't really nervous. *Now if it were Franklin*, he thought.

As the father continued his lecture, the teen rolled his eyes. "Why don't we have a séance and tell the founders thanks?"

"One more sarcastic comment like that and you'll spend the weekend in the hotel room."

"You're going to punish me just because I don't get a hard-on thinking about American history like you do?"

"Yes indeedy. And watch your mouth."

"Wouldn't the founding fathers oppose such tyranny?"

While Washington and Jefferson shook their heads, the mother prevented a confrontation. "Not another word out of you," she said to the teen. "Or else."

"Was Dad this big a gomer when you met him in college?" he replied. "Or did he evolve into a *National Lampoon* character?"

Washington thought of his spoiled stepson Jackie Custis as an annoyed sense of déjà vu filled him. *Dot*[45] *the brat!* he thought. *Cage him in the hotel! Do something! Don't make idle threats!*

The father seemed to agree with Washington, but like Martha centuries before, his wife once again protected the teen. She gave her son a pleading look as they approached the stairway. Humor your father, it said. The teen smiled acquiescence, cementing the truce.

Now that his son was subdued, the father once again stared at the Rushmore pamphlet ceremoniously. As he and his family began their ascent, he looked at his wife with great curiosity. "What do you suppose the founders would think of America today?"

---

45 Dot. Hit.

Once the family disappeared, Washington and Jefferson retreated into the woods and discussed what they had seen. "That man seemed rather immature," Jefferson said.

Washington nodded. "He needs a stiff dose of discipline."

"The parents treated him like a child. Could he be a child? Could social conceptions of maturity have changed?"

Washington thought of Jackie Custis again. "Most men will remain children as long as you let them. Though if you are correct, I hope jackanapes[46] like that 'lad' are the exception."

"The father's comments about us were quite laudatory," Jefferson said. "And they add weight to our circumstantial supposition that the American Republic still exists."

Washington nodded. "He mentioned liberties 'taken for granted.' Presumably, this means they survived in some form. 'National Lampoon' seems to corroborate this assumption with its implication of a free press. Is it a political satire, perhaps?"

Washington shrugged. "The father also wondered what we would think of this future. Further proof that our time transport experience is esoteric?"

"That seems logical," Jefferson agreed.

They discussed other, more trivial observations, then Washington said, "Tell me about this Louisiana Purchase."

"It was the toughest decision of my Presidency," Jefferson said. "And the most difficult political decision of my life."

Washington listened attentively as Jefferson outlined the fortuitous circumstances that led Napoleon Bonaparte to offer sale of the largest territorial addition in American history.

"I think this is as garden as it gets," Franklin said.

The Samaritan nodded agreement.

"No britches at all?" he asked.

"Sorry. It's tough to sell pants with Rushmore on them."

And these vulgar sarks are easier? "Is there a fitting room?"

"No."

Franklin guessed shirt sizes. He erred on the large side, then thanked the Samaritan for her help and continued shopping. The moment he left, she searched for air freshener.

---

46 Jackanape. Brat.

Franklin was curious about the current state of his profession, and couldn't resist a brief trip to the bookstand. He also knew Washington would crucify him if he didn't check for arms, so he visited a display case where replicas of archaic colonial weapons were sold. Franklin felt nostalgia, but the mementos also issued a stern warning; he knew that if he didn't integrate into this new world, he would be as obsolete as the wares that surrounded him.

"You have my approbation," Washington said, when Jefferson concluded his description. "In securing Louisiana, you secured America's future."

"Thank you, George. I appreciate such sentiments because they were not universal. The acquisition of Louisiana was disapproved by some who feared the enlargement of our territory would endanger its union. But who can limit the extent to which the federative principle may operate effectively? The larger our association, the less will it be shaken by local passions."

"So you still think Montesquieu[47] incorrect?"

Jefferson nodded. "His doctrine that a republic can be preserved only in a small territory has been proved a falsehood. The reverse is the truth. The larger the extent of a country, the more firm its republican structure, if founded not on conquest, but principles of compact and equality."

"How large is the extent of our country? Does it now encompass the whole North American continent?"

"I know not. But during my Presidency I initiated an overland expedition which reached our western coast."

"The final frontier," Washington whispered with awe. "You charted the final frontier?"

Jefferson shook his head. "Captain Meriwether Lewis and Lieutenant William Clark did."

As Jefferson described the two-year odyssey of colonial America's Columbuses, Washington's amazement continually increased. A veteran of multi-month surveying trips in the Virginia and Ohio regions, he was keenly aware of the courage required to venture westward into such a vast unknown. Lewis and Clark's feat staggered the imagination as surely as an airline!

"We need not know the boundaries of the current republic to be cheerful about its prospects," Jefferson concluded, "for it will take a hundred generations to fill even the Louisiana territories."

"That estimate seems overly optimistic."

---

47 Montesquieu. Charles-Louis Montesquieu. French political philosopher. His most famous work, *The Spirit of the Laws*, greatly influenced American intellectuals.

Jefferson thought a moment. "When one considers Watt wagons and airlines, probably. But it has been less than a dozen generations. The western lands should not have been filled. Could not have been filled."

"That much I concur with."

Jefferson nonetheless seemed concerned. "Our hope of America's duration was built much on the enlargement of the resources of life going hand in hand with the enlargement of territory. Men are disposed to live honestly if the means of doing so are open to them. Our manufacturers were as much at their ease, as independent and moral as our agricultural inhabitants, and they will continue so as long as there are vacant lands to resort to. For whenever other classes attempt to reduce them to the minimum of subsistence, they will quit their trades and labor the earth."

"And if the western territories are filled?"

Jefferson frowned. "I think our governments will remain virtuous as long as they are chiefly agricultural. This will be as long as there shall be vacant lands in any part of America. When they get piled upon one another in large cities, as in Europe, Americans will become corrupt as in Europe."

Washington considered Alexander Hamilton's prediction of an urban, manufactory America more realistic than Jefferson's rural, agrarian vision, but he did not reopen the rift. "This gloomy hypothetical will not dampen my enthusiasm for your tremendous accomplishments. When I think of the blood that has oft been spilled to acquire mere parcels, I cannot help but rejoice! Let the poor, the needy and oppressed of the Earth, and those who want land, resort to the fertile plains of our western country, the second land of promise, and there dwell in peace, fulfilling the first and great commandment!"

Jefferson agreed with this sentiment, but he also felt concern. The poor, the needy and oppressed of the Earth could fill a hundred Louisiana Territories or western frontiers in but a few generations; if America allowed unlimited immigration, it might squander the western cornucopia that was the foundation of its long-term prosperity.

Jefferson pondered this worrisome possibility, but did not dwell on it. Few men basked in the glow of Washington's approbation, and the Sage of Monticello savored the moment.

FRANKLIN OBSERVED the cashier while he waited in line. Some customers paid with notes, but others used small cards that were processed in some way and handed back. Futuristic promissory notes perhaps?

"Why'd you dress up like Ben Franklin at Mount Rushmore?" a man in line asked.

"I don't look like Washington or Jefferson or Lincoln," Franklin replied. "I look like Franklin."

"The costume seems real enough anyway."

"It isn't a costume. I'm Benjamin Franklin."

The man laughed. "And I'm JFK."

Franklin laughed with him, and wondered who JFK was.

The next two customers paid with notes, but the third used a card. "Debit or credit?" the cashier asked.

"Debit."

"Please enter your PIN."

As Franklin watched the woman touch numbers on the keypad, he quickly surmised what was happening.

Bloody amazing!

Did all citizens have such a card? Was credit now universal, or had it remained a luxury enjoyed primarily by the well to do?

The technology the tiny card utilized, and more importantly implied, continued to amaze Franklin, but there was also something ominous about the device. Surely stores checked bank ledgers before approving purchases. Surely this was why the woman entered a confidential cipher. Were individual banks contacted, or was there was a central repository of information about everyone? Wouldn't those that controlled such information control the society? Couldn't money jobbers create a system where specie was abolished or greatly reduced and accounting entries were the de facto currency? Where depreciation of the currency didn't even require one to print physical notes, but could be accomplished by mere bookkeeping?

These cards would give Jefferson a conniption, Franklin thought, as his turn for checkout came. He hid his amazement as the cashier used a pistol that expelled red light to read prices. He had *no idea* how it might operate, and though he knew there had to be a natural philosophic explanation, it nonetheless seemed magical to him.

Franklin hid his nervousness as he paid with hundreds, which the cashier scrutinized, then marked with a peculiar, blunt-tipped, featherless quill. He was grateful she didn't look back and forth between him and the notes the way tourists had Washington, Jefferson and Rushmore.

"$262.31," she said, as she counted out notes and coins. "Out of three hundred. $37.69 is your change."

Franklin took the bags in his free hand. They were made of slippery material that gave the simultaneous impression of being water resistant and durable.

Though trivial to other customers, the ticket the cashier handed Franklin was one of the greatest wonders he had seen so far. Or, more properly, the tiny press that printed it was. Each ticket was clearly unique, yet the type hadn't been changed even once! Franklin thought of the thousands of hours he'd spent lugging presses and resetting fonts and wanted to groan. At least the ciphers on the notes now made sense. Currency, pamphlets and books were probably printed with larger versions of the invention.

While counting his change, Franklin saw Washington's face on the one dollar note and responded with a guarded double take. He perused the other notes quickly. Lincoln was on the five, Hamilton the ten, a Jackson he recognized from the Presidential portraits the twenty. It seemed the greater one's stature, the smaller the denomination, which made sense; more numerous notes were more desirable from a memorabilia standpoint.

Though he enjoyed ribbing him, Franklin didn't mind being upstaged by Washington; the enormity of his contribution to the American existence was almost impossible to overestimate. George belonged on the one. Franklin was too ignorant to be sure, but Lincoln seemed a reasonable choice for the five. After that things grew confusing. Where was Jefferson? And besides military service in the revolution and championing the Constitutional Convention, what had Hamilton done to merit parity with the likes of Lincoln and Washington? Served as Executive? No. He hadn't been on the wall. If Hamilton was on a note, why not Madison, who had fathered *The Constitution* and been Executive?

I don't know the history that has transpired since I lived, Franklin told himself. *Or how the War for Independence has been depicted. I can't judge such questions accurately.*

But as he pocketed the currency that was also a photo album of sorts, and saw another customer pay with a promissory card rather than notes, Franklin was concerned for the first time.

"Did Franklin sail to Britain for those clothes?" Washington said.

"I think he prefers the tailors in France," Jefferson replied.

Washington grunted. "Perhaps I should have gone after all." The remark was borne of calm analysis, not hasty regret.

"Ben was the logical choice. We both know that."

"I hope nothing's happened." Once again, calm concern.

"Ben's no soldier," Jefferson said, "but he can be resourceful when circumstances demand it. And as a natural philosopher, he is perhaps more qualified to navigate this inventive age than you or I."

"I hope you're right."

So do I, Jefferson thought.

"Let's go see the Watt wagons yet again," Washington said. "And Ben hopefully."

"Look!" Jefferson whispered to Washington. "Niggers!"

An African-American family was descending the stairway. They were distant, and only their color was discernable.

"Slaves?" Jefferson said.

"I can't tell," Washington replied. "But we'll know in a tick. And don't talk. Concentrate on moving quietly."

Jefferson obeyed. Washington completed the approach quickly, and the voyeurs were perched behind the sculptor's studio in time to see their quarry's features grow more distinct.

"These niggers' clothes appear plusher than the masters'!" Jefferson gasped.

"We are ignorant of styles," Washington said. "And these are the first niggers we have seen. But their garments do seem opulent."

As the family neared the bottom of the stairway, their conversation echoed through the empty parking lot. "Don't believe what the white historians and school teachers tell you," the father said to his son. "Lincoln didn't care about slaves."

"Really?" the pie-eyed boy said.

The father nodded. "The Civil War was about money. The north had factories where paid workers manufactured goods, and the south had plantations where we picked cotton for free. Foreign countries made inexpensive manufactured goods that the south preferred to costlier equivalents made in the north. Rather than improve and compete, northerners convinced Congress to pass tariffs on these imports. Foreign countries retaliated by passing tariffs on exported American cotton, which they usually purchased. After the tariffs, cotton grown in other countries was cheaper than America's, so people stopped buying it." The father had clearly recited the sermon many times, and he whizzed through it smoothly. "The South seceded to escape the tariff. That's what the Civil War was about! Money, not freedom for our people."

"But Lincoln fr—" the son began.

"The *Emancipation Proclamation* was pure propaganda," the father said. "Men don't join wars about high tariffs. They die for causes. The North couldn't field enough soldiers to beat the South, so Lincoln cooked up his *Proclamation* as a public relations scheme. It worked. Suddenly the war was 'righteous' and volunteers were lining up for a chance to die."

"Washington and Jefferson both owned slaves," the mother said to her son. "Don't ever forget that."

Washington and Jefferson exchanged a glance.

"In the white world that means they put you on a fuckin' mountain!" the father growled.

"Don't swear in front of Michael, honey."

"Sorry." The father squatted and faced his son. "Sorry I swore, Mike. I shouldn't cuss, and neither should you." He reinforced the fact that swearing was wrong, asked his son to wait in the car, then spoke to his wife. "I'm glad we came. My father brought me here and taught me the truth and his father did the same. Somehow, hearing it at this monumental hypocrisy makes it sink in more."

Washington and Jefferson exchanged another glance while the wife nodded. This latent resentment seemed incomprehensible and deranged to whites, and she knew that in some subconscious way most trivialized it. She never grew vehement like her husband, but she nonetheless identified with what he was saying. All her people did to some degree, and Rushmore was a fundamentally different experience for a black. As was America.

The husband's eyes brimmed with anger as he looked up the stairway. "I'd love to go back and take care of those bastards!"

"What would you do?"

"Drop the motherfuckers off on Crenshaw, grab some barbecue, then come back and skullfuck the corpses."

The wife chuckled. "You scare me sometimes."

"Naw," the husband said. "Naw. That's not what I'd do. I'd get myself a tiny little plantation in the Caribbean or on some remote Greek island. Call it Cockacello[48]. I'd chain those motherfuckers up at Cockacello, put 'em to work, and give 'em the old Kunta Kintae. None of this George Washington or Thomas Jefferson shit! Naw. Those hypocrites would have African names! I'd have 'All Men Are Created Equal' tattooed on their backs in big-ass, black, block letters, brand 'em like cattle with a Malcolm 'X', whip 'em, rape 'em, and then get medieval on their asses!"

"Damn, Tyrone. You're harsh."

Tyrone's grimace turned even more pugnacious as he slowly shook his head. "I'm not harsh. What those motherfuckers did to us . . . now that's harsh."

Jefferson was going to shift his weight, but the second he moved Washington turned his head warily. The angry look in his eyes stopped Jefferson cold. "Don't move," he mouthed. Washington was totally focused on the clearing, and looked like a cat ready to pounce.

Thank Providence you're here, Jefferson thought, as he watched Washington watch.

---

48 Cockacello. Monticello was Jefferson's home. It is Italian for 'little mountain'. Mont, mountain. Cello, little. Cockacello is a mocking reference to the belief that Caucasians have smaller penises than African-Americans.

Tyrone put his arm around his wife, smiled, and kissed her on the cheek. "Brothers need to find some ebony mountain somewhere. Carve Malcolm, Martin, and Rosa in it."

Tyrone pulled away from his wife when he saw a white family nearing the bottom of the stairs. "Ebony and ivory livin' in perfect harmony, my ass!"

Their child was calling for its mother. Tyrone's wife grabbed his hand briefly, then entered the vehicle.

Before he did likewise, Tyrone thought of Mount Rushmore one last time and spat on the ground. "Somebody should blow this fucking thing up!"

THOUGH WASHINGTON and Jefferson were not surprised that niggers would have lingering resentment, the sheer vehemence of the hatred was nonetheless an eye opener. After the family drove off, Washington said, "I fear for Ben."

"And America."

"No philosophy for now."

"Ben opposed slavery late in life," Jefferson said.

"Do you think that would matter to a nigger like the one we just saw?"

"I didn't say that. But there are whites everywhere. They don't seem worried."

"Well I am."

WASHINGTON'S CONCERN for Franklin made him decide to wait near the parking lot indefinitely. Other black families came and went, and though none seemed spiteful, Washington and Jefferson were now subject to a kind of involuntary racial programming; every nigger they saw made them wary.

"Developments like this are why I always preach caution," Washington said.

"Preach away," Jefferson replied. "You'll not find me arguing."

"Anonymity is now paramount. If a group of niggers determined who we are, the results might be grim."

"While you are preaching, pray that Ben acquired weapons."

"I'll settle for his prompt return."

"Not me. I want a weapon. And not some archaic musket or pistol. I want an advanced one from this time."

"What of peace?" Washington's smile was mocking. "Have you abandoned your mantra?"

"Vindictive niggers are an exception. Especially since Gabriel's Conspiracy."

"A slave rebellion?"

"The most significant of my life. In 1800, shortly after I was elected President, a Virginia slave named Gabriel Prosser organized a large-scale uprising. The first portion of his plan called for the burning of Virginia's capitol and the capture of prominent hostages such as the Governor."

"By Providence!" Washington gasped. "Was he successful?"

"Nay. Slave informers leaked the plot, the Virginia militia was mobilized, and the uprising was quashed."

"A bold plan, nonetheless. Unusually audacious, for a nigger."

Jefferson nodded. "Gabriel was motivated by the rhetoric of the French and American revolutions."

"And your *Declaration*, perhaps?"

Jefferson frowned.

Washington joined him. He felt guilt, but only for a moment. Though he was in a progressive future, he had not discarded the survival reflexes of his racist past. Southerners like he and Jefferson lived on plantations where slaves outnumbered able-bodied whites by at least ten to one. The precedent of rebellion could not be tolerated, for even one modest success might lead to nationwide upheaval. "A punitive example was made, I hope."

"Of course," Jefferson replied. "Gabriel and 33 of his co-conspirators were hung."

"Co-conspirators. Slave informers." Washington shook his head, then sighed deeply. "What sort of nigger would sabotage his brethren's attempt to obtain liberty?"

"The kind I strived to own," Jefferson replied.

"Were I a nigger, I would die rather than turn Benedict."

Jefferson chuckled with dread. "Thank Providence you aren't a nigger. With a commander such as you leading a slave uprising . . ."

"Were I a nigger, I would have organized a nationwide insurrection. Every slave in the nation would have acted in unison, executing their masters at a predetermined day and time."

"I do not want to ponder such things. Thank Providence niggers were stupid. And devoid of a great leader like you."

"Not merely stupid," Washington said. "Something worse. When the British oppressed us, we risked all, and would have died rather than submit."

"It seemed inevitable that niggers would eventually mimic us and develop the same mindset." Jefferson's face contorted with fear as he juxtaposed events like Gabriel's uprising with the hatred he had just witnessed. "If that nigger had a few accomplices, he could have captured us, put us in his Watt wagon, and we'd once again be a part of the past."

Figuring it would end up drenched in sweat as he descended, Franklin decided not to wear his new shirt, and he regretted this decision the moment he exited the store. Two steps out, tourists closed in. Franklin answered the usual inquiries pleasantly, but also kept conversations shorter and tried to walk while he talked. George was probably livid by now.

New phenomenon continued to bombard Franklin.

Bright purple hair. Jewelry worn savage-style, piercing lips, noses, eyebrows. Dual-eyed spyglasses that did not require extension. Thin cigars that were rolled in paper rather than leaves, seemed to be produced en masse rather than by hand, and had unusual butts.

Every step brought a new realization, every glance a new experience, every fleeting word of conversation a new question. The First American stepped, and glanced, and listened, but most of all he learned.

FRANKLIN PAUSED BEFORE he approached the stairs to paid parking and glanced at Mount Rushmore one last time. Above him, George and Tom still stood sculpted in granite.

Franklin smiled.

All these people paying homage to a stone visage, standing under Tom and George's noses, totally unaware that the opposite was also true.

Franklin laughed. Then he walked away from his companions, and headed toward them.

THOUGH STILL PAINFUL, the descent was less excruciating than the ascent, and Franklin could think while he hobbled down the stairs. His mind ricocheted from topic to topic every few steps.

Clothing prices were reasonable.

Seemed reasonable. Invention could have lowered production costs, offsetting depreciation. So prices are tough to gauge.

Still, this money bought much, and will buy much, which is good for George, Tom, and I. But what of wages? How long would it take a citizen of this time to earn the money we hold?

At least my hundred wasn't the smallest denomination . . .

Maybe I shouldn't fret the promissory cards, Franklin thought. *Perhaps they are currency's logical evolvement.*

Am I not being progressive enough in my thinking?

Another step, another thought.

No.

No! Don't assume that safeguards exist. Jefferson's observation about human nature's invariance is astute.

It is awfully cynical and pessimistic to assume corruption before even studying the society.

But not unrealistic. And Jefferson is no pessimist.

Franklin took another step, and wondered about the clear glass walls that covered the gift shop. How did they weather winds and storms without breaking?

"What's in the bag?" an ascending tourist asked.

"A kite and a key," Franklin replied.

The tourist chuckled at the joke.

Franklin smiled back. *When in Rome . . .*

Franklin thought of the Watt wagon communicator, ticket press, artificial horns, promissory notes, cipher pads, red-light reader, and other wonders he had seen. What natural philosophic principles were utilized to create them?

Leyden jars stored electric fire that could be used to displace a magnet. Could one put letters on a compass instead of bearings and apply electric fire of differing strength to point at each letter? Or a coding system that utilized electric fire bursts of alternating duration and strength? This conceptualization was crude, but could these principles have been utilized in a more sophisticated way?

Franklin didn't know, but he nonetheless continued to brainstorm, and groped at other natural philosophic insights.

Franklin was careful to tread gently, with soft, almost tip-toeing steps, but he accidentally descended a step hard and his stone flared.

Dropping his bags, he grabbed his midsection reflexively, and winced. *Bloody bastard of a stone! If George is right and Providence sent us here, you'd think he or she or it would have seen fit to cure me!*

"Cool costume," an ascending woman said, as she and Franklin passed each other.

"Thank you," he replied, as he once again wiped his brow. *But actually it's rather hot.*

Her comfortable looking garments and vitality appealed to Franklin. He wanted to be rid of his old clothes suddenly. Wanted to dress like this era's citizens. And live like them.

While Franklin rested at a small clearing in the stairway, he stopped thinking about individual observations, and viewed his situation holistically and philosophically. He realized that the amount of time he'd been gone, be it on a trip to the shop or the future, wasn't important.

Invention was.

The advancements he experienced had accelerated Franklin's emotional equilibrium process, crystallizing his view not of the future, about which he still had infinite questions, but rather his own era. Franklin had no doubts that whether it was a second or a century behind him, whether he returned five ticks from now or never, he would forever view his old time as the past.

WASHINGTON SIGHED with relief when he saw Franklin's rotund form wobbling down the stairs. It was clear the journey had taken its toll. Washington wouldn't have thought it possible, but Franklin was descending slower than he'd climbed. "These last few rods will take him until morning," he groaned.

"At least he isn't being chased by a rout of niggers," Jefferson said.

"Chased?" Washington chuckled. "As if he could run."

WHEN FRANKLIN COMPLETED his descent, he sat on the lowermost step, waited for the lot to empty, then waddled into the woods and rejoined his companions.

"You took long enough," Washington said.

"Traversing the future isn't as easy as you might think."

"We founded another republic while you were gone."

"Yes, Martha."

"Watch it."

"Don't whine like a wench and I won't treat you like one." Franklin shook his head. "And you chide me for complaining too much."

Jefferson grinned broadly as he clasped Franklin on the shoulder. "My Rocinante returns."

"Still a Cervantes fanatic, I see. Help your decrepit horse sit down, Tom Quixote."

Jefferson obeyed, and settled Franklin against a tree. "What of prices and depreciation?" he asked.

"My notes were the smallest denomination."

Jefferson paled slightly. "No?"

"No." Franklin smiled. He handed Jefferson the ticket, and let him deduce his question's ambiguous answer.

"The ticket lists the year," Jefferson noted. "2001."

"And the exact time the purchase was made," Franklin added. He described the futuristic printer.

"Do you think Gregory's calendar[49] still reigns?" Jefferson asked. "Or have additional errors been discerned?"

---

49 Gregorian calendar. A reformed calendar established by Pope Gregory XIII in 1582. The previous standard established by Julius Caesar had overestimated the length of the year by 11 minutes and 14 seconds, creating a 10 day discrepancy by the time of Gregory's reforms. All three founders were alive when Britain and her possessions finally adopted this new calendar in 1752.

Franklin shrugged. "Maybe our old new calendar is the new old. Similar questions apply to chronometer conventions."

"Sales tax," Jefferson read. "A five percent sales tax!"

"Federal or state?" Washington asked.

"It doesn't say."

Washington's brow furrowed. "This is a significant uncertainty. The way taxes are levied is as important as their amount."

Franklin nodded. "In the original *Constitution*, indirect taxes were the primary source of Federal revenue. Did this change?"

"Not in my lifetime," Jefferson replied.

"This indirect sales tax is a federal tax then?"

"How could we assume otherwise?" Jefferson shook his head. "Five percent. Five bloody percent! A staggering burden!"

"Certainly strenuous," Washington agreed. "But worthwhile if it has perpetuated an efficacious union."

Jefferson's eyes flared. "Prior to the Revolution, what was our aggregate tax rate?"

"Outside of war time?" Franklin replied.

Jefferson nodded. "Especially the exorbitant French & Indian War, which would skew any estimate."

Franklin thought a moment. "Two to three percent. This would include external taxes imposed by Britain to enforce the Navigation Acts, internal provincial, county, and town taxes, inter-colonial taxes, and fees."

"Three percent. For *all* government. And futurity's Federal branch confiscates five?"

Franklin chuckled. "Let us avoid paroxysm until we determine futurity's tax rates conclusively."

Washington ran his hands up and down one of the shopping bags. "What is this strange substance?" he asked.

"I have no idea," Franklin replied.

"Not even a guess?"

"Not even a guess."

"That bulge looks like a weapon," Jefferson said.

Franklin smiled. "That's what the wenches tell me."

His companions shook their heads while Franklin brandished the bulge and held it out.

Washington accepted the axe, tested the edge with his fingertip, then said, "The blade seems grotty[50]."

---

50 Grotty. Shoddy.

"It is merely an ornament," Franklin replied. "But it'll have to do."

"Is that what you tell the wenches?" Washington laughed as he spoke to Jefferson. "Ben's roger isn't an ornament. It's a relic. A relic from an age long past."

At least my "relic" produced offspring. "We'll see if you're still laughing in five or ten years. And I think you've worn this pun out."

"I don't." Washington's laughter grew more mirthful.

"I thought we were the relics," Jefferson said.

Washington stopped laughing. "Only if unearthed."

Franklin dug into a bag and tossed two letter openers at Washington, who threw the axe into the air, deftly caught one opener in each hand, then tossed the one in his right hand toward his left. He caught the descending axe and the other opener simultaneously. The actions took but a second, and were nonchalant. "Muskets?" he asked Franklin.

"In the bags. With the cannon."

"Excellent. At least you have one piece of artillery that will fire."

Franklin laughed. "No firearms, George. Or swords. I purchased the wickedest blades they had."

Washington held the letter opener up and frowned. "Better than nothing, I suppose." He smiled at Franklin. "Sorry to sound like one of your wenches."

"I didn't hear you scream." Franklin handed Jefferson a letter opener, then dispersed pocket knives.

Jefferson smiled as he fiddled with the saw, file, and corkscrew protrusions. "Lighter and more finely crafted, but otherwise it is almost exactly like the Sheffield I carried centuries ago." Like Franklin with the pavilion architecture, he found this permanence comforting.

"At least this knife is functional," Washington said. "The blade is real, but alas too tiny to be of any practical use." He telegrammed the obvious simile with a smile.

"You slander like a Tory[51]!" Franklin laughed. "Though I'd be happy to unleash the kraken and disprove your feeble hypothesis empirically."

"To protrude from under that gut, it'd have to be a kraken."

"Can we please dispense with the vulgar fencing?" Jefferson moaned.

Washington obliged, and gave Franklin a quick summary of the encounter with the angry negro. He downplayed the tension, and wasn't much of a storyteller.

"What if the negro had noticed you?" Franklin asked.

"I would have thrown my teeth at him," Washington answered.

---

51 Tory. An American colonist who supported Britain during the American revolution. A loyalist.

Franklin laughed. "Fearless George."

"I was affrighted enough for both of us," Jefferson said.

How surprising, Franklin thought. "All the negroes I saw appeared to be freemen. Does slavery still exist?"

"The niggers we saw also appeared to be free," Washington replied. "And the angry nigger mentioned an 'Emancipation Proclamation' this Lincoln issued during the Civil War."

"An edict ending slavery?" Franklin wondered.

"A sensible assumption," Washington said. "Though whether it was accepted or successfully enforced is uncertain."

"Maybe the edict precipitated the Civil War," Franklin speculated. "Slavery is such an atrocious debasement of human nature that even its extirpation may open serious evils."

"Our niggers didn't seem to think slavery caused the conflict," Jefferson replied. "Though their perspective is just one. Bitterness could have tainted their interpretation of history."

"Every nigger we have seen has been free," Washington reiterated.

"That doesn't mean all niggers are free," Jefferson countered. "We are in the north. The persistence of southern slavery might explain the niggers' bitterness."

"The negroes I saw all seemed peaceful," Franklin said. "Of course, this was in public. In private, they may feel like the angry negro did. Whatever the negroes' feelings, I pray slavery has been eradicated in the whole nation. If so, America has removed a great pockmark from its complexion."

Washington rubbed his own pockmarks reflectively while he nodded. "There is not a man living who wished more sincerely than I did to see a plan adopted for slavery's gradual abolition."

Franklin narrowed his eyes and glared at Washington. "Gradual abolition. Akin of partially pregnant?"

Washington resented the remark, but knew Franklin was right, so remained silent.

"I pray slavery is as much a part of America's past as we should be," Jefferson said with sincerity. "But if it has not been abolished we should purchase niggers as soon as possible."

While Franklin chuckled morosely, Washington closed his eyes, pinched the upper part of his nose, and exhaled sharply. Jefferson didn't seem bothered by these reactions, but his companions knew better than to wonder what he might be thinking. Though rarely evasive in professional matters, in his personal life Jefferson confronted only what suited him.

"Slavery is nefarious," Franklin said. "We shall not purchase slaves even if they are available."

"Bu—" Jefferson began.

"We shall not purchase slaves! The moment you do, we part company permanently! I am not judging your past, but we shall not canker the future."

Washington spoke before Jefferson could respond. "This is not the time for such a discussion. Just be grateful we are armed, for whether freemen or slaves, this era's niggers represent a serious threat. Now enough dawdling. Let us don our new clothing and locate a tavern."

Washington and Jefferson laughed when they saw the red, white and blue starred and striped shirts; they didn't portray an American flag, but rather seemed to have been made from one.

"Subtle," Jefferson said. "We'll blend right in."

"Worth the wait?" Franklin asked.

"Sally Fairfax wouldn't have been worth a wait that long," Washington replied.

Jefferson peered into the empty bag. "No britches?"

"None were for sale."

"The same shirts for all of us?" Washington asked.

"I could go back if you like."

"Sculpting Rushmore probably took less time than that would."

Jefferson held up a shirt. He noted the short sleeves, casual collar, and three-buttoned aperture just below the neck. "These are horrific!" he said with a chuckle.

"A true affront to taste," Washington agreed.

Franklin laughed. "If you didn't like the flag, you should have asked Betsy Ross to design it differently."

"This from the man who wanted to make our national bird the turkey," Jefferson said.

"The bald eagle is a bird of bad moral character," Franklin replied, with mild indignation. "He does not get his living honestly. The turkey is much more respectable, is a true native of America, and is a bird of courage."

"I love the flag," Washington said. "And the republic for which it presumably still stands. But not as clothing."

"I assure you these were the most tasteful and inconspicuous sarks available."

Washington scoffed, "I find that difficult to believe."

"These sarks would scare scurvy away," Jefferson said.

"Would they even scare Fearless George?" Franklin asked.

"We'll know in a tick." Washington threw a shirt at Franklin. "You selected this 'fashion'. You parade it first."

WASHINGTON AND JEFFERSON laughed at Franklin the moment he returned. "You look like some jester," Washington said.

"One of the Queen's pets," Jefferson added.

"A large pet," Washington said.

"Stick it in your knickers!"

"I don't think its tongue is domesticated," Jefferson said.

"I'd heard the Franklin is hostile to royalty."

"And stupidity. But please, laugh while you can. In a few minutes we'll be a troop of jesters."

"You'll still be the King Jester though," Washington said.

"Don't you mean Executive Jester?" Franklin corrected. "And shouldn't we elect one?"

"You're the only one who hasn't served," Jefferson said. "You've got my vote."

"And mine," Washington added.

"Executive Franklin," Jefferson said. "I like the sound of that."

"As do I." Washington stood and began to change. "An Executive is accountable. The next time Ben takes half a solstice to do twenty ticks of shopping, we can impeach him."

WASHINGTON'S SHIRT was a little too small, and the pudgy Franklin of course looked ridiculous, but Jefferson's garment fit him well. He looked characteristically neat and precise.

"Not a bad start," Washington said. "We look futuristic from the waist up."

"Did you note anything else that may help us look more indigenous?" Jefferson asked Franklin.

"Perhaps you should conceal the axe," Franklin said to Washington. "I didn't see anyone touting a weapon."

Washington complied, and shoved it and their colonial clothing into the slippery sacks.

"Tell me of your trek," Jefferson said.

Franklin gave a quick, colorful narrative. "I was overwhelmed by the inventions and the opulence," he concluded. "Everything suggested wealth, abundance, excess. Especially the people. And the store! By Providence, the store! This Rushmore gift shop appears to cater to the common man, yet in many ways it shamed our most lavish boutiques."

"Luxury for everyone, even the common run." Washington nodded approvingly. "I like this new America."

Franklin played with his lips, and a thought. "I don't think what I saw is opulence to these new Americans. What we considered luxury is probably austerity in this time."

"If so, the rich of this future must live a dream," Washington said.

Jefferson smiled. "If the common run in this future live as well as the rich of our time, then perhaps America itself is the dream."

"The dream we always dreamed," Franklin said.

"Perhaps," Washington replied. "Like you, I always felt optimistic about America's long-term prospects, but we must not draw hasty conclusions."

"I find it pleasing to hope that moral philosophy has kept pace with natural philosophy," Jefferson said. "Hopefully this future's advancements have been used to end destitution and war rather than exacerbate them."

"I cannot mock such a wish," Franklin said, "however fanciful."

Silence. Everyone understood that only time and experience would prove or disprove their speculations.

Franklin's thoughts were drawn back to advertising. In the colonial world goods were comparatively scarce, and generally sold themselves, so advertising was of limited use. Many products Franklin had seen in the gift shop were adorned with bright colors, bold letters, catchy slogans, cute drawings and intricate packaging that seemed to imply a world where buyers were scarcer than goods and purchasing had to be induced.

On the surface, this seemed like a good development. Invention had clearly reduced the effort required to produce life's necessities. The human condition was drastically improved.

Yet . . .

Franklin told himself he was just being pessimistic again, but like the promissory cards, this concept filled him with a vague yet intense foreboding.

Franklin groaned inwardly. Subtle implications were eluding him. Subtle implications that would usually crystallize rapidly. Was the future that difficult? Perhaps. But Franklin knew he was beleaguered by pain, fatigue and the situation in general. He needed to rest, and think in leisurely circumstances, with a lucid mind.

"Let's get moving," Washington said.

"Where?" Jefferson asked.

"Keystone."

"We could ask a Watt wagon for a ride."

Washington shook his head.

"I hardly think obtaining a ride is an excessive risk," Franklin said.

"But it is a risk."

"As is having me hike three miles."

"Obtaining a ride may endanger all of us," Washington said. "Hiking endangers only you."

Franklin looked at Jefferson, who gave him a sympathetic look but shook his head. *Coward*, Franklin thought. *You're petrified by the negroes.* The thought of a three mile hike that would entail more needless suffering made Franklin angry, but he checked his temper, and was careful not to telegraph resentment.

"Are we agreed?" Washington said.

We? Franklin thought. He remained expressionless.

"Ben?" Jefferson said.

"The tavern awaits." Franklin sighed. *Hopefully I'll live to see it.*

"What's in that other bag?" Washington asked.

"Books. You can carry them. I'll hike, but I'm not going to burden myself with a single scruple[52]."

Washington accepted the sacks without comment. "Lead on, President Franklin."

"Franklin will suffice. Doctor Franklin, if you must."

"Yes sir, President Franklin."

"I shall never again respond to that address."

"Even if elected?"

Franklin pursed his lips and turned away.

"I am anxious," Jefferson said. "Answers await."

"So do more surprises, I'll bet." Franklin smiled as he gripped his walking stick and began to hike. "A mere shop flabbergasted me egregiously, almost beyond the thresholds of comprehension. Imagine the wonders we'll encounter in a settlement!"

---

52 Scruple. A very small unit of weight.

The founders stayed in the woods and followed the road away from Rushmore. They exposed themselves only during sign-scouting forays, but during one of these a Watt wagon screeched to a stop behind them. “Unbelievable!” the driver said, as he exited and approached. “I scoured the park looking for you, and here you are on the side of the road! We ran into a family you signed *The Constitution* for. I thought they exaggerated, but you do look *exactly* like the founders! Even without costumes!”

Washington gave Jefferson and Franklin a wary glance.

“My son’s nuts about you guys! Reads everything about the revolution he can find! Says he wants to be a politician, but I tell him to do something honest.” The father laughed, but stopped when the founders didn’t. “Look. I know it’s late, but would you put your costumes back on and talk to my son?”

“We are in a bit of a hurry,” Washington said.

The father removed his wallet. “If it’s a question of money?”

“We don’t need notes. We need garments and transportation to a tavern.” Franklin avoided eye contact with Washington. He could grow warm[53] if he wanted, but they’d been discovered, the risk was assumed, and he’d be damned if he would hike three excruciating miles without at least trying to reap the reward.

Franklin treated, and after terms were reached, the founders entered the woods. They whispered while they changed.

“Our Minister did well,” Washington said. “We’ll get to ride in a Watt wagon, Franklin will be spared the torture of a walk, and we’ll be spared the torture of a walk with Franklin.”

“I’m as elated as you,” Franklin replied. “So that quip will go unpunished.”

Washington turned away quickly as Franklin removed his shirt. “That glimpse was punishment enough.”

Jefferson also avoided looking.

---

53 Warm. Angry.

"I've got a new theory about our Puppeteer's motive," Franklin said, as he donned his colonial garments. "Maybe we've been brought to the future to be exhibits."

Afraid other Watt wagons might stop if they stood near the road "costumed," the founders made the family join them in the woods. The second encounter began like the first, with questions about historical clichés. The new boy was older and less intellectual than his predecessor, so his inquiries had a radically different flavor. "If you crossed the Delaware today would you bring Navy SEALs with you?" he asked Washington.

A futuristic Turtle? Washington wondered. The "Turtle" was a one-man colonial submarine powered by a hand-cranked propeller, but Washington amended this initial impression instantly. A Seal was probably a soldier specially trained in winter or water warfare. "If seals were available, I would have used them."

The child envisioned Washington in his colonial military uniform, hunched in the front of a speeding dinghy that zipped across the ice-filled Delaware. In the back of his craft, SEALs in wetsuits checked their automatic weapons and applied face grease. "Wicked, man!" he said. "Totally wicked! And the nuke? Would you have used it during the Revolution?"

Newk? Washington glanced at Franklin and Jefferson, hoping for help, but they were also ignorant.

"You could've just smuggled a nuke into London on a ship. Ba-boom! Long live the Queen!" The boy laughed.

"I honestly don't know what I would do with newks," Washington replied. "That is a difficult question."

"I guess it would be," the teenage daughter said. "For three men from the eighteenth century."

The founders nodded earnestly at the handsome, voluptuous woman. This was the first time she had spoken, and her comment heightened the sense of intelligence and intolerance that she conveyed. "So how'd you get here?" she asked.

"We came from the past," Franklin replied.

She laughed. "How else, right?"

Franklin ignored venomous looks from Washington and told a truthful account of their time travel experience.

"They certainly act well," the mother whispered.

The father nodded. "Whoever thought this gag up is a genius."

"Franklin is a nice twist."

"Maybe Rushmore's quartet are the regulars and they rotate an additional guest. Franklin one month, FDR another, maybe JFK or Hamilton the next."

The father smiled. “Who knows? If we ever visit again, Nixon or Clinton might be here.”

The wife shook her head disdainfully. Like many Rushmore tourists, she had mentally juxtaposed America’s Father and Honest Abe with modern Slick Willys and Tricky Dicks. Calling the exercise worrisome was crass understatement.

“I’ll bet you Einstein could answer your time travel questions,” the boy said.

“Where would we find this Einstein?” Franklin asked.

“He’s dead,” the boy said. “Isn’t he, Dad?”

“Yes. Einstein died decades ago.”

“Did you rape your slaves?” the daughter asked Jefferson.

“Sarah!” the mother said.

“Never,” Jefferson said calmly.

“What about Sally Hemings?” the daughter replied. “If she was free do you really think she would have slept with you?”

Franklin and Washington glanced at each other, and then Jefferson. Washington shook his head while Franklin chuckled quietly. Tom never ceased to amaze!

The daughter laughed at Jefferson’s wounded expression. At least the actors were having some fun with their roles! “Slavery was bad,” she said, like a parent scolding a child. “Right?”

Jefferson reminded himself that the haughty wench thought him an actor. He’d endured these slanders as President, and could certainly tolerate them now. “Yes. Slavery is bad. An abomination. America never should have embraced it.”

“Why’d you own slaves then?”

“My father left me plantations that were our family legacy. Slaves were the only way to run a plantation in my time.”

“Why didn’t you hire people that were free?” the boy asked.

“Freemen weren’t free,” Jefferson replied. “Or even cheap. When all expenses were factored in, they cost three times as much as slaves.”

“So,” the daughter retorted.

“Well if other plantations use niggers and I don’t, my crops cost three times as much and I can’t compete. The only realistic solution was to abolish slavery for everyone.”

The mother gave Jefferson a dirty look when the “N” word was used. He was concentrating on the boy and didn’t see it.

“Why didn’t you abolish slavery for everyone?” the boy asked.

“I tried,” Jefferson said, “and failed.”

"Why?"

Jefferson recalled his first attempt to fight slavery politically. Recently graduated from law school, a naïve Burgess of 24, he proposed legislation that would have given Virginians permission to free slaves. At the time, it was illegal to free a slave without permission from the Virginia legislature, and the privilege was only granted under extraordinary circumstances. Jefferson allowed the more senior Burgess Richard Bland to propose the legislation as a courtesy, and the vehement opposition was instructive. The bill was not simply defeated; Bland was denounced as a traitor.

Jefferson sighed. How did you explain such a mentality, and for that matter such a society, to a child several centuries in the future who seemed to consider nigger freedom an axiom? "People's thinking hadn't matured enough yet, lad."

"Why didn't you try to change your thinking?" The daughter smiled. "I mean their thinking."

"I did." Jefferson remained totally calm as he offered citations. He had proposed legislation abolishing slavery in Virginia. This failed, but while Governor, he convinced Virginia's legislature to become the first body politic in human history to abolish the slave trade. He drafted and championed The Ordinance of 1784, which would have made slavery and involuntary servitude illegal in all new American states. He also wanted all blacks to be educated at states' expense, and defended a mulatto[54] who sued for freedom pro bono. Jefferson was going to point out that these were remarkably progressive actions for his time, but the family's condemning glances made it evident a verdict was already rendered. Long ago, by historians perhaps?

"Why didn't you just abolish slavery when you were President?" the boy asked.

"Just abolish slavery? Just abolish slavery! You make it sound like catching a fish or learning Latin. Even if Providence intervened to pass such a law—and that's the only way it would have passed—the southern states would have seceded."

"Oh," the boy said.

Franklin found the scene humorous. Though Washington was disgusted by the miscegenation[55] accusation, he had sympathy for Jefferson because he knew his political summary was accurate. Abolishing slavery in their time was about as likely as a trip to the moon.

"But you honestly wanted the slaves freed?" the boy asked.

---

54 Mulatto. The offspring of an African-American and a Caucasian.

55 Miscegenation. Marriage, cohabitation or fornication between a Caucasian and another race.

"Why is it so hard to believe I opposed slavery?"

Accusing looks from the family again.

"Yes!" Jefferson said. "I wanted to free the niggers and dep—"

"I think we've heard enough!" the mother said. "Get over here Stephen! And you Sarah!"

Sarah obeyed instantly. Stephen crossed his arms and stood fast. The mother requested intervention with a glance and the father shook his head. To him, the notion that their children hadn't heard the "N" word was naïve. The discussion was useful when viewed as a history lesson rather than moral commentary. Jefferson's barbaric beliefs could be debunked after the fact.

Emboldened by Stephen's defiance, Sarah re-approached Jefferson. "Free the slaves and what?"

"Once educated and freed, slaves should be colonized to such place as circumstances render most proper. They should be sent out with arms, household implements, seeds, and pairs of domestic animals. We should declare them a free and independent people, and extend them our allegiance and protection until they acquire strength."

"A racist Noah's Ark, huh?" Sarah shook her head. "Doesn't that strike you as impractical? Maybe even naïve?"

"No."

"Plantation owners wouldn't even free their slaves, much less educate and provision them."

Washington and Franklin nodded glum agreement.

"Why not free the slaves and let them stay in America?" Sarah asked.

Jefferson shook his head with great severity. "A common question. Why not retain and incorporate blacks into the state? Deep rooted prejudices entertained by the whites. The thousand black recollections of the injuries they have sustained. New provocations. These and many other circumstances will divide us into parties, and produce convulsions which will probably never end but in the extermination of one or the other race."

Sarah grew more intrigued with every word. This was definitely a side of Jefferson you didn't get in history class!

"Nothing is more certainly written in the book of fate than that these people are to be free," Jefferson continued. "Nor is it less certain that the two races, equally free, cannot live in the same government. Nature, habit, and opinion have drawn indelible lines of distinction between them."

As the mother dragged her children away from the founders, Jefferson realized he had erred. "Sorry," he whispered.

"Apologize to Ben," Washington replied. "He's the one that will suffer on our hike."

"Diplomacy seems appropriate." Franklin approached the mother, who backed up. "Please just lend an ear, madam." She continued to retreat. "Don't be angry, madam. I realize his views are offensive, but this is honestly what Jefferson thought. The actor was just trying to portray him accurately."

"I don't care how historically accurate you're trying to be," the mother hissed. "This isn't a KKK rally."

"I know this isn't a KKK rally," Franklin said. *Whatever that is.* "And I apologize."

"I'm reporting you to the park."

"Please don't do that. We have families to feed. I'll talk to Jefferson about his language."

"So will the park."

"Please, madam. Don't make us victims of Jefferson's vile racism, as his slaves and your son were. Think of everything Washington and I have done for America, and have mercy."

She smiled at the pun, and softened. Franklin continued to schmooze. "Well . . . all right. But if anyone utters another word of profanity . . ."

"Then we deserve what transpires," Franklin said. He curried favor a little longer, then made an apologetic exit.

The mother watched Franklin curiously. She wanted to stay angry at him, but couldn't. It was less what he said than the humility in his manner, and the way he listened with such genuine sympathy.

Franklin approached Jefferson. "Not another word about slavery."

Jefferson nodded. Once the father saw this exchange, he released Stephen, who sprinted up and asked more questions. Franklin glanced at the wife. "I am afraid we must leave."

"Can we at least take your picture before you go?" the boy asked.

"How long will this picture require?" Franklin asked.

"A minute tops," the father said. He aimed his camera obscura.

"Could you give us a tick to talk?" Franklin asked.

The father acquiesced and the founders huddled together. "Having a portrait 'taken' is unwise," Jefferson said.

"I would prefer not to sit," Washington replied. "But refusing may arouse suspicion."

"Refusing may do more than that." Franklin summarized the encounter with the mother. "For now, we do whatever they want."

"Hopefully Franklin's telling Jefferson to watch his mouth," the mother said, as she watched the founders' conference. "Can you believe he said the 'N' word? In front of impressionable children? At a National monument? He sounded like some NAZI! And Jesus do they smell!"

"We have to give them a ride to town," the husband replied. He explained the negotiation.

"They're not riding in our minivan."

"I can't stow them on top. It's only a couple miles."

"They're not riding."

"I gave them my word."

"Well you'd better un-give it then."

"I'll leave you and the kids here and make two trips if you insist, but a deal's a deal. I'm keeping my word and giving them a ride."

The wife exhaled sharply. "Hurry up and take the pictures so we can be done with these creeps!"

THE FATHER PEERED into the camera obscura. "Say freedom!"

"Freedom!" his son chirped. He faced the founders. "You didn't say freedom."

The ever-sarcastic Franklin resisted the urge to suggest "nigger," and on the second try everyone advocated freedom. The father took dozens of pictures, then showed them to the founders using a futuristic light canvas on the camera obscura's back. They hid their amazement. The father had also taken close-ups of Rushmore, and when he shuffled back and forth between flesh and stone faces rapidly, the results were damning. "Are you descendants of the founding fathers?" he asked.

"I am not a descendant of George Washington."

"And I am not a descendant of Thomas Jefferson."

"Search a large enough population and you'll find someone that looks like anyone," Franklin said.

"True," the father replied. "Very true." He drew on a piece of paper and handed it to Franklin. "If you ever want the pictures I can e-mail them."

"Thank you," Franklin said.

As the founders entered the rectangular Watt wagon, the boy said, "What'd you guys wanna be when you were growing up?"

Married to Sally Fairfax, Washington thought. "Like my older brother Lawrence," he answered.

"That's not what I meant. What'd you want to *be*?"

"Moral. Brave. Well-mannered. Esteemed as a man of character and accomplishment by my countrymen and mankind."

The boy was slightly frustrated. "I mean like for a job."

"I wanted to be a wealthy landowner and a high-ranking military officer," Washington answered.

"I wanted to be a wealthy and famous author and natural philosopher," Franklin replied. *Who rogered gaggles of women.*

"Educated," Jefferson said. "Free. Happy." *Handsomer, funnier, more outgoing. And more confident with females.*

Franklin smiled slightly at Jefferson's ambiguous facial expression, and answer. Both had a strong undertow.

"But what'd you wanna do?" the boy asked Jefferson.

Something to make the world less cruel and savage. Something to uplift humanity from its depraved ways. Something to help end war, hunger, hatred and ignorance. Something that would propagate love, freedom, music, education, culture and most of all, peace. Jefferson conveyed vague intensity. "I didn't dream of a specific profession," he said. "I was the oldest male, and knew running my father's plantations would be a career, but . . . law was always a strong possibility. I knew I would be educated. Educated. That I would try to learn most everything and use this knowledge to benefit humanity somehow."

Such youthful hopes seemed simultaneously noble and foolish to the elder Jefferson, and he fought contradictory urges to cling to them and discard them. He knew he could never do the latter and exist without idealism. Even if he could, how did one explain abominations most adults would never truly face or dare to try and change to a lad? Even if it was possible, was it desirable?

Let this future be a noble and decent one! Jefferson thought. *Please!*

The boy was unsatisfied with Jefferson's inability to give a simple answer, but also sensed that one might never be coming. "What do you want to be when you grow up?" Franklin asked him.

"A time traveler," his sister quipped.

"A leader. Like you three." The boy frowned suddenly. "But politicians are all liars or crooks."

The lad continued to talk, and though the founders answered his questions, most of their attention was focused on the Watt Wagon interior and the father's driving.

"What hotel should I drop you at?" the father asked.

No one answered.

His son continued to talk, but the father knew this wasn't the primary distraction. In his rearview mirror, he had noted the actors' stupefied expressions and frequent glances at each other. The way their eyes' darted in unison to watch him change the radio station, or his wife look in the visor mirror. Right now they were staring out windows. Was Superman jogging next to the minivan? Trees were blowing by, but what was so special about that?

It was all very peculiar. The need to act had certainly passed. Yet they were still acting . . .

Strange. It almost seemed like . . . like . . . like what?

The actors were unconcerned about money but had no car or clothes. Had theirs broken down? With their clothes in it? Were they foreigners? Englishmen? That would explain their peculiar dialect. So would acting.

The father shrugged. Artists were eccentric creatures, and it didn't really matter; in another few minutes they would be the past. "What hotel should I drop you at?"

"The top of that hill would be fine," Washington replied, as he continued to peer out the window.

"Nothing I'd like more than a stroll." Franklin's smile was saucy.

Washington glared at Franklin. The father observed in the rearview mirror, and when Washington turned away to once again face the window, their eyes locked. Most people look away instinctively, but Washington continued to stare. The father felt fear. Instinct told him "Washington" would not start trouble, but that if it ventured his way he would be lethal.

As Franklin listened to the Watt wagon's artificial music, he pondered "E-mail." Could some equivalent of the promissory card ciphers be an "E-mail address?" And what of camera obscura images? If the father was to be believed, they could also be telegraphed. How?

Or was E-mail something more conventional? Delivery of ticketed images and letters by airline perhaps?

Am I being fancifully futuristic? Franklin wondered. He didn't know, but instinctually envisioned an interconnected camera obscura, ticket printer, and cipher pad. Was this a futuristic post office?

Franklin thought of the father shifting through the camera obscura images rapidly, then contemplated sound and fluxions[56], as he had many times in the past. Weren't all seemingly smooth, continuous phenomenon composed of smaller discrete ones? Had fluxions been used to transcribe sound? Did persistence of sounds in the mind give rapidly replayed yet discrete tones the illusion of seamlessness? And if so, couldn't the concept be extrapolated to the camera obscura? Like other colonial natural philosophers, Franklin realized that images persisted in the mind for a short time after being viewed. Couldn't a camera obscura capture images at regular intervals, display them quickly and exploit this persistence of vision to create the illusion of motion?

Franklin was dizzy with revelation. He also felt mild frustration. By Providence he needed to rest at a tavern and think! Of course, a tavern trip would probably answer many of these questions. And create scores more.

---

56 Fluxions. Colonial term for mathematical derivatives, and the calculus, which were conceived by Gottfried Wilhelm Leibniz and Sir Isaac Newton in the late 1600s.

The father stopped at the hilltop and Stephen exited the Watt wagon with the founders. “It was good to meet you,” Jefferson said to him. “And remember, politics can be an honorable profession.”

“I know one bad apple can’t spoil the bunch,” Stephen replied. “But what if all the apples are rotten? Can one good one make them better?”

Washington knelt and looked the boy in the eyes. “I wondered things like that often during The War.”

“Really?”

“Really. But I never faltered, no matter how rotten the situation seemed.”

“And if Washington had faltered . . .” Jefferson smiled. “One man can improve the world, lad. Never doubt that.”

Stephen was skeptical. “Maybe if that man’s one of you guys.”

The parents laughed.

“Surely this time has Washingtons and Franklins,” Jefferson said.

“I don’t know about that,” the father whispered. The mother and daughter nodded emphatic agreement.

“Great men see what is possible rather than what isn’t,” Franklin said to the boy.

“We could have assumed England was too strong to beat,” Washington added. “And then there wouldn’t be an America.”

“Instead we dreamed,” Franklin said. “And cynics laughed, and cowards stood idle, as they always do while men of principle strive for progress.”

The child smiled. Consumed with thoughts of the Pledge of Allegiance, aircraft carriers, and World War II movies, he swelled with what he only vaguely realized was pride. “Can you sign my *Declaration* and *Constitution*, like you did that other boy’s? And can you make the signatures look the same again?”

The founders obliged, then said goodbye to the child, who was shuffled into the Watt wagon by his mother. She didn’t say a word or wave goodbye.

“Thank you,” the father said. “That meant a lot to my son. And the signatures were impressive.”

“We draw them frequently,” Franklin replied.

“All part of our performance,” Jefferson added.

The father popped the trunk, opened suitcases, fished for clothes, then ceded the promised pants. The patrician Jefferson and the cherubic Franklin were both striking images, but his indelible final impression was Washington, who had turned to face him, flexing his enormous calf as he did. It had layered strands of sinew that resembled flank steak.

Rare, the father thought. *To see a man that old that fit. Not just that fit, that muscular.* Washington held out a hand and their eyes locked again. *His eyes are* exactly *like those in the paintings at Rushmore! Eg-zactly!* They shook hands. Washington's grip was pneumatic.

"We're done jobbing until the morrow," Franklin said. "So I'd appreciate it if you wouldn't tell other parents about us."

"No need to worry about that!" the wife shouted out the window.

The husband agreed more politely before he wished the founders well and reentered his Watt wagon.

"What's your trade?" Washington asked, as the Watt wagon began to pull away.

"I'm a cop."

THOUGH THE FAMILY'S Watt wagon had zoomed from sight, the town of Keystone was now visible in the distance. It was little more than a row of hotels, restaurants, and souvenir shops that skirted the right side of a downward section of road. Keystone existed solely to support Mount Rushmore tourism, and its worn-down buildings were littered with neon signs and advertisements.

After staring for a few moments, the founders entered the woods to change again. "What do you suppose a 'kop' is or does?" Jefferson asked as he undressed.

"I cannot fathom," Washington replied. "But the father was observant in a way that implied training. We made him suspicious."

"Hopefully not suspicious enough to snoop," Jefferson said. "Or report us to the park."

"We must be discreet at the tavern," Washington warned.

"We must also avoid the word 'nigger'," Franklin added.

Washington nodded. "If caucasians found it that offensive, can you imagine how the niggers would react?"

"Negroes, George. Though I wonder if even that is offensive."

"Sorry. Can you imagine how the negro family we saw would have reacted? The negro father?"

Discussion of negroes continued while futuristic garments were donned. The husband's pants fit Jefferson almost perfectly, but were a bit too short for Washington. Franklin was forced to wear the father's sweat pants; they were far too long, and ridiculously tight around the waist.

Washington and Jefferson mocked Franklin's comical appearance as the founders walked down the hill toward the town. Teasing soon gave way to more serious conversation.

"What is a KKK rally?" Washington asked.

"What is a KKK?" Franklin replied.

"A faction that seeks to re-institute slavery?" Jefferson suggested.

"How about E-mail?" Washington asked.

"It would have been nice to ask this Eye-in-Stein," Jefferson said. "Presumably, he was a futuristic Newton."

"We'll have to locate a futuristic Newton that still lives," Washington said. "Or find a library and get Ben to do some reading. I wish to learn about this newk weapon. And these Navy seals."

"What of Sally Hemings?" Franklin asked Jefferson.

"A topic for later," he replied.

Franklin shook his head slowly and firmly.

"As you know, she was a Monticello slave. During my Presidency, muckrakers alleged an affair between us."

"Was there one?" Washington asked.

Jefferson laughed. "But the mere accusation created a scandal. Especially because children were postulated."

"Why would they postulate children?" Washington asked. "Such libels would be simple to refute."

Jefferson acted as if Washington hadn't spoken, and addressed Franklin. "Other questions on this topic are best postponed."

This topic? The word choice irked Washington, as did Jefferson's reaction. He once again thought of Alexander Hamilton, who had often observed that the depths of Jefferson's hypocrisy were boundless.

A car raced by, creating a loud whizzing. The founders turned their heads in unison, and watched it until it vanished from sight.

"Amazing!" Jefferson said.

"Right ridiculous," Franklin agreed. "The speed stupefies."

"Keep moving," Washington said. "We cannot allow awe or rumination to impede our progress."

The founders gaped at other passing cars as conversation continued. After musing about the Watt wagon interior, having Jefferson quickly summarize turtles built in his lifetime, speculating about what Eye-in-Stein was famous for, and trying unsuccessfully to come up with Greek and Latin roots that might shed light on a newk, they turned their attention to the most worrisome issue. "What of the disparaging comments about politics?" Jefferson asked.

Silence.

"They reeked of Rome," Jefferson said.

"They did imply corruption and despair," Washington replied. "But we must be skeptical, as we were with the angry negroes, and ask if the family's impressions are accurate."

"Suppose they are accurate?" Jefferson said.

"Suppose they aren't?" Franklin replied.

"Please desist with the nursery taunts."

Franklin laughed. "I wasn't simply taunting."

"Hypothesize with us then," Jefferson chided.

Franklin stopped walking suddenly and faced his friends. "I view such speculation as extremely premature, but *if* the family is correct about the reek of Rome, then our presence here may have an unforeseen purpose, and would make much more sense."

Six

The SETTING SUN bled into the sky as the founders entered the outskirts of Keystone. They soaked up sensations in silence at first, but eventually conversation resumed. "It's nice not to be stared at," Franklin said.

"People are still staring," Jefferson replied.

"Not like they did up at Rushmore. These new sarks are less conspicuous."

"But still conspicuous," Washington said. "We will have to find other clothes."

"And other faces," Franklin added. "If you two wish to do anything but sit in our tavern room."

Washington nodded grimly. Tourists swarmed Keystone, and being in plain view made him nervous.

As he walked, Jefferson surveyed the architecture almost instinctively. "Its buildings say much about a civilization."

"What are these telling you?" Washington asked.

"They bemoan their sterility and beg for artistry."

"Some buildings are constructed for mere function," Washington said. "Not as works of art."

"Not in Greece," Jefferson replied. "Not in Rome. Most structures served both purposes. How is architectural taste to be formed in our countrymen unless we erect public buildings which are models for study and imitation?"

"You seem to vacillate on this point," Franklin joked. "Is this Rome, or isn't it?"

Jefferson smiled. "Architecturally? No, it definitely isn't. And that tells us something, doesn't it?"

"Keystone may not be representative," Washington said.

"I hope not," Jefferson replied, as an African-American family approached.

The founders hid their tenseness until the threat passed. "Why didn't you argue negroes' inferiority to negroes?" Franklin asked Jefferson.

The quip annoyed him. "We may be able to test my theories very simply. If large numbers of nigge—"

"Negro," Franklin corrected.

"If large numbers of nig-ro freemen exist, we can visit their communities and see if they exhibit a rate of development comparable with that of the rest of society. I have no problems subjecting my suppositions to empirical tests. I do not cling to my theories of niggers dogmatically, as so—"

"Neg-ro," Franklin corrected again.

"Sorry. I do not cling to my neg-ro views dogmatically, as some do religion. If I am wrong, I will admit so. Gladly."

"I believe it all," Franklin said with a chuckle. "Except the last word."

"Speaking of the last word, you're too used to having it."

Franklin laughed. "No one gagged you."

"Perhaps we should have," Washington replied. "If Ben hadn't charmed that wench, our situation might have become vexsome."

"I realized I was talking to a child," Jefferson defended. "I tried to avoid profanity and be polite."

Washington suppressed a sigh. Jefferson had a propensity to become engrossed in philosophical discussions, had doubtless been concerned with defending his reputation to posterity, and was perhaps emboldened by the family's assumption he was an actor, but even if one granted tolerance on all these counts, his behavior was still frustrating. Why risk such a conversation at all?

"It is easy to criticize my blunder with the omniscience of hindsight," Jefferson said. "But how was I to know 'nigger' was an insulting term? Especially to whites? It is simply a derivative of niger, which is Latin for black. Do caucasians now object to being called white? Indians, redskins?"

"Your general views about negroes offended the mother as much as the term 'nigger'," Franklin replied.

Washington shook his head. "You should secure the room," he said to Franklin, as they approached the first tavern. "Same rationale as the clothes."

THE DECADENT HOTEL was independently owned and had a primitive lobby typical of the breed. When Franklin entered, the clerk stood unenthusiastically, handed him a registration card, and said, "We've got vacancies."

Franklin was dismayed by the request for personal information. In colonial times you simply paid and slept. "All this just for a room?" he asked.

"Yes, sir."

Franklin grabbed a futuristic quill and considered fake names. Did the tavern verify addresses and identities, as the gift shop did the promissory cards?

Franklin filled the form with fiction and returned it to the clerk, who examined his calligraphic cursive with dismay. "You're supposed to print," he said.

"Sorry. Shall I draw another?"

Draw? "That's okay, man. It's all good." The clerk scanned the card. "Your zip code?"

Zip code? Franklin's response was a confused expression.

Who the hell doesn't know their zip code? "No car?"

What's a car? Franklin shook his head.

"I can't accept a credit card," the clerk said.

"I'm paying with notes."

Notes? "Are you British?"

Franklin shook his head aggressively. "American."

"Just wondering. We don't get a lot of 'Sirs.' "

He and Jefferson shunned tobacco, and Washington's dentures precluded it, so Franklin selected a non-smoking room. He had no idea what HBO or local calls were, and was about to ask when a loud ring startled him. Franklin watched the clerk use a device that touched his mouth and ear to have what was probably an E-mail conversation. Did E-mail stand for ear-mail, perhaps? Like the Watt wagon, ear-mail was unsurprising on one level, stunning on another. The clerk was reserving rooms for someone in the Floridas, but the conversation nonetheless took place in real time, without delays!

History might be different if King George[57] *had ear-mailed the colonies during the Revolution*, Franklin thought. *Or if I had ear-mailed Washington from France. Is this possible?*

The clerk concluded his ear-mail and began pressing buttons on its cipher pad. Franklin peered curiously.

"Can I help you Mister Steele?"

"How many numerals in the cipher?" Franklin asked.

"The cipher? You mean the phone number?"

"Yes."

Caustic remarks occurred to the clerk, but Franklin's earnest expression elicited sympathy, and he politely explained basic telephone concepts.

"And what of baths?" Franklin asked.

"In the room. Along with soap, shampoo, and towels. You've got electricity too. Running water's a buck a gallon."

Franklin removed his money.

"I'm kidding, man. You know, joking?"

Franklin felt foolish. He thanked the clerk again and left. When he was gone, the clerk laughed and reexamined his reservation card. *If Mr. Steele is from Philadelphia, he must have been livin' in a cave under it.*

---

57 George III. King of England from 1760–1820.

Jefferson and Washington had chosen the most inconspicuous spot they could locate and were waiting for Franklin behind a restaurant around the corner from the hotel.

Washington pondered security and wished for Hamilton, who was as smart and visionary as Jefferson or Franklin, but also a soldier. As a fourth? No. Not with Jefferson present. Instead of Jefferson?

The thought was enticing to Washington, who groaned inwardly. Jefferson was raised on a frontier plantation, was an excellent horseman, and had been taught to shoot and hunt, yet this hardly made a man a soldier, as his disastrous Virginia Governorship made clear. Jefferson was elected during the Revolutionary War, when hostilities were rampant, and Washington warned him that a British Army commanded by the brilliant and vengeful Benedict Arnold was approaching. He also made it clear that he could offer no aid. Jefferson did not prepare defenses adequately, the capitol Richmond fell, the state's legislature fled in shame, and huge sections of Virginia were ravaged.

Jefferson admitted his failure candidly in public and in distraught letters to Washington, whose fatherly response was dignified and forgiving. But he was in truth surprised and tremendously disappointed; the Sage of Monticello was not the General of Monticello, and Washington knew his fellow Virginian should never again be a wartime leader. So did Jefferson. He was re-elected, but refused the position and recommended a soldier.

As he saw another black family, and wondered if they hated whites, Washington once again hoped he didn't end up in a life-or-death situation with Jefferson or Franklin.

Jefferson saw the family too. "I never thought slavery was ethical," he said.

"Nor did I," Washington replied, "but in this future, we must face the truth. We were hypocrites. We are hypocrites."

Jefferson sighed glumly. "Especially me."

Washington nodded. The negro dilemma was prototypical Jefferson, but his personal hypocrisies, even the repugnant miscegenation, were secondary concerns at present. Jefferson rarely exemplified what he advocated, but his vision was uncanny. He had *always* opposed the release of negroes in their enslaving nation. Never mind that this was inhumane, or that negro resentment was justified, or a thousand other criticisms. Jefferson had prophesized the danger they now encountered.

In the future, the negro hazard seemed obvious, but in colonial times freed slaves generally hadn't gone headhunting. Many wise men like Franklin had advocated integration after emancipation. Washington had thought Jefferson's predictions unrealistic, and assumed the hatred would cool with time.

Of course, one family hardly represented broad opinion, resentment didn't necessarily equal violence, and in a few more centuries the hatred might dissipate totally, but this was a small consolation to Washington, who thought of Jefferson's other predictions and sighed.

"What's wrong?" Jefferson's earnest expression seemed almost feminine. "Can I be of assistance?"

Washington smiled. "Nothing. And no."

"Are you certain?"

"Yes." Washington surveyed Keystone. In hindsight, the assumption that civilization equaled safety was perhaps naïve. But how could they have foreseen bitter freemen negroes that were a more insidious threat than savages, wildlife or the elements? *We may never be safe*, Washington thought, *and this makes Ben and Tom much more of a liability.*

The black family entered a restaurant and disappeared from view. To Jefferson, the act symbolized both the death of slavery, and a relocation that had never occurred but should have. "Our risk in this nigger-ridden America will be perpetual," he said.

Washington pictured a negro assassin hiding behind a Watt wagon brandishing some futuristic weapon and nodded. "Especially if our true identities are ever discovered."

"No quips about building cabins or founding republics," Franklin said to Washington. "I didn't dally at all."

"What took so long then?" Washington asked.

"They demand an enormous amount of personal information." He related his fabrications and the clerk's questions.

"You didn't make this tavern hand suspicious, did you?"

"Relax, George. It is all good."

Washington smiled at the futuristic verbiage. "It isn't all bad, anyway."

Waning sunlight provided the only illumination inside the room, so the founders left the door open. All three realized that there were probably futuristic electric lamps, but no one knew how to operate them. A search commenced.

"There's a trigger on the wall," Washington said. He pulled it and the room was illuminated.

The founders gaped at the non-flickering light momentarily, then surveyed the room; it had a pair of parallel double beds, a squat dresser, a small table with two chairs, and a basin and counter situated next to a closed door.

After Washington locked the front door, the trio plunked down on the beds and let out sighs of relief.

"We are somewhat safe here." Washington smiled with satisfaction. "And we now have a base of operations."

"And we can rest," Franklin added, as he leaned back and lay down. "And bathe and eat and drink."

"And learn," Jefferson said.

Washington nodded. "We must educate ourselves quickly, for we shan't stay here long. This reprieve is only temporary."

Franklin let out a deep sigh. "Relax and enjoy it then."

THE FOUNDERS BASKED in their new sanctuary, then began to study it. Washington and Jefferson, anyway. Franklin was in pain from his exertions, and remained glued to the bed.

Washington examined the large box on the hutch. It was made of a strange material that reminded him of the Watt wagon interior and gift shop bags, and had a slightly convex glass front. "An enormous camera obscura?" he speculated.

"I don't know," Jefferson replied. "But it is placed prominently. It must be something of import."

"Ben?"

Franklin didn't even open his eyes. "If it isn't vittles or a wench or a cure for gout or stone, I don't care right now."

"Let me be the first to thank our natural philosopher for his penetrating insights," Washington said.

"Let me be the first to thank our General for hustling along and procuring vittles," Franklin responded.

Washington laughed. "You call me a General and command me like a Corporal."

"If only you'd obey like one."

"A General? You have a Congressional edict, I presume."

Franklin laughed.

Washington laughed back. Then he and Jefferson explored the necessary[58] like rambunctious children. They turned the faucets on and off, toggled the lights, and flushed the toilet repeatedly. A mirror made for a monarch! Hot and cold aqueducted water! An enormous bath and a toilet! All in a dilapidated room that seemed designed for the common run!

Two cabinets were next to the dresser. The smaller was stacked atop the lower, which hummed and appeared to be an ether cooler. The purpose of the smaller device was more elusive. When Washington began pressing beeping buttons on its cipher pad Franklin sat up. "You shouldn't do that," he said.

Washington ignored the warning.

58 Necessary. Outhouse.

"Don't be foolish," Franklin said. "It could be dangerous."

Washington hit the largest button on the device and the door popped open. He put one of his knives inside, closed the door, and then continued hitting buttons.

"The device may utilize electric fire," Franklin said.

"So?"

"Recall the key on my kite. It conducted electric fire."

Washington made sure Franklin couldn't see his smile. "So?"

"I'd test something inert. Cloth, water, food. Yes, food. The food you should have fetched. Something non-metallic."

Washington hit more buttons. A light inside the box turned on, and a humming commenced. "Everything seems fine to me."

Moments later, sparks formed and a sizzling could be heard.

"Not for long, perhaps," Franklin said, as he ducked behind his bed. "It sounds like lightning is forming."

Jefferson retreated into the necessary and peered out a slit in the door. "Turn the bloody thing off, George!"

Washington squatted and peered inside the device calmly.

"I didn't survive my electric fire experiments to be killed by your denseness," Franklin said.

"And I didn't survive the perils of war to be killed by yours." Washington glared at Franklin. "What is sauce for the goose is also sauce for a gander. You told that family we were from the past without consulting Tom or I."

Franklin wanted to mention the "JFK" experiment at the pavilion, but realized this would hurt his cause. "The family assumed us actors, George. As most citizens of this time will."

"Your gambit's success does not make it any less foolish."

The sparking increased. Blue flashes arced.

"I envision a cannonball blowing up," Franklin said.

Washington shrugged. "I've faced cannon fire."

"Stop the device!" Jefferson whined. "Please, George!"

"I want your word. Both of you. That the stupidity will stop and all future risks will be group decisions. Especially those that involve revealing our identity."

The sparking sounded like popcorn now. Washington heard it, but still calmly waited for a response.

"Fair enough," Franklin said.

"I also agree," Jefferson said. "Now stop the lightning!"

Washington popped the door open. The humming and sparking stopped, but he was leery of unforeseen danger and stood back.

"Be careful," Franklin said. "Your blade may be charged with electric fire."

Washington extended his forefinger and touched his knife once very quickly. "It's warm," he noted.

"So was my kite key." Franklin lay back down on the bed, closed his eyes, and let out a long yawn.

Washington and Jefferson continued their exploration of the room, and picked up the device on the nightstand next to Franklin's head. An unvarying tone could be heard.

"Any clues, Ben?" Washington asked.

With a smile of resignation about rest not taken, Franklin sat up and held the phone the way the clerk had. Sound entered his mouth, so he inverted the device.

"What is it?" Jefferson asked.

Franklin explained. By the time he'd finished, Washington and Jefferson were bug-eyed. "Instantaneous communication?" Washington gasped. "With someone scores of miles away?"

"If this invention can reach the Floridas from Dakota it could have connected Philadelphia and Monticello. I could have spoken with Martha while away." Jefferson smiled sadly. Despite the ideological victories, the Revolution was not a happy time. His wife had fragile health, especially where childbirth was involved, and in commuting to Philadelphia and Richmond to lend his talents to the cause, he had frequently been forced to leave behind a pregnant, bed-ridden soulmate he could only communicate with sporadically.

Franklin knew memories of his deceased wife were painful for Jefferson and tried to provide levity. "Half the joy of Paris was my wife's inability to contact me instantaneously."

Jefferson and Washington chuckled and shook their heads.

"How does this phone function?" Washington asked.

"I have an inkling," Franklin replied. "But my theory is involved. And could be incorrect." He nonetheless explained.

"You deduced the device before you saw it," Washington guessed.

"Yes."

Washington smiled. "What else have you deduced?"

"As ignorant as I am, teaching seems foolish and arrogant. I must learn first."

"So must we," Washington replied. "Especially about inventions like this phone that may aid us immediately."

Franklin explained what he knew.

"Ten digit ciphers?" Jefferson said. "Ten billion perms[59]? Large numbers of these devices must exist."

---

59 Perms. Permutations.

"Does a list of the ciphers?" Washington asked.

"A list is logical, and should have occurred to me while talking to the clerk. But I am ignorant."

While Jefferson and Franklin speculated about the total number of phones, and ultimately the number of Americans and humans, Washington opened the nightstand between the two beds. He saw a Bible and a yellow book; hoping to avoid a religious discussion with Jefferson, he removed only the latter.

"Where'd that come from?" Jefferson asked.

"Right under your nose. I believe it is a cipher list."

The phone spoke loudly, "If you'd like to make a call, please hang up and try again." Beep, beep, beep, beep, beep, beep . . .

"Make a call," Jefferson whispered. "A call may no longer be a physical visit."

Franklin obeyed the phone. He skimmed the cipher book, located a restaurant advertisement, and after failing to dial properly several times, consulted instructions printed on the phone and succeeded. In seconds, he was conversing with a voice who asked him what he'd like to order. "I'll have three roast beefs, bloody as a Yorktown lobster, mashed sweet potatoes, and a double Yorkshire pudding."

"Uh . . . we don't serve roast beef. Or lobster. Just pizza and subs and salads."

Pizza? Sub? Franklin thanked the voice and hung up. Then he opened the cipher book, skimmed other restaurants, called one, and ordered victuals. Washington reminded him to order something soft that he would be able to chew.

While Washington and Jefferson experimented with the phone, Franklin examined the large "camera obscura" and noted the small protrusions on the bottom of the invention. They were black like the rest of it, and difficult to see. Franklin began pressing them one by one.

"We're not going to contact France!" Washington said to Jefferson. "That might be costly, and even if possible, is frivolous. There are more practical contacts to make. Shops that will have garments. An airline, Watt wagon or horse that can transport us, and a library or book sh—"

Franklin hit the rightmost button and the device made a popping sound. Colored sunlight filled its screen and from somewhere inside it a deep voice boomed, "This is CNN!"

Washington and Jefferson dropped the cipher pamphlet and phone, fell into seated positions on the edge of the beds, and gaped. Franklin joined them, and the founding fathers took their first hit of modern America's most powerful drug.

The founders watched the living portraits in stupefied silence, until the phone interrupted. "If you'd like to make a call, please hang up and try again." Beep, beep, beep, beep, beep, beep . . .

"This 'phone' nags like a wench," Washington said absently. He hung it up without looking away from the living portraits.

Franklin laughed. "Who would have ever thought we'd be saying such things about machines!"

"Or seeing such things with machines!" Jefferson gasped.

"Is this a view of what's transpiring somewhere else in the world at this very moment?" Washington asked.

"The flowing sentences and glowing words seem to argue against that," Jefferson replied. "Unless they are superimposed forthwith."

"These living portraits could have been captured at some earlier time," Franklin said. "As our images were on the camera obscura. Though I'm not sure what is more amazing. Scribing reality, or communicating it across leagues instantly."

Washington remembered his Presidency, when he showed visiting Indian delegates their first painting; they touched it tentatively, expecting living objects, and took time to understand it was not real. *I am the savage now*, he thought.

The speaking woman seemed to offer insights, but the founders were too awestruck to truly hear, much less listen. The living portraits had a hypnotic grandeur, and mere dialogue, even informative dialogue, was trifling by comparison.

"By Providence, this is incredible!" Washington said. "I feel foolish saying such a thing, but this seems like sorcery!"

"Sorcery we must demystify." Franklin rose and examined the box. Washington and Jefferson craned their necks to see past him, and suggested he study the device without blocking the image, but he ignored their gripes and sleuthed.

Two strings exited the rear of the box and entered the wall. Franklin examined the lamps, cooler, and lightning box, and noted they had but one. By disconnecting these strings and trying to turn devices on, he realized they provided impetus.

"You look nervous," Washington said.

"Wouldn't you be?" Franklin pursed his lips. *I forgot who I was conversing with.*

"Do the strings contain electrical fire?" Washington asked.

"I don't know."

"Couldn't you perform a futuristic version of your kite experiment and insert a key into one of those wall slits?"

"That seems unwise." Franklin often made points with quick stories, and he narrated an experimental blunder in which he shocked himself senseless by discharging two Leyden jars intended for the electrocution of a turkey.

Franklin abandoned the wall slits and experimented with the second string. When it was unscrewed the box images turned to dancing dots, but with it attached they reanimated. "This string gives the portraits life," he concluded.

"How?" Washington asked.

"I know and I don't," Franklin replied. "Futurity seems to mail portraits through the string. Though they probably require a code or language to do so. A palette alphabet, if you will."

"You deduced this invention too!" Washington said.

Franklin shrugged. "I did and I didn't."

"Why don't you just build us an airline?"

"Don't be absurd. Now as to the composition of the individual images . . ." Franklin tapped his lip with his forefinger. "In France I met an obscure artist who painted with dabs rather than strokes to capture landscapes more realistically. He combined color specks that seemed disparate and random at first, but they gradually formed an image."

Jefferson nodded. In Paris, during his liaison with the painter Maria Cosway, he had associated with many artists in her social circle, and had observed the unorthodox technique. "You're saying this living portrait box does the same thing?"

"That is my theory, but it is hardly proven."

Franklin sleuthed again; he determined that the box's small protrusions shuffled the images and changed the volume levels, and that its sounds emanated from specific locations, as the Watt wagon's had. Unable to deduce further insights, he sat, content to join Jefferson and Washington and merely watch.

THE NEWS HEADLINES described domestic and international conflict. The former included overviews of White House and Congressional initiatives, while the latter focused on successful acts of violence and failed attempts at peace.

Clips of the President were shown. He was filmed at a summit shaking hands with a foreign leader. Facial close-ups of dialogue were also included.

After a few sound bites, CNN cut to another story. "He barely spoke a sentence," Washington said. "How am I to educate myself with such sparse information?"

"Perhaps that is not the goal," Jefferson replied. "Or perhaps information you consider sparse may be sufficient to a resident of this era."

Franklin nodded. "This appears to be a visual paper that summarizes many events quickly. Maybe conventional papers still exist. Presumably they contain the detail you desire."

The Congressional leaders seemed uninspiring, and their partisanship was pronounced. But the trio did not understand the current political climate or the issues being discussed, and they realized that more than any other topic, politics might not be what it seemed. They were careful to limit their judgment.

"There appear to be two political parties," Franklin said with concern. "Democratic and Republican."

Washington scowled, but Jefferson simply nodded. "I expected my Republicans to schismatize once they put down all things under their feet. And I always expected that whatever names the resultant parties might bear, the real division would be into moderate and ardent republicanism."

"You founded a political party?" Franklin accused.

Jefferson nodded. "Madison, I and others. To oppose the Federalists."

"How could you do such a thing?" Franklin asked.

Jefferson was unsurprised by this vehemence. Franklin hadn't lived to see the rise of United States political parties; to him, like most pre-19th-century Americans, party was synonymous with faction, and had an almost treasonous implication. Having observed the corruption and havoc political factions wreaked in Britain, most founders envisioned a republic with but one large "party" that worked for the good of the nation.

"I expect an answer," Franklin pressed.

"I formed the Republican party to defend freedom," Jefferson replied. "I will gladly discuss this later, but for now I wish to watch these living portraits."

Another news story was beginning. The founders listened at times, but mainly watched. The sight of artificial moving images was still shocking enough that their ability to focus on conceptual implications was hampered.

They noted camera flashes, microphones, modern furniture, and other futuristic phenomena, but didn't fixate on them as they might have a few hours before. Politicians were the present focus, not technology. Seeing living American representatives helped the reality of their situation settle more firmly.

"Our child has definitely survived," Franklin said.

"Though we still don't know what sort of a man it is," Washington replied.

Each founder analyzed information the living portraits provided and tried to answer this question.

Professional football highlights aired. The founders leaned forward slightly when they saw the rout of fans in the first coliseum. More than a dozen other contests in different locations were quickly shown, with armies of spectators.

"These events appear to be concurrent," Washington said.

Franklin nodded. "And all seem to be located in America."

"That means there must be whole colonies . . . colony upon colony watching these contests in person."

"Not to mention those that may observe it on this camera obscura," Jefferson said.

A slow-motion replay of an especially viscous hit was shown. Washington smiled when he saw Jefferson wince.

Franklin peered intently. "The fact that the rate of motion can be slowed seems to support my shuffling image hypothesis."

"Futuristic armor-clad gladiators . . . lionized by rabid masses . . . in dozens of American Coliseums." Jefferson smiled morosely. "At least Rome had but one."

"Are these spectacles government funded?" Franklin asked. "As the Coliseum was?"

"More importantly, are they meant to distract citizens from oppression and civil decline, as the Coliseum was?"

No one offered an answer, or even formulated one. There wasn't time. The living newspaper sprinted through other gladiatorial summaries, and the founders gave chase.

The first commercial break arrived, and sponsors tantalized visitors from the past with wares from the future. The founders were as interested in ads as programs, and watched attentively.

No one spoke or analyzed the phenomenon internally. The enticements cued their desires, and the founders sat lusting, imagining themselves eating, driving and dressing like the individuals in the alluring advertisements.

Stock quotes scrolled across the bottom of the screen while financial prognosticators analyzed the day's trading mania. A futures note also appeared.

"Futures?" Washington said. "Could this relate to our experience? Could the invention used to transport us help people predict or manage the nation's mercantile interests?"

"I still think this time travel is esoteric," Franklin said. "Future probably implies something more conventional. A forward merchandise contract? Perhaps some highly speculative venture that seeks funds but doesn't yet exist?"

"What is the Dow?" Jefferson wondered. "And I presume these galloping abbreviations are stock prices."

All three founders knew what stocks were. In early colonial America, brokers had met in restaurants, coffeehouses, and parks to sell securities.

"Did she say 'The New York Stock Exchange'?" Franklin asked.

"Yes," Washington replied.

"What of Philadelphia? It was the de facto American capitol. Britian's exchange is in London, after all. And France's is in Paris."

"The New York Stock and Exchange Board was formed late in my life," Jefferson said. "In 1817. It was tiny compared to America's first bourse[60], the Philadelphia, which was formed after both your deaths in 1800 to handle spiraling trade."

Washington and Franklin were once again unsurprised yet stunned. Prominent colonial nations had security exchanges, and though an American incarnation was considered inevitable, its future form was nonetheless stupefying. Jefferson had decades of historical experience his two contemporaries lacked, but even he found it almost incomprehensible.

"How many stocks are there?" Washington wondered. "Hundreds? Thousands?"

Franklin thought of the Coliseums, billion-potential phone ciphers, and profligate wares. "Hundreds of thousands?"

Analysts discussed a small "tek" stock that had lost a third of its value in a single day. "What caused the collapse?" Washington asked. "Some physical disaster like a fire?"

"A shift in opinion," Jefferson replied. "If these stock jobbers are to be believed."

"We received information by courier," Franklin said. "With these phones, and constant information reporting by this living-portrait device, perceptions could shift rapidly."

"As could stock ownership," Jefferson added.

Franklin nodded. "The velocity of the exchange must be tremendous."

As stock quotes continued to shoot by like bullets in a battle, Washington shook his head. "How could anyone keep up with it all?"

As AN ESPECIALLY buxom movie star exited her long Watt wagon, Washington's eyes dilated with lust. "By Providence are they handsome!"

"Yes they are," Franklin said. "And so is she."

"That's not what I meant," Washington replied. "Though I agree on both counts."

"Don't you mean all three?"

"I can't imagine . . ." Jefferson gasped.

"I can," Franklin replied.

"I've never seen such a twiggy woman with such gargantuan mammae," Jefferson said. "It seems decidedly unnatural."

"Pleasantly unnatural. I *know* that wasn't a complaint."

"Of course not, but . . ."

---

60 Bourse. European term for stock exchange. Bourse is French for purse.

"Her butt's fabulous too." Franklin arched a teasing eyebrow. "Everything on her is divine."

Jefferson normally would have rebutted the religious rib, but when he saw a stunning redhead that vaguely resembled his deceased wife, memories flooded him and he grew erect.

Washington imagined the glamorous Sally Fairfax exiting one of the luxurious Watt wagons, grew aroused, then felt guilt; he should be thinking of his temporal widow, not his first love.

While his friends immersed themselves in the past, Franklin remained firmly focused on the present. "Look at the dugs on this next wench. They're bigger than . . . bigger than . . ."

"You," Washington said.

Franklin laughed. "Excellent metaphor."

Franklin was checking on the status of the vittles, and as Washington watched him dial the cipher with what seemed like casual familiarity, awe once again filled him. "A few ticks ago this 'phone' was magical. After seeing the living portrait box, it seems almost trivial."

"I wonder what will seem trivial in a few more days," Jefferson said.

Franklin smiled as the phone rang. "And I wonder what will seem magical."

When CNN began to replay living portraits the founders had already seen, they changed images. Jefferson favored the *McLaughlin Group*, Washington a History Channel Civil War special, and Franklin was torn between a TLC Tornado program and *Baywatch*. Before a consensus evolved, the victuals arrived. Franklin had ordered four large pizzas, forty-eight chicken wings, two different types of bread sticks, a half-dozen foot-long subs, nine salads and a dozen drinks.

"You bought enough to feed a battalion!" Washington hissed.

"We can put surpluses in the cooler invention," Franklin replied. "The cost was trifling, and even if it wasn't, a small excess of vittles is far preferable to a shortage."

"We clearly have different conceptions of small excess and trifling cost," Washington said.

"Enjoy supper. You can chastise me afresh afterwards."

Washington decided this was good advice. Both portions. While he perused the victuals, and *paper* plates and boxes, he amused himself with fantasies in which he forced Franklin to consume their entire supply depot.

Jefferson distributed drinks. The founders marveled at the flexible, foamy white cups, then removed the equally amazing lids. Franklin's liquid was black, Jefferson's light green, and Washington's bright orange. All three drinks fizzed.

"Priestley's water?" Franklin guessed.

Jefferson nodded. "Probably."

"My memory is terrible, as always," Washington said. "How and when did he invent it?"

"Joseph demonstrated his artificial-spring-water apparatus to the London College of Physicians in 1772. His device proved that air could dissolve in water, but was not robust enough for mainstream use, so he suggested a more powerful incarnate which utilized pumps."

"It was built," Jefferson said. "Though not by him. Artificial spring water was first manufactured and sold by an English apothecary in the mid 1790s, shortly after your death."

"Is it still medicinal?" Washington asked.

Colonials believed natural springs had potent rejuvenative properties, and traveled great distances to bathe in them; artificial spring water was an attempt to transport the medicine to the individual rather than vice versa.

"The carvery worker called one of the drinks 'doctor's pepper'," Franklin said. "Might it not contain some peppers or herbs physicians use to heal? Another was called pep-see. Could it enhance vision?"

"That is plausible," Jefferson replied. "In 1820, alkali was added to soda water to enhance medicinal properties. Ginger improved the flavor."

"Does mine contain carrot or squash?" Washington wondered.

"There's only one way to obtain an answer," Franklin said. He and Jefferson smiled as the trio toasted Priestley. One of the most brilliant natural philosophers either man had ever met had been remembered! And one of his inventions was still utilized!

The founders drank deeply and grimaced immediately. "By Providence is it sweet!" Washington said.

"Enough sugar for a hogshead[61] of tea," Franklin added.

Jefferson nodded rapidly. "Conservatively."

"Is there a variety with less sugar?" Washington wondered.

"I cannot envision one with more," Franklin replied.

"Perhaps sugar is used to mask a potent medicinal flavor," Washington said. "This doctor's pepper or pep-see perhaps?"

"That would explain the vile taste," Jefferson replied. "What else but a medicine could be so noxious?"

"I distrust medicines," Franklin said. "Even futuristic ones. Until I know what this contains, I will imbibe no more."

---

61 Hogshead. A large cask or barrel that held 50–140 gallons.

Jefferson shared a similar sentiment, and followed Franklin's lead immediately. Washington joined the herd, and the founders drank water.

"Since we lack suitable drink, I suggest we have some lactic with our meal." Franklin smiled mischievously as he located *Baywatch*.

THE FOUNDERS HAD watched snippets of *The Drew Carey Show* and *Cheers*, and were now viewing *Friends*.

"These plays are unusually terse," Washington said.

"And lowbrow," Jefferson replied. "The humor seems plebian, the ironies obvious, the plots predictable."

"One could say the same thing of Cervantes or Sterne," Franklin teased.

Longing and sadness filled Jefferson as he thought of his wife Martha. They both loved Laurence Sterne's *Tristam Shandy*, and had recited their favorite passages to each other on her deathbed.

"These plays are moronic," Washington agreed. "Yet people are laughing. You can hear it clearly."

"The dialect is confusing," Franklin noted. "And we don't know enough about this culture to understand many of the jokes. Or truly appreciate the characters."

"Thankfully, perhaps," Jefferson said. As usual, he was eating sparingly; he had sampled a tiny smidgeon of each food, and was now perusing the salads. Franklin shoved the remnants of a piece of pizza into his mouth and joined his friend.

"These greens look sickly," Jefferson said. He was used to the vine ripened tomatoes, luxurious lettuces, and other verdure from his Monticello gardens. The pale, half-dead vegetation before him seemed niggardly by comparison.

Franklin nodded agreement as he peered at the tiny wineskins of dressing. He squeezed one. Nothing came out. "I don't see a lid or spout."

"Nor I," Jefferson replied, as he sorted through the small pile. "Ranch. Italian. French. Fromage bleu."

"Le fromage des rois et des papes," Franklin mumbled.

"Et maintenant, comme il se doit, aussi celui du peuple," Jefferson replied.

"Bleu cheese I can read," Washington said. "Translate the rest of your exchange, if you would be so kind."

"The cheese of kings and popes," Franklin repeated.

"And now, fittingly, also commoners," Jefferson once again replied.

Washington nodded. He knew French royalty like Emperor Charlemagne were quite fond of Roquefort "bleu" cheese, and had heard Lafayette lament its scarcity in America.

"Thousand Island," Jefferson continued.

"The Thousand Islands?" Franklin asked.

This was a group of more than 1,500 tiny isles in the St. Lawrence River between New York and Canada.

"Perhaps," Jefferson said. "They were surveyed in 1818."

"Or perhaps the name implies a diverse conglomeration of spices and ingredients. From the Indies, Arabias, and other locales that were undiscovered in our time. There may be entirely new animals, vegetables, and dishes for us to consume!"

"Just what you need," Washington said. "Another justification to eat."

Franklin laughed. "I'd prefer another justification to roger. But you diverted the baywenches."

"I cringe as I utter this, but I'd rather you ate."

"Baywenches?"

"That would be a diet, I suspect."

"But the few times I broke my fast . . ."

"At your age you'd probably break something else."

Franklin laughed. "Cruel, George. Cruel."

When Jefferson and Franklin reached for the same packet of French dressing, Washington smiled. "Francophiles."

Colonial America was a crude nation that lacked the refinement found in great capitals of the world like Paris. Both Jefferson and Franklin were smitten by French architecture, art, food, its scholars and philosophers, and most of all her people. This led to criticisms. Some questioned whether Franklin functioned with sufficient impartiality as Minister Plenipotentiary to France, and was securing the most favorable terms. As Secretary of State, Jefferson favored France to Britain, and similar questions were raised.

"I am a Francophile, George," Franklin said. "Though also an Amerophile."

"Live in France and experience the grandeur of her culture before you mock it," Jefferson suggested.

"I was not mocking her culture," Washington replied, "or her grandeur. But rather your unwavering loyalty to her."

"As she supported our revolution and made our independence possible, France is more America's mother than England," Jefferson retorted.

Neither man said anything more. Franklin was intrigued by the contentious exchange, but did not want to ignite conflict, so he quelled his questions. He gave Jefferson the French dressing, and selected the unknown ranch. This decision seemed symbolic. Why come to the future and eat foods from the past?

Franklin opened the wineskins with a knife. He and Jefferson winced when they took their first bite of salad. The dressings had a foreign aftertaste. Had palates changed? Franklin and Jefferson didn't know, but they shunned the noxious dressings like the sugared soda water, scraped them off, and ate their salads plain.

Sitcoms grew tiresome, so the founders watched *Survivor.* The show began with summaries of previous episodes' "crises": fatigue, wet clothes, cold meals, even bugs! Then competitions that emphasized practical survival skills like playing memory and standing in place were reviewed. The shows concluded in true Darwinist, Call-of-the-Wild fashion; the episode's "victim" was determined by taking a vote.

"Survivor," Washington scoffed. "When I heard the title I envisioned rugged woodsmen enduring real hardship."

Lewis and Clark would be appalled, Jefferson thought.

"I'd love to release a savage nearby and see who survives," Washington growled.

Franklin and Jefferson smiled and exchanged a glance.

"I traveled from Virginia to Ohio with fewer supplies than these fools," Washington said. "Dusk till dawn every day through savage-infested forests."

As he watched the show, Franklin was reminded of a 1744 negotiation with the Six Nations, a coalition of Iroquois tribes that bargained with America, Britain and France collectively. Virginia had offered to educate savages, but they refused, noting with genuine disgust that other natives returned from white colleges unable to build shelter, endure hunger or cold, run, hunt or fight. The white education and lifestyle rendered them useless for wilderness existence, and proved ruinous.

A female "survivor" worn down by the "hardship" was shown crying. "What is a wench doing in the wilderness?" Washington asked. "Sniveling isn't going to feed anyone, wench! Stop burdening the party with your feeble emotions. Return home and man the pot and fireplace!"

"Is that what you said to Martha while she suffered with you at Valley Forge?" Franklin asked.

"She was a guest, not a member of the expedition."

Franklin and Jefferson laughed as Washington's scathing criticisms continued. "Nine people who can't start a fire between them? They don't deserve to survive!"

The founders had finished eating and were cleaning up.

"Parchment plates," Washington said. "Had you suggested such a thing two days ago I would have heckled."

Franklin and Jefferson nodded. Paper was exorbitant in colonial America, so exorbitant that no colonial would think of throwing it out. The founders therefore wiped off their plates, refolded their napkins, and stacked both neatly.

"You're sure there wasn't a surcharge for the parchment plates?" Washington asked.

"Positive," Jefferson replied. "I checked the ticket."

While stacking the clear silverware, Franklin paused, flexed a fork, and once again shook his head with amazement. "Like balsa, but better. The windows at the pavilion make more sense."

Washington took in the room's myriad wonders and chuckled. "I'm glad something does."

The Real World was worse than *Survivor.* Individuals lived in a house together, aired petty grievances, fought about trivial disagreements, and vied to be liked.

"I am reminded of the sycophants in French and English court," Franklin said.

"Why would people sit in their own houses, watching other people live in a house?" Jefferson asked.

No one knew. But no one changed the channel.

Washington rubbed his aching eyes. "How long have we been watching?" he asked.

Jefferson checked the clock. "It is 10:18."

"Almost three hours?" Washington gasped.

"Tempus fugit[62]," Jefferson said.

Franklin laughed. "Time has certainly flown today!"

"We frittered away *three hours*!" Washington said.

"It felt like *much* less than that," Jefferson replied.

Franklin nodded. "These living portraits are entertaining."

"And insidious, it would seem."

When Washington turned the television off, Jefferson and Franklin objected. "No griping," he said. "And no more living portraits until we have planned our actions for the morrow."

Washington knocked on adjacent rooms' doors to make sure there were no eavesdroppers, then the conference began. Washington took the lead, chaired, and decided they would count their notes first. All currency was placed in the center of the bed. Franklin donated the coins and smaller bills he had accumulated. "George is on the one," he said.

62 Tempus fugit. Latin. Time flies.

Everyone examined the note. "It is good to see such a small denomination," Jefferson said. "This assuages my inflation concerns slightly."

Washington seemed more interested in Lincoln's five than his one, and smiled broadly at the ten. "Hamilton!"

"Hamilton." Jefferson scowled. "Who's on the next denomination, Benedict Arnold?"

Washington gave Jefferson a dirty look as he held up a twenty. "Andrew Jackson. Congressman Jackson?"

Jefferson nodded. "And General Jackson. Also President Jackson, most likely, despite my opposition to his candidacy."

"Two terms," Franklin said. "After John Quincy Adams. I saw him on the Executive portrait display I described."

"What is the largest denomination?" Jefferson asked.

"I saw nothing larger than my hundred," Franklin replied.

"Is Tom on any notes?" Washington asked.

"Not that I saw," Franklin said.

Jefferson shrugged. Like his companions, he considered notes trivial relative to inclusion on Rushmore.

The founders guessed at an ascending-denomination coin order: penny, dime, nickel, quarter. The "one cent," "five cents," "dime," and "quarter dollar" markings settled the issue. "United States of America," "Liberty," "e pluribus unum[63]" and "In God We Trust" reinforced previous conclusions. Faces were difficult to discern, but rudimentary sleuthing revealed that Lincoln was on the penny, Jefferson the nickel, and Washington the quarter. The dime's small size and unknown silhouette made it intriguing.

Jefferson was happy that he and Monticello were on the nickel. It was one thing for a man to be remembered, but the architect in him realized the feat was even rarer for a structure.

"You and Lincoln are the only two individuals on Rushmore, notes, and coins," Franklin said to Washington.

"I will have to study Lincoln," Washington replied.

Franklin nodded. "We all will."

Franklin and Jefferson began to discuss the backs of the notes, but Washington intervened and made them count. The founders had started out with $100,000 but now had slightly less.

"We have adequate funding for the short term," Washington said. "Though we must still be frugal."

"Holding all of our wealth is risky," Jefferson said.

---

63 E pluribus unum. Latin. Out of many, one.

"If taverns require personal data, banks must," Franklin said. "They may request papers and verify them instantly."

"Will we need papers to travel?" Jefferson asked.

"Probably," Franklin said. "I suspect life will be very, very difficult without them. Which presents a dilemma. Will we reveal our identities, or assume fraudulent ones?"

"Do we want to remain anonymous?" Jefferson asked.

"Yes," Washington replied. "If time transport is esoteric, and we reveal ourselves, we might be assumed ripe for Bedlam."

"I concur," Franklin said. "Until we have determined the climate that would greet us, anonymity is preferable."

"Anonymity requires fraud," Washington said.

"Assuming fraudulent identities does not concern me ethically," Franklin said. "Not in circumstances this unusual. But these portrait papers may be perilous to counterfeit."

"I recommend we table this matter," Washington replied, "pending investigation of paper requirements in the morrow."

This was agreed upon, as was Washington's proposal that the money be divided into four portions: three small amounts each individual would carry, and a large reserve that would remain in the room.

"We must procure more potent weapons," Jefferson said.

"We should also burn our archaic garments," Washington added.

Franklin nodded. "This era's advanced natural philosophy might be able to prove that they are more than mere costumes."

"What of pretending to be ourselves?" Jefferson said. "This ability may be useful in unforeseen ways."

"We can always acquire or construct costumes," Washington said. "Though I would prefer to avoid self impersonation unless absolutely necessary. We made this 'kop' suspicious already. Who knows who he or his wench might have contacted?"

"What if we are discovered and asked to prove our identities?" Jefferson replied. "I would hate to rot in Bedlam or gaol[64] wishing we'd kept our garments."

Discussion continued. Jefferson wanted to save and hide the garments, but was outvoted. They would be destroyed.

A physician visit was contemplated. If Franklin's gout and stone could be improved the party would be more mobile. Washington's dentures and Franklin's spectacles would also have to be replaced, as they presented risks

---

64 Gaol. Jail.

similar to the garments. Unfortunately, none of these actions seemed wise near Rushmore.

"We must leave this region," Franklin said.

Washington nodded aggressively. "This is our singular priority. We must tailor all other actions to facilitate it."

"Where to go?" Jefferson asked. "This 'Rapid City' the Rushmore pamphlet mentioned?"

Franklin emptied his bag of books onto the bed and unfolded a United States map. As they had left different American geographies, each founder noted different features, but they all studied the map diligently, hoping to extract useful information as rapidly as possible.

Washington whistled. "Our child has indeed grown! Is this all the result of your Louisiana purchase?"

"Louisiana Purchase?" Franklin asked.

Jefferson outlined the central third of America between the Stony Mountains[65] and Mississippi River, then explained quickly.

"What a tremendous accomplishment!" Franklin said. "You more than doubled the size of the Union!"

Washington nodded agreement. "What of this Hay-way-eye?" he asked. "This All-ass-kay?"

"After my time." Jefferson explained the 1819 Adams-Onis treaty, in which America purchased Florida and the Pacific Northwest from Spain. This was the only other acquisition he had knowledge of.

"The Virgin Islands?" Franklin arched a suggestive eyebrow.

Washington and Jefferson chuckled and shook their heads.

"Is Canada still French?" Washington wondered.

"It definitely isn't American," Jefferson said. "The map makes that clear."

"Canada would have been a valuable state," Washington said.

"As would Mexico," Jefferson replied. "And Cuba. Madison, Monroe and I tried to expand The Empire of Liberty, I assure you."

"Empire of Liberty." Franklin smiled at the oxymoron. "A term you concocted?"

Jefferson nodded. "As you know, empires are traditionally built through colonialism in which a ruling country acquires and exploits possessions. When these inevitably revolt, as we did, the empire collapses. America's Empire of Liberty would acquire land through purchase rather than conquest, make new territories equal states rather than subservient colonies, and would therefore be moral and sustainable."

"An 'Empire of Liberty' filled with slaves?" Franklin said.

---

65 Stony Mountains. Rocky Mountains.

Jefferson sighed. "Must you distort every view with the spectacles of slavery?"

"This seems to be the habit of futurity."

While Jefferson nodded glumly, Franklin wondered if the Empire of Liberty was another case where the Sage of Monticello espoused one principle but pursued another. And what of posterity? It seemed naïve to think the mightiest colonial empires would evacuate North America peacefully. Were "sales" made under duress? Had America become a behemoth through a series of Louisiana Purchases or French & Indian Wars?

"Look to the northwest, George," Jefferson said. "A state is named after you."

Washington maintained a neutral expression. He enjoyed posterity's homage, and knew his pre-eminent historical position was deserved, but colonial gentleman considered it vulgar to profess a desire for, or love of, homage. Public service was to be undertaken for idealistic reasons, and genteels were expected to espouse the chivalrous notion that the satisfaction of doing one's duty was the only necessary reward. "Is there not a state named Jefferson, Franklin, or Hamilton?"

"Don't be worn down by the world's injustices," Franklin replied. "I'm sure Tom and I have a county or two named after us."

Washington knew that Franklin had received homage comparable to his in France, and that his ribbing, though perhaps borne of mild resentment, was generally just good-natured mocking. He took it as such.

"The parcel north of Virginia also bares your name," Franklin said. "The national capitol, I presume?"

Jefferson nodded.

"Isn't there a state named West Washington?" Franklin asked. "North Washington? South and East Washington? Central Washington? How about Washington Washington? Surely a cardinal direction has been named after you?"

"I doubt it," Washington replied.

"I don't." Franklin laughed. "I'm surprised the nation wasn't renamed The United States of Washington."

"That is vulgar. It makes America sound like a monarchy."

"A stranger who studied its nomenclature would never suspect otherwise. A mountain, a note, a state, a coin, a capitol. You've even eclipsed Lincoln. It seems that 'future generations' have indeed given 'the richest and most lasting monuments to the name of Washington.' "

Washington smiled wistfully. His first victory in the Revolutionary War was Boston, which he liberated from the British, and her mayor bestowed the prophetic wish upon him. "Boston. What a misleading experience. If all my victories had been that easy . . ."

Jefferson and Franklin smiled with admiration. None of Washington's victories were "easy."

Washington touched D.C. on the map. "Two centuries later and it survived!" His smile grew more rueful as he thought of the difficult battle the issue of a national capitol had created. States wanted the capitol near them to exercise influence, funding had been inadequate, the infighting furious. Washington understood that the establishment of a capitol was a critical part of solidifying the union and creating a sense of national identity, and he had championed the cause personally. It was his most cherished pet project. One he'd felt certain he would never see completed. "I wonder what it looks like."

"Washington?" Franklin said. "Tall, serious, and rather ugly, frankly."

"Ben Frankly?" Washington replied.

Franklin laughed. "Time transport has definitely honed your wit."

Washington stared blankly as he attempted to hybridize past plans with future inventions and conceptualize the capitol. Doing so was difficult, and though he knew his visualizations were probably inaccurate, he nonetheless tried.

"You're not going to see your capitol by peering into the map," Franklin said.

Jefferson laughed. "It is almost reassuring to know there is something this civilization hasn't invented."

"All ingenuity has limitations," Franklin said.

Washington cast a sidelong glance Ben's way. "Even yours?"

"I stand corrected."

Washington chuckled. "D.C. seems a logical destination."

"You mean Washington D.C.?" Franklin said.

"D.C."

"The map says Washington D.C."

"Saying it seems pretentious."

"You could just call it My D.C.," Franklin suggested.

"That's humble." Washington smirked ever-so-slightly. "I think *Washington* D.C. should be our final destination."

"Thank you, George," Franklin said.

Jefferson laughed.

"Washington's D.C. seems logical," Franklin agreed. "What better place to gauge the state of a nation than its capitol?"

"Washington D.C.," Washington corrected. "Not Washington's D.C."

"Washington's D.C. then?" Franklin said to Jefferson.

"There, as here, we may be conspicuous," Jefferson said. "Washington's D.C. may have portraits and statues of us."

"Or George, at least." Franklin grinned. "But since you addressed the capitol properly, I shan't argue."

"Sorry, George," Jefferson said.

Washington waved a hand dismissively. "Continue. Please."

"Philadelphia, New York, or Boston may be better choices. We may be somewhat familiar with them. Or a settlement built after our time, where memories of us are less prominent. In such a place we could explore and learn more easily."

"I advocated selection of a final destination because it might affect our intermediate one," Washington replied. "As long as an eastward vicinity is agreed upon, we can table the matter."

"Rapid City then?" Franklin asked.

Washington examined the South Dakota region of the map, then nodded. "It contains the airline, is the largest settlement within a great distance, and is one of the closest."

"How will we travel?" Jefferson asked. "We may need papers to use airlines or Watt wagons, and I doubt we can cadge rides across the country."

"Notes can circumvent laws," Franklin said.

Jefferson smiled. "Are we to scheme like fugitives?"

"For the short term, we may have no choice."

"We must scheme to stay anonymous until we understand more about this era," Washington said. "Are we in agreement then? We leave for Rapid City as soon as prudently possible?"

Jefferson nodded. "Rapid City."

"And then we must travel East," Franklin said. "To the colonies we once knew."

"AMAZING, DON'T YOU think?" Franklin shouted while shoughering. "Even the commoners in this era can bathe daily!"

Franklin and Jefferson nodded. In colonial times cleaning usually entailed a sponging of the face and hands. The preparation of a bath was a labor-intensive undertaking that only the wealthiest individuals could afford, and as everyone knew that excessive washing destroyed the skin's natural oils and made one susceptible to disease, even those with means only took baths a few times a year. A few heretics embraced the radical notion that regular washing improved health, and pursued ostracized bathing regimens. To varying degrees, Jefferson, Franklin, and Washington held such unorthodox views.

"This artificial rain is better than a bath!" Franklin continued. "A suitable complement to the artificial lightning."

"Don't shout references to the past!" Washington hissed.

Franklin was soon singing *Such Merry As We Have Been*, one of the simple Scottish songs he loved. Washington and Jefferson laughed at their friend's horrendous voice.

"I'm glad Ben's here," Washington said.

Jefferson smiled. "He is always good company."

"What do you make of our situation?" Washington asked.

Jefferson turned away from *Inside Politics*. "I don't know, George. The question seems premature."

This interaction aside, the two men watched the TV in silence. It persisted for several minutes, growing gradually tenser.

"I'm sorry, George," Jefferson finally said. "About the Samson remark."

Washington's eyes grew cold. "As I told you the first time, it is the past. Leave it there."

"After this discussion, I will honor that request, but you must hear me out. We have disagreed, but it was never my intent to voice private matters publicly."

"That was the result."

Jefferson wasn't surprised by this initial reaction. Washington could be pragmatic in pursuit of the public good, but his personal life was a vastly different matter. A man who crossed him was almost never forgiven. "The ruin of our friendship remains one of my great regrets."

"You ruined it."

"You died so suddenly, so unexpectedly. Fate denied me a chance to apologize in our past, but she has bequeathed a future opportunity I cannot forsake. I swear on my wife's soul I never wanted the letter published. I apologize for the harm this injustice brought you. Please forgive me."

Washington remained cold and said nothing. Jefferson felt humiliated, but he also craved Washington's approval, and was about to offer another apology when Franklin shut the water off. "Divine!" he said through the door. "Absolutely divine! This is the best my gout has felt in years!"

Why do I feel guilty? Washington wondered. *Tom is wrong!* He knew that Jefferson would not lie about such a grave matter, nor apologize unless he meant it, but his strict sense of justice nonetheless recoiled. Washington had never felt such remorse or ambiguity when punishing or deriding other men, even great ones who were personal friends like Hamilton or Knox.

What was it about Jefferson? His childish, almost feminine sincerity? His seemingly insecure need for approval? The fact that he acted like a scolded puppy?

And he had invoked his wife! Washington hated to admit it, but because he knew what she meant to Jefferson, this moved him.

"I believe that hike helped," Franklin said from the bathroom. "It's beneficial to get the blood pumping. I feel like I just returned from my yearly journey."

Franklin was a sedentary man whose responsibilities often kept him chained to the office. Once a year he vacationed for a week, and the exercise travel entailed usually left him feeling revitalized. Later in life, as his responsibilities increased and his health declined, he often skipped his holiday, and he felt its absence contributed to his ailments.

"If you exercised daily you would enjoy this feeling daily," Washington chastised. "Why wait for a sabbatical?"

"I know," Franklin said. "I didn't exercise before the gout and stone struck, and deserve little sympathy."

"Not to worry, none is forthcoming." Washington mustered discipline. There would be no forgiveness for Jefferson, not because he had emotional feelings one way or another, but because doing so would be unjust.

Franklin exited the bathroom naked. He was a collage of pale fat folds, varicose veins, and knobby gout protrusions that made it seem like rocks were stuffed under his skin. And of course there was his enormous gut, which looked even larger unclothed and seemed to swallow him.

"Please dress," Washington said.

Franklin shook his head. "Don't worry, George. I'm not trying to show you the kraken."

"I realize that," Washington said. "But that doesn't make the sight of you starkers[66] any less revolting."

Franklin shrugged and sat down. He was immune to modesty, and behaved as if clothed.

Jefferson chuckled. "I had almost forgotten this ritual."

Franklin believed there might be a disease-causing agent in sweat, and reasoned that sweating more and washing these agents away would lead to better health. A colonial physician had compared his sweat production while clothed and naked, and reported a doubling in the latter state. Franklin therefore spent time each morning and night sitting naked to maximize perspiration.

"I'll never forget this ritual," Washington said. "Unfortunately. This scene is seared in my mind like a camera obscura image."

"In this future, my 'odd' habits may be the norm."

"I hope not," Washington said.

"But if they are, we must board with baywenches."

While Jefferson laughed, Washington shielded his eyes, walked past Franklin, and prepared to bathe. He removed his dentures gingerly, like a

---

66 Starkers. Naked.

surgeon extracting a bullet, and sighed with relief as he placed them on the counter. Crude and cruel, the dentures contained tiny metal springs, and looked more like a torturer's tool than a physician's remedy. Washington stripped down to his under breeches, twisted his midsection several times and touched his toes spryly. He was sensitive about his lack of teeth, and disliked conversing without his dentures, so he scurried into the necessary quickly.

WASHINGTON ALSO SANG *Merry As We Have Been* while showering, but absolutely howled the words. Franklin laughed. "George is as subtle as ever."

Jefferson also laughed. "Subtlety doesn't win wars, I suppose."

"Does it make for a successful Presidency?"

"Overall, yes. Yet . . ." Jefferson sighed. "Oh, Ben! Hamilton and the Federalists tried to make America an oligarchy, and Washington let them."

"George treats you differently than he once did," Franklin said. "He is polite, but there is less warmth."

Jefferson glanced away and shrugged.

I need a history book, Franklin thought. "What of the Federalists? They continued to support nationalized power?"

Jefferson nodded. While *The Constitution* was being drafted, debated, and ratified, there were two main factions, Federalists and Anti-Federalists. The Federalists supported *The Constitution* and the Anti-Federalists opposed it.

"Your Republicans replaced the Anti-Federalists?" Franklin asked.

"Yea and nay. We upheld *The Constitution* and the limited government it enumerated. This meant opposing the Federalists, and their government."

"The American government."

Jefferson nodded, sighed, then summarized the great problem of his Secretary of State tenure: Alexander Hamilton. Hamilton and Jefferson had dipolar views about America and human nature. Jefferson feared concentrated power, had an optimistic view of people's inherent ability to self-govern, and therefore favored a republic where most power was given to individuals and states. Hamilton favored a strong federal government; he felt the wealthy had to work with the state rather than against it if a nation were to prosper, thought most people were impulsive and easily corrupted, and wanted an elected aristocratic class to hold most power.

Hamilton was Washington's Secretary of the Treasury, Jefferson his Secretary of State. His two most gifted advisors vied for their President's ear, and their basic philosophical differences meant that they disagreed about *everything*.

"Hamilton and I were daily pitted in the cabinet like two cocks," Jefferson concluded. "Especially about the war debts. They were the most pressing problem in Washington's first administration. Hamilton felt the answer was federal assumption and a national bank to fund the federal debt."

"By assumption, you mean the federal government would assume ownership of state-held war debts?"

Jefferson nodded. "And responsibility for repayment, obviously."

"Was repayment to be proportional to arrears?"

"Perspicacious as always, Ben. Unlike the north, southern states were financially stable, and had paid off large amounts of their debts. A scheme that did not account for this fact and taxed all states equally to pay the assumed national debt would effectively transfer wealth from the southern states to the northern. Southern states opposed the assumption bill on this ground, and it did not pass."

"And the Union?" Franklin said.

"The north and south both threatened secession. Openly."

"In the first year of Washington's Presidency?"

"The second, actually. Legislating takes time. And I thought you'd be more surprised."

Franklin shook his head sternly. "The Constitutional Convention is fresh in my mind."

Jefferson smiled. "I forgot. So we faced dissolution of America in its second year of existence. Even Hamilton sensed the magnitude of our predicament, and was dejected and haggard."

"The resolution?"

"Compromise. I brokered a meeting between Hamilton and Madison."

"Was Madison a member of Washington's cabinet?"

"Sorry," Jefferson said. "I keep forgetting to put things in context. Madison was a Virginia Representative who led Republicans in America's first Congress. The bill determining the capitol's permanent location was pending. Hamilton convinced Madison to allow passage of the assumption bill. In exchange, Federalists agreed to appease the Southern states by situating the capitol on the Patowmac."

"What were your feelings on the matter?"

"I had just returned home after five years as Minister to France. You know how foreign America seems after a prolonged absence."

Franklin smiled. "Do I ever."

Jefferson chuckled. "I didn't feel knowledgeable enough to pass judgment at the time, but I was generally supportive. In hindsight, I realized that Madison and I were duped by the Secretary of the Treasury, and made a tool for forwarding his schemes. Of all the errors in my political life, this has occasioned in me the deepest regret. I failed to realize that the central issue wasn't debt, or the capitol, but states' rights. If states repaid debts, creditors would owe allegiance to them and prevent federal intrusion into their affairs out of self-interest. But if the federal government assumed these tasks, loyalty would shift to them. Hamilton shrewdly foresaw this."

"And you failed to anticipate such an obvious consequence?"

Jefferson sighed. "Yes. Hamilton duped me, as he has many others. Though his true intent became apparent soon after when he submitted his proposal for The First Bank of the United States to Congress."

"What did he propose?"

"A privately owned banking monopoly with exclusive power to set the price and supply of a 'private money'. A 'private money' Federal and state governments would accept as payment for all taxes and duties. The First Bank of the United States was basically a duplicate of the Bank of England, and predicated on similar fraud."

"Hamilton's behavior seems contradictory. He advocated honest money at the Constitutional Convention. Aggressively."

"He also advocated a President for life little different than a monarch," Jefferson said. "Perhaps he and the Federalists defended honest currency at the Convention with premeditation, hoping to avoid competition for a national bank they would later use to enrich themselves. Or maybe Hamilton was corrupted. To individuals defrauded by his national bank, such technicalities make little difference."

"Perhaps he thought he was doing right and erred."

"A man of Hamilton's brilliance? Preposterous."

As preposterous as you failing to see the implications of the assumption compromise, Franklin thought. Yet he agreed with Jefferson. Hamilton's brilliance was inarguable.

"Despite fierce opposition from Republicans, Congress passed the national bank legislation," Jefferson said. "Only Washington's signature was needed to enact it, but Madison's vehement opposition on grounds of constitutionality made him wary."

Franklin nodded. Madison had fathered *The Constitution*, and was an expert on the history of government and law. His opinions about Constitutional matters were thus highly regarded.

"Washington consulted his cabinet for opinions," Jefferson continued.

"What was yours?"

"I consider the foundation of *The Constitution* as laid on this ground: that 'all powers not delegated to the United States, by *The Constitution*, nor prohibited by it to the States, are reserved to the States or to the people.' "

"That sounds like the second *Article of Confederation*[67]," Franklin said.

"It is the tenth amendment to *The Constitution*. Sorry for the lack of context again. As you know, Anti-Federalists agreed to ratify *The Constitution* only if a *Bill of Rights* similar to Mason's *Declaration of Rights*[68] would be passed immediately by the first Congress. Madison drafted the bill and ten of its amendments were ratified. I'm sure you have questions, but defer them please."

Franklin nodded. "We must examine *The Constitution*, though."

"Yes. Now as I was saying . . . I consider the foundation of *The Constitution* as laid on this ground: that 'all powers not delegated to the United States, by *The Constitution*, nor prohibited by it to the States, are reserved to the States or to the people.' To take a single step beyond the boundaries thus specially drawn around the powers of Congress, is to take possession of a boundless field of power, no longer susceptible of any definition."

"And Hamilton disagreed?"

Jefferson nodded. "He argued that there were implied as well as expressed powers. That to accomplish certain constitutionally delegated powers, the government had others that were implied. Say what you will about Hamilton's character and ill-conceived views, but he was a formidable adversary who could speak and draw well. He actually made this 'implied powers' doctrine sound reasonable."

"Who would determine what's implied?"

"There's the rub," Jefferson said. "Hamilton's doctrine would institute a Congress with power to do whatever would be for the good of the United States; and, as they would be the sole judges of the good or evil, it would be also a power to do whatever evil they pleased."

Franklin shook his head gravely. "This is a most troubling development."

"Yes. As you noted when we first examined the notes, the incorporation of a bank and the powers assumed by legislation doing so were not delegated to the United States by *The Constitution*. They were not among the powers specially enumerated. Nor does *The Constitution* give the federal government the right

---

67 *The Articles of Confederation* were the first American constitution. Ratified by the Continental Congress in 1781, six years before *The Constitution* was drafted, they embodied colonial disenchantment with British centralized authority and established a loose confederation of sovereign states rather than a strong central government. The second article stated, "Each state retains its sovereignty, freedom, and independence, and every power, jurisdiction, and right, which is not by this Confederation expressly delegated to the United States, in Congress assembled."

68 Once hostilities with Britain erupted, colony constitutions designed for British monarchial rule were obsolete, and. many states called Constitutional Conventions that foreshadowed the national. At Virginia's convention in June 1776, George Mason proposed his *Declaration of the Rights of the Citizen*, which was ratified. Like many of the staunchest Anti-Federalists, Mason opposed *The American Constitution* because it did not contain similar guarantees.

to emit bills of credit[69]. Without amendments explicitly granting these powers, they should have been denied on grounds of constitutionality."

Franklin couldn't nod fast enough. The delegates at the Convention understood the dangers of national debt, bank monopolies, and paper money[70]. Provisions legalizing such ills existed in early drafts of *The Constitution*, but after being vehemently denounced, they were expunged.

"What finally happened?" Franklin asked.

"Washington signed the bill and began siding with Hamilton and the Federalists on most every issue. I resigned as Secretary of State at the end of his first term and opposed his administration. Unfortunately, the precedent of implied powers was established, and for the balance of my life it grew ever more entrenched. If it has persisted, I shudder to imagine how powerful the federal government has grown."

Franklin thought of the promissory cards. He knew he had much to research before commenting, but he too felt fear. Jefferson's agitation about the notes now made much more sense. A national bank hadn't simply been formed. *The Constitution*'s most fundamental intention—the enumeration of specific federal powers that could not be expanded, except by amendment—seemed to have been subverted.

THE MOMENT JEFFERSON turned on the water to take the last shower, Franklin said, "What happened between you and Tom?"

"Just a moment. I've barely got my teeth in." Washington winced while he adjusted his dentures gingerly. With them in, he looked more puffy-faced and serious. "Clothe yourself while we talk. I thought it better not to mention my conflicts with Tom. They are the past."

Franklin began to dress. "Think of me as a historian."

Washington laughed. "Tom told you about his disagreements with Hamilton?"

Franklin nodded. "And the implied powers argument."

"Jefferson opposed every attempt to strengthen the federal government. With zeal that was often excessive."

"Why?"

"I don't know. Because he was in France when we floundered under *The Articles of Confederation*, and did not see anarchy like Shays' Rebellion first hand?"

Franklin remembered the turbulent pre-*Constitution* period vividly. *The*

---

69 Emit bills of credit. To circulate debt as money.

70 Paper money. Another colonial term for bills of credit. Paper money in the colonial context does not mean all notes made of paper, but those not backed by a commodity.

Articles of Confederation favored states rights, and created a federal government too weak to perform basic functions like defense. The result was a slide toward anarchy epitomized by Shays' Rebellion, a Massachusetts tax uprising. Massachusetts paid its immense Revolutionary War debts by levying steep agricultural taxes and confiscating the land of farmers who could not pay them . . . Until Revolutionary War veteran Daniel Shays led an uprising of 1,200 disgruntled farmers who forced the state's Supreme Court to adjourn before approving confiscations. Though crushed by a proprietor's army en route to the federal arsenal in Springfield, Shays' state rebellion threatened the nation's security, and to many concerned Americans, it exemplified the chaos that would ensue if federal powers were not strengthened. The episode was one of the major impetuses for the Constitutional Convention that began three months later.

"While in France, Tom maintained diverse correspondence and was well informed of American events," Franklin said. "Absence, or even ignorance, cannot explain his stance. And he was among those who advocated a stronger federal government than the *Articles of Confederation* provided."

Washington nodded. "Tom's great weakness remains slavery, and loyalty to the south and Virginia. Though his objections were often principled, he opposed a strong national government because it might force southern states to abolish slavery."

Franklin winced. "That would mean the loss of his beloved Monticello."

Washington nodded again. "Never forget that when talking to him."

"Do you believe Hamilton wanted to institute a monarchy?"

"As he made plain at the Convention, Hamilton favored a constitutional monarchy. And he had his illicit affairs and corruptions, just like Jefferson."

"Was he corrupted by ambition?"

"That he was ambitious I shall readily grant, but it was of that laudable kind which prompts a man to excel in whatever he takes in hand. He was enterprising, quick in his perceptions, and like Jefferson, his judgment was intuitively great."

"Why did they disagree so often then?"

"Inherent temperament notwithstanding, the root cause lies in upbringing, I would guess. Hamilton's childhood imbued him with a fundamentally pessimistic view of human nature, Jefferson's gave him an optimistic opinion."

Hamilton had been orphaned in the West Indies when he was eleven. At an age when Jefferson was learning to read Latin and play the violin amid the opulence of the Virginia gentry, Hamilton was toiling in abject poverty. Through self-discipline, hard work, and enormous innate talent, he succeeded in joining the wealthy elite, but his journey was a great struggle. Hamilton had seen the darker side of human nature firsthand, and he regarded Jefferson's rosy assessment of man as pathetically naïve.

"Who was right?" Franklin asked.

Washington laughed. "You act as if you're interviewing Providence. On many issues, my humble answer is both. They balanced each other, and provided diverse perspectives that were indispensable to me when making difficult decisions. I didn't realize just how indispensable until they'd both resigned. In their absence I felt . . ." Washington scowled as he thought of his second Presidential term. *Abandoned.* "It's the past, Ben. I want to spend my last years enjoying this new world, not bickering about decisions that can't be undone."

"You didn't answer my question."

Washington smiled. "Hamilton advocated policy that would have created monarchy, Jefferson anarchy. I wasn't going to let either man have his way. The middle road between their views was Republicanism. I used their strengths for America's benefit, and limited the damage their weaknesses could cause."

Franklin also smiled. Washington was no philosopher, lawyer, or orator, but he was an adept judge of men. "What of your dispute with Jefferson?"

"It began with Jay's Treaty."

"John Jay?"

"Yes. I appointed him the first Chief Justice of the Supreme Court."

"A wise choice." Franklin could not think of a better selection. Jay was universally regarded as a man of temperance and wisdom. He esteemed Jay enough to make him an executor of his will.

"Jay also served as Envoy Extraordinary[71] to England and negotiated a treaty near the end of my first Executive term," Washington explained. "He secured agreements for trade, evacuation of the Crown's North American frontier posts, and most importantly, perpetuation of our neutrality. As our war debts were monstrous, commerce was a major concern. We were not secure as long as Britain had troops near our borders. And I was determined to avoid entangling alliances that would draw us into the bloody European quagmire.

"Unfortunately, Britain was still the strongest nation in the world, and this enabled her to force humiliating terms. But Jay's treaty was far superior to no agreement, and its fundamental accomplishment, securing peace that would allow our infant republic to concentrate on internal development rather than external warfare, was a great one.

"The treaty was unpopular, especially to Republicans, who preferred a pact with France for ideological reasons. In a letter to a neighbor, Phillip Mazzei, Jefferson criticized the treaty. And me!" Washington clenched a fist. "I still

---

71 Envoy Extraordinary. Minister Plenipotentiary.

remember his exact words: 'It would give you a fever were I to name to you the apostates who have gone over to these heresies, men who were Samsons in the field and Solomons in the council, but who have had their heads shorn by the Harlot England.' "

Still hypersensitive about your reputation, I see. Despite your poor memory, you recite trivial affronts verbatim. Franklin resisted the urge to chuckle.

Washington stood, and with palpable effort, controlled his anger. "Mazzei printed the letter overseas, and it soon littered every paper in America, becoming the most singularly discussed morsel of political gossip. I don't care about the personal affront . . ." Washington saw Franklin's dubious expression, and smiled. "I cared about the personal affront, but not as much as the political one. The letter undermined me. And more importantly, my efforts to build a republic."

"Adam's inauguration must have been cozy."

"I was polite the day before yesterday," Washington said. "As was Tom. The republic needed unity at its first transition of leadership. In a world where succession is usually determined by birth or battle, this was something special. Something that transcended our differences. We both realized it."

"Do you still hold a grudge?"

"I no longer consider Tom a friend, but I will not allow emotion to impede necessity. Unity is our great strength, as it is America's. Jefferson has talents we may need."

"I'm surprised Tom opposed a peace treaty," Franklin said.

"He became a zealot late in my life," Washington replied. "A French theorist who embraced principles of government which would lead infallibly to licentiousness and anarchy. Hopefully his tenure as President made him more ap—"

"I am a zealot when defending liberty," Jefferson said, from inside the necessary. "And some principles shouldn't be compromised."

Washington and Franklin hadn't heard the shower stop, and were surprised by the interruption.

Jefferson exited the necessary wrapped in a towel. He resembled a wet kitten; unclothed he seemed even more gangly, and his saturated hair no longer hid his ears, which jutted diagonally, challenging his nose for supremacy. Freckles had bred like microbes, peppering his entire body. Though Jefferson's skin sagged, he was more muscular than one who'd seen him clothed would have thought. "History settled these arguments conclusively," he said to Washington. "Long before we lived."

"I don't care who was right or wrong," Washington replied. "America survived somehow. That's all that matters to me."

"Has the American *republic* also survived?" Jefferson asked. "Has freedom? Have the principles we outlined in *The Declaration* and *Constitution*?"

What I wouldn't give for a nigger, Jefferson thought, as he folded his clothes sullenly. He knew slavery's demise should bring him joy, but instead it scared him. He had never prepared a bath, cooked a meal, made a bed or pressed a shirt, and beginning to do these things in the twilight of his life was daunting.

As was the prospect of survival in an emancipated world. Slavery's end had always been theoretical for Jefferson. He was sure it would come about, but not in his lifetime. He would not make the sacrifices emancipation entailed.

Jefferson sighed deeply. *I deserve this*, he thought. *To be truthful, I probably deserve much worse. If living my last years without servants is my only penance, I have cheated fate.*

This philosophical mindset evaporated quickly in the scalding intensity of Jefferson's fear. He recoiled when he thought of the time he would have to waste on menial tasks. Time better spent in study. And what of an estate? Even with futuristic inventions, how would he build something as sublime as Monticello, and live in the style he was accustomed to, if he actually had to pay workers?

His selfish reaction forced Jefferson to confront his hypocrisy. He and other southerners opposed emancipation because they refused to forsake the luxurious lifestyle slavery perpetuated. Their treatment of niggers was despicable and evil. How ironic that in a slave-filled past this truth could be ignored, but in a free future it was glaring!

Once his denial hibernated, Jefferson was wracked by guilt. His remorse about slavery had never been a gnawing anxiety, but rather a stabbing anguish triggered by associations that highlighted the difference between his utopian ideals and hypocritical actions. Jefferson hated these searing moments, and it chilled him to think that every time he folded a shirt, washed a dish, or saw a free nigger, he might face one.

"There's no need to fold our old garments, Tom," Washington said. "We'll be destroying them in the morrow."

"I know," Jefferson replied. He continued anyway, put the folded garments in the dresser, then surveyed the room. The disorganization annoyed him perpetually, like an aggressive mosquito. Soap bars were strewn across the counter, the nightstand drawer was open slightly, and a towel was hung without first being folded.

As he stacked the soap, Jefferson watched Washington and Franklin in the mirror. They didn't seem to mind the work. Which made sense. Franklin had fended for himself early in life while a commoner. Though accustomed to slave servants, Washington had a high tolerance for all adversity, and his military expeditions made him self-reliant.

Jefferson sighed again. His companions' cheerful acceptance of their labor exacerbated his own dissatisfaction. He didn't just mind the work. He resented it.

Washington saw Jefferson carefully hanging a towel as if it were the centerpiece of some monarch's necessary, and smiled slightly, but said nothing. Jefferson worked until everything in the room was meticulously arranged. Then he stood near the door, surveyed the orderliness, and smiled with satisfaction.

Franklin was the only remaining chaos. While peering at his hundred dollar note, he froze suddenly. "Of course!" he said, as he hobbled across the room and opened the door. "I can't believe I didn't think of it earlier."

"Where are you going?" Washington asked.

"You'd approve of this trip, I assure you."

"I'll take you at your word," Washington said. "But if you don't return I need to know where to search."

"The tavern lobby."

"WHAT CAN I do for you, Mr. Steele?" the front desk clerk asked.

Franklin held out a hundred dollar bill. "I need to locate a natural philosopher."

"Natural philosopher?"

"I require tutelage in the history of invention. I wish to learn how implements like TVs, airlines, and phones operate."

"You need a scientist or engineer. And I'm not promising you he's social, but I know your boy."

Franklin brandished another hundred. "Is this sciencist or enginear available early in the morrow?"

The clerk scanned the lobby, made sure no one else was around, then tried to take both hundreds.

Franklin released one. "The other is yours when you introduce me to this sciencist."

"And my boy?"

Franklin fanned several hundreds. "I'm a fair man. You're certain he's smart?"

The clerk nodded quickly. "I grew up with the guy. He's a total whiz. He was building radios while we were still riding big wheels. Got a 1540 on his SATs. 790 Math."

Ray-dee-ohs? The clerk clearly considered these achievements impressive, so Franklin nodded approvingly.

"Why don't you give me a few minutes to get a hold of him," the clerk said. "I'll call you in your room."

"Agreed. But before I vacate I need smaller denominations." Franklin placed several hundreds on the counter.

The clerk smiled slightly as he changed them. Who would have thought a disheveled oddity like Mr. Steele was loaded?

WASHINGTON HELPED FRANKLIN into the room, and shut the door behind him. "I am quite curious," he said.

"So am I," Franklin replied. He sat on the bed and sorted his notes by denomination. "The cipher that differs note to note may allow us to estimate the money stock. Let's start with your note. Eight digits, plus the single alphabetic prefix and suffix. Making the reasonable assumption that language and number conventions have not changed, that gives 10 possible perms for the cipher and 26 for the letter . . ." Franklin grabbed a parchment and quill, and began ciphering[72] feverishly. "67.6 billion unique ciphers. Or 67.6 billion one-dollar notes."

Jefferson sat down and handed everyone a five. It had an extra letter in its alphabetic prefix. Eight ciphers, three letters. 1.7 trillion unique ciphers.

"By Providence I hope you are wrong," Jefferson said.

"So do I," Franklin replied.

Jefferson peered at the notes intently. "Yet . . ."

Franklin nodded. "It makes sense. The ultimate defense against counterfeiting. Giving each note a unique cipher."

The process was repeated with each denomination. Franklin was a slow cipherer, so Washington performed most of the calculations. A list was soon assembled:

Denomination	Number of Ciphers	Total
1	67,600,000,000	$67,600,000,000
5	1,757,600,000,000	$8,788,000,000,000
10	1,757,600,000,000	$17,576,000,000,000
20	1,757,600,000,000	$35,152,000,000,000
50	1,757,600,000,000	$87,880,000,000,000
100	1,757,600,000,000	$175,760,000,000,000
Total	8,855,600,000,000	$325,223,600,000,000

72 Ciphering. Performing mathematical calculations.

All three founders were now petrified. Almost 9 *trillion* notes totaling over 325 *trillion* dollars!

"This may not be as grim as it seems," Franklin said. "Our enumeration probably represents a theoretical maximum. The ciphers would likely be made excessively large so that unique identifiers were never exhausted. Also, one would expect small denominations to be much more numerous than large."

"A small comfort," Jefferson replied. "Even if we assume a thousand-fold error, a money stock of 325 billion dollars is still affrightening. The bankers and money jobbers must be emperors by now!"

No one argued. During times of economic prosperity in colonial America, tens of millions of dollars circulated. Egregiously irresponsible, rapid depreciations to almost 650 million dollars had decimated the economy. Even if America's population had grown to some absurd level, say 25, 50 maybe even 100 million people, and wares rained from the sky . . . A depreciation to 325 billion dollars defied comprehension, and was so staggeringly large that the founders would have dismissed it as a joke or the ravings of a lunatic in any setting besides the future.

Franklin sighed deeply. "This estimate may still be too large, but its general magnitude, even with errors, suggests two conclusions. The American currency has been depreciated relentlessly, and *The Constitution* has either been unwisely amended or circumvented."

"Hopefully, we erred," Washington said. "Maybe this cipher has some other purpose."

"You erred," Jefferson replied. "But not about the ciphers. If a private national bank controls a circulation this large, the money jobbers have probably subjected America to depreciations that make our old ones seem trifling."

"SOMETHING ABOUT THOSE actors wasn't right," the wife said to her husband. The children were asleep and they were tossing and turning in the uncomfortable hotel bed, trying to mimic them.

"They were lying about something, but seemed like honest men." The cop shrugged.

"Honest men who were lying. You sound like Jefferson."

Another shrug.

"Doesn't the dishonesty bother you?"

"If I let every liar I encountered get under my skin I'd go crazy."

"Nothing's sacred anymore," the wife said. "Not even a place like Mount Rushmore. Kooks like those actors make it more like Roswell or *The Rocky Horror Picture Show.*"

The cop sighed. "They're the past. What difference does it make?"

"They could be child molesters for all we know."

"You're pretty cynical sometimes. They weren't child molesters. They were good men."

"Good men who lie."

"Yes."

"You can't be sure. We should report them to the police and Rushmore, just in case. Wouldn't you feel terrible if I was right and something happened to someone else's child?"

They aren't fucking child molesters! "Let's just go to sleep."

"You've got their fingerprints on the pen and documents. And their pictures. When we get home why don't you see if they have records?"

Silence. The husband gritted his teeth.

"Are you telling me they didn't make you suspicious?"

Of course they did. But if I admit that you'll keep me up all night. The wife kept nagging, and seemed determined to do so anyway. Finally the husband rolled over and said, "If I contact Rushmore and the local police before we leave tomorrow, and run their prints when we return home, do you promise not to bring this up for the rest of our vacation? Not a single word?"

"Yes. And I don't see why you're being so rude ab—"

"Good. I'll do it then."

Franklin's enormous girth made him the logical person to have his own bed, and when he passed gas loudly while starkers, the matter was settled decisively.

The window was more contentious. Franklin opened it, as was his routine, and Washington objected immediately.

"We must have fresh air," Franklin retorted. "Would you risk disease?"

"Would you risk a mugging? And won't the cold, damp night air cause disease?"

Franklin knew Washington was expressing the typical colonial view, which held that fog or miasma could cause illness somehow. "I believe the causes of colds are totally independent of wet and even of cold. Diseases are probably transmitted by some particular effluvia in the air."

"The window will nonetheless stay closed."

Jefferson smiled. Washington would never compromise security, but he was wise enough not to refute Franklin's natural philosophy views.

An air-expelling invention below the window seemed to make it superfluous anyway. The futuristic fan could also alter the room's temperature. Franklin realized a similar device must have been used in the Rushmore gift shop, and experimented.

"I can't believe you haven't collapsed," Jefferson said.

"Nor can I," Franklin replied. "But these are hardly typical circumstances. My mind is racing and my excitement is incurable. I am exhausted, yet manic."

"It is past midnight," Washington said. "We must sleep. And would you get into bed or put some breeches on!"

As he obeyed, Franklin sat on the inside edge of his bed and gave Washington the worst possible view.

"Are you trying to make me purge?" Washington asked.

The phone rang. Franklin remained in place and answered, denying Washington salvation. After a terse, unrevealing conversation, he hung up and said, "I have secured an appointment with a sciencist in the morrow."

"Sciencist," Jefferson said. "You mean a scholar?"

"A natural philosopher. Futurity seems to have narrowed our definition of science."

"Sciencist," Jefferson whispered. "Science. Scientia, Latin for knowledge. Present participle of scire, to know. Sciencist . . . Sciencist . . . Scientist would make more sense, but . . ."

Franklin expected Washington to chide him for not consulting the group, but he said, "Excellent. While Tom and I investigate, you can receive tutelage."

"Hopefully, in the late morrow or after the noon. This scientist did not give an exact arrival time, so I may be able to slumber at leisure and recover from today's exertions."

Washington sighed with relief when Franklin finally hid himself under the covers. As Franklin placed his spectacles in the nightstand drawer, his hand brushed a book, which he held within inches of his face. "A Bible."

Jefferson sighed. "The note cipher, and now religion. Not an inspiring end to the day."

Franklin put his spectacles back on. "It is a King James. The Old Testament. The New Testament. Genesis, Revelations. It appears to be the same book we knew. So it is not merely religion that has survived, but Christianity."

"Does this surprise you?" Washington asked.

"No," Franklin replied. "The Christian mythology we knew survived for 1700 years. Two more centuries is hardly a shock."

Washington offered the Bible to Jefferson. He refused. "The thickness tells me all I need to know for now."

"What do you mean?" Washington asked.

Jefferson ignored the question. His eyes grew sad. "Foolish, I know. But I had hoped . . ."

Franklin nodded. "That reason might have prevailed conclusively?"

"Or prevailed somewhat. But it is too late for such thoughts."

"Tonight you mean?"

Jefferson chuckled morosely. The Bible made him envision the religious oppression that ruled and was the rule for most of human history. Were the scriptures a harmless hotel amenity, or had America regressed socially, as it appeared to have monetarily? Were church and state reunited? Had the clergy resumed its power jobbing? Had there been other Inquisitions and Crusades? Did natural philosophers once again hide from religious oppressors who suppressed truth to perpetuate mysticism? Jefferson would not assume without proof, but as a student of history, he was aware that this possibility was a real one, and the Bible brought him no comfort.

Silence while the founders situated themselves in bed. Exploration had finally ceased, and the mood shifted, becoming more philosophical.

"Killed by a throat ache," Franklin said to Washington. "Ironic, after everything you've survived."

"Providence wasn't going to spare me forever."

"Why did he spare us this long?" Franklin wondered. "There must be a reason."

Silence.

Thoughtful silence.

"Humor a restless old friend with predictions of the future," Franklin said.

"Predictions of the future." Jefferson chuckled.

"It would be useful to enunciate our expectations for later reference," Franklin said.

"Ever the natural philosopher," Jefferson replied.

Franklin smiled proudly. "Yes."

"Natural philosophic advances are the most significant futuristic observation," Washington said.

"They are certainly our most indelible initial impression," Franklin agreed. "But I want predictions, not observations."

"Whether predicting or observing, natural philosophy is still the predominant factor," Jefferson replied. "As I previously stated, I believe the daily advance of science will have enabled futurity to administer the commonwealth with increased wisdom."

"Or oppress with greater alacrity," Franklin countered.

Jefferson's nod seemed pained. "No one wishes the spread of information among mankind more than I. And no one has greater confidence in its effect towards supporting good government. But, I fear, from experiences of the last twenty-five years, that morals do not advance hand in hand with the sciences."

"Are we wiser, or aren't we?" Washington asked.

"Perhaps both," Jefferson replied. "I expect our axiom of inalienable rights to have proliferated. Though it would be foolish to think we will find Ou Topos[73]."

"What will we find?" Franklin asked.

"All discussions of the American Republic must begin and end with its sacred and inviolate law, *The Constitution.*"

"Amendments?" Franklin said. "Another Constitutional Convention?"

"The natural philosophic revolution which has engulfed the world may have antiquated our *Constitution,*" Jefferson replied. "It may have been rewritten, not merely amended."

"An intriguing and unsettling proposition," Washington said. "An America whose *Constitution* is not the one we drew."

"Is your pride wounded?" Franklin teased.

Washington bristled. "Of course not."

"Mine is." Franklin chuckled. "How many amendments do you predict?"

Jefferson laughed. "Is this one of French Court's parlor lotteries? You and George helped draft *The Constitution*, not I. I should be quizzing you."

"You have three decades' experience with its implementation we lack," Franklin countered. "Not to mention political vision which eclipses ours combined."

"I would refute the latter supposition. In your case."

Franklin laughed at Washington's sour expression.

"No constitution was ever before so well calculated for extensive empire and self-rule," Jefferson said. "Our government is destined to be the primitive and precious model of what will change the condition of man over the globe."

"Will change, or has changed?" Franklin asked.

Jefferson shrugged. "Once again, both?"

"What of the government's anatomy?" Washington asked. "Do you predict the same species?"

"Though the American genus should still be respublica[74], I pray the species is new. An immortal constitution must be amended to keep pace with advances

---

73 Ou Topos. Greek. Ou, no. Topos, where. Nowhere. The Latin equivalent is Utopia. A Utopia is a fictional, ideal commonwealth whose inhabitants exist under seemingly-perfect conditions. The phrase originated with Sir Thomas More's 1516 philosophical satire: *Libellus . . . De Optimo Reipublicae Statu, Deque Nova Insula Utopia (Concerning the Highest State of the Republic and the New Island Utopia).*

74 Respublica. Latin for republic. Res, thing. Publica, of the people.

in science and experience. We must not mimic European governments who resist reformation until the people undertake it with force."

"Slavery?" Washington asked. "The Civil War?"

"Perhaps." Jefferson nodded. "Probably. But I was making a broader point. Unless the mass retains control over those entrusted with government power, it will be perverted to their own oppression and to perpetuation of wealth and power in politicians and their families. Whether our *Constitution* hit on the exact degree of control necessary is yet under experiment."

"Or perhaps was yet under experiment," Franklin said.

"Yes. Perhaps was. A sobering thought."

"Did anything you observed after my death make you think America might revert to genus monarchia?" Franklin asked.

Jefferson shook his head. "We were educated in royalism. No wonder some of us retained that idolatry still. Our young people were educated in republicanism. An apostasy from that to royalism is unprecedented and impossible."

"Are you perhaps being overly optimistic?" Franklin asked.

"I make no claim to omniscience."

"The apostasy's form, if there were one?" Franklin asked.

"Genus oligarchia."

"What worries you most?" Washington asked.

"I abhor war," Jefferson replied. "It is the greatest scourge of mankind. I hope America has not wasted its energies in destruction and has avoided implicating itself in European affairs, even in support of principles it means to pursue. We can enforce principles by peaceable means, if our public councils are detached from foreign views."

"There is naiveté in this view," Washington replied, "but also wisdom. Against the insidious wiles of foreign influence, the jealousy of a free people ought to be constantly awake. History and experience prove it is one of the most baneful foes of republican government."

Jefferson nodded. "I am for free commerce with all nations, political connection with none, and little or no diplomatic establishment."

"Except for France," Washington said sourly. *You hypocrite.*

"Like Franklin, I am a Francophile. But I am not for linking ourselves by new treaties with the quarrels of Europe, entering that field of slaughter to preserve their balance, or joining her confederacy of Kings to war against the principles of liberty."

"What if Europe is now a confederacy of republics?" Franklin wondered.

Jefferson raised one of his bushy eyebrows. "Hmmm."

"What if your beloved Republican France was overrun by the confederacy of Kings?" Washington said. "I doubt you would still preach the same doctrine."

Jefferson's eyebrow became an arch.

"Hmmm indeed." Franklin chuckled. "Is Jeffersonanity fraught with the hypocrisies of other religions?"

As Jefferson frowned, Washington smiled. He enjoyed forcing the Sage of Monticello to grapple with his hypocrisies.

"Our suppositions were hypothetical," Franklin soothed, "and perhaps offered more to make sport than spurn philosophical revelations."

Our suppositions, Washington thought. *Ben apologized for my caustic remark, but grouped it with his to lessen the offense to me.* Washington knew such masterful use of subtle language was instinctual to Franklin. How many battalions of this brilliance had he employed to secure French support?

"Peace," Franklin begged. "Peace! If I could ask only one thing of American history, it would be peace!"

"It certainly seemed possible," Washington replied. "It remained only for the states to be wise to prevent being made the sport of European policy. Hopefully, heaven gave them wisdom to adopt the measures necessary for this important purpose."

"I believe we will multiply and prosper until we are powerful, wise and happy beyond what man has seen," Jefferson predicted. "Europe will no longer make sport of us. Rather, we may shake a rod over the heads of all which may make the stoutest of them tremble."

"Shake a rod," Washington said. "Or perhaps a newk?"

"Whatever we shake, I hope our wisdom grows with our power, teaching us the less we use it, the greater it will be." A sudden frown from the Sage of Monticello. It conveyed rare cynicism. "I hope improving the mind and morals of society may lessen its disposition to war, but of its abolition I despair."

"America will always need Washingtons," Franklin agreed.

Washington smiled ever so slightly.

"Our new *Constitution* was established, and had an appearance that promised permanency, but in this world nothing can be said to be certain except death and taxes." Franklin raised a finger belatedly. "And time transport."

Washington and Jefferson laughed.

"Death and taxes," Franklin repeated. "What would cause the former?"

"The latter," Jefferson replied. "Certain forms of government are better calculated than others to protect individuals' natural rights and guard against degeneracy, yet even under the best forms, those entrusted with power gradually pervert it into tyranny. The natural progress of things is for liberty to yield and government to gain ground."

"Had you observed this natural progress?" Franklin asked.

Jefferson nodded. "America is not incorruptible. Corruption was making sensible though silent progress."

"Its form?" Franklin asked.

"After its Revolution, a nation goes downhill. Government grows accepted and does not need to resort every moment to the people. They are therefore forgotten and their rights disregarded. They forget themselves but in the sole faculty of making money, and never think of uniting to effect a due respect for their rights. Corrupt leaders then purchase the people's voices and make them pay the price."

Washington's grimace reminded Franklin of a clenching fist. When he spoke, he seemed to be shooting words. "Government is not reason, it is not eloquence, it is force. Like fire, a troublesome servant and a fearful master. Never for a moment should it be left to irresponsible action."

"We have missed much more than a moment," Franklin replied. "What is the worst scenario you can envision?"

"The greatest calamity would be submission to a government of unlimited powers," Jefferson said. "When all government, domestic and foreign, in little as in great things, is drawn to Washington as the center of all power, the checks provided by one government on another will be rendered powerless. This is a despotism as venal and oppressive as the one we separated from."

An anvil of a nod from Washington. "The spirit of encroachment tends to consolidate all branches into one, creating, whatever the form of government, a real despotism. A just estimate of the love of power and proneness to abuse it which predominates the human heart is sufficient to satisfy us of the truth of this position."

"That is why economy is an important republican virtue, and public debt a most fearful danger," Jefferson added. "To preserve our independence, we must not let our rulers load us with perpetual debt. We must make our election between economy and liberty, or profusion and servitude. America must never run such debts that we must be taxed in our meat and drink, necessaries and comforts, labors and amusements, callings and creeds, labor sixteen hours in the twenty four, give the earnings of fifteen to the government, and find the sixteenth insufficient to afford us bread. It would shatter my heart to see Americans with no time to think, no means of calling the mismanagers to account, gladly obtaining subsistence by riveting the mismanagers' chains on the necks of fellow-sufferers."

Jefferson was passionate about his topic, and had spoken with emotion. He panted slightly as his rant ended.

"It will be interesting to speak to history," Washington said.

"It will," Jefferson agreed. "Though history, in general, only informs us what bad government is."

"Hopefully America has changed this."

"Perhaps. The system of government which kept us afloat amidst the wreck of the world has probably been immortalized in history. But the political history of man always has been, and no doubt always will be, a struggle of the masses against the forces of tyranny."

"Tyranny is your prediction then?" Washington asked.

"I know not what to expect. Or predict. I do believe America's future happiness depends on the maintenance of our revolutionary principles. As long as they prevail, we are safe from everything which can assail us from without or within, for whenever our affairs go obviously wrong, the good sense of the people will interpose and set them right."

"Any non-political predictions or hopes?" Franklin asked.

"Culture," Jefferson said. "My zealous good wish is that United States artists may give an innocent and pleasing direction to accumulations of wealth which would otherwise be employed in the nourishment of coarse and vicious habits."

"What of you, George?" Franklin said. "What hopes have you for your child?"

"The establishment of civil and religious liberty was the motive which induced me to the field. The object was attained, and it remains my earnest wish and prayer that America's citizens make wise and virtuous use of these blessings."

"And what would you consider a virtuous use?" Franklin inquired.

"Like Tom, I rejoice in a belief that intellectual light will spring up in the Earth's dark corners. That freedom of enquiry will produce liberality of conduct. That mankind will reverse the absurd position that the many were made for the few. And that men will not continue as slaves in one part of the globe when they can be freemen in another. Especially with airlines and Watt wagons that simplify emigration."

"Is that a hope or a prediction?" Franklin asked.

"A prediction, I hope. It is uncertain whether our Revolution is ultimately a blessing or a curse." Washington paused and reflected. "With America's fate the destiny of unborn millions has certainly been involved. No country ever had it more in its power to attain liberty's blessings than a United America. Wondrously strange and much regretted it would be if it neglected the means and departed from the road Providence pointed to so plainly. I cannot believe it will ever come to pass."

Franklin pursed his lips. "What if it did come to pass?"

"The foundation of a great Empire was laid. Providence will not leave its work imperfect."

Franklin laughed. "Perhaps we are Providence's solution to an imperfect work."

Washington tensed. "I know you jest, but the thought of spending my few remaining years in public service is oppugnant."

"So if future America pleaded, you would refuse to serve?"

Washington's deep exhalation was more of a growl. His eyes narrowed as compassion drained from them. "The foundation of America was not laid in the gloomy age of ignorance and superstition, but at an epoch when the rights of mankind were better understood and more clearly defined than at any former period. At this auspicious time, the United States came into existence, and if its citizens are not completely free and happy, the fault will be entirely their own."

Franklin nodded. Jefferson nodded. Washington nodded. Optimism filled the room. The founders did not know what they would find, but they chose to hope for the best.

"I would hear Doctor Franklin's predictions," Jefferson said.

Franklin let out a long yawn. "I am tired."

"None of your diplomat's antics," Washington pressed. "Have we kept our republic?"

Franklin smiled. *The Constitution* was drafted in secret, and when he and the other delegates finally emerged from their multi-month ordeal, a member of an anxious crowd asked him what sort of government had been crafted. "A republic," he replied, "if you can keep it." Like so many of his sagely snippets, it was widely quoted, and soon considered the definitive one-clause synopsis of the Convention.

"You both piloted the American ship," Franklin said. "I never even saw it. How could I possibly prognosticate?"

"Surely you have some thought," Washington said.

Franklin recounted his study of flies drowned in wine that were revived by the sun. "I always wished to invent a method of embalming drowned persons so they could be recalled to life. Having an ardent desire to observe the state of America in a few hundred years, I felt being immersed in a cask of Madeira wine would be preferable to an ordinary death."

"You often imbibe enough that the effect is probably the same," Washington said.

Franklin laughed. "In my fantasy, I and a few friends would be recalled to life by the solar warmth of my dear country."

"Your fantasy . . ." Washington whispered.

"I never thought we would live to see the American result," Jefferson echoed.

Silence as the founders pondered what an enormous gift they had been given.

"A pithy story, Ben," Washington finally said. "And entertaining, like all your narratives. But not a prediction."

"A prediction, then. If our *Constitution* succeeded, I do not see why Europe would not form a federal union and one grand republic of all its different states and kingdoms, by means of a like covenant."

"Did our *Constitution* succeed?" Washington asked.

Franklin thought a moment. "I always believed *The Constitution* would be well administered for a course of years, but could only end in despotism, as all other forms have done before it. People eventually become so corrupt they require despotic government, being incapable of any other."

"How long a course of years?" Washington pressed.

Franklin shrugged and smiled. Washington and Jefferson continued to badger him for prognostication, but his only responses were witty evasions. Finally, they gave up. Washington hid the notes, then placed an axe under his pillow and a knife on the nightstand.

"You'd better hope George doesn't have any dreams about chopping wood," Franklin said to Jefferson. "Or redcoats."

Washington pulled a trigger instead of blowing out a candle, an act symbolic of the entire day and situation. A roaming, random, stream-of-consciousness conversation filled the darkness. The day's experiences were discussed and analyzed until even Washington was droopy eyed. After they once again wondered about the Puppeteer's motive, the founders finally slept, and their first day in the future slipped into the past.

AT 7:58 A KNOCK woke Washington. The soldier's habit of sleeping lightly had never left him; he rose immediately, grabbed his axe, and crept up to the door. "Identify yourself."

"I'm the front-desk clerk's friend. You hired me for science lessons."

Washington kept the chain bound, opened the door fractionally, inched an eye past its edge, and peered at the caller. He was careful to show as little of himself as possible.

"Hello, sir. I'm Paul. Am I supposed to teach you?"

Washington relaxed somewhat as he sized up the obese, bookish sciencist. "This is the proper room, but your pupil has not yet risen. Just a moment, please." Washington closed and locked the door, then slid a twenty dollar note under it. "My apologies for the delay. Please break your fast at the carvery to the north. Your pupil will be along in a few ticks."

WASHINGTON'S KNOCKS WERE quick and impatient.

"I can only crap so fast, George," Franklin said through the door. "I've got a bloody stone!"

Sitting on the toilet, Franklin looked like an elephant on a bar stool. An amazed elephant. He was used to outhouses, buckets, and chamber pots, and had also been privileged enough to use some of the world's first toilets, tiny, crude metal crucibles that seemed made for a midget or a monkey. The luxurious necessary he sat upon shamed them all!

"What an advancement this is, George! Better than TV, Watt wagons, and airlines combined!"

"I was hoping to experience the wonder myself," Washington said. "If you would end your reign."

"You'll have to overthrow me."

"My bravery has limits. Not even a savage could stand that smell."

"It's this futuristic food. It has given me diabolical dysentery." Franklin held a piece of fluffy chamber paper between his fingers, and petted it like animal fur. *So soft! Far superior to corncobs, mussel shells, and melon husks!*

"Do you require a newspaper?" Washington asked. "Or do I need to fetch a stick or some leaves?"

"No."

"I would offer wool or lace, but we have none. Perhaps one of my stockings?"

Like toilets, these were luxuries that only royalty and ultra-wealthy colonials enjoyed. "Thank you for the generous offer, George. But parchment is provided."

The First American smiled as he wiped. He was not being lewd or perverted. The necessary and its inventions seemed like a divine blessing to him.

Franklin wondered what to do with the soiled parchment. The water hole in the throne seemed small; he decided not to risk a conspicuous malfunction and placed it in the rectangular refuse container instead.

Washington knocked on the door again. "Do you intend to bivouac? The natural philosopher is waiting."

Franklin finished up, stood, and played with the necessary's shiny trigger. It roared, and with surprising force and velocity, water whisked his excretion away. As he once again shook his head with amazement, Franklin thought of Bethlehem, the first aqueduct in America, and the steam-powered water-pumping station Jefferson had mentioned. Such facilities were probably ubiquitous.

Still a colonial who viewed paper as exorbitant, Franklin had used miniscule squares, and feces coated his fingers. Like many from his era, he had often been forced to wipe bare-handed, and was not disgusted. Rather, he was once again grateful and amazed, this time for the sink, which saved him the need to drag his hands along the ground, procure leaves, or pump well water.

When Washington finally stormed into the bathroom, he found Franklin hunched over the necessary. He had removed the lid and was observing the innards while pulling the trigger. "A clever invention. Look at the buoy that aqueducts the water. And feel the parchment, George! Compared to what we used, it's like cleaning your arse with Rose petals!"

Washington tugged Franklin out of the bathroom by an arm. "If you aren't dressed in two ticks, I'll kick you out the door starkers!"

FRANKLIN CRINGED as he looked in the mirror and saw his American flag shirt, sweat pants, and Mount Rushmore cap. He reminded himself vanity wasn't the primary concern—not looking like Ben Franklin was.

"No more dallying," Washington said, as he dragged Franklin toward the door like a disobedient child. "You groom and dress slower than a wench preparing for a ball."

"At least let me take a tick and gather my thoughts!"

"Fine." Washington released Franklin. "But only a tick."

"I've got the phone cipher, knife, and notes."

"One of us will be in the room all day in case you telegraph," Washington said. "Here are some extra notes. If you can purchase wares that may aid us, do so."

"No long tirade?" Franklin grinned. "No threats or dire warnings?"

"A rescue in this future may be impossible, so please don't take *any* unnecessary risks. You may not believe this, but I actually want to see you again. And for Providence's sake, please be frugal! Once these notes are gone . . ."

Franklin nodded gravely. "So is a large measure of our freedom."

FRANKLIN ENTERED the carvery and picked out the hunched, scholarly scientist immediately. *Time can't alter some things*, he thought, as he sat down. "How do you do? I'm terribly impolite."

The scientist laughed, they exchanged names, then several minutes of obligatory small talk ensued. Eventually Franklin said, "Tell me about your education."

"I have a Bachelor's in applied physics and I'm pursuing a Master's in electrical engineering," Paul replied.

"You can summarize the sciences and teach principles which underlie the TV, airline, and other inventions?"

"Yes," Paul said. "Within reason, I certainly can."

"Tell me then," Franklin said. "Since . . . well . . . arbitrarily, let's say since America was created. What were the dozen most significant inventions?"

Paul thought a moment, then said, "In no particular order, the plane, computer, nuke, combustion engine and car, polyphase electrical power, transistors, plastic, genetic engineering . . ." A pause for thought. "Rockets would be up there. The laser and television, too. What else? Radio, I guess, and . . . well . . . that's a good start."

"Would you be kind enough to explain them one by one?"

"Are you serious?"

Franklin laughed. "You look overwhelmed."

"That's a lot of ground to cover."

Franklin took a sip of his terrible tasting tea, then handed Paul $200. "I have all day. How about you?"

PAUL EXPLAINED the combustion engine during breakfast, and afterward he led his student out of the classroom and into the lab, where he popped his car's hood and pointed out the things he'd described. Washington and Jefferson watched from the window, and Franklin made eye contact with them occasionally.

After the lesson concluded, Paul said, "Your learning would progress faster if I showed you the things I'll be describing, but that'd mean a drive to Rapid City."

"How long would that take?"

"About a half hour."

"You could return me to my tavern before the sun sets?"

Tavern? "Yes. I don't see why not."

"Let us proceed to Rapid City then."

As they entered the car, Steele examined *everything*. As if it were all somehow new. "Where you from?" Paul asked.

"Boston, originally."

"And your profession?"

"I don't like deception, so let us make a rule. You don't ask me personal questions, and I won't lie."

Paul was taken aback, but said nothing. Like most people, he bowed to boldness to avoid confronting it. "Fair enough." He started the car, then opened a CD to put in his stereo.

"What is that?" Franklin asked.

"Mozart. You've heard of him, right?"

Franklin smiled. "Yes. I meant the thin wheel."

"Oh. That's a CD?"

"See-D?"

"Yeah. A compact disc. You from Boston, or Mars?"

Do humans live on Mars, or was that an absurd figurative? "That was a personal question. So this compacted disk contains Mozart?"

Paul let the stereo answer. Hearing one of Mozart's *Serenades* made Franklin contemplate his own, and his heart wept with longing as he remembered Anne-Catherine Helvetius, widow of the renowned French Philosopher Claude-Adrien Helvetius. They had become close friends almost immediately when he arrived in France. The bond strengthened so much Franklin proposed in 1780, but Helvetius refused, citing loyalty to her husband's memory. When his Minister Plenipotentiary tenure ended, she begged Franklin to spend the rest of his life in France, but he wanted to die in America and returned home.

Ah, Helvetius! Franklin longed. *I would cross continents to see you once more! Were you here, nothing would stop me! Not two stones, not twelve!*

Franklin smiled as he remembered some of the happiest days of his life. By Providence Helvetius had wit! And education! And intellect! Combined, they created a charisma so beguiling it made her body and beauty seem trifling!

If I travel to scores of times I'll be lucky to meet one such woman! Franklin thought, as he examined the CDs Paul kept in a book-like case. "Music is scribed on the shiny, uniform sides?"

"Yes," Paul answered.

"How?"

"A laser etches it onto the CD."

"This lay-sir is one of the inventions you mentioned?"

"Yeah." Paul noted Steele's odd inflection, and realized he had regurgitated his pronunciation. "Laser. L-A-S-E-R. Light Amplification by Stimulated Emission of Radiation."

Steele looked totally lost.

Paul retranslated the acronym slowly, then smiled. "It's a mouthful, but don't be intimidated. The underlying principle is simple. Normal light is out of phase and contains different frequencies. Lasers isolate a narrow frequency range and synchronize the phases, creating a highly intense and directional light beam th—"

"Sorry to interrupt," Franklin said, "but you lost me."

"You don't know much about science, do you?"

Franklin smiled. "No." *Not anymore. Did I ever?*

"Do you know what light is?"

Franklin hesitated. The nature of light was a mystery that caused heated debate among colonial natural philosophers. Sir Isaac Newton thought light was composed of tiny particles called corpuscles, and advocated this model in 1672. Christiaan Huygen proposed a viable wave theory in 1690, but Newton was so prestigious that this work was discounted. Newton's corpuscular theory was orthodox in the colonial world, but a few heretics like Franklin and Euler favored Huygen's wave theory.

"Do you know what light is?" Paul repeated patiently.

"I must own I am much in the dark about light. Teach me as you would a simpleton or child. Please."

"I guess we should begin with light waves," Paul said. "You see, light i—Did I say something funny?"

"Joyous, not funny." *Light waves. Light waves! To futurity, one of our most vexing natural philosophy questions is mere preamble!* "I enjoy learning. Pardon my inadvertent interruption. Please continue instructing."

As he pulled onto the highway, Paul obeyed, and began a rudimentary tutorial on the electromagnetic spectrum.

WHILE WASHINGTON and Jefferson waited for Franklin to exit the carvery, they read the yellow pages and scribed useful ciphers. By the time he and the natural philosopher drove away, Washington was on the Ts and Jefferson was making calls.

"Airlines could transport us to Boston, Philadelphia, New York, or Your D.C!" Jefferson said, as he hung up the phone. "Today! We could leave after the noon, and be almost anywhere in America before the morrow! If we had a 'credit card' to purchase the ticket, that is." He checked his notes. "And we would need a passport, 'driver's license,' or other 'valid picture ID' to obtain our tickets."

"Call several airlines," Washington said. "I realize the requirements are probably uniform, but we must be thorough."

"THE REQUIREMENTS are uniform," Jefferson said. "An airline is not an option for now."

"What of these buses?" Washington replied. "And if that fails, here are ciphers for something called a taxi. Perhaps that could transport us to the Eastern colonies."

"RAPID TAXI," a gruff voice said. "Where you goin?"

"I'm not sure," Jefferson replied. "Could you quote taxes to Washington D.C., New York, Philadelp—" Jefferson stared at the phone with confusion. "Did he terminate the conversation, or did the phone experience an erratum?"

"THIS 'BUS' IS VIABLE," Jefferson said. "We can purchase tickets with notes and without papers. A 'bus' can take us most anywhere in America, though it is much slower than the airline. It would take us two days to travel to the eastern colonies."

"That long?" Washington replied.

They laughed.

" 'Taxis' are chauffeured Watt wagons that also do not require papers. Though they are not used for long-distance travel, one could transport us to the Rapid City bus terminus."

"Can a taxi be chartered in the evening?"

"Yea. Until two in the morrow."

"Excellent," Washington said. "We will travel to Rapid City late tonight, after most Rushmore visitors are asleep."

"WE'LL BE TRAVELING with all our notes," Jefferson said, as he once again hung up the phone. "Banks require exhaustive information. And papers."

Washington was hammering out pushups, moving up and down like a piston. "As Franklin predicted. No bank tirade?"

"Nay. But I can't believe the thieves make it so arduous to give them our money."

"Arduous for us. Probably not for a future citizen."

Jefferson was impressed by Washington's strength, but did not comment on it. "Franklin was correct about the difficulties we would encounter without papers. They are a necessity."

"Then we must determine a way to obtain them."

As Paul's car raced through the outskirts of Rapid City, Franklin was teased by fleeting views of myriad new phenomena. He felt excited yet frustrated. It would be nice to examine something for more than a moment!

The car bounced over a bump and Franklin winced.

"You look petrified," Paul said. "Am I scaring you?"

"Is it safe to travel so fast?"

"We're just under the speed limit."

Speed limit? Speed limit. Interesting. Most interesting. "I am uncomfortable, but there is no need to slow down."

Franklin knew fear and pain were a small price to pay for such speedy transport. On horseback, this journey would take a healthy colonial almost a day.

Rapid City's size was tough to gauge. *Everything* was foreign, and the car's astronomical speed distorted Franklin's sense of distance. "How many people live here?" he asked.

"Rapid City's pretty small. 65,000, plus or minus 5,000?"

A "pretty small" city twice the size of Philadelphia, old America's largest! Franklin resisted the urge to whistle. "What is new America's most populous city?"

"New America?"

"Sorry. What is America's new most populous city?"

"New York? LA? Chicago? I'm not sure."

"How many people?"

"I don't know. 5 million, plus or minus 2 million?"

5 million? Franklin looked at his tutor like a lunatic.

"That may be high," Paul said. "But only by a million."

Only by a million? Franklin knew it might make Paul suspicious, but he nonetheless whistled. *The United States population was approximately 2 million in 1750, and hovered somewhere near 4 million when The Constitution was drafted. The entire population of the America I knew now inhabits a single city!* Franklin felt a familiar sense of overwhelming amazement, and as he continued to peer out the window, he was grateful Paul left him to his thoughts.

Wal-Mart seemed larger than a colonial palace to Franklin, and its endless conglomerations of futuristic vendibles stupefied him relentlessly. Paul found this perma-awe amusing. Analogues like *The Gods Must Be Crazy*, *Crocodile Dundee* and *Stranger in a Strange Land* came to mind frequently.

Paul realized his student was starting from scratch, and helped him shop accordingly. While they browsed toiletry bags, Franklin said, "Is this Walled Mart a storage facility that provides goods for several colonies or a region of the nation?"

Colonies? "No. Stores like this exist in every city."

"So these wares are a tiny fraction of America's total?"

"Yes."

"Less than one percent?"

"Easily," Paul said. "Probably less than a ten-thousandth of one percent. Maybe less than a hundred thousandth."

Though he had a vague appreciation of the enormity it implied, the statistic wasn't meaningful to Franklin, so he tried a different approach. "How many shirts do you own?"

"Fifty, plus or minus five? And you?"

A commoner with more garments than a wealthy colonial! "This is my only shirt. Though I'm hoping to rectify that."

One shirt. From Rushmore. "No problem. Though we won't do much clothes shopping here. Except for stuff like socks. We'll buy you one outfit so you blend in more, then head to the mall."

Franklin selected three different toiletry bags and wallets. "Don't lose me," he said, as he followed Paul through the maze of aisles. "I may never find my way out."

Paul laughed. "You're a trip, man."

"A trip where?"

Paul laughed harder, then explained "trip's" modern meaning. "I'll keep my eye on you. You have arthritis pretty bad, huh?"

"It could be worse. One's lot can always be worse."

"Have you been to a doctor? Or tried medicine?"

Franklin wanted to ask about gout and stone cures, but feared this might hint at his identity. "There's no cure for old age. Now tell me. How are so many wares produced?" *How have Whitney's musket methods been improved?*

Paul thought of the money he was making and quelled questions. "Mass production was pioneered by Henry Ford . . ."

"Why are there so many soaps?" Franklin asked.

"What do you mean?"

"Are these soaps fundamentally different in some way?"

Paul shrugged. "No, not really."

Franklin confirmed that soap was still soap, the cleaning agent man had been using from time immemorial. It did not contain futuristic improvements that eliminated pockmarks, cured gout or made your roger bigger. Natural philosophy had not induced a complexity that might justify variation. "So if these soaps are essentially all the same, why make thirty 'different' types?"

"They're made by different companies," Paul replied. "Competing companies."

"Who make them at different factories?"

"Yes."

"But this mass production you described means just a few factories could make all the soap that is needed."

"I suppose. Maybe even one factory."

"Why not do that?"

"Because one company that produced all soap could charge whatever price it wanted and gouge people. If there was only one brand of soap, it might cost two or three times as much."

Brand. A most enlightening term. Franklin envisioned cattle; they were all the same, so differentiated by markings.

Paul's reasoning seemed sound, but Franklin was bothered. He felt strongly attracted to the soaps with the flashier packaging, even though the drab brands cost half as much.

After checking with Paul, Franklin opened several boxes and compared soaps. He perceived parity among the products, and therefore selected the inexpensive "brand."

As Paul led him through the mall, Franklin juxtaposed past and present continually. He remained perpetually cognizant of the fact that colonial production methods and goods were savage when compared to futuristic equivalents.

"D-cup?" Franklin said, as he held the bra up and twisted it every which way. "A natural philosophic measurement of the amount of lactic emitted?"

Like the woman who turned away in disgust, Paul thought Steele was making a crude joke. Until he saw his student's analytical expression. "Geez," he muttered.

"Gs?" Franklin peered past the largest bras, the sparse Es, into the surrounding aisle. "Where?"

Franklin had opened several boxer-brief packages and was trying to determine a size for Jefferson.

"Aerodynamics makes airplanes possible," Paul said.

"These breeches are much too small. Air-o-dye-what?"

"Aerodynamics. The study of moving air." Paul tried to stifle his impatience. Did a guy this ignorant expect to learn aerodynamics while shopping for underwear? "Airplanes operate on the principle of lift. Take a ball. It's symmetrical, so as it moves air flow is the same on all sides."

Franklin caught on immediately. "A non-symmetrical shape. Newton's third law. And these breeches are too big. Something that creates pressure differences in the surrounding fluid."

"Uh, yeah. That something is a plane or artificial wing. Thus the name 'airplane'." Using a small notebook from the cart, Paul diagrammed the air flow around a wing.

Franklin extrapolated the concept instantly. "An automobile engine attached to the wing could generate a horizontal impetus. If the air plane moved rapidly enough, the increasing pressure difference might generate an upward lifting force which exceeded the vehicle's weight. Assuming the wind didn't tear it apart."

Paul eyed Franklin shrewdly. "That upward force is lift. And planes have to be made strong. You didn't go to college?"

Franklin smiled ruefully. "No."

"It's too bad. You learn quickly."

Franklin shrugged. "I do not dwell in my past. So who invented this air plane, and when?"

"The Wright Brothers. At Kitty Hawk in 1903."

"Right as in right and wrong?"

"Wright with a W." Paul smiled as he began to explain. He'd never realized how many rudimentary concepts and facts he took for granted until today.

"Couldn't you construct an air plane that creates lift without forward motion?" Franklin asked, while Paul loaded their Wal-Mart purchases into the car. "By moving air past the wings instead of the wings past the air? Or putting wings on some sort of . . . wheel and moving it instead of the entire vehicle?"

"Yeah, you could. It's called a helicopter." Paul was almost dazed with surprise. "I know I'm not supposed to ask these sorts of questions, but I have to. Is today the first time you've been exposed to the concepts I'm teaching?"

"Yes."

"And you honestly never went to college?"

"No."

"And you've never seen a helicopter?"

"No, I've never seen a hell-uh-copped-tur."

"Not even in DaVinci's sketches?"

Franklin chuckled. "No."

"So you've never seen Da Vinci's sketches?"

"No."

Paul shook his head slowly. Though he believed Mr. Steele, it was nonetheless unbelievable. Less than an hour after learning the theory of the wing, he had *deduced* the helicopter! Who in the hell? How in the hell? What the hell! *I feel like I'm teaching freakin' Da Vinci!* "Are you some kind of genius?"

"Classifications like that serve little practical purpose."

Paul laughed as he started his car. "That sounds like something a genius would say."

"In the future, I'll try to be thick."

Paul laughed harder. "I don't think you'll be successful."

"Do ANY CARS utilize steam engines?" Franklin asked.

Paul was pumping gas. *Steam engines?* "No. Petroleum runs all cars."

"How many of these cars exist?"

"At least 100 million, worldwide. At least."

"This civilization must use large amounts of petroleum."

This civilization? Where was Steele from? Was he Amish and entering society for the first time? An accident victim plagued by selective amnesia? "This civilization is addicted to petroleum. It is the world's most important commodity."

"What about food, garments, or lodging?" Franklin asked.

"Petroleum provides energy for machines that produce those necessities. In a certain sense, it is more fundamental."

"Where does it come from?"

"The Middle East, mostly."

"Middle East. The term seems somewhat contradictory."

"There are a lot of contradictions in the Middle East."

"Cite a few. Please."

"Let's stick to petroleum science and avoid the politics."

"As you wish. Is this Middle East a seafaring nation that breeds whales like livestock and farms them for oil?"

Paul thought of *The Purple Rose of Cairo*[75]. Had Steele been conjured from a Melville novel? "Oil is obtained from underground reservoirs."

Franklin realized he had erred suspiciously. Whales were the primary source of oil in colonial times, but a world with 5-million-person cities could probably kill every whale on Earth and still be wanting. Franklin felt a stab of concern as he extrapolated this resource reasoning, and wanted to

75 *The Purple Rose of Cairo.* A Woody Allen motion picture in which a movie hero exits the screen and enters the real world.

pursue it, but Paul's shrewd expression made him wary. Better not to wander. "Underground oceans of oil. The source of natural seeps[76] which humans have been discovering since antiquity?"

Paul nodded and explained oil drilling. As he listened, Franklin contemplated petroleum politics. Had this Middle East exploited its petroleum bounty to create an enormous empire with a Northern East, Southern East and Middle East? Did it exist in lands his time had known, or some newer new world? Were futuristic wars fought for petroleum instead of spices, gold, or bread?

Paul accidentally overfilled his tank and a tiny geyser of fuel shot out. While Franklin watched it pollute a puddle, a starting truck ejected a black cloud that caused him to cough. After he recovered he said, "This petroleum seems to dirty the world."

"Have you ever seen a smelting factory or a coal plant?"

Franklin shook his head. "Are they nearby?"

"No. But make time to see one some day. I think you'll find the experience . . . educational."

"You seem sad and ambivalent."

Paul smiled. How to summarize humanity's destruction of the Earth's ecosystems? In some ways, Steele was like a child.

An eighteen wheeler spewing fumes pulled into the station. "Man is destroying the world by using so much petroleum." Paul smiled sanguinely with eyes that seemed old. "But I guess all progress comes at a price."

"So TELL ME more about this Tom Edison," Franklin said, as they pulled out of the gas station. "And this Nick Tesla."

"Nikola Tesla. Do you know anything about electricity?"

Franklin smiled. "A little."

Paul began his lesson, and explained rudimentary concepts like positive and negative charge, condensers, and conductors to the man who coined the terms.

FRANKLIN'S INADVERTENT BUFFET didn't seem appropriate for breakfast or brunch, but Washington refused to wastefully purchase more victuals. "I envy Ben," he said, as he pulled his pizza out of the microwave. "He is seeing this new world."

Jefferson thought of his old one. He pictured the usual Monticello breakfast, and Monticello itself, with longing. Sweet Virginia ham. Fresh baked pastry. Tea or coffee. Some mornings, served by Sally Hemings.

---

76 Natural seeps. Spots where underground petroleum oozes slowly to the surface and forms a pool.

Washington picked up his overheated pizza and dropped it quickly. "Amazing!" he said. "The lightning box boiled the cheese in less than a tick! How long do you suppose a turkey or roast beef takes? Fifteen ticks? Twenty? Are most foods cooked with this lightning rather than fire or water?"

"That's a question for Ben. Shall we watch TV while we sup?"

Washington turned it on, and as they ate, he and Jefferson continued to eliminate their ignorance.

"So MANY UNFAMILIAR nations," Jefferson whispered, as CNN's international summary aired. "So many exotic cultures."

"Perhaps other colonies revolted," Washington said. "Or old nations splintered."

"Or newer worlds were discovered."

Television continued to gallop, and a cereal commercial soon bragged that it contained a full day's supply of the United States Recommended Daily Allowance.

"United States Recommended Daily Allowance," Washington parroted. "Advocated by a government department which regulates vittles or medicine, perhaps?"

"If the government prescribed our medicine and diet, our bodies would be like our souls during the Revolution's bleakest moments."

CNN returned and showed a dictator who refused to let United Nations arms inspectors examine his chemical weapons.

"Did she say United Nations or States?" Washington asked.

"Nations," Jefferson answered.

"A dialect change?" Washington wondered. "A new nickname for America perhaps?"

"Perhaps Europe emulated us as Franklin predicted."

"Europe was comprised of nations rather than states. The nomenclature would make sense. But America seems to be a member of these United Nations. Is the world now a federation of countries?"

"If so, the union is as tenuous as America's was initially," Jefferson replied. "All parties involved seem to dislike and distrust each other."

"What are chemical weapons?" Washington wondered. "And weapons of mass destruction? Newks?"

"We must look beyond mere aggression and its implements." Jefferson's bushy eyebrows sprung together and his expression grew introspective. "United Nations. The United Nations. A World Senate? Has it an Executive? One man elected to represent all of humanity? Communicate with all of humanity?"

Jefferson was dazed by the monumental implications of the proposition. Analogues occurred to him incessantly, stimulating myriad questions and perpetuating a steady backdrop of mental chatter.

The Sage of Monticello sat in a contemplative funk for several minutes, then rose with gravitas. "I think I finally understand the true power of futurity's telegraphs."

"Are you referring to natural philosophic principles?" Washington asked.

"Political principles." Jefferson raised the phone receiver, peered at it, hung up, then watched the television warily. "Telephones let anyone talk to anyone, but living portraits probably let some one influence everyone."

"Would you like me to take a turn making calls?" Washington asked, as breakfast concluded.

Jefferson remembered how spent he was after vacating the Presidency. "My two decades of retirement eclipse your two days. I deserve the work."

The reasoning was logical, and Washington felt no need to offer insincere disagreement, though he wondered if Jefferson was currying favor to promote forgiveness. "I wish I could ride or hunt! My first free time in eight years and I'm gaoled in a tavern!"

"I would suggest the TV," Jefferson replied. "But my calls will take several more hours." The phone investigation had proved time consuming, both because of its thoroughness, and because Jefferson's ignorance required him to inundate the people he called with questions. "Amazing though, if one ponders it. This TV and phone allow us to explore our new world from the inside of a room."

"Speaking of explorers, I wonder how Franklin is faring."

"Well, as he always seems to, would be my guess." Jefferson dialed the phone. "Perhaps you should read or nap."

Washington accepted the first suggestion willfully and the second inadvertently; while Jefferson quested for papers, he explored his dreams.

Like most members of *papyrus peddlus*, the bureaucrats Jefferson spoke to seemed indifferent to grueling governmental inefficiency and its victims, and could explain contradictory regulations without ever seeming cognizant of their absurdity. The present call was archetypal. "How does one obtain a social security number?" Jefferson asked.

"Are you an American citizen?"

"Yes."

"Then you probably already have one."

"What if I was never assigned one?"

"How could that be? Did you immigrate here?"

That's one way to put it. "No."

"You were born in America?"

"Yes. But I'm . . . old."

"You just need to prove your age, place of birth, and identity."

That's all? Jefferson closed his eyes and rubbed his eyebrows. "How do I do that?"

"The identity and age are the easiest. If you have a valid U.S. driver's license or Passport or . . ." She rattled off a list of acceptable documents. Jefferson had investigated most of them, and knew that each was required to obtain the other. He was trapped in a self-referencing conundrum. "And my place of birth? How do I prove that?"

"A birth certificate."

"How would I obtain that?"

"From the state where you were born."

Virginia. "And what would my country require?"

"I said your state of birth, not America. And it varies. Can a hospital confirm your birth?"

The "hospital" of my birth was Shadwell plantation, my father's home. It burned down in 1753 while I was building Monticello. Even if it hadn't . . . "A hospital cannot confirm my birth."

"How about your doctor? Can he provide verification?"

Dr. Robley Dunglison, who was 27 in 1825. "My physician is dead."

"You have a documentation problem."

That's stating it mildly, Jefferson thought. The wording perturbed him. These futuristic bureaucrats had a knack for obtuse euphemisms.

The conversation proceeded, but eventually reached the predictable end result. Jefferson was tempted to ask the bureaucrat how to obtain counterfeit documents, but refrained.

He didn't dwell on his defeat. There were other victories to strive for: bifocals, dentures, cures for gout and stone, book stores, garment shops, libraries, barbers . . .

Like most men eventually trusted with large tasks, Jefferson had always been fastidious about the small ones, and he continued to phone diligently as the morning wore on.

As HE ENTERED the mall, Franklin gaped at the ceiling, which stretched above him like a cathedral's. Paul led him to the lighted map and its X.

"You are here." Franklin laughed. *A store so large it has to be mapped!* In his youth, before he became a soldier or inherited Mount Vernon, Washington was a surveyor, and Franklin envisioned young George delineating the mammoth interior with his theodolite[77].

"What's so funny?" Paul asked.

"Everything and nothing. Just one of those moments. You have some idea what is fashionable?"

"Yes, but you don't want me picking out clothes. We'll ask salespeople for help."

"I need garments that are . . . timeless. Garments that won't become obsolete quickly. I prefer function to aesthetics. But I want something that will . . ." Franklin hesitated.

"Something that will blend in rather than stand out?"

Franklin smiled. "Exactly."

FRANKLIN BROWSED CLOTHES in several of the trendier stores, but nothing seemed functional enough to him. Paul suggested they walk the mall until something caught his eye. That something was American Eagle.

"How about it?" Paul asked.

American Turkey it is. Franklin beamed as they approached. "I've got a good feeling about this one."

AS THEY ROAMED a large electronics store, Paul showed Franklin everything from video cameras to beepers to subwoofers, and explained how they operated.

"So this electromagnetic radiation allows inventions like telephones, TVs, and car alarms to function?" Franklin asked.

"Yes," Paul replied.

"You said the sun's ultraviolent light darkens people?"

"Ultraviolet. Like the flower or color. But yes."

"Surely these other radiations have some effect on the human body. Or life in general."

Paul was once again impressed by Steele's intuitive ability to make penetrating deductions. "There are severe negative effects. Look at the air in front of you. Invisible conversations, letters and images are blowing by. Your body is an antenna that picks them up just like TVs and radios do."

"Then why can't I hear them, read them, or see them?"

Paul wondered if the comment was a joke. "Because you can't decode the signals. But in another hundred years, who knows? And I don't give much thought to the negative health effects because I can't escape them. I would never give up the luxuries electromagnetic inventions provide. Without them, we'd still be living like middle-age knights or colonial Americans."

77 Theodolite. A surveyor's tool. It includes a swiveling telescope that can be angled vertically.

Franklin looked around thoughtfully. "I see your point." *It would be tough to go back.*

"THEY SEEMED LIKE nice guys," the cop said. "To be honest, I probably wouldn't have bothered you if my wife hadn't nagged. Sorry to make you fill out a report. It's probably nothing."

The Keystone police officer was inclined to agree, but he was thorough, and wasn't willing to dismiss another cop's instincts completely. The trooper was blaming it on his wife, but was clearly suspicious himself. "And you said they looked like Washington, Franklin, and Jefferson?"

"*Exactly* like 'em. I swear to Christ, if I didn't know the founders were already dead, I'd have thought it was them."

"Well it won't hurt to lift some prints off the camera and pen and run them. We're usually informed of special events, but I'll double check with the park and make sure no performers were booked. If none were, we'll make a few extra patrols, and if we see the 'founders' we'll question them. It's illegal to perform without the approval of the park, so if they have criminal histories or are belligerent, we'll also have an excuse to arrest them."

FRANKLIN WAS GETTING his hair cut. "So this frequency modulation is superior to this amplitude modulation?" he asked.

"In absolute terms, no. Remember that there are tradeoffs. Amplitude modulation travels farther, but frequency modulation has better signal quality."

"YOU SAID THAT radio waves cannot circle the world, as Magellan did."

"Right," Paul replied. "Radio waves travel in a straight line, and the Earth's surface is spherical."

The salesperson returned. "We've got all three shoes in your size."

Franklin looked at Paul. "Another soap situation. Are the more expensive brands most individuals are purchasing superior?"

"Probably not. Or only slightly. And certainly not superior enough to justify the price differential."

After Franklin made the economical selection, he wondered why most people did otherwise. Unlike the drab soap, the inexpensive shoes seemed just as flashy and futuristic as their competitors. What attribute made people happily pay such exorbitant premiums for them?

As the salesperson approached with the shoes, Franklin said, "How is it possible to receive signals from the other side of the world if radio waves cannot circle it? Is the signal forwarded by ground communicators repeatedly?"

"That and satellites."

"Saddlewhats?"

As he thought of the final frontier, Paul ran his fingers through his hair and sighed. *Where to begin?*

Franklin stopped walking suddenly and faced Paul with an incredulous expression. "America landed a man on the moon?"

"Yes," Paul said nonchalantly. "In 1969."

Only two centuries after I lived! "Humans live on the moon?"

"I thought maybe you had been living on the moon."

Franklin laughed.

"No. Humans don't live on the moon. We went and returned. Just a couple of quick, exploratory visits."

A couple of quick visits. He makes it sound like riding up to Boston. "Why didn't you tell me this at breakfast?"

"Perhaps I should have," Tom replied. "But there was so much ground to cover. We could talk for weeks and still not cover everything you wish to learn."

"Details. Please give me more details. How did man manage to stand among the constellations? A highly advanced plane with an enormous car engine?"

"In a spaceship. JFK and the Apollo Project. But before we get into all that, I've got a question for you. Where in the fuck have you been living?"

"What does fuck mean?" Franklin asked,

Paul laughed and shook his head. *Who in the fuck hasn't heard of the word fuck?*

"So a combustion engine can't operate in space because there's no oxygen," Franklin said.

"Or air. Thus the term space." Paul was once again intrigued. Steele seemed extremely hesitant when discussing combustion, as if confirming something he suspected.

"Oxygen," Franklin whispered. "Acid former."

"Is that what it means?" Paul asked.

"In Greek."

"You speak Greek?"

"No."

Paul's glance questioned, but Franklin simply smiled. Combustion was a mystery for most of his life, and like other colonial natural philosophers, he thought matter contained phlogiston, a "fiery substance" that caused an object to warm or burn if released. Joseph Priestley discovered "dephlogisticated air" in 1774, and by 1785 Antoine-Laurent Lavoisier renamed the gas oxygen, making it the backbone of his revolutionary respiration and combustion theories. Franklin observed both friends' experiments, corresponded with them, and developed an accurate understanding of oxygen and fire a few years before the Constitutional Convention. He had expected combustion to spawn breathtaking advancements, yet he once again felt humbling awe as they eclipsed his conceptions.

"You are the one who is speaking Greek," Franklin joked. "You said this space shuttle is an extremely advanced, rocket-propelled air plane?"

"Crudely stated, yes. Though I wouldn't call the shuttle extremely advanced. The military has craft that make it seem like a wooden wagon."

Franklin shook his head at the metaphor. *A space plane is primitive?* "And what are these more advanced craft called?"

"UFOs, for now."

"UFO?"

Paul did his best to answer the question, and scores of others, but his pupil was frequently confused. "I realize the technologies I'm describing are difficult to envision," he consoled. "If you ever get a chance, you should visit the Air and Space Museum. It's the best place in the world to learn the history of flight and aircraft."

"Any preferences?" Paul asked, as they drove past several fast food restaurants.

"Anything but this Burger Monarch," Franklin said.

"I'm going to let you decide. I've tried 'em all before."

"What makes you think I haven't tried them all before?"

"Pardon my presumptuousness." Paul laughed.

Franklin joined him. Until an image from a fast food TV commercial supplanted his other thoughts. Franklin felt a strong urge to choose the advertised restaurant, but resented the psychological usurpation and eliminated it from consideration. "Is one carvery superior?"

Paul shook his head. "It's like the soap and the shoes. They try to make it seem different, but it's all the same slop."

"Tasty slop," Franklin said, as he ate his fries. "So this special relativity says what?"

"That the speed of light is the same in all frames of reference."

"All frames of reference?"

"Under all conditions. It's a fancy way of saying that the speed of light is *always* the same." Paul resisted the urge to chuckle. Normally, giving someone as uneducated as Steele a relativity overview during lunch would seem absurd.

This wasn't normally.

"How do you like your salad dressing?" Franklin asked.

Paul shrugged. "Fine. I suppose."

"It does not taste acrid to you?"

"No. Why do you ask?"

Franklin shrugged. "I know we covered this, but light is considered a wave?"

No way am I getting into quantum mechanics and particle/wave duality. Uh-uh. "It's a wave. For purposes of this discussion, anyway."

"So light is a wave, but its speed is always the same. This creates a paradox, does it not?"

Paul smiled and nodded. "I hate to keep saying this, but you catch on quickly." So quickly that Paul had grown more than merely suspicious. Steele had learned centuries of science in mere hours, and had demonstrated a consistent, almost unnerving ability to hone concepts to their core principles. That someone could be so staggeringly intelligent and so strangely ignorant was a dichotomy he could not reconcile. "Yes. Relativity creates a paradox. Many paradoxes, in fact. Yours relates to wave mechanics. In any fluid in which waves propagate, currents or eddies can exist; these can speed waves up or slow them down. And if the density of the fluid varies, waves in regions of lower density travel faster."

Franklin nodded rapidly. "How is this paradox resolved?"

"Special relativity is another way of saying there isn't a fluid."

"What?"

"Special relativity is another way of saying that light waves don't propagate through a fluid."

"I realize my understanding is rudimentary," Franklin said. "And that Newtons like this Eye-in-Stein must have given these topics prolonged consideration. But in the ocean there is water. Without water there wouldn't be waves."

Paul nodded. "You're wondering how light waves can exist if space is empty. Special relativity ignores that question. Just accept that light waves propagate through nothing."

"May not all the phenomena of light be more conveniently solved by supposing universal space filled with a subtle elastic fluid?"

"You're talking about the luminiferous aether. The light propagating aether. Many 18th and 19th century scientists believed in it, and the corpuscular theory of light, but both have been experimentally disproven."

"You're sure?"

"Positive." Paul laughed. "You're a trip, man. This morning you didn't know what light or atoms were, and now you're second guessing Einstein?"

Franklin smiled. "If it soothes you, I'll wait until the morrow. But experience, and some experiences, have taught me to question all assumptions. Even Eye-in-Stein's."

FRANKLIN WAS PEERING into one of the camping store's many glass cases, perusing knives. "How many people are there in the world?"

"Where'd that come from?" Paul asked.

"I was contemplating killing." The comment made the clerk nervous. "Philosophically," Franklin soothed.

"6.3 billion, plus or minus 100 million?"

Franklin's eyes bulged. "6 *billion*?"

Paul nodded. "And climbing fast."

"Mass production has been applied to people, it seems."

Paul laughed. "I've never heard it phrased quite like that."

WHILE THEY WAITED at a red light, Paul explained signals and signs, yellow lines, and other traffic control mechanisms. As he listened, Franklin watched a destitute man shuffle aimlessly near a bench. "Are mass production and these other inventions able to provide for 6 billion people?" he asked.

"Yes and no." Paul turned the stereo down, made eye contact and explained the grim reality; most of the world lived worse than colonial slaves had. "Though the capacity to feed, clothe, and house every human on Earth exists. For now. World population is increasing so rapidly this luxury will not be indefinite."

Paul studied Franklin's face. Like a complex wine, it was a mix of many ingredients. Disappointment. Resentment. Sadness. Anger. Everything but surprise. "Aren't you going to ask why resources aren't distributed more equitably?"

"Could you answer?" Franklin asked.

"I can teach you about science. Now human nature . . ."

Franklin's sardonic smile gave his face additional textures. "This is one thing I don't need you to explain. Natural philosophy evolves. New inventions are promulgated. But human nature is the same in all frames of reference."

THE CALLS WERE finally completed, though before Jefferson and Washington analyzed the new information, they unwound by watching TV. On *Jerry Springer*, two obese, adulterous wenches were trying to maul each other while their gigolo of a mate gloated. A squad of *enormous* guards prevented the melee. The wenches would sit for a spell, exchange guttural insults, then attempt another attack.

"I am reminded of rams," Jefferson said.

"Rams are smarter," Washington replied. "And smaller."

Jefferson laughed. "Surely the program has other elements?"

Both men grew optimistic when another trio was paraded. Like their predecessors, they sat, exchanged insults, and then attacked. Jefferson and Washington exchanged bemused expressions and simply shook their heads.

During a peaceful lull, Springer moved in like a lion tamer and asked agitating questions. His circus animals responded as if trained and charged. As the crowd erupted, a brief shot of Springer showed him grinning slyly.

For Jefferson, mild amusement had turned to disgust. "What sort of primitive civilization would consider this vulgarity entertainment?"

"We now return to *As The World Turns*," the TV said.

"A natural philosophy tutorial?" Jefferson wondered.

It wasn't. *Guiding Light* didn't offer spiritual advice, *General Hospital* had no real doctors, and *Days of Our Lives* wasn't a contemporary history summary, but Washington and Jefferson watched the plays anyway because they conjured pleasing memories of lost loves and wives, and were enjoyable. For the first few ticks anyway.

"This melodrama grows tiresome," Washington said.

"As does the obsessive focus on courtship and rogering," Jefferson replied. "These plays are probably designed for a wench audience."

Jefferson nodded. "Inventions may have simplified the management of a household. Perhaps wenches watch such programs while their babies take afternoon naps. Or while supper cooks."

As Washington changed the channel, he thought of Martha, who, like most planters' wives, had spent her days managing large portions of the plantation. "Surely futuristic wenches can find more productive ways to spend time after the noon."

"One would hope," Jefferson said. "But a large number of these plays and advertisements seem to cater to them."

Oprah also seemed designed for wenches. The all-wench audience made this obvious when it was finally shown, but Oprah's bedside manner telegraphed the reality long before. She doted on her guests' every word and gushed with sympathy, no matter what was said. The mention of the minutest hardship resulted in an outpouring of empathy from her and the crowd.

These aspects were merely annoying, but what made Washington and Jefferson almost unable to watch was the glaring lack of intelligence. Oprah's questions were invariably fluffy and insubstantial. The methodical questions that occurred to Washington and Jefferson were never the ones she asked.

"Mindless emotion," Washington said, as Oprah asked another menstrual question.

Jefferson nodded. "Fascinating, though. It is interesting to see large numbers of women in such an unrestrained setting and experience their palpable lack of reason."

"True. Such an opportunity did not exist in our era."

"And would not have existed. Even if we had these living portraits."

Washington nodded. White women in colonial America were a step above a slave, but a step below a male. Marriage was their focus, and once betrothed, they surrendered all property and most rights to their husbands. Though a husband had to provide for a wife, and could not kill or permanently injure her, she had to obey him implicitly, and focus on childrearing and household management. Professional careers and politics were the exclusive privileges of males.

"Thank Providence wenches can't vote though," Jefferson said. "I shudder when I think of the 'rationale' they might use in selecting leaders."

"Women couldn't vote. We don't know that they can't."

THE PHONE RANG and Washington pounced. "Ben?"

"Richard here."

Paul smiled at Franklin's terseness. *Ever heard of hello?* he wondered. *Probably not.*

"How goes the day, Richard?" Washington asked.

"Well."

"Can you talk?"

"No."

Washington listened while Franklin explained what little he could, then said, "Where are you heading next?"

You'd have a conniption if I told you. "I'm not sure."

Washington wished Franklin well and hung up. "Ben is at the natural philosopher's home and will return soon after sunset."

PAUL WAS DRIVING Steele back to Keystone. "What's next?"

"A trip to Rushmore?" *Sans the excruciating ascent.*

"I grew up here so I've been like a jillion times," Paul said. "But you know what's weird?"

"What?"

"I never get sick of it."

In modern clothes, Mount Rushmore was a much more enjoyable experience for Franklin. His limp attracted a few glances, but no one seemed to suspect his identity.

They entered from paid parking, and Paul paused in front of the Mount Rushmore gift shop. "Do you want to go in?" he asked.

"No," Franklin replied, as he thought of the Samaritan. "I am interested in the Visitor Center."

"What about the mountain itself?"

Franklin smiled. "That too."

As Franklin peered at Rushmore for the second time, a diminished sense of awe pervaded. *Absurd*, he thought. *Remaking mountains in the images of men. Yes, absurd. Absurd, and excessive, and perhaps even vain. But nonetheless impressive. Both the result and the intent.*

Franklin gaped until his thoughts abated, then he and Paul headed into the Visitor Center, which contained display cases and podiums that described Rushmore's creator Gutzon Borglum, its construction and preservation process, its portrayal in evolving American culture, and its four icons. Franklin and Paul concentrated on the latter, proceeded in chronological order, and examined Washington's podium first.

"Washington had cold-hearted eyes," Paul said.

Franklin nodded slowly, with great emphasis. "Yes."

"You can even see them in his life mask[78]."

"You can probably see them when they're closed."

"Not the type of man you'd have wanted to cross."

Franklin's nod grew severe. "Most certainly not."

Jefferson's podium contained a reproduction of John Trumbull's *The Signing of the Declaration of Independence*. Paul was trying to identify figures in the painting, and this made Franklin nervous because he was displayed prominently in its center with the other four drafters.

"Jefferson and Franklin are pretty obvious," Paul said.

"Yes," Franklin replied. *One would think.*

"But who's that really short dude?"

John Adams. "I do not know." Franklin suppressed a smile. Adams had been sensitive about his height, desirous of praise, and had often bemoaned his lack of recognition relative to other Revolutionary leaders; his lot as an

78 Life mask. An exact replica of a living person's face made by applying plaster to it.

unremembered "really short dude" would have riled him up thoroughly, and as Franklin envisioned his probable response were he present and able to speak freely, it took effort to maintain composure.

"I wish the painting were bigger," Paul said. "I can't figure out who anyone is."

Not just in the painting, thankfully. "Didn't John Adams help with *The Declaration*?"

"Yeah, yeah. Adams. But I can't ever remember those other two guys."

Roger Sherman and Robert Livingston. "Nor can I."

"And who's that guy sitting on the other side of the table?"

John Hancock, President of the Continental Congress. "It is difficult to tell. The side profile reveals little."

"This boring you or something?" Paul asked.

"No," Franklin said. "Not in the slightest."

"You seem kind of quiet. We can move on if you're bored."

"I assure you I am not bored."

Paul tried to identify individuals in other portraits. Franklin recognized most, but continued to give incorrect answers. Though he remained careful, his worry was generally replaced by enjoyment. Franklin had *always* loved teasing and lampooning, and the future seemed to provide ample opportunity for such pleasures.

FRANKLIN STOOD HYPNOTIZED by the Lincoln podium. Paul laughed. "Not bored anymore, huh?"

"No," Franklin said absently. "Not at all."

Franklin read every word on the podium twice, then stood motionless peering into Lincoln's eyes.

"You flirting with him?" Paul asked.

Franklin shook his head. "Trying to measure the man."

ANOTHER FIVE MINUTES passed. Franklin hadn't moved.

"You ready?" Paul asked.

"No," Franklin replied. "You must be bored by now. But please let me flirt with Lincoln for a few more moments."

Moments became minutes, and still Franklin remained intrigued. Like other Rushmore visitors, he marveled at the achievements of eras and Presidents he had never known.

ROOSEVELT INTERESTED FRANKLIN far less than Lincoln; he read his podium once, then he and Paul walked down a hallway that led to a long, backlit glass mural that provided an overview of America's first 150 years. To its immediate left, in enormous backlit letters, was a quote:

> The four American presidents carved into the granite of Mount Rushmore were chosen by sculptor Gutzon Borglum to commemorate the founding, growth, preservation and development of the United States. They symbolize the principles of liberty and freedom on which the nation was founded. George Washington signifies the struggle for independence and the birth of the Republic; Thomas Jefferson the territorial expansion of the country; Abraham Lincoln the permanent union of the states and equality for all citizens; and Theodore Roosevelt, the 20th century role of the United States in world affairs and the rights of the common man.

The central portion of the mural was an enormous collage that interlaced images of key historical figures and events with descriptions. It was colorful, and brought history to life.

As Franklin peered at a newspaper headline that announced the secession of the south, he wished Washington and Jefferson were present; the Visitor Center would have accelerated their learning.

Franklin examined the mural thoroughly, then turned around and faced four large, backlit plates. Each contained a quote, and Franklin read the first:

> The preservation of the sacred fire of liberty and the destiny of the republican model of government are justly considered as deeply, perhaps as finally staked, on the experiment entrusted to the hands of the American people."
>
> George Washington
> First Inaugural Address
> April 30, 1789

Franklin was drawn to the word experiment. He observed the other Americans reading the mural. They seemed like humble, decent people. Franklin shared their sense of humility; he was in the future, in circumstances that should have enabled him to judge the accuracy of Washington's inaugural prophecy, yet from an intellectual perspective he felt surprisingly and glaringly impotent. Did the fire of liberty still burn? Had the republican model of government been vindicated?

> We hold these truths to be self-evident, that all men are created equal, that they are endowed by their Creator with certain inalienable rights, among these are life, liberty, and the pursuit of happiness."
>
> Thomas Jefferson
> Declaration of Independence
> July 4, 1776

Self-evident truths. The wording once again made Franklin cognizant of his ignorance.

"All men are created equal," an ancient-looking black woman whispered. "All except slaves."

The words caught Franklin's attention because they were spoken without bitterness. He tried to examine the hunched woman without being rude, and noted her brittle body and weathered face. Her viny hand clasped a cane.

She looks like she was alive during the War for Independence, too, Franklin thought. "Nothing is created perfectly," he said to her. "All things err. Even Thomas Jefferson, George Washington, and others. And even America."

Franklin saw hatred in the eyes of the young black man escorting the elder, but she smiled and peered up at him with vibrant eyes that twinkled like gems. She cupped his hand in hers, and said, "Time heals all ills. Even imperfection."

Franklin smiled as the woman walked off. *So do repentance and forgiveness.*

> It is rather for us to be here dedicated to the great task remaining before us—that from these honored dead we take increased devotion to that cause for which they gave the last full measure of devotion—that this nation, under God, shall have a new birth of freedom—and that government of the people, by the people, for the people, shall not perish from the earth.
>
> Abraham Lincoln
> Gettysburg Address
> November 19, 1863

"This Lincoln belongs on Rushmore," Franklin whispered.

"What'd you say?" Paul asked.

"Was Lincoln as great a leader as Washington or Jefferson?"

"He's the only President that comes close."

Yes, Franklin thought. *Lincoln deserves many laurels for slaying the kraken we couldn't.*

Or wouldn't.

> We, here in America, hold in our hands the hopes of the world, the fate of the coming years; and shame and disgrace will be ours if in our eyes the light of high resolve is dimmed, if we trail in the dust the golden hopes of men.
>
> Theodore Roosevelt
> Address at Carnegie Hall
> March 30, 1912

The quote increased Franklin's interest in Roosevelt; it suggested vision and morality, yet seemed borne of concern. "Has America trailed the golden hopes of men in the dust?" he asked Paul. "Has it dimmed the light of high resolve, to its shame and disgrace? Or did it secure the fate of the coming years and prove itself worthy of the world's hope?"

Paul thought a moment. "It has done both."

"I HAVE NEVER seen a more foreign sight!" Jefferson said.

"Why would a veterinarian wear a toga?" Washington asked. "And why cover one's mouth?"

Jefferson shrugged. "The ambience is so bright. So clean. The devices se—what is that?"

A rhythmic beeping coincided with the movement of a blue blip on a tiny television. Washington and Franklin gasped as the doctor unsheathed a catheter so thin it could barely be seen. He stuck it into the retriever, which went limp soon after. Then the operation proceeded.

"It is dormant as if drunk!" The remote fell from Washington's hand as he relived his excruciating hip operation. He saw scores of screaming soldiers being cut and cauterized with bones and bullets clenched in their teeth. "By Providence! The lives such advancements must save! The suffering they must prevent! Unfathomable! To *sleep* through such anguish rather than enduring it!"

"It's too bad Ben isn't here to see this."

Jefferson turned away immediately when the surgeon made his first incision. Blood had always made him queasy.

Washington sneered at Jefferson and watched the procedure unflinchingly. "All this for a mere dog! Imagine the wonders futurity employs to save humans!"

Franklin and Paul browsed books in the small store in the Visitor Center. Franklin's selection contained quotes by Rushmore's creator, sculptor Gutzon Borglum:

> We believe the dimensions of national heartbeats are greater than village impulses, greater than state dreams or ambitions. Therefore we believe a nation's memorial should, like Washington, Jefferson, Lincoln and Roosevelt, have a serenity, a nobility, a power that reflects the gods who inspired them and suggests the gods they have become.

The Gods they have become?

The Gods they have become.

The Gods they have become!

Franklin's chagrin grew as he read the words repeatedly.

Franklin and Paul left the mural area, entered the adjacent theater, and watched a movie about Rushmore's construction. Seconds after it began, Franklin whispered, "Are these moving images truly real? Or are individual portraits being shuffled rapidly?"

"The latter," Paul said. "The continuity is an illusion."

"What of the 'real' physical objects I see? People, cars, birds. Is their continuity an illusion too?" *And might this conundrum help explain time transport somehow?*

Paul laughed and shook his head quickly, more out of a desire to avoid the conversation than as an answer. "Let's just watch the movie."

After the movie, Franklin and Paul sat on the benches in the outdoor amphitheater. Franklin concentrated on people more than the sculpture. Most visitors beamed with pride, curiosity and, most of all, love.

Love for men they had never met.

Love for the child those men had borne.

And gratitude for both.

"I'd like to just sit here awhile," Franklin said.

Paul was staring at the mountain. "Fine with me."

Franklin also perused the book he'd bought and read Gutzon Borglum's quotes. One in particular gripped him:

> As for sculptured mountains—Civilization, even its fine arts, is, most of it, quantity-produced stuff: education, law, government, wealth—each is enduring only as the day. Too little of it lasts into tomorrow and tomorrow is strangely the enemy of today, as today has already begun to forget buried yesterday. Each succeeding civilization forgets its predecessor, and out of its body builds its homes, its temples. Civilizations are ghouls. Egypt was pulled apart by its successor; Greece was divided among the Romans; Rome was pulled to pieces by bigotry and bitterness much of which was engendered by its own empire building.
>
> I want, somewhere in America, on or near the Rockies, the backbone of the Continent, so far removed from succeeding, selfish, coveting civilizations, a few feet of stone that bears witness, carries the likeness, the dates, a word or two of the great things we accomplished as a Nation, placed so high it won't pay to pull them down for lesser purposes.

The passage inspired Franklin, but he didn't like the assumption that America would collapse eventually and was doomed to be a slave to historical precedent. Franklin knew no previous civilizations had escaped this servitude, but he nonetheless refuted Borglum's logical assumption dogmatically.

America must endure! he thought. *Freedom must endure! It must become permanent, ingrained in the human psyche as surely as this Sphinx and Rushmore are ingrained into the Earth!*

Paul noted a resolve in Franklin's expression he found odd, but didn't comment. "If you could meet one person on Rushmore, who would it be?" he asked.

"Lincoln," Franklin said.

"I'd pick Washington or Jefferson. One of the original founders. But I'm not sure which."

"Jefferson," Franklin said. "Either man could regale you with historical stories and insights. But this aspect aside, I suspect Washington would bore you somewhat."

Paul laughed at the absurdity of the concept. "I always wondered what made Washington such a great General."

Franklin knew silence was his wisest answer, but nonetheless said, "Washington wasn't a great General."

Paul laughed. "You're a trip, man."

Franklin smiled. "A trip where?"

Paul laughed harder. "If Washington wasn't a great General, how'd he win the Revolutionary War?"

"Washington was *totally* fearless and incorruptible, had grace and physical stature, and was one of the best horsemen in the world, which was important for officers who commanded from the saddle. He was every soldier's model, and his appearance and deeds inspired hope, trust, and loyalty in men. Only a handful of leaders in all of history have been granted such motivational prowess."

"Did Eisenhower have it?"

"I do not know." Franklin peered at Washington's sculpture. "Washington was exceedingly cautious, and avoided *all* unnecessary risk, no matter how slight. He rarely gambled, and never hastily, but when he did all potentials were considered and he was unusually daring."

"Like crossing the Delaware."

Franklin nodded. "Washington was also a man of incomparable resolve. Once he committed fully to a goal, only death could deter him. And since he did not fear it . . ."

"That's why he stuck it out at Valley Forge. Or during the entire Revolution, for that matter."

Franklin nodded again. "Men of lesser mettle would have crumbled or succumbed to mutinies. Washington survived Valley Forge, and scores of equally vexsome trials, through sheer will. He willed himself, and his army, to persevere."

"And that's not greatness?"

"Washington is a great man. An exceptional President, seemingly."

"Seemingly?"

"An exceptional President. But he was a mediocre General."

"What makes such a great man a mediocre General?" Paul asked.

"Though intelligent, Washington is no genius. Given reliable analysis by brilliant advisers, he usually makes wise decisions. But he is a man of minimal creativity and rudimentary education who often lacks the capacity to derive the reliable analysis himself. Washington is a competent General when given sufficient time for counsel, but when circumstances deny it, and he is forced to make rapid strategic decisions, the results are usually dismaying. This shortcoming cost America dearly."

"But he won the Revolutionary War!"

"The French deserve as much credit for the victory as Washington and his Army. He persevered until French assistance arrived, and this staggering accomplishment should not be trivialized. But we must not romanticize heroes as history often does. Men like Caesar and Alexander demonstrated a consistent ability to achieve victory in almost any military situation. Washington lacked this genius. America had generals with more brilliant military minds and superior battlefield records than him."

"So one of them should have commanded?"

"No. Definitely not. Most certainly not."

"Why?"

"None of them would have displayed, or in fact did display, Washington's unwavering obedience to civil authority."

"Washington sounds interesting," Paul said. "If I could meet anyone on Rushmore it'd be him."

Franklin resisted the urge to smile.

"People always talk about being honest and courageous," Paul said. "But how many men really do it?"

Franklin smiled. "I suppose Washington's character does have a timeless appeal. But that doesn't mean he is more interesting than a multi-disciplined puzzle like Jefferson."

"I'm sticking with Washington anyway."

"Fair enough. You probably shouldn't place too much stock in my opinions anyway. It's not like I knew the men."

"What about Jefferson?" Paul asked. "What was he like?"

Franklin shook his head. "I won't even attempt such a discussion."

"It doesn't have to be involved like Washington. Just a quick overview."

Franklin laughed. "Jefferson cannot be described quickly or easily. He defies categorization. And to most men, comprehension. I could paint you a picture of any other revolutionary figure with a few broad strokes, but not Jefferson."

Paul pressed, and Franklin began to describe the Sage of Monticello, until the pavilion speakers said, "Ladies and Gentleman, our national anthem." The entire crowd stood. "*Oh! Say, can you see, by the dawn's early light, What so proudly we hailed at the twilights last gleaming?*"

Everyone faced Mount Rushmore and many individuals placed their hands over their hearts. Two men to Franklin's left offered crisp military salutes.

"*Whose broad stripes and broad stars, through the perilous fight, O'er the ramparts we watched were so gallantly streaming?*"

As the song progressed, a tingling filled Franklin. He didn't know what battle or war the song commemorated, but it nonetheless tugged at his emotions and filled him with pride.

The singer's voice moved up an octave. "*And the rocket's red glare, the bombs bursting mid-air, Gave proof through the night, that our flag was still there.*"

Franklin swelled with joy, both because America was something he helped create, and because it had been created at all. Looking around, he saw that others were moved. The emotion was palpable.

"Oh! Say, does that Star-Spangled Banner yet wave, O'er the land of the free . . . and the home . . . of the . . . brave!"

After the national anthem concluded, leaving seemed fitting to Franklin. Not just Mount Rushmore, but the entire region of the country. He felt a sense of closure.

"The five percent tax rate definitely isn't an erratum," Jefferson said, as he compared the restaurant, hotel, and gift shop tickets.

"Perhaps America's two to three percent is the anomaly," Washington replied. "This was the rate prior to our Revolution. Afterwards, our newly confederated states were denied British bounties[79] and Royal Navy protection. Higher merchandise prices and defense outlays tripled the typical rate."

"Six to nine percent is an accurate appraisal for the period prior to the Constitutional Convention," Jefferson agreed.

"Futurity's taxation levels could be less than ours. Or at least comparable." Jefferson's smirk irritated Washington. "If you disagree, say so."

"You could be right," Jefferson replied, with the tone of a man humoring a fool. "If this indirect tax is the primary federal funding mechanism."

Franklin and his instructor were walking toward paid parking when a voice from the vicinity of the gift shop shouted, "Paul? Is that you? Hey, Paul?"

Franklin's heart sank when he saw the Samaritan hurrying toward them. *Stay calm*, he told himself. *Paul will suspect after talking to her, but they can't prove who you are. No matter what happens, you are a Franklin impersonator. An actor.*

I'll have to be a right good one, to convince them I am such. Especially Paul, a natural philosopher who may know that time travel is possible!

"Small world," the Samaritan said, as she drew close. "Hey, Mr. Franklin. You found some garden clothes, I see. Do you have a kite and a key yet?"

"Still questing."

The Samaritan laughed at Paul's stunned expression. "I didn't think you'd be that surprised to see me. What's it been? Five years since high school?"

"Yeah. I guess. How do you know Mr. Franklin?"

---

79 Bounty. A subsidy paid or concession granted to producers of certain commodities. The British Empire regulated the trade and production of its colonies with a complex system of tariffs and bounties.

As the Samaritan summarized their gift shop encounter, Franklin grew more nervous. He knew Paul was recalling scores of their conversation snippets and piecing things together.

"You look like a slave just walked over your grave," Washington said to Jefferson.

No response. The Sage of Monticello stared blankly as money jobbers debated the markets. Stocks once again sprinted across the bottom of the screen. Millions, even billions, flowing to and fro.

Washington normally respected privacy, but Jefferson was probably gleaning insights that would never occur to him. He waved a hand in front of the Sage of Monticello's face. No response at first, but finally Jefferson looked over.

"A shilling for your thoughts," Washington said.

"My thoughts are shillings," Jefferson replied. "Notes, to be precise."

Washington glanced at the television. "What vexes you?"

"Depreciation."

"That seems unrelated to the stock market."

"I pray you are right," Jefferson responded.

"Why wouldn't I be?"

"What causes depreciation?"

"Printing more notes."

"Why is this done?"

Jefferson's arrogant tone irked Washington, but he played along. "Funding. Governments which cannot levy higher taxes print additional notes and spend them. As more notes now exist, each is worth less, so purchasers pay more for the same wares."

"An astute appraisal," Jefferson said. "But one that makes a fundamental assumption."

Washington thought hard, but could not deduce it.

"That the notes circulate." Jefferson peered at the television. "Postulate a nation of dupes conned by stock and money jobbers. Further suppose a corrupt government which prints new notes relentlessly, but schemes to delay the suffering this inevitably causes."

"How would a government do this?" Washington asked.

"Encourage stock market speculation which would siphon quantities of notes equal to new government emissions."

As Washington's jaw dropped he envied Jefferson's intellect. "Money invested in stocks would be removed from circulation and newly-emitted notes would replace it! The total number of notes would appear to remain constant, and there would be no net depreciation!"

"Or depreciation would ravage much more slowly. For the short term."

"By Providence!" Washington gasped as he realized the inevitable long-term consequence. "Could such an apocalypse transpire?"

"I hope not," Jefferson sighed, "but the avarice of money and stock jobbers has always been boundless." A dour chuckle. "I admit that paper money has some advantages, but its inevitable abuses also cannot be denied. By breaking up the measure of value, rampant depreciation eventually makes a lottery of all private property. I always believed this was one of those cases where mercantile clamor would bear down reason, until it was corrected by ruin."

"Good luck, Mr. Franklin," the Samaritan said, before she kissed Paul on the cheek and left.

"Where to, Mr. Franklin?" Paul asked.

"It's Steele, not Franklin. I'm an actor."

Paul smiled. "You know a lot about Jefferson, Washington, and the American Revolution. For an actor."

Franklin shrugged. "I'm a student of history."

"Not 19th or 20th century history. Not the Civil War. Or Lincoln or Roosevelt."

Franklin's smile seemed lubricated. "The American Revolution was my focus. Such knowledge is useful when portraying Benjamin Franklin."

Other remarks occurred, but Franklin knew from his diplomatic experiences that it was better to project confidence and say as little as possible when employing subterfuge. Each additional word was a risk. Only liars justified.

Paul smiled at Franklin then resumed the trek to the car. He was suspicious, but not certain.

Does he know time transport is possible? Franklin wondered. *If current natural philosophy considers it impossible will he ignore it, or his instincts?*

If he believes I am me, what will he do?

Attempt a cross examination?

Try to trick me into admitting my identity?

Franklin's fear increased.

No. He is a natural philosopher. He will try to prove his hypothesis. Empirically. Using futuristic inventions I am ignorant of and do not know how to thwart.

"You seem tired," Washington said to Jefferson.

"There is no time to be tired. But yes, nightmares hampered last night's doze. It is absurd to still be plagued by them."

"Guilt about slavery?"

Jefferson stiffened. "No."

"Are you sure?"

"I have rarely sacrificed sleep to slavery."

"What then?"

Silence.

Washington knew better than to press. Getting reticent Jefferson to talk was like opening an oyster with a feather.

They channel-surfed in silence, pausing on a program that documented the opulent lifestyles of futurity's rich and famous.

"Such concentrated wealth seems incompatible with republicanism," Jefferson criticized.

"You sound like some bitter peasant," Washington replied. "The sage I knew was a staunch defender of property rights."

"I still am."

"Contemplation of your nightmares has made you grumpy."

"Yes." Jefferson listened to some Trump magnate's debt woes and resisted the urge to frown. "Yes, it has."

"The concentrated wealth you criticize existed in our time. At places like Mount Vernon and Monticello."

"If slavery was eradicated, Monticello and Mount Vernon could no longer exist . . ."

Jefferson looked like he might cry. Washington shrugged as he thought of losing Mount Vernon. He loved his old home, but not as fervently as Tom loved his. Monticello was Jefferson's mistress, his soul set in stone. At least it had been.

"Our homes are irrelevant, Tom. We cannot reclaim them if they are history."

Jefferson forced a smile. "We are time pilgrims who must truly begin life anew."

Washington nodded. "A seemingly absurd undertaking for men of our age."

An aerial view of a manicured estate revealed gardens eerily reminiscent of Monticello's. Washington figured this would depress Jefferson more, but he snapped out of his funk.

Washington once again knew better than to ask. Jefferson was acting like a widow. Surely he had realized Monticello was gone. Was the reality sinking in belatedly perhaps? If so, why did he seem liberated by the loss of Monticello?

"This future isn't so bad," Jefferson chirped. "An exotic vacation is all."

Washington grunted. "I fear we have been brought here to do more than just vacation."

PAUL WAS DRIVING Franklin back to the hotel. Franklin didn't like taking such a risk, especially after the Samaritan encounter, but since this was his last conversation with Paul, he asked the gnawing question, "Is time travel possible?"

"Relativity allows for time dilation," Paul replied. He explained that time slowed at extremely high speeds. If two twins were placed on objects moving at two disparate velocities, say a planet and spaceship, they would age at different rates. The spaceship would have to be moving near the speed of light for the effect to be pronounced, but if it did so for an extended period of time, and then returned to Earth, the astronaut would be years younger than his terrestrial twin.

"This twin experiment has been performed?" Franklin asked. "The craft has been built, accelerated near the speed of light, and returned to Earth with a younger pilot? On the moon trips perhaps?"

Paul smiled. "No. Not exactly. The effect has been confirmed empirically, but not in the way you described. Super sensitive atomic clocks have been placed in planes that circled the Earth and the predicted time dilations were observed."

Atomic clocks? "There are air planes that can circle the Earth at the speed of light?"

Paul sighed. "No. No. Nothing even approaching it. The clocks are the key. They measure seconds to like ten decimal places, and note *extremely* minute time variations."

Franklin nodded. "You said the predicted time dilations were observed? The effect has been quantified mathematically?"

"Yes," Paul said. "By Einstein. And Lorentz."

"Has anything traveled at the speed of light?"

"Subatomic particles like electrons have come very close."

"I meant a tangible object. A chair, a hen, a person."

"No," Tom said. "Nothing that large has ever traveled at or near light speed. The twin experiment is an allegory that makes time dilation easier to understand."

It's not doing its job, Franklin thought. Like most, he struggled to understand relativity. It seemed to muddle the meaning of time, transforming it into something almost magical. Was time truly a dimension akin to length, width or height? Could this fourth "dimension" actually expand or contract like a wad of taffy? This helped Franklin envision time dilation, but in purely physical terms it seemed ridiculous. As did every other physical visualization he attempted.

Franklin remained lost in relativity's absurdities longer than he would have liked, but eventually his scientific instincts reasserted themselves. "What causes time dilation?" he asked.

"Moving faster."

"I need a more fundamental answer. *Why* does moving faster slow time? Or more specifically, *how* does velocity affect time? What is the underlying *physical* mechanism that causes time to slow when one speeds up? *Physically*, besides their velocities and their time passage rates, what is the difference between an object moving at the speed of light and one that is moving slowly?"

"I don't know," Paul said.

"You don't know, or no one knows."

"Both, I think."

Franklin wasn't sure if he should be encouraged or discouraged by the ignorance. "Is this time dilation considered literal time transport?"

"No," Paul said. "Not in the H.G. Wells sense of the word. Changing the rate of passage of time is different from instantaneously transporting yourself to a different time."

"Is the Wells time travel possible?" Franklin asked.

"Probably not," Paul said. "Unless physics is incorrect about its most basic assumptions. Some esoteric theories may allow time travel, but even if they do, it will probably be decades and perhaps centuries before empirical tests are performed."

"Suppose time transport is possible," Franklin said. "What limitations would exist?"

"Time travel creates all sorts of absurd paradoxes." Paul eyed Franklin suspiciously. "For example, suppose you go back in time and kill your parents. How did you exist?" Paul cited several other similar conundrums, then concluded, "In general, these paradoxes are created by traveling to the past and making changes that would alter the future."

It took great effort, but Franklin refrained from asking the next, logical question.

"*Bad boys, bad boys, whatcha gonna do, whatcha gonna do when they come for you?*"

Jefferson searched for a new play after *Crossfire* ended, and stopped on *Cops* as the credits rolled.

"Wonderful," Washington said. "We made a constable suspicious."

"At least we know what a cop is now," Jefferson replied. "We should watch this play sometime and determine what weapons constables have at their disposal."

Washington nodded sternly as an airplane ad aired. "You are now free to move about the country," it promised.

"We are free to move," Jefferson said. "But the question is where?"

Both men stared the United States map and felt overwhelmed. They had no way to research large numbers of cities and pick an optimum location.

"It would be unwise to travel to a destination we know nothing about," Washington said.

Jefferson nodded. "Hopefully Ben has acquired knowledge that solves this problem. If not, I still favor a city we knew such as Philadelphia, New York, or Your D.C."

"Ben was revered in Philadelphia, and we all may be in D.C."

"New York, then? Tentatively?"

Washington nodded. "When does the bus depart?"

"In the morrow at 9:45 am. We would arrive in New York on September 9th."

"Excellent. We'll visit physicians on the 10th, and can be exploring by the morning of the 11th."

"It's been an educational day," Franklin said, as they pulled into the tavern parking lot. He tried to give Paul another hundred dollars in twenties, but he refused it.

"You've been more than generous, Mr. Steele. I can't possibly accept any more money. And I can teach as late as you want tonight."

"I think we're both worn out," Franklin said. "I would like to retain your services in the morrow, though."

"The proper term is tomorrow. When you say morrow you make yourself conspicuous."

"Tomorrow then? At the same time?"

"Sure."

They had stuffed Franklin's purchases into three backpacks, and as Paul unloaded them, he saw an eye peer out Franklin's room window. *Washington's!* he thought, as a chill spread through him. "Should I put them in your room?"

Franklin smiled. "Right outside the door will be fine."

Paul obeyed, then faced Franklin. "Who are you? Honestly?"

"I told you I don't like lies. See you tomorrow?"

"Yeah," Paul said. "See you tomorrow."

"Will you be ready to second guess Eye-in-Stein by then?"

Paul laughed. "You're a trip, man."

Franklin smiled as Paul started his car. "A trip where?"

WHEN FRANKLIN ENTERED the hotel room, he found an anxious Washington waiting. "A fruitful day?"

"Yea. I met Lincoln."

Washington's eyes bulged. "What?"

Franklin smiled. "Just jesting."

"What did you actually do?"

"Well, I began the day by visiting Rushmore."

Washington's eyes bulged again. "What?"

Another smile. "Just jesting."

"Killing[80]," Washington said. "I see you procured indigenous clothes."

"Among other things. This day was invaluable. Perhaps priceless."

Washington brought the futuristic packs into the room, then tried each one on. Though filled with wares, they were *extremely* comfortable. "How much did you spend?"

"Much. But I was sensible. You will be pleased."

Washington expected Franklin to unload the packs and give a narrative of his day, but he hobbled across the room and stood next to Jefferson instead. "I'm back, Tom."

Jefferson didn't look up, or move. "Yes."

"What are you reading?"

"*The Constitution*. It is an appendix in one of the books you purchased yesterday. I intend to systematically research political changes. This seemed a logical place to start."

Franklin nodded as he sat. "Alterations?"

"The articles seem the same, but it has been amended 27 times. Including *The Bill of Rights*."

"Give us a quick summary."

Jefferson perused the amendments quickly. "We will skip *The Bill of Rights*, as George and I both lived to see it ratified, and you saw it rejected at the Constitutional Convention."

---

80 Killing. Hilarious.

Franklin nodded. "The 13th amendment, then."

"The 11th, actually. As I mentioned, only 10 of Madison's 12 amendments were ratified. The 11th amendment was ratified during Washington's Presidency as a response to Chisholm vs. Georgia. Chisholm was a South Carolina resident who sued Georgia to recover property it impounded from him after the war. The United States Supreme Court ruled on the case, as mandated by *The Constitution*, and ordered the property returned, creating an uproar. The notion that any individual could drag *a state* into federal court and have the national government intervene in its affairs was distasteful to many states. So they ratified the eleventh amendment. It removed cases in which a state was sued by individuals from the jurisdiction of the federal courts."

"State power versus national," Franklin said.

Jefferson nodded. "An important precedent. Or attempt at one. The states disliked a federal action, and negated it."

Washington read over Jefferson's shoulder. "The electors shall meet in their respective states and vote by ballot for President and Vice President, one of whom, at le—"

"Amendment 12," Jefferson said. "Election of Presidents and Vice Presidents. Ratified after you both died, while I was President. In response to the Revolution of 1800."

"The Revolution of 1800?" Washington said with concern.

Jefferson smiled. "My Presidential election. In choosing me over Adams, the nation rejected Federalist oppression and reaffirmed Republican principles. No blood was spilled, but tyrants were nonetheless overthrown."

"Adams was that bad?" Franklin asked.

Jefferson nodded crisply, then summarized the Revolution of 1800. At the time, constitutionally mandated electors voted for two candidates, and did not specify which vote was for President or Vice President. The person with the most votes became President, the runner-up Vice President. Jefferson, the unanimous Republican Presidential candidate, chose Aaron Burr as his running mate.

"Burr," Washington growled. "You nominated him?"

"The decision was pragmatic," Jefferson replied. "Burr controlled New York's electors. I needed them to win."

"No matter what the consideration, he was unfit for such a high office."

"In hindsight, no one can refute that claim, but my options were sparse. Federalists you emboldened were defiling the republic, and wresting power from them was my priority."

"I warned you about Burr after I forbade his copying of your papers," Washington said.

Burr served in the American Army during the Revolution. Washington recognized his brilliance and made him a part of his inner circle, until he entered his office one day and found Burr sitting at his desk reading confidential papers. After a *stern* reprimand, Burr requested and received a transfer. Washington never trusted him again, and during his Presidency, when he learned that Jefferson was allowing the New York Senator to copy sensitive documents, he banned the practice instantly.

"You warned me about Burr," Jefferson said. "And I warned you about Federalist tyranny. I move we table this discussion. The focus is *The Constitution*."

"Agreed," Washington said. "But we will revisit it."

"Through a mistake in voting, Burr and I received the same number of electoral votes. It was assumed he would defer to me, but Federalists supported him, and he chose to vie for the Presidency. The election was thrown to the House of Representatives for a vote, as *The Constitution* prescribes."

"We did not foresee factions when drafting *The Constitution*," Franklin said. "The loophole seems obvious now, but . . ."

"An unfortunate oversight," Jefferson replied. "Most Federalists had been voted out of office, but until their term expired and a newly-elected Republican majority took the reins, they controlled Congress. My position was precarious. I had to rely on the integrity of my deposed enemies to secure my election. Unfortunately, a multi-month deadlock prevailed and there was talk of an interim Federalist president."

"Your response?" Washington asked nervously.

"I was the people's selection. Their will could not be usurped. A President pro tempore[81] was a fatal precedent, that, once set, would be artificially reproduced and end soon in dictator."

"Your response?" Washington was anxious.

"I met with Federalist leaders, and openly and firmly assured them that the day such an act passed, the middle states would arm, and that no such usurpation, even for a day, should be submitted to." Jefferson smiled ever-so-slightly. "This shook them."

Washington chuckled at the understatement. The Federalists must have been stunned when the gentle-natured Jefferson, one of the world's staunchest pacifists, a man widely regarded as a coward, threatened to enforce his election with bloodshed. Washington smiled with admiration. Jefferson had always possessed vision, but a President needed courage and will as well, and Washington had always felt him suspect in these regards. *I would have doubted your resolve*, he thought.

81 Pro tempore. Latin. Time being. A temporary or interim official.

"My threat to call another Constitutional Convention, to reorganize the government, and to amend it, frightened the Federalists further." Jefferson smiled again. "No interim President was appointed. I was elected by the House. Without bloodshed. The twelfth amendment was ratified to close the constitutional loopholes that cornered me. It makes electors cast separate votes for President and Vice President, and requires tie-breaking House of Representative votes to take place immediately after deadlocks are discovered."

"The integrity of elections is the integrity of the republic itself," Washington said. "Your refusal to compromise this sacred principle was an act of greatness."

"I agree," Franklin said. "To think our errors almost elevated a man the people did not choose to the Presidency!"

"Thank you," Jefferson said. "I regard the 11th and 12th amendments as refinements to the original *Constitution*. They were ratified early in American history, and corrected oversights made when drawing it."

"If those were our only oversights, we can count ourselves lucky," Franklin said.

"We weren't that lucky," Jefferson replied. "Slavery was abolished in 1865."

"Thank Providence!" Franklin exclaimed.

Washington nodded sternly. "Confirmation of what we suspected."

"The niggers were freed immediately after this Civil War," Jefferson said. "Amendments 13, 14, and 15 outlaw slavery, bestow citizenship on all individuals born in America, and grant niggers suffrage."

"Bestowing citizenship and suffrage was wise," Franklin said. "If slavery were merely outlawed, negroes might have been oppressed insidiously."

"Perhaps they still are," Washington replied. "We assumed slavery was abolished recently. If negroes have been free citizens for more than a century, why was the father so bitter?"

"The niggers will always be bitter," Jefferson said. "No matter how justly they are treated by our posterity. That is why they should have been freed and deported, not freed and granted citizenship."

Franklin smiled sadly. "Racism hasn't been vanquished from men's hearts, but its expulsion from *The Constitution* is an enormous evolvement. Amendment 16 is next, I believe."

Jefferson tensed. "Amendment 16. 'Congress shall have power to lay and collect taxes on incomes, from whatever source derived, without apportionment among the several States, and without regard to any census or enumeration.' "

Silence.

Stunned silence.

Petrified glances were exchanged.

" 'Direct taxes shall be apportioned among the several states which may be included in this Union, according to their respective members.'[82]," Franklin quoted. " 'No capitation, or other direct, tax shall be laid, unless in proportion to the census or enumeration herein before directed to be taken.'[83]"

"The 16th amendment negates both clauses," Jefferson said.

"Unwisely," Franklin replied. "It destabilizes the tenuous state and federal power balance we so carefully crafted."

Washington nodded. "I favor a strong national government, but not this strong. Only states should levy capitations."

Jefferson seemed like he might cry. "How could the people have allowed such tyranny?"

"They must have supported the amendment if it was ratified," Washington said. "Unless America is plagued by tyrannies most overt."

"How large is the national tax on income?" Franklin asked. "Perhaps it is tolerated because it is miniscule."

"Doubtful," Jefferson replied. "Though it may have been ratified under that premise. And the enumeration isn't the point. Granting such power to the federal government is unconscionable."

Franklin and Washington nodded vigorously.

"A government granted such power would press relentlessly to increase it," Jefferson continued. "The end result would be wealth redistribution, erosion of personal liberties, an entrenched bureaucracy, and pervasive corruption." He sighed deeply. "This is the road to Rome. A fundamental subversion of our most cherished republican principles."

"I am inclined to agree," Washington said.

"As am I," Franklin added. "Though I am reserving judgment somewhat. We must study the empirical consequences of this tax, and learn how it is implemented. And why. At present our knowledge is almost entirely theoretical. The 17th amendment?"

"Direct election of Senators."

---

82 Article 1, Section 2, Part 3 of *The United States Constitution*. To apportion is to "divide and distribute proportionally." Suppose the federal government needed $1,000,000, wanted to obtain it through a direct tax, and the Union had only two states, Virginia and Pennsylvania, with populations of 900,000 and 100,000 respectively. Prior to the 16th amendment, it had only one choice: levy a $900,000 tax on Virginia and a $100,000 tax on Pennsylvania. As Pennsylvania had 10% of the nation's population, it only had to pay 10% of the total tax. The federal government could not require a geographically larger or wealthier state to pay a larger burden, tell a state how to raise the funds, nor circumvent the states and tax individuals directly.

83 Article 1, Section 9, Part 4 of *The United States Constitution*, which denies Congress specific powers. A capitation, or head tax, is a direct tax levied against individuals. This clause prevented Congress from varying the rates of direct taxes.

"This makes America more democratic and less republican," Washington said.

"It also weakens the states further," Jefferson noted.

Washington and Franklin nodded. In the original *Constitution*, state legislatures elected Senators. Senators elected by state legislatures would be expected to strongly support states' interests; thus they would check unwarranted growth of competing federal power.

"Is the House still directly elected?" Washington asked.

"Yes," Jefferson replied.

"And the Executive?"

"Electors. Still. As originally prescribed."

"So the entire legislative branch is now completely democratic." Washington's brow furrowed. "Another troubling development. With Congress completely subservient to the whims of the masses, injustice and tyranny are much more probable."

"Don't you mean inevitable?" Jefferson replied. "And if Congress has the power to directly tax income, the masses may be subservient to them, not vice versa."

"Election and taxation discussions consumed days at the Convention," Franklin said. "We should table these topics and revisit them. I wish to review the amendments quickly and obtain a broad sense of the republic's evolvement."

"Evolvement may be a misnomer," Jefferson said.

"The republic's state?" Franklin quipped.

"The republic's states appear to have been spayed. But as you requested, this topic will be tabled. The 18th amendment outlawed spirits nationwide in 1919."

"America outlawed ale!" Franklin gasped. "What sacrilege! What blasphemy! What . . . what . . . what could they have possibly been thinking? Was the whole nation ripe for Bedlam?"

Washington laughed at Franklin's appalled expression. "And I thought Jefferson was disgusted by the federal capitation."

"I'm no toper," Jefferson said, "but criminalizing spirits seems inappropriate for purely philosophical reasons."

"And practical ones," Washington said. "If merchandise is desired, it will be provided. By miscreants, if outlawed."

Jefferson scanned amendments he hadn't read. "The 21st amendment rescinded the ban in 1933."

"I don't suppose the 16th was rescinded," Washington said.

Jefferson laughed morosely. "Revolutions usually require decapitations, but the opposite is also true."

"This 21st amendment should encourage you a little," Franklin replied. "If it can be rescinded, others can."

"A federal capitation will be more difficult to abolish than a spirits ban."

"Hopefully the people hate federal capitations more than they love spirits," Franklin said.

Jefferson's smile was cynical. "Hopefully. The 22nd amendment prevents George and I from running again. Presidents can only serve two terms."

Washington let out a long sigh of relief. "Thank Providence!" He clasped his hands and looked skyward. "Thank bloody Providence!" Another deep sigh. "Thank Prov-i-dence."

"My sentiments would be the same," Jefferson said. "Were America not plagued by depreciation and a federal capitation."

"America probably wouldn't have ratified the 22nd amendment unless a President served more than two terms," Franklin said.

As they envisioned a power-jobbing President who tried to usurp power and become a Caesar, the founders grew nervous.

"I always disapproved the perpetual re-eligibility of the President," Jefferson muttered, as he consulted a list of Executives in a different appendix. "It created the potential for dictatorship. Jackson, Tyler, Polk. Taylor, Fillmore, Lincoln. Grant, Garfield. None more than eight years. Ah. Just a moment. The Franklin Delano Roosevelt from the pamphlet served 12 years. Until 1945. This amendment was ratified in 1951. It was probably a response to his three terms."

"I approve of this amendment heartily," Washington said. "If *The Constitution* is obeyed, no future Executive will become a dictator."

"Several amendments have increased the scope of suffrage," Jefferson continued. "The 19th gave women the right to vote." He looked at Washington. "The 23rd gave Your D.C. Presidential electors, the 24th abolished poll taxes, and the 26th extended suffrage to everyone 18 years of age or older."

Franklin laughed at his friends' sour expressions. "Posterity has crafted a nation whose suffrage is the embodiment of *The Declaration*'s ideals. Yet you both seem distraught."

"Also overwhelmed," Washington said.

And frightened, Jefferson thought. *Bitter niggers and emotional wenches could outnumber rational white males, dwarfing our influence in elections. The uninspiring leaders we observed on TV now make much more sense.*

"I am neither distraught nor overwhelmed," Franklin said. "I am happy! Negro and wench equality are logical evolvements for humanity!"

A brief discussion of each suffrage amendment ensued. Then the 20th and 25th Amendments, which altered term dates and succession procedures for the Executives, were reviewed.

" 'If the President-elect shall have died, the Vice President-elect shall become President,' " Washington read. "Which Presidents did not complete terms?"

Jefferson obtained the answer from the appendix: William Harrison, Zachary Taylor, Abraham Lincoln, James Garfield, William McKinley, Warren Harding, Franklin Roosevelt, John Kennedy and Richard Nixon. "Roughly 20% of our Presidents," he said. "Excluding Vice Presidents who replaced them."

"The family mentioned three impeachments, including Nixon and Clinton," Franklin recalled. "Nixon is on your list, Clinton is not. It seems reasonable to assume that Nixon was impeached, and Clinton was tried and acquitted."

"Even if a second President was impeached, the statistic is still disquieting," Washington said.

"Natural death from illness?" Jefferson hoped. "Old age?"

Franklin shook his head. "Doubtful. One would expect this era's advanced natural philosophy to minimize illness, extend life, and make assassination easier."

"America is more democratic." Jefferson thought of the French Revolution and its government by guillotine. "Could passionate mobs have executed Presidents?"

"This should be a research priority," Washington said. "What use are elections if one in five is circumvented?"

What use are elections if niggers and wenches are a majority? "The 27th and final amendment," Jefferson concluded. " 'No law, varying the compensation for the services of the Senators and Representatives, shall take effect, until an election of Representatives shall have intervened.' "

"One of Madison's failed *Bill of Rights* amendments," Washington observed.

All three men knew of it. A Congress that set its own pay created a conflict of interest most founders had recognized.

"This was probably meant to check knavery in a Congress that has trodden the path of Parliament," Franklin predicted. "An amendment eliminating compensation and its attendant corruption would have been preferable."

"Unrealistic," Jefferson replied. "Once the idealistic fervor of revolution passes, most amendments would be reactionary rather than visionary."

"Ending with Madison's amendment seems fitting," Washington said. "Now tell me. What do you think of the new *Constitution*?"

They all deliberated.

"Our *Constitution* is successful," Franklin answered. "We could all fault specific amendments, but their miscellany and multitude indicate a government that has implemented radical change through the rule of law rather than revolution."

"I must abstain," Jefferson said. "My negative feelings about the income capitation taint my view of the whole."

"And you, George?" Franklin asked.

"The 16th amendment aside, liberty has prevailed. *The Constitution* appears to have preserved most of the freedoms we enumerated, and facilitated their expansion."

"What a gift!" Franklin laughed. "I signed *The Constitution* two days ago and am viewing its evolvement as many centuries later!"

"A gift, and perhaps a burden," Washington replied. "You are the only person in this room eligible to be President."

FRANKLIN OPENED the first backpack like some priest performing a ritual and removed three leather wallets. He had placed a $1 bill in Washington's, a $2 bill in Jefferson's, and a $100 bill in his own.

"Is the purse containing the hundred dollar note mine?" Washington asked with a grin.

Franklin laughed. "Being revered has its disadvantages."

Jefferson removed his $2 bill and examined it.

"Your note is used infrequently," Franklin said to him. "Though legal currency, it is circulated in tiny quantities that make it more of a collector's item than a barter tool."

This uniqueness seemed to please Jefferson, who peered at Trumbull's *Signing of the Declaration of Independence* on the back of the note.

The painting reminded Franklin of his Rushmore visit; he still had to relate the Samaritan debacle.

Franklin distributed digital watches, explained the features, and smiled as Washington and Jefferson pressed the light repeatedly. "I did the same thing with my amputee chronometers."

"Amputee?" Washington asked.

"Handless," Franklin replied.

Clothes were next. After they changed, the founders examined themselves in the mirror. They wore casual slacks, plain t-shirts, generic flannels and fleeces, and tennis shoes.

"There is enough variation in color and style that we do not appear suspiciously uniform," Franklin said.

Jefferson nodded. "We now seem indigenous."

Washington tucked his new knife into his belt and saw that his long fleece hid it completely. "You did well, Ben. Very well."

Franklin distributed additional bags of clothing. "Three outfits each," he said.

"The cost?" Washington asked.

"Trifling. This civilization grows garments as grass." Franklin described the massive stores he'd been in, then explained their clothing's futuristic features. Their coats were waterproof, the shoes were designed for physical activity, and the fleece was warm yet quick drying.

"This 'fleece' feels like wool, yet unlike wool," Washington said. "What animal or plant is it produced from?"

"None," Franklin said. "It is created."

"Created?" Confusion contorted Washington's face. "How?"

"I didn't comprehend the natural philosopher's explanation." Franklin distributed baseball caps and sunglasses. "The spectacles are styled to accentuate facial features, so I procured a large variety. I spared no expense on implements that can help us conceal our identity."

"A wise decision," Washington tried on a pair of sunglasses and pulled back reflexively as the room became dark. "One could stare at an eclipse wearing these!"

Jefferson was equally impressed. "These shame our times' tinted spectacles. This era's ingenuity is boundless!"

The electric razors and hair clippers enthralled everyone, even Franklin, who had already seen them. He and Jefferson tried out toothbrushes while Washington looked on with longing, then the trio experimented with deodorant, colognes, Q-tips, nail clippers and other toiletries.

"Varnish?" Washington held up the can with puzzlement.

"For your wooden teeth," Franklin replied.

Washington chuckled while Franklin unpacked a radio and plugged it in. Futuristic music alternated between high and low notes rapidly. The female singer was marginal.

The lack of harmony soon grated even Washington, the only member of the trio that wasn't a musician. Franklin tuned in an orchestra station while he explained electromagnetic radiation.

"So where is this 'signal'?" Washington asked.

"The air," Franklin said.

"I see nothing," Washington replied.

"The signal cannot be seen. But it exists."

"I comprehend your explanation of a 'signal' transmitted through a string," Washington said. "But through the air?"

Franklin repeated one of Paul's lessons; he raised and lowered the antenna, put the radio in places like a drawer and the bathroom that blocked the signal, and let Washington and Jefferson observe the degradation in sound quality. Then he explained cell phone basics, including signal strength and finite minutes. As papers and a "credit check" were needed for frugal phones, he had purchased three of the comparatively expensive pre-paid variety; they would be used only for important matters, and calls would be brief.

As their cell phones might be their only method of contact if they were separated, Franklin wanted to be sure Washington and Jefferson both knew how to use them. He exited the room and dialed Washington, who answered but remained silent. "Is this President General Washington?" Franklin asked.

"Where are you?" Washington replied.

"France."

"I wouldn't doubt it."

Jefferson peeked out the window and saw Franklin just as his phone rang. He answered it. "Is this President Sage Jefferson?" Franklin asked.

"Is this President Franklin?"

"Hold the phone closer to your mouth," Franklin said. "I didn't hear you."

Jefferson obeyed. "Is this President Franklin?"

"Don't be lewd." Franklin hung up and reentered the room. Washington noted that the phones were not plugged in like other devices, and wondered about power. Franklin showed him the battery, and the plug-in charger.

"How does this futuristic battery work?" Jefferson asked.

"A new branch of natural philosophy called chemistry. I understand little of it."

As Franklin unpacked tiny "Mag-Lites" and "LED headlamps", a "portable compact disc/mp3 player" and music "CDs", "Power Bars", "plastic" bottled water, "multivitamins", absurdly tough yet light knives, and other seemingly endless wonders, Washington and Jefferson grew overloaded. A new *Constitution*, suffrage for all, an income tax, potential Presidential assassinations, TVs, phones, radios, geared shavers, "created" fabrics, tiny batteries, eclipse spectacles, invisible signals . . . Not to mention the scores of revelations and gaggles of questions about their effects on warfare, learning, government, recreation, family life, rogering, medicine, agriculture . . .

It was too much for almost anyone to synthesize.

Franklin smiled when he saw his friends' frazzled expressions. "Those devices were a mere prelude," he said, as he removed a digital camera from his bag. He taught Washington and Jefferson how to take pictures and scroll through them.

"I would have traded Monticello for a few camera obscura images of my wife," Jefferson said.

"Camera," Franklin corrected. "Not camera obscura. We must learn to use futuristic diction. When we do not, we might as well be wearing our colonial clothes. And what would you have given to record your wife using this?"

Franklin removed a portable video camera, demonstrated it, then relaxed while his friends spent several awestruck ticks scribing reality.

"I would have traded Mount Vernon for one of these," Washington said, as he filmed Jefferson. "Imagine having scribed Cornwallis' surrender, my wedding to Martha, Sally Fairfax, the Constitutional Convention, my inauguration . . ."

Franklin smiled. Washington's childlike excitement was rare enough to be uncharacteristic. "Posterity would probably barter more than Mount Vernon for such images."

"I would have trained Jupiter[84] to use this device," Jefferson said. "Then I would have scribed Martha for days on end. Weeks on end!"

"How about Sally Hemings?" Franklin teased.

Jefferson's eyes flared with resentment, but he gained control immediately and said, "Would you have scribed your mistresses?"

"Absolutely. And my wife. Though I doubt my recordings would have been suitable for posterity."

Washington and Jefferson shook their heads while Franklin turned off the video camera and plugged it in to charge. "I purchased many ingenious new inventions today," he said, as he removed a laptop computer from his backpack. "But this final discovery excited me the most, and will help us inestimably. It is called the internet."

Franklin explained what he knew about computers while the laptop booted, but Washington and Jefferson were too stupefied to really focus. Franklin understood. He had responded the same way hours before when he'd first seen a computer.

After he connected the phone line to the modem, Franklin tried to log onto the internet using a desktop shortcut Paul had created. He was unsuccessful, and had no idea why. Paul had typed rudimentary troubleshooting instructions, but navigating windows was like sailing without a sextant; Franklin was hopelessly confused almost immediately.

Paul's room contained posters of naked women, Stonehenge, the Pyramids, a nebulae, an atom bomb explosion, an *X-Files* UFO close-up that proclaimed "The Truth Is Out There," and a piped Sherlock Holmes who insisted, "When you have eliminated the impossible whatever remains, however improbable, must be the truth." The Hounds of the Baskervilles were behind Holmes, sniffing out the improbable truth, seemingly.

---

84 Jupiter. A slave who was Jefferson's lifelong valet and traveling companion.

The truth about Steele might be way the hell out there, but Paul felt certain it was nonetheless out there. He had adhered to Occam's razor and considered the mundane explanation first. If Steele wasn't Franklin, then he looked *exactly* like him, had the same medical ailments, had aged in the modern world while remaining totally ignorant of everything since 1800, had learned more about the colonial era than several history PhDs, and was a first-order genius who had squandered his talents to become a vagrant actor with an interest in time travel.

This was clearly improbable, but was it possible?

Paul sighed as he juxtaposed diametric beliefs. Steele was Franklin, but time travel was impossible.

Which hypothesis was incorrect?

Could either theory be tested?

Was some *Jurassic Park* historian scenario more realistic?

And what if Steele actually was Franklin? What then?

Paul's cell phone rang. *Speak of the founder,* he thought, as he answered.

"This computer is most vexsome," Franklin said. "Are you certain the softwear you inserted is not erratum prone? That my use of your internet ciphers at a new location is practicable?"

"Positive, Mr. Steele."

"As I've said, call me Richard."

Saunders?[85] "We'll get it figured out." *Mr. Franklin.*

JEFFERSON ASKED ABOUT the strange pinging and screeching sounds, and Franklin explained that they were the computer's language. Using this alien voice, it could speak to similar devices anywhere in the world. Franklin's smile was giddy. "This machine is a library, a mathematician, a natural philosopher, a sage, a dictionary, a printer, a lawyer, an accountant . . . Everything but a carpenter. And the world, which is now an interconnected web of such devices, is a large brain."

"What do you mean, a large brain?" Washington asked. "Are you saying it thinks?"

Franklin smiled. "You'll see."

The web connection was established and the Yahoo home page loaded. It contained pictures, advertisements, and headings for calendars, jobs, news, maps, weather, companionship, art, science, education . . .

"Yahoo?" Jefferson said. "Swift's Yahoos[86]?"

---

85 Saunders. Richard Saunders. Franklin's pen name. He wrote his famous *Poor Richard's Almanac* under the pseudonym.

86 Swift's Yahoos. Creatures encountered in Jonathan Swift's 1726 satire *Gulliver's Travels.* Yahoos are warring, hedonistic, materialistic brutes that the human protagonist begrudgingly recognizes as men.

Franklin shrugged. "If so, an intriguing connotation. And a clever one."

"Is this 'brain' a futuristic, worldwide newspaper?" Washington asked.

Franklin's smile widened. "That, and more. No colonial metaphor could adequately describe what you are about to see."

Franklin stood, made Jefferson sit in front of the computer, then spoke like a jinni granting wishes. "What would you like to know?"

"What can I ask?" Jefferson replied.

"Anything. And I do mean *anything*."

"Monticello," Jefferson said. "What's become of it?"

"Type it in," Franklin said.

"The entire question?"

"Just Monticello."

"By 'type' you mean press these letter protrusions, as you did?"

"Yes."

Jefferson obeyed with a gruelingly slow hunt and peck. He spoke the letters as he typed them. "m-o-n-t-i-c-e-l-l-o. The m is lowercase. Is that acceptable?"

"Yea. Now hit 'Enter'."

"You mean type it out?"

"Nay," Franklin said. "On the right there is a key that says 'Enter'. Press it."

Jefferson obeyed and the image disappeared instantly. Another reappeared slowly, a piece at a time.

"Why is this so much slower than the TV?" Jefferson asked. "As the TV's images move, one would assume it to be slower."

"The television image is communicated continually," Franklin explained. "The image you are receiving is only sent when requested. It takes time to retrieve and send it."

"And this is all done by these computer machines?"

Franklin nodded. "Yes."

The entire page was soon visible. Text jumped out at the founders:

> Monticello on eBay Find Monticello items at low prices. With over 5 million items for sale every day, you'll find all kinds of unique things on eBay - the World's Online Marketplace.
> www.ebay.com

The *World's* Online Marketplace? Find Monticello items? Monticello existed! Monticello existed? If it still did, was it being auctioned or sold? Jefferson felt consuming panic. He read feverishly:

TOP 20 WEB RESULTS out of about 612,000

1. Monticello official site. Learn about Jefferson's home and life.
Features visitor information as well as a biography and a day in
the life of the third president.
www.monticello.org - 17k - Cached - More pages from this site
Category: Virginia > Charlottesville > Historical Museums and
Memorials > Monticello

Franklin laughed as he read. "I bet visitors would enjoy a narrative of your day today. Or yesterday."

Visitors. Historical Museums and Memorials. Jefferson sighed with relief. Monticello probably wasn't being sold.

"20 results out of about 612,000," Washington read. "Does that mean . . . it couldn't mean . . . what does it mean?"

Franklin explained that each of the 612,000 "results" was a different "page" whose information could be accessed *instantly*.

"You can't be serious?" Washington replied. "612,000 of these computers with information about Jefferson's home?"

"Some computers contain scores of 'pages', so the actual number isn't that large. And though 612,000 'pages' contain the word 'Monticello', I wouldn't assume they all discuss Jefferson's home."

"How many of these computers exist?"

"Millions. Most American homes contain a TV, phone, and computer. Governments and businesses also own many."

Washington shook his head extremely slowly. He seemed ready to speak, but no words exited his open mouth.

Jefferson's mind raced. If there were 612,000 Monticello "sites," what of more practical topics? Why not create "sites" for Congressional minutes and legislation? For courts? For business records and transactions? Why not for everything? Jefferson realized the first "Yahoo" "site" was probably intended to provide easy access to this "everything," and he reeled mentally as implications dawned.

Franklin instructed him in the use of the mouse, and though he moved it clumsily, Jefferson was able to click on the first Monticello link. As information appeared, Franklin once again emphasized that it was transported from a distant location.

"Monticello perhaps?" Jefferson hoped. Franklin helped Jefferson surf, and obtain conclusive confirmation. "Monticello still exists!" A pause while he read. "In pristine condition!" Another pause. "As a kind of park or museum, like Rushmore!"

"Your return probably wasn't anticipated," Franklin speculated.

Jefferson stood, turned quickly, and hugged Franklin suddenly. "Monticello lives! It lives!"

While Jefferson continued to celebrate, Washington said, "What of Mount Vernon?"

"Have a try," Franklin suggested.

Washington sat, surfed, and confirmed that Mount Vernon's fate was the same as Monticello's. Though pleased, he was not ecstatic like Jefferson.

"Is there a junction for Martha?" Washington wondered.

"There's a page for *everything*," Franklin said, as he plunked down on the bed and began removing his shoes. "Most of the knowledge humanity has amassed can be accessed."

As he clicked on one of the 883,000 "results" generated by a search for his wife, Washington once again shook his head with awe. "This world's one large brain is that of a genius."

"A genius who can teach us," Franklin said. "I suspect our knowledge acquisition shall soon be a tantivy[87]."

ALL IS OVER. I have no more trials to pass through. I shall soon follow him.

Martha had spoken the words shortly after his death, and Washington felt chagrin as he stared at the computer and read them. His wife seemed to lack the will to live without him, and had made good on her promise three years after he had passed.

Would suffrage, a profession, or other rights and interests besides servitude to me have given you a more optimistic outlook? Washington wondered. *Greater self-reliance, perhaps?*

The more he pondered the matter, the more uneasy Washington grew. It was disquieting to realize he may have unknowingly oppressed his beloved wife as surely as he had his slaves.

All is over. I have no more trials to pass through. I shall soon follow him.

The computer articles reinforced this theme of servitude. Martha was remembered as the wife of Washington. Nothing more.

All is over. I have no more trials to pass through. I shall soon follow him.

Like Franklin, Martha had that rare ability to make her own happiness, to bring cheer to any situation, no matter what the circumstance. Washington had drawn strength from her positive attitude during times of bleak adversity,

87 Tantivy. A rapid, barely-controlled gallop or ride.

and he regarded her support as an indispensable underpinning of his success. *Their* success.

All is over. I have no more trials to pass through. I shall soon follow him.

No, my love. I shall follow you. Though hopefully not soon. For I suspect a few trials still await me.

Jefferson knew Washington was callous about death, but he nonetheless marveled at his coldness. This was his wife of almost forty years! How could he read about her passing without sighing, slumping, or shaking his head? Had he already accepted the fact that she was history?

If I had left a living wife behind perhaps I would display such detachment. Jefferson admired the practicality of Washington's response. *Why fret over a death that he didn't experience, that has been a memory for more than two centuries? A death that had to occur sometime.* "I wish I had been plucked from a time when my Martha still lived."

"Such thoughts are frivolous," Washington replied.

"And torturous," Franklin added. Contemplation of his wife could depress Jefferson severely, and he wanted to avoid the situation, for reasons practical and compassionate.

"I wish I could have read about Martha's death rather than living it. As George is. I wish our Puppeteer had ex post factoed my life's greatest agony and allowed me to bask in pleasant memories."

"You can bask in pleasant memories without the aid of Providence," Franklin said. "The choice is yours."

Jefferson's tortured grin suggested otherwise.

While reading articles about his wife on the computer, Jefferson surprised everyone by smiling.

No portrait of Martha Wayles Jefferson is known to exist . . . Jefferson destroyed every letter they had exchanged shortly after her death . . . only two of their letters survive . . . Jefferson had deep antipathy to publicly relating anything about his personal life . . .

Yes I did! Jefferson thought. *Yes I do! But I never thought I'd be reading a primary cause of my antipathy!*

Jefferson stared at the Yahoo home page. "Typing my own name seems inappropriate for some reason."

"Surely you wish to know more of your place in history?" Washington said. "And your death."

"Of course. But I am also . . ." Jefferson thought of Sally Hemings and foreboding filled him. "What would you be remembered for? If posterity could only know three of your deeds, what would you have them be?"

"Wenching," Franklin answered. "Adultery. And drinking spirits. And you, Tom? Sally Hemings and your flight from Tarleton are obvious, but I struggle for a third. The 'dysentery' which kept you from delivering your *Summary View of the Rights of British America*?"

"Walker," Washington suggested.

"I haven't heard of this," Franklin said.

"Nor shall you now," Jefferson responded.

"I'll receive my fire," Franklin said. "The Hutchinson Letters and Cockpit, fleeing home and deserting my brother, and the attempted seduction of Ralph's milliner."

"I'd have to choose . . ." Washington hesitated. "I don't know what I'd choose."

Franklin laughed. "I would mock any other man for pretension. Viscously."

"I'm trying," Washington said. "Honestly."

Franklin laughed harder.

"When I was a young man, I decided certain principles would guide my life and be inviolate. Looking back, I cannot think of a single time I breached this treaty with myself. I blundered more frequently than I would have preferred, but these erratum were the result of deficiencies in understanding, never morals or courage." Washington's expression was compunctious. "I am sorry."

Franklin stopped laughing. "For all of humanity, I accept your apology with gratitude."

"Thank you, Ben. But surely there must be som—ah, yes! Slavery!"

At first, Washington seemed pleased to have actually found an answer, and Franklin once again chuckled. But his joy was fleeting, as was Washington's regret. Whatever his weakness, slavery had perished, and wasting emotion on the issue now was frivolous.

"*The Declaration*," Jefferson said. "*The Virginia Statute of Religious Freedoms* and the University of Virginia. By these testimonials that I have lived I wish most to be remembered."

"General," Washington said. "President. *The Constitution*."

Franklin peered at Washington with veneration. "You won our freedoms on the field of battle, supervised the creation of *The Constitution* designed to safeguard them, constructed the government that has perpetuated them, and then nurtured that government through its infancy. I salute you, sir."

"Thank you again, Ben. I can think of no man whose salutations mean or meant more. Now what of you?"

Jefferson and Washington were both curious. Franklin's accomplishments were the most varied and his decision was therefore the most difficult.

"Minister Plenipotentiary," Franklin answered. "Natural Philosophy. And my testimony before the Committee of the Whole. Now enter your name, Tom. I wish to know when you died."

Jefferson obeyed and skimmed his biography. "I died on July 4th, 1826. One year and four months from the time I left."

"The 50th anniversary of *The Declaration*," Franklin noted. "A fortuitous death, if there is such a thing."

That was Hamilton. "Our Puppeteer definitely had hindsight as an advantage," Jefferson said. "I was also transported after my primary contributions to the republic were made."

"Conjure George's biography," Franklin requested, as he sat next to Jefferson. He laughed when the "Washington" search was returned, and read the hits aloud. "Washington's *Post*, Washington's State, Washington's University, Washington's *Times*, Washington's D.C, Washington's Capitols, Washington's Wizards, Washington's Redskins, Washington's *Monthly*. Your obscurity remains an affront. Your name returned a mere 68,000,000 hits."

Jefferson typed "George Washington," and the founders were soon reading a biography that contained a posthumous character summary drawn by Jefferson.

Franklin read it aloud, and took frequent breaks to rib both Washington and the author. " 'His mind was great and powerful . . . as far as he saw, no judgment was ever sounder.' " He laughed heartily. "A most ambiguous compliment."

"My writing has been abridged," Jefferson defended. "You are misrepresenting my words."

"I'm merely letting them speak. 'His integrity was the most pure, his justice the most inflexible I have ever known, no motives of interest or consanguinity, of friendship or hatred, being able to bias his decision.' " Franklin smiled expansively. "The oasis of sincerity."

"I'm sure you'll find employ in this time as a propaganda minister," Jefferson said.

" 'It may be truly said that never did nature and fortune combine more perfectly to make a Samson great.' "

Washington's jaw tightened at the term.

"I drew man, not Samson." Jefferson glared at Franklin, whose mockery was hampering Washington's potential forgiveness.

"I know you meant well, Tom," Washington said.

"Thank you," Jefferson replied.

Washington's biography was laudatory, and Franklin mocked it with impunity. Jefferson's was a different matter. After summarizing his major achievements, it went for the jugular:

> Long regarded as America's most distinguished "apostle of liberty," Jefferson has come under increasingly critical scrutiny within the scholarly world. At the popular level, both in the United States and abroad, he remains an incandescent icon, an inspirational symbol for both major U.S. political parties, as well as for dissenters in communist China, liberal reformers in central and eastern Europe, and aspiring democrats in Africa and Latin America. His image within scholarly circles has suffered, however, as the focus on racial equality has prompted a more negative reappraisal of his dependence upon slavery and his conviction that American society remain a white man's domain. The huge gap between his lyrical expression of liberal ideals and the more attenuated reality of his own life has transformed Jefferson into America's most problematic and paradoxical hero.

Franklin's sudden absence of mockery was glaring, especially to the apprehensive Jefferson. As he had lived the longest, his biography contained revelations that Washington and Franklin were unaware of. Revelations that embarrassed him.

"History has not been kind to you," Franklin noted.

"Nor has it been unjust," Washington countered.

"I wish I could disagree," Jefferson said glumly. "But as always, George speaks the truth."

Franklin had urinated, and was about to sit down and read his own biography when Washington swooped in and stole his seat. "Allow me," he said, with a broad grin.

Franklin lay down on the bed. "I know you're the father of your country. But I really don't need a bed time story."

Washington read anyway. "Benjamin Franklin was a jack of all trades and a master of many. No other American, except possibly Thomas Jefferson, has done so many things so well . . ."

Franklin craned his hands behind his neck and exaggerated his smile. "Read on, George. All night if you like. With a protagonist this admirable I doubt I'll be able to sleep."

"Does posterity know what a dandy Ben is?" Jefferson asked.

"One of the trades he mastered, clearly." Washington continued to read, and though he and Jefferson mounted a unified assault, neither could muster insults as flairful as Franklin's. Eventually they abandoned their Waterloo of wit. Washington rose, turned the computer back over to Franklin, and said, "I'll leave you alone with yourself."

Franklin had just finished his biography. "They wrote almost nothing about my death," he said.

"Nor ours," Washington replied. "Though I'm sure narratives are available. We only examined the perfunctory summaries."

"Cyclopedia printers should plan on our return to the future and write their articles accordingly."

Washington laughed. "Good luck with that."

"There were minor errata in my biography, but few major ones. Were yours generally accurate as well?"

Washington and Jefferson nodded, the latter morosely.

"It is chilling to review history articles about oneself," Franklin said.

Washington nodded. "Reading about yourself in a paper is one thing, but I find articles drawn by posterity almost . . . almost . . . a tad bit . . . frightening."

"To me they seemed somewhat sacrilegious," Jefferson said. "I almost felt like . . . not a criminal, not a conspirator, but . . . an intruder. Reading my biography almost made me feel that we shouldn't be here."

"We won't be here much longer," Washington replied. "It is eight of the clock now. After the town tames, we must commute to Rapid City."

While Jefferson tangled himself in the World Wide Web, Washington mimicked Franklin and lay on a bed. "You don't seem especially anxious to use this computer," he said.

"Nor do you," Franklin replied.

"I am champing for another turn. But Tom reads and learns faster. It is sensible to allow him more ticks initially."

Franklin nodded. "I used the natural philosopher's computer today, so it is not as nouveau to me."

"Nothing seems as nouveau to you."

"I was as surprised as you, the first time I saw many of these wares."

"You are also a natural philosopher accustomed to studying new inventions and discoveries. This skill seems to give you a pronounced advantage in adapting to this future world."

Franklin smiled. "I too feel overwhelmed. My day was long, and this barrage of new discoveries was as draining as it was exhilarating."

"What of your tutor?" Washington asked.

The question was vague, but Franklin understood its crux. Washington was concerned about discovery.

Franklin summarized the Rushmore visit and the encounter with the Samaritan. Washington surprised him by listening in silence. "Foolish," he accused, when Franklin finished.

"Perhaps. I will not defend my actions, nor will I apologize for them. I was trying to learn."

"Don't you mean teach?"

"The natural philosopher stared at my portrait and didn't recognize me, George. After that, a discussion of you and Tom hardly seemed an absurd risk."

Washington's entire body tensed as anger coursed through him. It took great effort, but he contained his temper. "Has Paul deduced your identity?"

"He suspects. But I don't think he can reconcile his suspicions. And I don't believe he'll act on them."

"But if he did?"

"I don't think he will," Franklin speculated. "In any event, my purchases grant us a certain mobility."

"Which we must now utilize immediately. Suppose your scientist acts on his suspicions. Suppose the family we angered is comparing our camera obscura images to those found on "sites" on their computer? Suppose futuristic inventions we have no conception of are being employed in investigation as we speak?"

"I don't dispute these risks. Nor shall I attempt to trivialize them."

Washington and Franklin glanced at each other, and without uttering another word of discussion, began packing.

As THE PICK-UP truck approached a traffic light and slowed, the wind's turbulent howling abated and conversation once again became a reasonable proposition.

"The interior of a taxi would have been preferable to the exposed exterior of this vehicle," Franklin said.

Washington scowled. "Your visit to Rushmore denied us that luxury. The family knows we do not have a car. A constable trying to find us might consult taxi pilots."

Jefferson lacked Franklin's fat, and Washington's acquired elemental immunity. "I'm fa-fa-fa-freezing," he shivered. "Old m-m-m-men grow ch-ch-ch-chilled very easily."

"You cast the tie-breaking vote in favor of this decision," Franklin said. "So stop sniveling."

Jefferson stopped his teeth from chattering long enough to say, "I didn't know it'd be this cold."

"Sorry," Franklin said, as the stoplight turned green and the truck once again accelerated. "I don't speak shiver."

THE TRUCK STOPPED at the Wal-Mart and Franklin annoyed Washington by asking the driver if he could shop with him. He glanced at the First American's shrinking form with concern, then faced Jefferson and said, "What do you think of this future so far?"

"A premature question." Jefferson replied. "I have barely left our tavern rooms."

"With this TV, computer, and phone, you have nonetheless explored this world. In some ways, more than Ben. My mind is no match for yours, Tom. We've had strong disagreements, but I've always respected your intelligence."

What about the rest of me? Jefferson thought.

"You're an optimistic man," Washington said. "Why are you so negative about a society which seems so free and bountiful?"

"The notes, first and foremost."

"Besides the notes."

"This 16th amendment petrifies me. It could ruin a republic single-handedly, even if the currency were honest."

"Besides the notes and this tax on income."

"Hardly trivial omissions. They constitute the bulk of my concern."

"Humor me. Please."

"The violent gladiator contests, the enormous variation in Watt wagons, the family's remarks about education and politicians being corrupted, the nigger family's hatred, the television advertisements, Franklin's soap description, nigger American citizens, and of course, the notes and the income capitation."

"For every negative you list, I could mention a positive. The invention, the republic's mere existence, the prosperity."

"You misunderstand me," Jefferson said.

People who misunderstand you, Washington thought. *There's an exclusive junto.*

"This new civilization possesses many admirable traits," Jefferson said. "I did not metamorphose into a pessimist, but I have focused on problems. In battle, do you not give attention to weakening lines rather than those routing the enemy?"

Washington nodded. "Fair enough."

"I have confidence in my assessments, George. We are discovering follies which result in labefaction whenever they appear in history, without exception.

The causes which effect the ruin of nations may seem different from era to era, but they do not really change."

"Could natural philosophy advancements alter a society so much it became an exception? Might new rules apply?"

"A theoretical possibility," Jefferson conceded. "To accept it, I require decisive proof, and as that is absent, I will adhere to the timeless lessons history teaches. The nation which thinks itself an exception most quickly proves the rule."

Washington smiled.

So did Jefferson. "You are still skeptical. Suppose Cicero had been brought to our old time. He might have marveled at cannons, telescopes, and printing presses, noted that life had become easier and more luxurious, and assumed he was in a golden age. We realized corruption existed, and would have disagreed with him."

"That allegory is too simplistic," Washington replied. "It does not translate into our situation exactly."

"So you think, because you are awed by futuristic natural philosophy, like Cicero. But who can judge their present with omniscient objectivity?"

"Geniuses like you and Ben, I'm hoping. Once you understand this civilization more fully."

"Perhaps. But the humble and more realistic answer is no one. That is why we turn to history for guidance and wisdom."

"What does history teach that concerns you so much?" Washington asked. "Please educate me."

Jefferson peered at Washington with great intensity. "One of history's paramount lessons is that republics can endure only if they avoid corruption by those two great temptresses, empire and bureaucracy." A deep sigh. "It is odd to admit this to you, a man incapable of fear. But I am affrighted, George. Grievously affrighted. All morning I wanted to research notes and taxation but could not bring myself to do so."

Washington knew the answer, but nonetheless asked, "Why?"

"I fear America may have become an oligarchy's Elysium[88]. Free reign to depreciate currency *and* a direct, non-apportioned capitation? With either mechanism in place for an extended period of time, tyranny would take root. With both?" Jefferson shook his head rapidly.

"We suspect depreciation. It has not been proven. And we don't know the rate or methodology of the capitation."

"Skepticism can be a form of thickness."

---

88 Elysium. Roman heaven or paradise.

Washington glared.

Jefferson returned his glance evenly. "You still don't understand, do you? The most significant observation about *The Constitution* is what we didn't find. There is no amendment creating the Department of the Interior, or social security, whatever it is. No amendments that address airlines, Watt wagons, televisions, or other equally amazing advancements we have not seen, and could not have foreseen. Advancements government must have adapted to."

"The boundless field of power you prophesized."

"Yes! Implied powers are plants of rapid growth. If they remain rooted, America probably developed a most baneful vice: the habit of granting government new powers without amending *The Constitution*. If so, each new natural philosophy development, internal crisis, or external threat would grant government excuse for further usurpations."

Fear seized Washington's stomach and he felt a sudden chill.

"Our peculiar security was the possession of a written *Constitution*," Jefferson concluded. "I pray you, Hamilton, the Federalists, and futurity have not made it a blank paper by construction."

"So I am to blame for all of futurity's blunders?"

"You are certainly not blameless. Insatiable implied powers gorging on a boundless buffet of depreciation and capitation!" Jefferson's brow furrowed and his face glowed. "Such authority must never be given to government! No matter what the pragmatic necessity or idealistic intent! How could posterity be so foolish?"

"There is no need to grow warm," Washington said calmly. "Or loud."

Jefferson fumed silently.

"Anger is never without a reason," the returning Franklin counseled, "but seldom with a good one."

Jefferson smiled, and calmed. Franklin listened intently while the driver babbled about his divorce, and asked frequent questions that kept him focused on the narrative.

"So you predict empire and bureaucracy," Washington said, as the truck began moving.

Jefferson nodded. "I fear that as we research history and come to understand the republic's current condition, we will be appalled by what we find."

WASHINGTON DID NOT want the truck driver to know their destination; despite Franklin's objections, he insisted they be dropped almost ten blocks from their new hotel. Franklin was soon hobbling, so Washington carried his pack.

Though people they passed glanced at their backpacks, and Washington, whose muscularity and grace always elicited admiration, the flabbergasted stares they had endured near Rushmore were history. Even Washington relaxed somewhat.

Franklin's gout and stone made the ten-block trek seem like ten miles, but he did not complain and was unusually upbeat. The taverns he spied near the new hotel were of course coincidental.

Nine

THE NEW HOTEL room could have been the old; it looked the same, and the founders' previous activities had resumed, merely transferred to a different location.

The truck ride and walk aggravated his ailments, so Franklin used the computer immediately. At Paul's, he was unable to research critical topics because they would have created suspicion. Topics like gout, whose Yahoo search result was now being displayed:

> Gout cure . . . gout pain disappears like magic . . . topical cream for gout . . . total gout suppression therapy . . . MayoClinic.com: Gout . . . What is gout? . . . causes and symptoms of the illness, which is one of the most common forms of arthritis, as well as treatment options and self-care.

Two sentences leaped off the screen at Franklin:

> Goutin guarantees fast results. Be pain free in as little as 24 hours.

The second period was especially glaring. Why wasn't it an exclamation mark? It seemed haughty, and implied that the cure was trifling. Be pain free in as little as 24 hours. Yawn.

As he clicked a link and began to read, Franklin chuckled. A disease that had crippled him for more than a decade could now be cured in a day? A single bloody day!

> A small number of people with gout develop kidney stones . . .

Franklin leaned forward anxiously and clicked the kidney stone link. *Please!* he thought. *Let there be a cure for this too!*

> If you've ever passed a kidney stone, you're not likely to forget the experience—it can be excruciatingly painful.

Franklin laughed. *Thanks for the revelation. And if you've ever not been able to pass a kidney stone? For five years? If you'd endured trotting horses and a trip across the Atlantic in a tossing ship? How would you describe these "experiences"?*

> What's more, kidney stones (renal lithiasis) are a fairly common disorder and there's evidence these stones have plagued humans for millennia. Scientists have found traces of kidney stones in mummies more than 7,000 years old.

Franklin was once again awed and amused. Tidbits like this littered his reading, and were very telling. This civilization hadn't just determined the exact cause of stones, and cures, and methods of prevention. They'd traced them back to people that were probably older than the Bible.

As he read, Franklin continued to encounter futuristic terms that were meaningless to him:

Amino acid cystine, X-rays, arthritis, protein, calcium . . .

Might as well write those in Hebrew, he thought. Luckily, the articles appeared to be aimed at commoners, not natural philosophers, and meaning could be discerned without a clear understanding of the terminology.

FRANKLIN AND JEFFERSON were comparing their gout and stone notes, and explaining their discoveries to Washington. "Physicians called urologists specialize in treating stones," Jefferson said. "The most advanced remedy is called EWSL."

"What does EWSL stand for?" Washington asked.

"Something I cannot pronounce or comprehend. EWSL is advanced even for this time, and is a new invention. It uses sound to break the stone into tiny pieces that can be expelled. But it is not always effective. If it fails, riskier options like surgery are available, but these should be a last resort for a man of Ben's age, weight, and physical condition. Three urologists recommended EWSL as an initial remedy."

"Can Ben obtain the treatment in the morrow?"

Franklin shook his head. "EWSL only exists in major cities. Including Boston, Philadelphia, New York, and Your D.C."

"But the stone can be cured?" Washington asked.

"Yes," Jefferson replied. "The urologists seemed certain."

Franklin's sigh was orgasmic.

After he completed his medical research, Franklin typed "starkers" into the Yahoo search prompt. Hits for everything from Tokyo bands to dictionary definitions to gothic lingerie companies were returned. Franklin typed "starkers wenches."

"Really, Ben," Jefferson said. "Sometimes you are incorrigible. Do you honestly think humanity would squander an invention this powerful on starkers wenches?"

"Hopefully. I haven't lost all faith in the species. And you sound like Abigail Adams."

Abigail Adams was second President John Adams' wife. A staunch Quaker, she was mortified by France's promiscuousness, rampant prostitution and adultery, and Franklin's shameless flirtation with bold French women such as Helvetius.

Five starkers wenches hits were returned. "There have to be others," Franklin said.

"Adding a single word reduced your results from more than 10,000 to 5," Washington noted.

Franklin nodded. "Narrowing the scope of these searches takes great skill. Especially since dialect has changed."

The present problem was archetypal. If there were images of starkers wenches to be had, futuristic synonyms would have to be used to find them. Franklin checked online dictionary and thesaurus definitions of starkers and wenches, then typed, "naked women."

"1.5 million hits?" Jefferson gasped. "That's more than . . . more than . . ."

"More than anything I've seen so far." Franklin laughed. "For once, humanity did not disappoint."

"How vulgar," Jefferson said. He nonetheless sat down and pulled his chair closer. So did Washington.

"Really, Tom," Franklin said, as the first image loaded. He imitated Abigail Adams' expression and voice and waved an index finger reproachfully. "Sometimes you are incorrigible!"

"Shouldn't we be researching the government?" Jefferson asked. "Or natural philosophy? Or history?"

"Probably," Franklin replied.

Jefferson blushed at the sight of the two entangled starkers wenches. "They aren't really . . . each other? They can't . . . ahhh . . . how vulgar!"

"Yes they can!" Franklin said. "And yes they are! Look at this next one!"

Jefferson turned away and covered his eyes, but Franklin's jovial laughter made him curious. He opened a slit in his fingers and peered through. "How lewd!"

And your affair with Hemings wasn't? Washington thought.

Franklin chuckled. "It is lewd. Lusciously lewd. Lavasciously lewd. Langu—"

"Your meaning is discernable," Jefferson said. "Barely."

"Such smorgasbords are not lewd. And you could have sampled such fares in France. If you had followed my advice."

"You mean lead."

Franklin laughed. "Two score later and still a prude! After all this time, tell me you could at least greet one of my mistresses without scurrying away like a frightened child."

"I never scurried away like a frightened child. Adultery makes me uncomfortable."

"That I'll agree with. My mistresses always found your reaction amusing. And it wouldn't have been adultery for you in France! You were single! It would have been moral!"

"Not as bad as adultery, I grant you. But rogering multiple women at once is certainly immoral."

Washington's views were more moderate than those of his companions. He was aroused by the less vulgar images, saw no harm in viewing them, and wasn't conflicted like Jefferson. But he strongly disapproved of the *actions* Franklin advocated, especially adultery, and though he knew his friend was a lost cause in this regard, his sense of integrity demanded at least one disapproving comment. "Were you Emperor of the libertines?"

Franklin laughed. "President, not Emperor. Haven't you heard the proverb that rogering other wenches is not adultery if you are on a different continent than your wife?"

"Proverb sounds a bit optimistic," Washington replied.

"Axiom?"

"Definitely not. And I had heard country, not continent."

Franklin shrugged. "Even better."

An hour later, the founders were salivating from hunger as well as lust. Franklin stood, made no attempt to hide the enormous erection that deformed his pants, and said, "Shall we take some air and sup at a carvery?"

Washington decided not to comment. Franklin's roger wouldn't be a distraction for long. Not at his age. "Having food delivered here is safer."

"Going out would be more enjoyable," Franklin replied. "And more educational. Surely you tire of being caged in a room."

"What we tire of is unimportant," Washington countered.

"We're no longer near Rushmore," Franklin said.

"Yes we are."

"Is there a city on the Continent safe enough for supper?"

"Don't be absurd."

"Heed your own advice."

"Changing garments didn't eliminate our risk."

"Nothing will," Franklin replied. "Shall we become hermits?"

"My guiding strategic principle has always been to err on the side of caution."

"We're not planning a military campaign, George. This is supper we're talking about."

"This discussion is fruitless," Washington said.

"And meatless, breadless, and aleless."

"But not gutless. You could live on yours for a year. So stop acting like you've been at Valley Forge."

"We disagree and are both intractable," Franklin said.

"That much I concede."

Franklin and Washington looked at Jefferson, who said, "I vote to have food delivered. For selfish rather than strategic reasons. I wish to continue using the computer."

WASHINGTON LET FRANKLIN order dinner, but while the phone rang, he said, "No gluttony. One meal with modest remnants. If a buffet arrives, you'll be leaving."

"Can I sup on the buffet first?"

Washington laughed. "Don't make me knock you back to our past."

"Yes, you can help me," Franklin said into the phone. "I'll have eleven large pizzas."

Washington sighed as he approached.

Franklin grinned. "Just quizzing. One pizza and breadsticks."

Washington sat back down.

"Sixteen orders of breadsticks."

Washington stood.

"Sorry again. Make that one order of breadsticks."

Jefferson chuckled and shook his head. An ignorant observer would think he was seeing children, not two of the most prominent statesmen in American history.

"WHY THE SULLEN expression?" Franklin asked Jefferson. "Did more uninvited portraits of starkers wenches appear? I've told you to view them as gifts, not intrusions."

Jefferson shook his head, but said nothing.

"Slave got your tongue?" Franklin asked.

"That was his roger, not his tongue," Washington quipped.

Franklin chuckled under his breath as he approached Jefferson. The Sage of Monticello had entered "Treaty of Paris" into the computer, and was fixating morosely on the result:

Treaty of Paris, 1763
Treaty of Paris, 1783
Treaty of Paris, 1814–1815
Treaty of Paris, 1856
Treaty of Paris, 1898
Treaties of Paris, 1919–20

Descriptions followed. Franklin knew of the 1763 Treaty of Paris that ended the French & Indian War, and negotiated the 1783 vintage that concluded the American Revolution, but was ignorant about the newest quartet. "The 1814 treaty ended The Napoleonic Wars," he read. "You lived these?"

"And kept America out of them. They occurred during my Presidency." Jefferson shook his head. "Napoleon." A sigh. "The conflict was archetypal European madness."

"Thank Providence America had a wise leader like you who knew the value of neutrality," Franklin said.

Jefferson's eyes grew more despondent.

Now thoroughly intrigued, Franklin perused more quickly. The 1856 Paris peace ended a Crimean War involving Russia and Europe. No mention of America was made. "1898," he read. "The end of the Spanish American War. It may be foolish, but I feel pride seeing America mentioned as an equal to Spain."

"I felt it too," Jefferson conceded. "Momentarily."

Franklin nodded understanding as worry crept into him. Along with Britain and France, Spain was one of the colonial world's three major imperialist powers. "Was America defending against Spanish aggression, or did it become an imperialist?"

Jefferson shrugged. "I intended to research that question."

Intended? Franklin read the final entry, the Treaties of Paris, 1919–1920. Treaties. Plural. All other entries were singular. "Treaties of Paris ending World War I." Franklin glanced at Jefferson. "World War?"

Jefferson's smile was sanguine. "Not The World War, but World War I."

"You postulate a second? A third? A sequence?"

Jefferson shrugged again. "I'm affrighted to read more."

Franklin read the remainder of the entry. "The Treaties of Paris, 1919–1920, were ratified in six separate locations. Six separate treaties! A disheartening implication. The American Revolution and French & Indian Wars were massive, yet a single treaty ended each." Franklin paused. "Massive by our old reckoning of war perhaps."

Jefferson nodded. "The Napoleonic Wars dwarfed our Revolution or even the French & Indian Wars, but still only required two treaties."

"A World War," Franklin whispered. "A World War. A conflict so massive, so pervasive, that six major treaties were necessary to end it."

The First American peered into the Sage of Monticello's eyes and saw fear reflected back. Both men envisioned hyperbolic carnage created by armies utilizing futuristic inventions.

"Like trying to picture the airline," Jefferson said. "My conceptions feel fallacious and primitive, but I lack the prescience to correct them."

Franklin nodded. "A frustrating feeling. I have the vague yet intense sense that my visualization should be more sinister."

"Perhaps our inability to envision such scenes is proof of our humanity," Jefferson said.

"Or our ignorance."

"By Providence!" Washington gasped.

Franklin and Jefferson assumed he was commenting on World War. Until they turned and saw him scurrying up the bed to obtain a closer view of the television. Grateful for a reprieve from their morbid contemplation of war, they joined him.

"A wench Senator!" Washington said.

"United States or Amazonia?" Franklin joked.

"The former, I fear," Washington answered.

"C-span," Jefferson read.

"Though well shy of a C-cup," Franklin replied.

Washington and Jefferson were not familiar with bra sizes, so Franklin explained, but by the time he finished, the humor of the moment was lost.

"She looks decidedly masculine," Washington observed.

"I envisioned a wench in a dress," Franklin said.

"I envision the wench in a home raising children," Jefferson replied.

"Posterity clearly does not," Franklin countered.

Silence. Uncomfortable silence. As they watched the wench stand among her male superiors and speak about politics, the founders confronted their growing discomfort.

"Freed slaves I almost expected," Washington said. "Independent wenches with professions would be shocking enough. And I suppose it is inevitable that wench voters would eventually elect one of their own. But a bloody wench Senator!"

"Only once a month," Franklin replied. "Though hopefully not when treaties are being debated."

All three founders laughed heartily.

"Look at her masculine garments," Jefferson said. "She mimics males! As if trying to pass herself off as one. How unseemly."

"Logical, I suppose," Washington replied. "A shrewd wench trying to earn respect from males would beguile with her intellectual accomplishments rather than her physical wiles."

"A truly shrewd woman would do both," Franklin said. "She should be dressed like a baywench."

"In the United States Senate?" Washington replied. "That seems undignified."

Franklin laughed. "What could be more undignified than a wench Senator?"

"You seem distraught," Washington mocked. "Isn't this the wench equality you termed 'a logical evolvement for humanity'?"

Franklin pursed his lips. "Who raises her children?"

"Not a husband," Jefferson said. "What sort of eunuch would let his spouse govern while he played the wench?"

"Does she have a husband?" Franklin asked. "Or did she eat him like a mantid?"

"Perhaps she has a wife?" Jefferson said. "Have the courser vices of antiquity also been brought to the future?"

"Can two women now reproduce?" Franklin sprouted a perverted grin. "That would be fascinating to observe. Speaking as a natural philosopher."

Washington rolled his eyes.

"There are other intriguing possibilities in that vein," Franklin continued. "For a wench who takes the vein. A tarty strumpet could roger the federal electors and become President."

Washington and Jefferson once again laughed.

"The same principle might be applied to local elections," Franklin continued. "Male candidates gave spirits to voters, but a wench could improve the spirits of voters."

"Wenches have suffrage," Jefferson said. "What of them?"

"The Senator's husband? His reward for tolerating his wench? Or perhaps we change the term to wenches' sufferage?"

Washington and Jefferson laughed again. Franklin continued making quips until he exhausted his repertoire. Given his wit, this took many ticks. When he finished, the founders were no more comfortable with or accepting of wench equality. Like slavery centuries before, it was a repugnant reality they chose to ignore for a time.

"Amazing!" Jefferson said, as a male Senator spoke. "Every citizen can oversee government, be educated about its activities, and ensure its integrity! The advance of science truly allows posterity to govern with greater wisdom!"

Washington smiled. This was the Sage of Monticello at his best and worst. Optimistic, idealistic, and naïve.

"Legions of Americans might be scrutinizing our Senators at this very moment!" Jefferson continued.

"Americans may be watching their representatives," Franklin said, as he exchanged a knowing glance with Washington. "Or perhaps they prefer Survivors and baywenches."

"I WISH WE COULD sample other foods," Washington said.

"All commissaries that deliver serve such fare," Franklin replied. "Had my request been granted, so would yours."

"Little Caesar's," Washington read. "Julius Caesar?"

Jefferson's brow furled as he peered at the endearing pizza-box caricature. "Caesar was a tyrant and should be portrayed as such."

Franklin laughed. "I'm sure that would sell pizzas. Forget the praetexta[89]. Let's just pray."

"For what?" Washington asked.

"Et tu, George. Perhaps a carvery also bears your name and visage. Surely your portrait shames Caesar's."

"Et tu, Ben. Perhaps you're the cherubic caricature, not I. Our next meal may be from Big Franklin's. Or Big Ben's?"

Franklin took a large bite, flexed his belly outward, then smiled with his mouth full. "Whow's that wor a waricature?"

Washington and Jefferson laughed.

"Merchants will exploit anything and anyone for profit," Jefferson said. "Then and now, it seems."

"One of the few things time probably hasn't changed," Franklin replied, after he swallowed. "If Caesar were here he'd probably demand a share of the profit."

"An interesting conjecture, Big Ben."

"Yes, George, it is. Could Caesar be here?"

"Such tyrants belong in the past," Jefferson said. "Washington non alia iacta est.[90]"

---

89 Praetexta. A purple-bordered toga once worn by Roman magistrates and priests. It was a sign of status.

90 Washington non iacta alea est. Iacta alea est is Latin for "the die has been cast," the infamous quote spoken by Julius Caesar when he crossed the Rubicon River with his army and seized the city of Rome. This crossing was forbidden by Roman law, and in doing so, Caesar usurped power, murdering the Roman Republic. Washington non iacta alea est means Washington would not cast the die. That is, Washington would never usurp power.

Franklin smiled. "Our American Cincinnatus[91]. What is it Chastellux[92] wrote? 'He has commanded the army for seven years and still obeys Congress: more need not be said.' "

"I agree with Chastellux," Washington whispered. "More need not be said."

"I must respectfully disagree," Jefferson replied. "The moderation and virtue of a single character probably prevented the American Revolution from being closed, as most others have been, by a subversion of that liberty it was intended to establish."

A lesser man would have gloated, and a younger Washington might have telegrammed pride, but the elder American Father did neither. "You speak of Franklin?" he teased.

Franklin exhaled sharply, and pursed his lips so tightly his cheeks creased. *Absurd*, his expression said.

"I speak of Lewis Nicola," Jefferson replied.

Washington's eyes burned with anger as he recalled Nicola's 1782 letter. Written not by a British enemy, but an American officer! Colonel Nicola had asked him to create and head a United States Constitutional Monarchy.

"King Washington it would have been," Franklin whispered. "If you had acquiesced."

Jefferson nodded. "Support for such folly was more widespread than it is comfortable to admit."

"Would you have opposed me?" Washington asked Franklin.

"Of course. But not successfully. No one could have."

"Nicola could not have found a person to whom his schemes were more disagreeable," Washington hissed. "When I assumed the soldier, I did not lay aside the citizen. Instead of thinking myself freed from all civil obligations by the mark of confidence command represented, I constantly bore in mind that as the sword was the last resort for the preservation of our liberties, so it had to be the first to be laid aside when those liberties were firmly established."

"This is an important historical point," Jefferson said. "Has your priceless precedent of obedience to civilian authority endured?"

"If it had not, America would not have," Franklin replied. "And the fact that Caesar belongs in the past doesn't mean he resides there. One could apply similar logic to our situation."

"Logic and our situation still seem oppugnant[93]," Jefferson replied.

---

91 Cincinnatus. Lucius Quinctius Cincinnatus. Famous Roman farmer-soldier who accepted appointment as Dictator in time of national crisis, vanquished enemies that threatened Rome, then relinquished power and once again became a private citizen.

92 Chastellux. Chevalier de Chastellux. French military officer and philosopher who was third in command of the French forces at Yorktown.

93 Oppugnant. Opposite or opposing.

"To the natural philosopher as well as us." Franklin explained time dilation and special relativity. His rudimentary understanding and easily confused companions forced him to dumb the topic down. He concluded with an admission; asking about time transport was risky, but the knowledge obtained had been worth the risk by the most cautious reckoning.

"So this era's natural philosophy cannot explain how our travel here might have been facilitated," Washington said.

"Correct," Franklin responded.

"And no time travel invention exists?"

"Correct again," Franklin replied. "There is also no theory. A future natural philosopher has not derived laws of time transport the way Newton did mechanics and gravitation."

"What of these past paradoxes?" Washington asked. "Do they also result from travel to the future?"

"I wanted to ask that question, but it seemed too risky.

"It is good to know your audacity has some limit."

"I do not think transport to the future creates paradoxes," Franklin said. "In an absurdly technical way, our presence here seems logical."

"If travel to the past creates paradoxes, we can never return home," Jefferson reasoned.

"I would not want to," Franklin said. "Except for a quick visit. And I might not chance that, for fear of being stranded in our past."

"We are from the past originally," Washington noted. "Would returning be different for us than someone born in this time?"

"We now have knowledge of the future which we could use to create paradoxes," Jefferson said.

"What if this knowledge is eradicated prior to return?" Washington asked. "Our present memories contain contradictions, after all."

"We must concede our ignorance," Jefferson said. "To the totally ignorant, anything is possible and nothing isn't."

"We're bastards," Franklin laughed. "Temporal bastards."

"Bastards or not, we're most probably marooned," Jefferson replied.

"Permanent citizens of the future perhaps," Franklin said. "But the term marooned has a connotation I refute."

"You refuted my diction, but not my supposition. Do you think we can return to our past?"

Franklin shook his head. "Like us, I think nature abhors ex-post-facto laws[94].

---

94 Ex-post-facto laws. Retroactive laws which criminalize acts that were not illegal when committed. Ex post facto is Latin for "from a thing done afterward." *The United States Constitution* states, "No Bill of Attainder or ex post facto Law shall be passed." In Article 1, Section 10, Clause 1, it further decrees, "No State shall . . . pass any . . . ex post facto Law." American state and federal governments are denied the power.

But I do not think paradoxes are the most fundamental point. You are thinking like a lawyer rather than a natural philosopher, pondering time transport in theoretical rather than mechanistic terms. This seems to be an erratum. To me, the day's most intriguing revelation is time dilation. This future's natural philosophers have quantified the effect, but cannot explain the causative physical mechanism."

"You believe the time dilation impetus might also facilitate time transport?" Jefferson blurted.

Franklin smiled as he grabbed another slice of pizza. "Possibly. Time will tell. Now enough of my rudimentary speculations. What did you two emaciates do today?"

"You're certain futurity discards parchment plates after one use?" Washington asked. "The practice seems extravagant."

As Franklin nodded, he thought of the cocoons on most wares, the destitute citizen at the street corner, and Paul's description of global poverty.

Washington flexed his powerful arms and the pizza box compacted as if hit by a cannon. "This future requires adjustment," he agreed. "I don't think I'll ever be able to throw parchment out without feeling profligate."

Jefferson nodded and peered at the brimming trashcan. "We have produced more waste in a day than Monticello did in a fortnight."

"What is done with all this parchment excrement?" Washington wondered. "Is it destroyed?"

Jefferson shook his head. "It must be reused somehow. A civilization this advanced couldn't possibly be so wasteful."

While dinner settled, Franklin made a terse dash through the description of his day. Many of his risky decisions aggravated Washington, but he was too engrossed in the narrative to chide. Ben certainly could tell a story!

"The progression of knowledge and invention has been phenomenal," Franklin concluded. "This remains my most fundamental impression. In our era it was possible for a genius to be knowledgeable in most scientific, military, and political fields, but in this one, such a task would be folly for scores of Newtons. This future is awash in oceans of information that could drown a scholar; we will have to be *very* selective about what we choose to learn."

"A division of labor would be useful," Washington suggested. "I could focus on military history and wars."

"Natural philosophy would be logical for me," Franklin reasoned.

"I'll handle politics and government," Jefferson said. "And provide a general historical overview."

"Don't stray too much," Franklin warned.

"I won't, and that admonition is useful for all of us. Curiosity can be powerful, but we must be disciplined in our research and adhere to our chosen topics."

"All of natural philosophy?" Franklin laughed. "I wouldn't have time to stray even if I wanted to."

As Jefferson organized the room with typical meticulousness, Franklin took one of the long, hot baths that were his only real reprieve from the pain of his gout and stone. The ability to do so by merely turning a handle once again highlighted the difference between past and present.

While he bathed, Franklin read the multi-colored *USA Today*. There was a national newspaper! Printed in color! In colonial times most national publications were government mouthpieces. Was this *USA Today* independent? Franklin didn't know enough about futurity to tell, so he read with skepticism.

A first amendment editorial piece caused Franklin to pause suddenly. "There is one incident I forgot to mention," he yelled.

After Washington and Jefferson approached the necessary, Franklin summarized the quote in which Rushmore's sculptor had likened them to gods.

"The comparison is offensive," Jefferson groaned.

Franklin laughed. "I thought you'd be flattered. Is this not proof of Jeffersonanity?"

"If these moderners think us Gods, then hopefully they have obeyed our Bible, *The Constitution*."

"That sounds like dogma," Franklin joked.

"Whatever you term it, the comment increases my desire to stay hidden," Washington said.

"Gods can wish for anonymity," Franklin replied. "But if they returned to the world they had created, wouldn't they eventually stand out and be discovered? And once discovered, how could they avoid being worshipped?"

While Franklin resumed his reading, Washington surfed the web. He wanted to learn more about the fate of his nephew Bushrod, his obese stepson "Tub," his Secretary of War and close friend Henry Knox, Lafayette, Hamilton, and others, but researching potential destinations was more important. Washington wondered about his loved ones while the New York City web page loaded.

When Jefferson finished cleaning, he joined Washington.

"You pilot the computer," America's Father commanded. "You can insert words faster and have a knack for phrasing queries precisely.

Jefferson obeyed. "How shall we proceed?" he asked.

"We shall assemble a large list of potential destinations, and study them one by one."

"ARE YOU DONE?" Jefferson asked politely.

Washington shook his head. Jefferson read much faster than him, and had completed most articles well before him.

Washington finished reading about Las Vegas, checked it off the city list, rose, placed his hands on his lower back, stretched by leaning backward, then rubbed his eyes. "Don't you have a headache?"

Jefferson shook his head absently. "Though wonders like the Hoover Dam and Grand Canyon are alluring, none of the Western settlements seem like wise destinations."

"Our time was nonetheless well spent. What we suspected we now know."

WASHINGTON BEGAN the meeting with the unsettling question, "Shall we stay together?"

"Why would we part?" Franklin replied.

"Do you wish to split?" Jefferson asked.

"No," Washington replied. "But logic demands this course be considered. More importantly, offered."

"Unity is still our great strength," Jefferson said. "As it was the colonies'."

"I doubt better companions are to be found in any time," Franklin added.

Washington nodded, summarized the internet city search quickly, then said, "New York still seems the optimal destination."

"I favor Your D.C. to the Newest York," Franklin replied. "These Smithsonian Museums could save us weeks of research, and would be an ideal place to see history."

"And for history to be seen," Washington countered. He picked up the city list. "There are a dozen locations I would risk before D.C. And I still favor New York."

"Were New York not an option, I would also favor D.C.," Jefferson said. "But the former is safer, contains everything we need, and most of what we want."

"New York, then," Washington said. "We leave in the morrow."

"SCORES OF TICKETS to New York and Your D.C. are still available and should be in the morrow," Jefferson said, as he hung up the phone. "Taxis are also available beginning at 6:00 AM."

Washington's eyes bulged with awe as the computer's futuristic press scribed its first page. "By Providence this magic press is tiny! And fast! I could never draw that quickly!"

Franklin thought of the faster printers he had seen and smiled.

"What amuses you?" Jefferson asked.

Franklin answered while he examined the sheet:

Greyhound
TICKET CENTER
① Where ② When ③ Schedules ④ Fares ⑤ Buy

Your Selections

Travel	From	Date	To	Miles	Passengers
One Way	Rapid City, SD	9/7/01	New York GW Bridge, NY	1892	1

Location & hours info: Rapid City, SD | Location & hours info: New York GW Bridge, NY

To change your selections, go back to previous steps.

Select Departure Schedule for Friday, September 7, 2001

Select	Departs	Arrives	Duration	Transfers	Carrier	Schedule
◉	09:45a	10:45a	1d, 23h, 0m	3	JL	0702
			d=day h=hour m=minute		JL: JEFFERSON LINES, INC.	

"Jefferson lines?" Washington said.

"GW Bridge?" Jefferson replied.

"Eventually we will encounter something that doesn't bear your names," Franklin joked. "Or more improbably, something that bears mine. A gaol maybe? Or an asylum or brothel?"

"This is our ticket?" Washington asked

"No," Jefferson said. "But this will simplify the purchase of our tickets."

Washington smiled as he watched the press scribe. "This device probably simplifies a great many things."

Paper had to be fed into the press one sheet at a time, and though Franklin had significant difficulty succeeding in this task, he still seemed like a shaman to Jefferson and Washington.

The next sheet contained a list of New York tourist attractions: Carnegie Hall, the Empire State Building, the Federal Reserve Bank, the Aquarium, the Stock Exchange, Rockefeller Center, the United Nations Headquarters, the World Financial Center, and the World Trade Center.

"All is packed, sans the computer and the morrows' garments," Washington said.

"What now?" Franklin asked.

Washington smiled as he turned on the TV. "We relax."

"You fought in the clone wars?" the young man said.

Clone wars, Franklin thought. *Clone. Didn't Paul mention the term clone in passing once? Could Clone Wars be a dated term for World Wars?*

"I was once a Jedi Knight the same as your father," the white-haired man replied.

Jed-eye Knight, Washington thought. *Yet he wears no armor and no weapon is visible. He must have a weapon.*

"My father didn't fight in the wars," the young man said. "He was a navigator on a space freighter."

"That's what your Uncle told you. He didn't hold with your father's ideals. He thought he should stay home. Not gotten involved."

Washington and Jefferson exchanged a knowing glance. Lesser men had encouraged them to not get involved, to choose the seeming comfort of cowardice, never understanding that truly great men can never find solace in a lesser path.

"I wish I had known him," the boy said.

"He was a cunning warrior, and the best star pilot in the galaxy. I understand you've become quite a good pilot yourself. And he was a good friend. For over a thousand years the Jedi Knight protected the galaxy. Before the dark times. Before the Empire."

Is a *star pilot one who pilots ships among stars?* Washington wondered. *Are airlines the futuristic equivalent of a knight's horse?*

"How did my father die?" the boy asked.

"A young Jedi Knight named Darth Vader, who was a pupil of mine until he turned to evil, helped the Emperor hunt down and destroy the Jedi Knights. He betrayed and murdered your father. Vader was seduced by the Dark Side of the Force."

"The Force?"

Franklin pressed his glasses up on his nose and leaned forward intently.

"Yes, the Force is what gives a Jedi Knight his power. It's an energy field created by all living things. It surrounds us. Penetrates us. Binds the galaxy together. Which reminds me."

While Washington squinted and gaped at the surrounding air, Franklin pondered the electric fluid. Its resemblance to this "Force" was striking.

"Your father wanted you to have this when you were old enough, but your Uncle wouldn't allow it. He thought you'd follow Obi-Wan on some idealistic crusade."

The old man handed a metallic cylinder to the boy. "What is it?" he asked.

Washington's jaw hung slack and his eyes glistened with excitement. *Yes, what is it?*

When the boy activated the device, a bluish, cylindrical bolt of lightning leaped out, and persisted. The thunderous, foreign sizzling that accompanied the unsheathing caused Franklin to snap his neck back, but Washington simply gasped.

"It is a lightsaber. The weapon of a Jedi Knight. Not as random or clumsy as a blaster. An elegant weapon for a more civilized age."

World Wars in a more civilized age? Franklin thought.

As the boy swung the elegant weapon, Washington's eyes grew large. He seemed to salivate.

Franklin smiled. "Jeteye George?"

"Why did he sheath the lightning saber?" Washington growled. "We only saw it for a moment!"

Franklin watched the remainder of the scene, and was fascinated by the whistling AreToDeeTo oddity the old man talked to, but Washington could think of nothing but lightning sabers. He saw battles re-fought by colonials and redcoats utilizing the bluish weapons, and envisioned himself as a humbly-robed, modern Paladin who wielded it against enemies of the republic.

Washington shook the cobwebs of fantasy away, and stood purposefully. "I must obtain a lightning saber, and become expert in its use. No matter what the cost or the inconvenience."

"Who better to become a JetEye?" Franklin said. "You are an elegant weapon suitable for a civilized age."

"Elegant or no, I must find one."

A civilized age? Franklin pursed his lips. "I wonder, is this play fictitious?"

"The language and character names did seem allegorical." Washington shrugged. "No matter. Whether allegory or history, it used a prop that was undeniably real."

Franklin nodded. "I assumed posterity would tame lightning. But like other futuristic inventions, these sabers astound. When he unsheathed it! I've never heard such a sound!"

Franklin and Washington probably could have discussed the two minutes of play for as many hours, but when the commercials ended and the *Star Wars* resumed, they leaned forward and watched intently.

Jefferson envied Franklin's seeming ability to control his curiosity. He wanted to unwind and watch the TV, but could not abandon the internet. *I must learn all I can tonight*, he told himself. *There will be time enough for sleep on the bus, where I will not have use of the computer.*

"Are you finally researching taxation?" Washington asked.

"I was about to. What has you so excited?"

"A futuristic saber," Franklin answered. "Do I need to hide somewhere while you read about taxes?"

Jefferson smiled. "Pray that I was wrong and George and Hamilton were right."

"What's the worst you can envision?"

"For the national income capitation, or all taxes?"

"All taxes. Federal, state, and municipal. Internal and external. Direct and indirect. Surely this future's physiocrats have compiled some aggregate."

As was his nature when contemplating anything political, Jefferson assumed a philosophical perspective, and pondered historical precedent that included ancient Greece's 2–10% excise taxes, Caesar Augustus' 5% inheritance tax, and Julius Caesar's 1% sales tax. He knew civilizations began with low tax rates that facilitated an early period of growth and prosperity; as taxes were inevitably increased, late-stage corruption and decline resulted.

Taxation. More than any factor except external invasion, it would determine the American lifespan. Would the United States thrive for millenniums, or mere centuries? After two hundred years of existence, was it still in a prosperous era of low taxation, or a corrupt late-stage decline?

"We paid a two to three percent tax rate before the Revolution," Franklin said. "And six to nine percent prior to the Constitutional Convention. But I never lived to see America's early levels."

"The rich alone used imported articles, and on these alone the whole taxes of the General Federal Government were levied." Jefferson smiled. "The poor American who used nothing but what was made within his own farm or family, or within the United States, paid not a farthing of tax to the General Government."

Franklin nodded. "Your prediction?"

Jefferson thought a moment. "My initial inkling is a question rather than an answer. An educated, free people view taxation in terms of principles, and are apt to reject the most modest tax if it is not ethical. For the ignorant and enslaved, acceptance is a pragmatic accounting exercise rooted in material realities. If America is dominated by the former taxes will be low, and if it is filled with the latter they will be high."

"I asked for the worst you can envision."

Jefferson tapped his lanky index finger on his lip. The gesture was decidedly feminine. "I am trying to think like a tyrant, but doing so is difficult."

"Just imagine you're at Monticello," Franklin suggested.

Jefferson glared, but did not retort. "To constrain the brute force of the people, the European governments deem it necessary to keep them down by hard labor, poverty and ignorance, and to take from them, as from bees, so much of their earnings, as that unremitting labor shall be necessary to obtain a sufficient surplus to sustain a scanty and miserable life."

"The common run of this era does not seem to live a scanty and miserable life," Franklin said. "A significant percentage of their production could probably be tithed and they would still enjoy an existence our common run would consider luxury."

"The underlying principle is nonetheless the same," Jefferson countered. "A talented tyrant has an acute sense of the maximum tax level his serfs will tolerate."

Washington shook his head. "Once they abandon principle, a people will tolerate endless usurpations."

"A corrupted populace will tolerate excessive usurpations," Jefferson agreed. "But not endless usurpations. The most oppressed people still have a snapping point."

"What is futurity's snapping point?" Franklin asked.

Jefferson sighed deeply. "This era's natural philosophic advancements are difficult to account for. It would be foolish to simplistically assume that the tax rates we considered excessive are so to futurity. As you observed, physical necessities can be obtained with less work, so higher tax rates might be tolerated. Also, inventions like automobiles, computers, and airplanes may mandate civic expenditures which our era was immune to." Another sigh, then a tick of silence. "Drastically lower rates have historically led to revolts, but . . . All taxes, federal, state and municipal, internal and external, direct and indirect . . . Twenty percent."

"Twenty percent!" Franklin whistled.

"You asked for the worst I can envision."

"I won't do that again." Franklin laughed, then frowned. "A twenty percent confiscation! From the common run!"

"That would be tyranny for any run," Washington agreed.

"Your guess?" Jefferson said to Franklin.

"Like you, I had great difficulty assigning a cipher, but any guess I made would have been *well* under twenty percent."

"As would mine," Washington added. "Your prognostication staggers the faculties."

"Enough speculation," Jefferson said. He typed his query, and hit enter.

The founders leaned forward expectantly and a palpable tension filled the room. The trio realized that its aggregate tax rate was the most fundamental indication of a republic's health and character. The barometer would transcend time and natural philosophic change, giving an immediate sense of the size of government. As government could gain power only at the expense of individuals, a society's tax level was also a direct measure of how much liberty its citizens enjoyed.

The web page finally loaded. As they read it, the founders' jaws dropped open and color drained from their faces.

"THE LIEUTENANT wants us to be on the lookout for George Washington, Benjamin Franklin, and Thomas Jefferson," the lithe cop in the passenger seat said.

"That some kind of joke?" his muscular partner asked.

"No, man. Not at all. Apparently, a family complained." He summarized the incident.

"Probably tourists who watched *Point Break* or *North by Northwest* too many times."

"One was a cop."

"Really?"

"Really."

"Maybe that B&E at the hotel was Lincoln," Muscles suggested.

"Sounds more like Roosevelt's M.O."

They laughed.

The patrol car passed the hotel the founding fathers had stayed in, and headed up the hill to Rushmore, which soon became visible.

"That's a trip to think about though," Lithe said. "If the founders were really here . . . What do you think they'd do? Try and reform things?"

"They'd suck it up and work and pay taxes like everyone else."

Lithe laughed. "Imaginative as always."

"I know you just moved here, but I grew up near Rushmore. I've had this conversation like a jillion times."

"That means you should have some pithy insights," Lithe said. "Come on, man. Don't play possum. What do you think?"

"I think this is modern America for you. They've got us looking for Washington and Jefferson when we should be arresting fucks like Clinton and Bush."

"These rates must be an erratum," Washington said.

"Satire?" Franklin suggested. "A joke?"

"Hopefully," Washington replied. "Let's check several sources."

Thomas Jefferson felt ambuscaded. Not sobbing took great effort. A 10% to 38% federal income capitation! 6.2% for the Social Security he had phoned! Yet another 1.45% for something called Medicare! State income capitations were as high as 9%, in addition to state sales taxes that topped out just below 8%! Local property capitations siphoned another 1–3% of the common run's income, and additional taxes tithed liquor, tobacco, gasoline, cars, licenses, airline tickets, phones, roads, imports, corporations . . . He found so many taxes he stopped searching for new ones.

Franklin patted his friend on the shoulder as an act of consolation. He tried to concoct a comment to provide levity, but nothing came to mind.

Jefferson laughed morosely. "When you have nothing to say things are definitely grim."

Franklin peered at the list and noted the 18–55% federal estate tax. "I said death and taxes, not a death tax."

"It appears that people are being taxed to death," Washington replied.

"And after it. Even the undiscovered country no longer offers a reprieve." Jefferson closed his eyes and cradled his forehead in his hand. "A local, state, and federal Cerberus[95]. Three blankets of government, each smothering people more than the last."

"It's not a hydra yet," Franklin said. "I don't see a global tax. You'd think in a world this taxhappy, this United Nations would tithe also."

"Taxhappy." Jefferson shook his head.

Franklin forced a smile. "One of the natural philosopher's terms. An oxymoron for this new time."

"35% of the output of the entire American nation!" Washington read with stupefaction. "More than four months of the nation's labor, per annum!" He leaned forward and punched the wall suddenly. "As Surveyor of Culpepper County, I paid one sixth of my income to the College of William and Mary."

"That was a fee paid to the Crown as compensation for a lucrative wealth-generating appointment," Jefferson said. "These are uniformly applied taxes."

Washington nodded. "Had you told me American futurity would pay two to three times my one sixth rate, I would have thought you ripe for Bedlam."

---

95 Cerberus. In mythology, the three-headed dog that guarded the entrance to Hades.

"From two to three points, to two to three score." Franklin shook his head. "Paying taxes so onerous would make one ripe for Bedlam."

Washington swallowed hard, and nodded.

"You look ill," Franklin said.

"I feel ill," Washington replied. "That the common run would submit to such tyranny is unfathomable"

"The most chilling reality is not the rates," Jefferson said, "but their acceptance. Why are Americans not rebelling?"

"Don't you mean protesting to Congress?" Washington chided.

"I'm reminded of Parliament, when I told the King there could be no taxation without representation. One must be careful what one wishes for." Franklin pursed his lips so tightly they turned red. "We could have submitted to the Townsend, Sugar, Stamp, and Tea taxes which precipitated the Revolutionary War a dozen times over. Our burden would still be less than futurity's."

Jefferson nodded. "It would have been better to accept the bad government offered us from beyond the water without the risk and expense of contest."

FRANKLIN AND WASHINGTON stewed for a stretch, but were soon drawn back into the Star Wars. They seemed grateful for the diversion.

Sitting alone in front of the computer, Jefferson sighed. Thinking about taxation made his chest tight.

Might as well learn about all the tyranny in one dose, he thought. The Sage of Monticello loaded the Federal Reserve web site. In mere ticks, his worst fears were confirmed.

"1913," JEFFERSON WHISPERED to himself. "In 1913 the Federal Reserve Act was passed. 1913! By Providence, I hope I'm wrong."

"About what?" Franklin asked.

Jefferson typed his Yahoo query feverishly. "The 16th amendment. When was it ratified?" His knee jackhammered anxiously. "Please. Providence. Please!" Yahoo once again had a flair for the dramatic, and took several more seconds to load. "The 16th Amendment was ratified in 1913. The same year the Federal Reserve Act passed."

Franklin's smile was sad. "A coincidence?" he joked.

As Jefferson relived the National Bank argument, he glanced at Washington. *The Republic owes its existence to you. How ironic that the same will be true of its demise! Why did your one great error have to be so monumental?*

Jefferson was struck by a sudden and powerful urge to lash out at Washington, to chastise him for his folly. *When you are angry count to ten before speaking*, he told himself. *One, two, three . . .*

"What is it, Tom?" Washington asked.

Eight, nine, ten. Jefferson felt no calmer. He sighed again and tried unsuccessfully to tune Washington out. *When you are extremely angry count to one hundred before speaking. One, two, three, four . . .*

"Speak, Tom," Washington said. "Please."

"They won. By Providence, they won." Jefferson's eyes were embers and he channeled his dejection into the empty tapestry of the wall. "I can feel the onset of one of my head achs."

Both Franklin and Washington were familiar with the ailment. For the bulk of his life, Jefferson enjoyed exceptional health, except for crippling migraines that surfaced during times of intense stress, and often incapacitated him totally, leaving him bedridden.

"I am sorry your achs still plague you," Franklin said.

"They haven't since I vacated the Presidency."

"Relax," Franklin said.

"I'm trying. But in the maw of tyrannies like these, doing so is difficult."

PAUL WAS SURFING the web, trying to determine if Benjamin Franklin had left fingerprints or DNA at places like Independence Hall in the 1700s. When he saw Steele or Franklin "in the morrow" he intended to make historical allusions that would make the latter nervous, record and photograph him, procure skin or hair samples, obtain signatures, and have him touch as many objects as possible.

This is insane! Paul told himself for the umpteenth time. *Steele isn't Benjamin Franklin! You've lost it!*

Maybe Steele is Franklin, maybe he isn't. But I've frittered entire days away on far more frivolous activities like video games and porn. If Steele's Steele, and not Franklin, I'm out an evening. Big deal.

Paul covered the technical bases, then closed his eyes and tried to think like a detective instead of a scientist. *If I was Benjamin Franklin, and I suddenly found myself in the future, what would I do?*

I'd remain anonymous while I educated myself.

Remain anonymous . . .

Remain anonymous . . .

Paul hit himself on the forehead with his palm. *If I'm Ben Franklin, I certainly wouldn't spend a second day with someone who might know my identity! I'd tell him we'll meet tomorrow but stand him up.*

Paul scowled at his uncertainty. Science was easy, but people were perplexing.

If I'm Franklin, I'm smart, which means I'm careful, especially in a future I don't understand. I vacate the hotel room my tutor knows the location of and head . . . head where?

Paul called the hotel, and rang Franklin's room several times. No one answered.

Paul cracked his knuckles, then a beer, and paced the room anxiously. *If I'm Franklin, where would I be?*

THE MOOD GREW morose. Even Franklin could not muster cheer. "We stagnate," he said. "And should find social environs."

"Taking air might ease my migraine," Jefferson said.

"If it aids your health, I would endure a trip to the pub."

"How selfless," Washington replied.

Franklin smiled. "Anything to assist a friend."

The usual caution argument began, but Franklin preempted it and said, "Don't bother with the usual objections, George. Just answer one question. Is this a democracy?"

"Our exploration should be run as a military operation, by a commander who is obeyed unquestionably."

"That wasn't my question. And I suppose that commander would be you?"

"I am the logical selection."

"Commanders must be appointed. Democratically. Would you ignore civil authority and usurp power?"

Washington's eyes narrowed. Franklin laughed. "That was a bit unfair."

"A bit?"

Franklin laughed harder. "Pennsylvania's army was a democracy. Companies elected their officers, officers of the companies elected regiment officers, and officers drew up rules of law and conduct which the men would sign, and was then binding."

"Pennsylvania's *militia* was a democracy. *Colonel* Franklin. Your militia enjoyed an excess of supplies and enlistment, and a shortage of desertion and combat. You had to defend against pockets of savage encroachment and isolated Spanish and French privateer molestations, not attack the most disciplined army in the world. It is a *Plain Truth* that if my army had invoked such misplaced idealism, we would never have won our independence."

"A *Plain Truth*, eh?" Franklin chuckled.

Washington smiled. Long before the Revolutionary War, Franklin's home state Pennsylvania was threatened by French and Spanish privateers and savages, but political infighting and general shortsightedness in the populace prevented it from mounting a defense. Concerned, Franklin published a 1747 pamphlet called *Plain Truth*, which outlined the foolishness of Pennsylvania's actions and advocated a private militia if the government failed to fund one. Franklin held meetings with influential citizens, galvanized public support, and succeeded in raising a statewide force of several thousand men. Philadelphia appointed Franklin commander of their regiment, and he served a brief stint as a Colonel before turning command over to a more qualified professional soldier.

"We are not your army," Jefferson said to Washington. "I prefer voting on an issue by issue basis. Like a polis[96]."

"Let's vote then," Franklin said. "The first order of business is the pub." He and Washington both peered at Jefferson.

"I favor a pub visit. If Washington attends and he and I determine the departure time."

"Leave a tavern before closing?" Franklin scoffed. "I see tyranny has once again reared its ugly head."

"Caution certainly hasn't," Washington said.

"You are outvoted."

"Our polis is ruled by a mindless mob," Washington growled. "Decisions like this epitomize the failings of democracy."

"If only we were a republic, and you our elected leader," Franklin mocked. "You could protect us from ourselves."

"Are you and Tom to command?" Washington replied. "O praeclarum custodem ovium ovium."

Jefferson smiled slightly. Washington had regurgitated his previous quote and substituted the second ovium for lupus. An excellent protector of sheep, sheep. The sentence was grammatically incorrect, but he did not want to push Washington any further.

"We are not sheep," Franklin said.

"But I am your shepherd if wolves threaten."

Washington considered incapacitating Jefferson and Franklin; though physically feasible, and highly desirable, the action was nonetheless unrealistic for moral reasons. So was Jefferson's polis. Washington knew he would be consistently outvoted by his philosopher companions, who had always gotten along well and had identical views on many issues.

"The tavern is within rods," Franklin said. "The walk will only take a few ticks, even for me."

"Caution accrues," Washington warned. "As does folly. This is ill advised."

Franklin smiled as he donned his coat. "Isn't democracy a wench?"

---

96 Polis. An ancient Greek city-state. Poleis were self-governing nations whose small size allowed them to implement one of the purest forms of democracy ever to exist. Utilizing a "town-hall" meeting style, the people commanded a council that performed all legislative, judicial, and executive functions. All major societal decisions were made at such meetings by direct votes of the masses.

THE PUB WAS DIM, smoke-filled and rustic. It seemed designed for outdoorsmen, and the chubby suburbanites that filled it appeared out of place.

Patrons peered at the founders when they entered. Interest in Franklin and Jefferson faded quickly, but Washington's regal stature elicited periodic stares.

"You should ply your hard-earned expertise and order the spirits," Jefferson said to Franklin.

Washington selected a table in a shadowy corner that provided a clear view of the door. He and Jefferson sat and observed Franklin as he approached the bar.

"Do you have ID?" the bartender asked.

"Eye-dee?" Franklin replied. The portrait cards came to mind, but why would they be necessary for ale? Remnants of the 18th amendment perhaps?

"Just kidding." The bartender smiled. "What'll it be?"

"What do you recommend?"

"Budweiser's the most popular beer in America."

Franklin noted the "King of Beers" tap. "No."

"We've also got Corona, Guinness, Sam Adams, Hein—"

"Did you say Sam Adams?"

"Yep."

"As in American patriot Samuel Adams? As in, founder of the Sons of Liberty, drawer of the Circular Letter and organizer of the Boston Tea Party Samuel Adams?"

"I guess. I couldn't give you his bio. I just pour 'em."

"Three Samuel Adams." *That would have made the British cringe! One caused them trouble enough!*

While Franklin grabbed his beers, a young man standing next to him said, "Two pitchers of Bud."

"I need to see your ID, junior."

He imitated Franklin's perplexed expression. "ID?"

"I don't serve fetuses."

The man walked away from the bar dejectedly. Franklin walked with him. "I thought the 18th amendment was repealed."

"It's been twenty years of Prohibition for me. One more year till the promised land. Unless I get a fake ID."

"Is that difficult?"

"Naw, but I wouldn't risk it. There're enough places that don't card." He shook his head. "It's crazy though, if you think about it. I can't buy a beer in the country I might die defending!"

As he thought of time travel, Franklin agreed that the situation was preposterous.

"WHO IS YOUR new acquaintance?" Washington asked, when Franklin returned to the table.

"A soldier. In the Air Force."

"*Air Force*?" Washington replied.

Franklin nodded. "A modern military branch whose purview is airplanes and the sky, I presume. Maybe it has Eagles or Falcons that rival the Navy's Seals."

"Not Turkeys?" Washington quipped.

Franklin chuckled.

"The soldier seemed to like you," Jefferson said.

"I honed my diplomatic skills in pubs."

"I thought it was brothels," Washington replied.

Franklin laughed. "Those too. Wenches drive harder bargains than the most miserly ministers."

"No wine?" Jefferson asked.

"I would also prefer it," Washington added.

"None that I saw," Franklin replied. "But I think you'll approve of my ale selection." Washington and Jefferson examined their beers with bemused expressions. "It was Samuel Adams or the King of Beers. Not a taxing decision."

"Did you say the King's Beer?" Jefferson asked.

"The King of Beers. Superlative, not possessive."

"A rather tasteless descriptor."

"We'll never know if the same is true of the ale." Franklin stared at Adams' portrait and smiled wistfully. "Though radical, Sam was a true patriot. It's a shame his brewery failed. The ale was delicious."

Each man related tales about Adams, whose great knack was agitation. "Who else would have had the audacity to term the death of five men a Boston 'Massacre'?" Franklin asked.

The chuckles dissipated quickly. Recalling Adams made the founders remember their past, their lives, and their past lives. The nostalgia was palpable.

Franklin raised his beer. "To Sam. And other old friends who have 'past'."

"To Sam!" Three ales clinked and the founders drank deeply.

WASHINGTON SCRUTINIZED everyone who approached their table, offered endless admonitions to talk softly, and changed topics if someone seemed close enough to listen.

Jefferson observed niggers. None of the whites seemed to consider their presence odd, much less objectionable! Jefferson once again felt guilt about his inability to embrace equality, but couldn't quell his instincts, which told him niggers should be serving spirits, not drinking them.

While his friends fixated, Franklin continued to peruse women. His present quarry was a ravishing redhead in her mid twenties. "May I roger her back at the room?" he asked.

Washington shook his head, as he had for the previous several wenches. "You could be her grandfather."

"Don't you mean great, great, great, great grandfather?"

Washington chuckled. "That doesn't alter my crux. What would you do with her? Or try to do with her?"

"To her as well as with her." Franklin's face became an innuendo. "Though the things I envision would be inappropriate for a granddaughter."

"I wish John were here to chastise you," Jefferson said.

Franklin imitated the dour Adams skillfully. " 'At the age of seventy-odd, Franklin has lost neither his love of beauty nor his taste for it.' "

Jefferson and Washington laughed. They had both listened to Adams' appalled tales of Franklin's exploits. His disgust was usually funnier than the conquests themselves.

"If John had only learned to enjoy life more. He had a penchant for turning the pursuit of happiness into a morbid struggle." Another attractive woman walked by and Franklin sighed. "Speaking of morbid struggles. If you won't let me bed wenches, I might as well learn from males."

"It's they who won't let you, as well as I."

Franklin laughed, then sighed. "There are times when I could do without your honesty."

ADAMS' ANESTHESIA HAD numbed Franklin somewhat, and as he walked away, his limp was less pronounced. Washington smiled at the sight. "Ben is the only man I know who drinks and walks straighter."

"It would have been interesting to know him when he was a Water American," Jefferson replied.

In his youth, Franklin was a fit, ambitious man who shunned alcohol. After running away from home and traveling to Britain, he took a job at a large publisher that employed more than fifty printers. These British coworkers drank as much as six pints of ale per day on the job, and mocked the abstinent Franklin, calling him a "Water American". The printers claimed the ale gave them strength, but Franklin found the habit detestable, not to mention costly. He bought bread instead of ale, and saved the difference, which he often lent to broke coworkers who had exhausted their credit at local pubs. Printers were required to carry heavy form types up flights of stairs; one form type at a time was the norm, but Franklin gained notoriety by consistently carrying two. His coworkers were surprised to realize the "Water American" was stronger and wealthier than them. Franklin was always on time, always clearheaded, worked fast, and quickly acquired a reputation for diligence, prudence, and frugality; his boss favored him with special, lucrative jobs, and soon promoted him.

"At least spirits disgusted Ben at some point," Washington said. "I doubt they were ever repugnant to these commoners."

"Or most commoners, unfortunately."

At the bar, four men dropped shots in beers and slammed them. Jefferson and Washington watched with disdain. Neither man had ever felt the need to drink to excess, as the bulk of the common run did, and the behavior was foreign to them.

"Intemperance," Jefferson said. "Of all calamities, this is the greatest."

Washington nodded. "If I had a shilling for every soldier who returned from leave so sullied by whiskey that he was useless for days . . . or a pound for every promising officer who squandered his future in a bottle . . . Not to mention the scores of men my army disciplined for abandoning their posts to imbibe."

"At least ale is now favored. I am glad this beverage has become common instead of the whisky which used to kill a third of our citizens and ruin their families."

Washington nodded again. "I long to meet people. As Ben is. It will be good to leave in the morrow. And stop staring at the negroes. They are beginning to notice."

"I cannot help it," Jefferson replied. "I encountered free niggers in the North and in France, but for some reason they are more glaring here."

"Negroes," Washington corrected. "And learn to help it, lest they decide to instruct you in the art."

"This Air Force is fascinating," Franklin said, as he sat back down.

"Tell me everything you learned!" Washington replied.

"Vicarious regurgitation grows tiresome. You should be conversing with the soldier, learning in ticks what may take days otherwise. As I did with the natural philosopher."

Washington shook his head. "Too risky."

"Are you afraid?" Franklin teased.

"I am as scared as you are sober."

Franklin laughed. "I figured you might invoke your caution mantra, so I obtained the soldier's e-mail address. But why come to a pub if you're not going to meet anyone?" Franklin leaned forward and whispered. "Or the future, for that matter?"

"I didn't choose to come to the future," Washington replied. "Or this pub. I'll socialize eventually. When we're in a safer location."

"And I'll be done socializing," Franklin said, as he walked toward a group of middle-aged wenches. "Eventually."

Franklin talked to the women for almost a half hour, until they left for another bar. Several hugged him goodbye, and they made him promise to meet them later at their new location.

"Time hasn't reduced your ability to charm wenches," Jefferson said, as Franklin returned.

"Or your shyness around them," he replied. "Why did you not join me?"

"I was thinking."

"Thinking or fretting?"

"Both, I suppose. I am haunted by visions of the tyrannies this taxation must fund."

"We came here to prevent a migraine," Franklin said.

"I cannot stop pondering banking and taxation."

"I can."

"Are you not concerned?"

"Shall we convene a Constitutional Convention tonight? Relax and have a few ales. Or a few wenches. That bux—"

"Has anyone ever told you that you look like George Washington?" a voice said.

As he tensed, Washington tried to seem relaxed. "A resemblance has been noted on occasion."

"On occasion?" The stranger laughed while he completed his approach. "It's uncanny. And of all the places to meet you! Near Rushmore! Are you one of Washington's ancestors?"

"No, I am an actor who portrays him. My companion portrays Jefferson."

"Jefferson" offered a perfunctory nod.

"Do you work for Rushmore? I didn't see you at Rushmore. They aren't producing a play or something I missed, are they?"

"We are capturing images for an advertisement," Franklin said.

"Washington and Jefferson in front of Rushmore. Interesting. Who do you work for? Are you being filmed or photographed? And when? I'd love to bring my family and watch. Maybe catch you in costume. Will Lincoln and Roosevelt be there?"

Franklin answered questions and the tourist replenished them repeatedly. He eventually offered to buy the annoyance a drink, steered him toward the bar, then sent him packing with typical suaveness. When he returned, Washington said, "We're leaving immediately."

"Concur," Jefferson added.

Franklin followed without objection. "We need to visit the next pub anyway. The wenches await."

"So does a bus in the morrow," Washington growled.

"Every second here is a gift." Franklin switched to a whisper. "Suppose you woke up in the morrow back in 1797. What memories would you have, sans the inside of a room?"

"It is foolish to treat each day like one's last."

"You choose the other extreme, and act immortal. For Providence's sake, George! We are in a New World! Do you think Columbus sat in his boat when he discovered America?"

"What Columbus would have done is irrelevant. And if he had discovered the undiscovered country, he would have exercised greater caution."

"This future could be a finite gift. We must not squander it."

"Or our lives, freedom, or anonymity."

"Let the polis decide."

Washington sighed both before and after he was outvoted, and resigned himself to the assumption of additional unnecessary risks.

THE FOUNDERS FOLLOWED Franklin's wenches, pub-hopped, and eventually settled at a larger bar with a modest-sized dance floor, billiards, darts, and plenty of tables. It had space, yet was cozy.

The founders were sitting in a booth peering at the futuristic beeping dart board when a man walked by their table and did a double take. "Holy shit you look like George Washington! It's like Rushmore came to life."

"So they tell me," Washington replied dryly.

"Looking like Washington is hardly what I'd call a compliment," Franklin said.

Washington scowled and Jefferson smiled.

Washington answered the man's questions casually, told him they were actors who imitated the founding fathers, and gave polite yet terse answers that made it clear he wasn't feeling conversational. The man took the hint and didn't linger long.

"How many people have recognized us now?" Jefferson wondered. "Seven? Eight?"

"I told you," Franklin said to Washington. "We have nothing to worry about."

"Fooling a few individuals does not mean we have nothing to worry about. What if we stumble upon a historian? Or a cop? We should be in the room. In a new town, I will gladly socialize."

"I'll believe that when I observe it."

In colonial times, toasting was a more prominent and significant custom, and it was considered rude to refuse one; when Franklin raised his glass, Washington and Jefferson felt obligated and took small swallows.

"I need to ratify a Prohibition of sipping," Franklin groaned.

"I can't drink up the Delaware like you, Ben. Though I wish you hiked the way you drank."

Franklin laughed. "I wish drinking improved my hiking."

"How can you drink so much with a stone?"

"It provides incentive to imbibe. I have to be numb when I piss this much ale. Better to have the alcohol knock me out than the pain."

"I feel like we're back in Raleigh tavern again," Jefferson said.

"Hopefully this time we won't have to hatch a revolution," Washington replied.

Jefferson thought of the capitations and notes, but said nothing.

"Come on, George," Franklin said. "Take one drink that isn't wenchly. For Martha. For America. For your men. For bloody posterity. For something."

Washington raised a beer and took another tiny sip. Franklin rolled his eyes and groaned again. "Why come to the pub if we're just going to sit here like old men?"

"We are old men," Washington answered.

"You don't hike like an old man," Franklin retorted.

"And you sure as Providence don't drink like one."

Franklin laughed. "That's the spirit, George. You don't have to get wet like me, but let's drink an ale together."

Washington raised his bottle, and glanced at Jefferson, who also raised one. "To being unknown," he whispered.

"To being unknown," Franklin said.

Jefferson looked off into space suddenly. He once again thought of the capitation and the notes. *We should fight these tyrannies, not hide. We should announce ourselves to the world!* "To remaining unknown," he said flatly.

Washington fixed Jefferson with a steely glance. "And staying that way."

As Franklin dragged him toward another group of caucasian women, Jefferson remained distracted by an attractive nigger across the bar. She had just kissed a white man.

In public.

On the lips.

Deeply.

Jefferson knew Washington was watching from across the bar, and was careful not to telegram his disgust. As the nigger wrapped her arms around the caucasian's neck and they kissed again, he stifled amazement. In colonial America, such vulgarity would have been *unthinkable*.

More kisses for the nigger, and memories for Jefferson, who recalled the Hemings scandal during his Presidency, and French Minister Maurice Talleyrand. After Talleyrand scandalized Philadelphia by appearing in public with his mulatto mistress, he was blackballed from upper-echelon colonial society.

"Nice to meet you," a woman in her mid twenties said. "Mister?"

"Lincoln," Franklin answered. "Benjamin Lincoln. And you can skip the Mister. This is Thomas. Thomas Hamilton."

Jefferson scowled momentarily, then noted that the wenches seemed confused by Franklin's flirtation, as other women a quarter their age were.

"So, what do you do?" a different wench asked.

"I'm a printer," Franklin said. "Mr. Hamilton here is a priest."

When "Father" Hamilton once again scowled, the women realized Lincoln was probably teasing.

"I swear to Providence he's a priest!" Franklin said.

"And the Sam Adams in his hand?"

"He's just drinking tonight to treat a migraine."

"What gives him migraines?" a woman asked.

"Abstaining and being a priest."

The women laughed, and warmed up to Franklin slightly. He had seemed like a crusty old pervert at first, but that stereotype was fading quickly as his wit manifested.

Jefferson's participation in the conversation remained half-hearted because the nigger wench buzzed at the periphery of his vision. Guilt flared in him.

Here stood the world of equality he had championed in his youth, yet he still felt shock rather than joy, and nurtured an ingrained racial chicanery that remained instinctual.

As THE FOUNDERS headed to the bar's exit, they approached a small group of African-Americans whom Jefferson glanced at.

An innocuous action, seemingly.

A glance.

Jefferson did not stare, or glare, and in fact tried to hide his feelings.

But some contempts cannot be concealed.

The African-Americans saw Jefferson's disdain, and exchanged knowing glances. Modern racism wasn't the jail of slavery, segregation or lynching, but a white-padded room of affirmative action and political correctness. It was caucasians who feigned equality publicly while sabotaging it in their boardrooms and hearts. Honkeys who whispered nigger rather than shouting or abolishing the word, and whipped you with their eyes.

As Jefferson flogged the African-Americans again, the murky loch of his soul was illuminated momentarily, and they saw the monster clearly. This was no rabid Klansman, but an educated patriarch who seemed to transcend the emotion and ignorance most bigotry was based in. His glance was chilling because it indicted with empirical detachment. *I look down on you because reason demands it*, his eyes seemed to say. *I would prefer to respect you, but doing so is not logical.*

Jefferson lashed them yet again, and the African-Americans exchanged harsh glances. Though he dressed plainly, the racist had the bearing of an aristocrat, and was clearly refined. Old money, probably. The accrued wealth of generations, of nest eggs bequeathed by grandparents who had worked for themselves rather than masters.

To the African-Americans, Jefferson epitomized the kinder, gentler, new-and-improved bigotry that was a daily and lifelong affront; insidious, yet pervasive, it was a cunning oppression as degrading as a back seat on a bus, but far more difficult to combat.

Three staccato glances.

Mere seconds.

Then a spectacle-wearing African-American stood, faced Jefferson, and said, "What are you looking at?"

The nigger's cultivated English surprised Jefferson as much as his sudden intrusion. Every other futuristic nigger he'd heard spoke guttural, animalistic slang.

"Don't ignore me," the African-American said calmly. "I asked what you were looking at?"

Jefferson was petrified, and it showed. "I meant no insult," he stammered, as he made a beeline toward the door. "I apologize if any was construed."

Spectacles stepped in front of Jefferson. "That wasn't an answer."

As pub activity stopped and patrons stared, Washington joined Jefferson. He seemed to flow rather than walk, exuded calm confidence, and stared with eyes that could freeze a flame.

Jefferson's fear diminished greatly when Washington stood at his side, and the African-Americans could see why. The man was obviously not a fighter. He was a killer.

As Spectacles' companions assembled behind him, Jefferson apologized again.

"I don't want an apology," Spectacles replied.

"What do you want?" Washington asked

"To never receive dirty looks in the first place. Or insincere apologies for them. But I'll settle for the truth."

"Any slight my companion leveled was inadvertent," Washington said.

Spectacles exhaled contemptuously and shook his head. The African-Americans behind him snickered.

Washington surveyed the five stout negroes calmly, and said, "I would prefer to avoid violence."

"Is that what you think?" Spectacles replied. "That every black man who demands equality is looking for a fight?"

"We are sorry," Jefferson said again.

"Stop apologizing!" a dreadlocked African-American growled. "'Cause you don't mean it! You keep talkin' that bullshit, I'll make you sorry!"

"God damn right!" a bald African-American said. "You say one more word, I'll fuck you up. You heard me?"

Washington glanced around quickly. There was no way to the door, and even if there were, Franklin and Jefferson would be fodder en route and outside the bar. Washington considered his limited options, then said, "My friend looked at you the way he did because he considers you and your race inferior."

African-American eyes bulged like boners. Jaws freefell.

Washington balled his fists and raised his arms near his waist, high enough to attack more quickly, but low enough that they would not provoke aggression. "You said the truth is all you require. I have reluctantly given it to you."

His companions prepared to attack, but Spectacles raised a halting hand. How did you best bigotry? With the pacifism of MLK or a nuclear MX retaliation?

Spectacles peered into Washington's eyes. He saw callous honesty, not hatred.

"Fuck this!" Dreadlock brandished a beam of a fist. "I'm gonna beat these motherfuckers till they look like the Elephant Man!"

"No!" Spectacles barked sternly. He glared at his posse, then faced Washington, "I want to hear your friend admit it."

Jefferson paled and his eyebrows quivered. Washington resisted the urge to roll his eyes. Jefferson was truly a pitiful sight, one that might have been humorous under different circumstances.

"I do not think you inferior," Jefferson said.

"Then why do you look at us like circus chimps?" Spectacles replied.

Silence. Jefferson formulated many appeasing answers, but feared they might backfire.

"You're lying," Spectacles said.

"I am not."

"Yes, you are."

"No, sir. I must respectfully disagree."

On it went. Jefferson stammered a succession of apologies that made the African Americans progressively angrier.

Washington didn't know what to do. Both speaking and remaining silent seemed to anger the negroes. They couldn't flee. Violence seemed inevitable.

"Our friend will never make the admission you request," Franklin interrupted, "because he is a quixotic introvert, coward, and hypocrite."

Jefferson bristled.

The African-Americans smiled and relaxed slightly.

"You won't believe me," Franklin continued, "but were he younger and less prone to serious injury, we would allow you to administer a corporal, though not capital, punishment. A whipping, perhaps?"

Jefferson scowled. *I always instructed my overseers not to whip or beat my slaves, except in the most severe circumstances.*

"You're right," Bald said. "We don't believe you."

"I need this man healthy," Washington replied. "If need be, I will best you all to keep him that way."

Two African-Americans laughed, but Spectacles and Dreadlock remained stone faced, for they realized Washington was neither posturing, nor afraid.

"I am truly sorry for what we did to your people," Washington said. "And I give my oath never to administer a future injustice." A crisp nod that conveyed the respect of a bow. "This will be our final apology and will have to suffice."

Silence.

Tense silence.

As was often the case before a battle, thoughts sped, time slowed, and the air seemed to thicken.

Washington raised his arms slightly higher. He was willing to apologize, and because he had owned slaves and wished to remain anonymous, even be demeaned somewhat. But he would not boot-lick. *If the negroes knew we were slave owners from the past, their pugnacious attitude would be just. But they don't, so it isn't.*

As he peered at the five negroes and contemplated a fight that would seriously injure Jefferson and Franklin, Washington was seized by a sense of the bizarre. It was odd to face negroes who were equals rather than property. A slave behaving in such a manner would have been beaten, at best. Of course, this was why few slaves would have behaved in such a manner. Excepting uprising or anarchy, an analogous situation in the colonial south was *inconceivable.*

Spectacles assessed Washington, decided he was being genuine, then stepped out of his way. "That sincere sentiment in the heart of every caucasian is all I and my people have ever wanted."

Jefferson scurried toward the door, but it was impossible to approach it without also seeing the niggers, and out of fear, he glanced at Bald.

Lightning once again illuminated the loch. Bald lunged within inches of Jefferson's face. "Don't look at me like I'm your motherfuckin' house nigger!"

That was your grandfather, Jefferson thought, as he cowered like a battered wife and scurried forward. Immediately after thinking the thought, he was ravaged by guilt.

Bald raised a fist and seemed ready to maim Jefferson, but Washington flowed forward quickly with a wary glance. Bald saw something primal and pitiless in Washington. He lowered his fist not out of fear, but because he had a sudden realization: as this man was truly unafraid, he did not need to offer false apologies.

Washington was behind Jefferson in an instant, and cleared a path to the door with a glance. The trio hurried through and entered the safety of the night.

"I'm SURPRISED NO ONE in the pub drew a weapon," Franklin said, as the founders double-timed it away from the bar.

Washington and Jefferson nodded. Colonial Americans who witnessed a fight might not have intervened, but at least a few would have drawn pistols or knives so they were prepared for any eventuality.

"Perhaps George's prowess was a deterrent," Jefferson said.

"Or perhaps no one was armed," Franklin replied.

"A whole tavern?" Washington scoffed. "Preposterous."

Franklin and Jefferson didn't argue, but something had to account for the seeming molestability of futurity's residents.

"I saw no light sabers," Washington said.

"Perhaps they possessed more portable and powerful weapons," Franklin theorized.

"We return to the room," Washington commanded. "No votes, no arguments." He glared at Jefferson. "And no looking at negroes. Even if one turns white."

"I'll try."

"Do more than that," Washington growled. "And don't insult me with such weak words again."

LIGHT SPRAYED FROM streetlamps, and as the founders walked under them, their shadows danced. They were blocks from the bar, but still miles from their hotel.

While their shepherd tried to hail a cab, Franklin and Jefferson rehashed the confrontation with exhilaration that bordered on bravado. Washington remained nonchalant about the trivial incident and kept the chastising to a minimum. Caution had been validated, and would now be easier to enforce. This made the encounter almost worthwhile.

Franklin sensed Washington's pleasure and took a dim view of the inevitable long-term consequence, but Jefferson remained somewhat dazed. A nigger had threatened him! Interracial futurity was truly the asylum he had prophesized!

"You are distraught," Franklin noted, as he hobbled along. "Take comfort in the fact that the slaves you owned were probably more so."

"Am I supposed to find that amusing?"

Franklin laughed. "At least one of us does."

"America should have exiled the niggers the moment it freed them!" Jefferson hissed.

"Negroes," Franklin corrected.

"Niggers."

Washington's gait slowed and he glanced to his left warily. He was raising his hand for silence when a shadow once again danced. This time the whiteness that sprayed out was a man. A man with a gun. "Rabbit ears, motherfucker!"

"Rabbit ears?" Jefferson replied. "I am unfamiliar with your dictum."

"He's unfermiliar with our dictum," the Caucasian said, in a mocking, nasal voice.

Jefferson quivered as a shadow emerged from the shadows. The gargantuan nigger moved with fearsome grace, had arms like horse shoulders, and held a squarish, futuristic pistol.

"I don't think they want a history lesson," Franklin said, as he emptied his pockets.

"The watch too," Shadow commanded. "And the cell phone."

Franklin obeyed.

"The Grand Wizard here better flip them pockets too!" Caucasian said, as he aimed his gun at Jefferson.

Trembling, the Sage of Monticello obeyed.

Shadow turned his gun on Washington. "Give it up, bitch."

Washington's underbite jutted and his jaw muscle twitched. He peered into Shadow's cold eyes and saw a murderer.

"No IDs," Caucasian muttered, as he rifled through Jefferson and Franklin's wallets. "But all kinds of Benjamins. Fuckin' A! Goddaaaamn! These motherfuckers are rollin'!"

"Let me get that outya, or I'll put one inya." Shadow cocked his gun.

Washington knew capitulation was the wise course. They had the bulk of their funds in the room, and would not be broke, but the loss was nonetheless significant. And there was the principle. Cowardly acquiescence irked George Washington.

Shadow stepped forward confidently, extended his right arm, and placed his gun against Washington's forehead. "This is only a robbery. Don't make it a homicide."

Washington waited calmly. Experience was his ally. He knew all men in such situations had to survey their surroundings. Shadow could not stare at him indefinitely.

Having placed guns on craniums during myriad criminal enterprises, Shadow knew there were similarities of response. *Everyone* cowered, backed-up, or pulled their head away reflexively, even drug-crazed, penitentiary-hardened gangbangers. Everyone except this rod-backed quarry, whose contemptuous eyes bored with relentless pressure.

"Surrender your notes, George!" Franklin yelped. "For Providence's sake!"

Shadow pressed the gun harder. Washington resisted and kept his head straight. As his forehead throbbed, his eyes narrowed, becoming lizard-like.

Fucked up! Shadow thought. *I've got the drop on the motherfucker and I'm scared!* He wanted to retreat, but he realized his fearsome prey was also a fearless predator.

Each passing tick gave Washington confidence. Only amateurs hesitated.

"Let's just take what we've got and roll," Caucasian said.

"Naw. Fuck that!" Shadow's trigger-finger tensed, and so did he. *What kind of stone-cold motherfucker stares into a gun barrel and acts like he's in control? Just give me your goddamn money!*

When Shadow's eyes darted toward his partner, Washington ducked his head to the right and swung his left arm outward, diverting the gun.

The instant Shadow felt his weapon move, he fired. The gun roared inches from his face, but Washington did not flinch, nor did he reach for his left ear when the shot grazed it. Instead he pressed forward, clasped the barrel with his left hand and reached over with his right to control the gun hand. Shadow brought his unused arm forward on top of Washington's.

A shot rather than a laser, Franklin noted. *Are Star Wars' blasters fictional? Are light sabers?*

Breath bounced between Washington and Shadow as they grappled. Joined, they bobbed like a single, cumbersome creature struggling to keep its balance. The fulcrum of their precarious pivoting was the gun, which both men struggled to contain and control.

Shadow felt like a mountain battling the shearing force of wind and rain, gradually but inevitably being bested by his elemental opponent. *This guy is a fucking Titan*, he thought with dismay. *How can someone so old be so strong?*

Franklin and Jefferson noted Shadow's stunned expression. He was hardly the first to underestimate Washington's prowess. Jefferson recalled the story of Virginia's strongest man, who having bested all other competitors, taunted young Washington while he was reading under a tree; Washington rose, pinned him in moments with marrow-jarring force, and ignoring the cheers of the crowd, returned to his shade and book. Franklin remembered the forty-year-old Washington throwing the bar a huge margin farther than a conglomeration of athletes half his age. Other founders would have recalled other examples, but all knew Washington's strength was that rarest of legends: one that is impressive dressed in the naked truth, without makeup.

Though their conflict felt like minutes to Washington and Shadow, it was mere seconds. When Shadow fired his gun, Caucasian turned and aimed at Washington. As the shot would be point blank, there was little doubt about the result.

Jefferson wanted to charge forward bravely, but some physiological response overrode this desire. He felt physically ill suddenly, and stood motionless.

Franklin told himself to ignore the pain of gout, stone, and perhaps death, and ran toward Caucasian while screaming at the top of his lungs. His lame sprint was a plod. Caucasian turned and fired three shots. One sailed wide right, one whizzed past Franklin's head, and the third struck him in the chest just next to the armpit.

Jefferson gasped as Franklin fell back. The shock of his friend's shooting helped the Sage of Monticello overcome his cowardice, but he remained paralyzed by a combat weakness as fatal as fear: uncertainty. What to do? Fodder forward like Ben, leaving Washington two invalids to care for?

The rear portion of the pistol moved back and forth repeatedly, Franklin noted, as he careened downward. *Fascinating! Futurity's pistols are complex machines!*

Washington heard the shots; though only a few feet away, they were distant and peripheral. Killing his enemy was his only focus.

Washington had used his strength advantage to steadily improve his position and leverage against the gun. He freed it with a simultaneous twist and yank, then backpedaled immediately to prevent Shadow from retrieving it. While doing so, he heard a body hit the ground behind him and sensed a blur of motion to his left. Washington raised his gun arm while turning toward the motion.

After shooting Franklin, Caucasian turned back toward Washington.

The two men were turning toward each other simultaneously.

Washington was quicker. His weapon bored down while Caucasian's rotating turret was still fifteen degrees away.

Caucasian's surprise was complete. His partner played in the CFL and on a few NFL practice squads, and had bulked up in the pen'. How had an old man overpowered him so quickly?

George Washington hesitated long enough to make sure he wasn't shooting Franklin or Jefferson, then pulled the trigger. The shot was point blank. Caucasians' brains leapt out the side of his head and clung to the alley wall.

Washington felt no nervousness, no excitement, no remorse, no sense of shock or disgust. This was war, and he had long ago been desensitized to it. He was calm yet focused, and turned immediately to face Shadow, who grimaced but flexed and moved forward.

Washington was used to one-shot colonial pistols; presuming the gun useless, he threw it toward Caucasian's cadaver.

Shadow's eyes glowed with hope as he accelerated toward the airborne gun. *The pistol has fired repeatedly*, Washington realized. He knew he could not reach the weapon first, but nonetheless prepared to charge. By the time Shadow procured it, he would be upon him and their old melee would resume.

Washington was about to attack when he pictured Obi-Wan Kenobi slicing off an arm with his light saber. He envisioned Shadow using the weapon to dissever his charging form, and hesitated.

Shadow capitalized and caught the gun.

Washington was calm. As he noted the cowering form of Jefferson, he remembered his first few times in battle during the French & Indian War, when he saw other men petrified, felt more composed, and realized he was different.

Washington also pondered Providence. He flashed back to the Forbes campaign, when two close-quartered American lines accidentally fired at each other and he rode into the smoky crossfire and stopped the shooting; men on both sides fell, but he was unscathed. Washington relived scores of similar situations instantaneously. Always conspicuously brave in battle, he displayed daring bordering on folly, yet while those around him died in droves he had been spared. So many times, in so many manifest ways, he knew Providence had protected him for some divine purpose.

Washington now knew that purpose was to win the Revolution, found America, and shepherd its infancy. Providence had spared him so he could enshrine the liberties America was destined to propagate to all of humanity.

Yet that had been accomplished. Or had it? Had Providence brought him to the future, or was it some other force? Perhaps Providence was no longer protecting him.

The prospect was unsettling, but cowardice was not an option to George Washington. Early in his life, he had vowed to always be courageous. The common run liked to mythologize this ability, but it was primarily the result of unrelenting discipline. Initial iterations had not been easy, but each act of bravery built on the last, making the next easier, until the habit was ingrained and doing anything else was unthinkable.

George Washington was constantly mindful of the fact that it would only take one act of dishonor to permanently tarnish his fastidiously groomed reputation. A single instant of weakness would be remembered more than decades of sacrifice. Thus, as he stared down the barrel of the peculiarly square futuristic pistol, America's Father felt stark fear. He could not allow his reputation to suffer injury. Death was preferable.

"You're tough." Shadow smiled and his gold incisor sparkled in the streetlight. "But you ain't tougher than Teflon."

As Shadow aimed the gun, the dark voice that plagues all men spoke to Washington, telling him that because he was anonymous, he could flee without damaging his reputation. Washington smiled sardonically. Time travel and futurity had provided the most alluring justification for cowardice he had ever encountered! He was only mildly tempted. Fear of the public and posterity's condemnation had strengthened a bravery that was not always altruistic, but Washington was also motivated by a more fundamental desire to be true to himself. If he stood cowering like Jefferson, he would become a bundle of self-loathing and contradiction like Jefferson.

These were the things swirling through George Washington's mind as he peered into Shadow's eyes and charged. He saw the gun flash repeatedly as his massive legs propelled him forward like a panther pouncing from a trampoline. He felt a shot sail by the right side of his head, another graze the right side of his arm, yet another sneak under his left armpit.

Unnerved by a closing menace that seemed half Ray Lewis and half Baryshnikov, Shadow fired his last several shots hastily. "Motherfucker," he hissed, as he threw the empty gun away and brandished a monstrous knife. "You a ghost?"

Washington stopped and reached for his sword instinctively, but groped at air. He drew the knife Franklin had purchased. Tiny compared to Shadow's, but better than nothing.

Washington had meleed savages, knew knife fights were much more dangerous than sword or pistol, and was not pleased by the prospect. Had his enemy been a professional soldier or savage, he probably would have attacked, but neither would have surrendered a pistol as easily as Shadow had. Washington knew strength and courage were not a substitute for training and experience, and therefore waited for his opponent to err.

Shadow noted the vertical scar on his enemy's left cheek. Small, but too crudely healed to be the result of surgery. From a knife fight? Shadow inched forward, then raised his blade and lunged, slashing diagonally at Washington's jugular with a sword-like stroke.

While Washington flashed through a catalogue of butchered cowards and neophytes who had tried to parry knives from the perimeter, he reminded himself that the counterintuitive cardinal rule of melee is to keep your enemy close, where he can be killed and his weapon controlled. When Shadow slashed downward, Washington therefore steeled himself for inevitable injuries, moved in, grabbed Shadow's knife hand with his left, and simultaneously chopped at his forearm with his knife. It split open like a log hit by an axe and blood gushed.

Jefferson stifled amazement. Though he had often heard men describe Washington's battle prowess, he had never seen it, and on one level, this situation was a wish fulfilled. Washington's movements were an unfathomable combination of power *and* speed. Jefferson knew he could move nearly as fast, but his blows would inevitably lack power. Conversely, his strongest blows were his clumsiest. It was apparent from Washington's expression of exertion and the way his muscles flexed that he was attacking with maximum force. Yet his movements were also a ballet!

As Washington's knife cleaved his forearm, Shadow gasped with pain and dropped his blade. Washington slashed downward and filleted Shadows's neck, then opened him from crotch to chin with a blur of an upward stroke.

Jefferson once again stifled amazement. Washington's three lightning slashes seemed like one continuous, choreographed gesture!

Shadow's incisions popped open and reflective, milky flesh was visible for the brief instant that preceded the geyser of blood. Like Caucasian, the last thing he saw were Washington's frigid, pitiless eyes.

Washington's combat instincts short-circuited compassion during the battle, but now that it was over tension ebbed from him and his humanity returned.

Only an evil maniac could take human life in close quarters without some sense of abomination, and as he stared at the maimed corpses, Washington felt it.

But only for a moment. A deeper sense of justice quickly prevailed. The cadavers were hardly victims.

Washington collected himself, then turned, glanced at Jefferson with contempt, and knelt next to Franklin.

"Too bad the shell didn't hit my paunch," Franklin said. "It would have just bounced off."

Washington frowned. Blood flowed out the First American's wound steadily. The shot had penetrated his chest just inside the armpit, directly under the shoulder. Washington stood and began removing his shirt.

"Of course, a cannonball would probably bounce off," Franklin continued, as Jefferson knelt and entered his view. "Hello, Tom. Let me be the first to commend your courage."

"Are you angry?" Jefferson replied.

"I'm ecstatic. I love dying."

"I am sorry," Jefferson said.

Franklin glanced at the corpses. "You are not to blame. Crime is the fault of the criminal."

Washington ripped a strip from his shirt, knelt, and pulled it under Franklin's shoulder. His arms flexed vigorously as he tied the tourniquet. Franklin closed his eyes, winced, and gritted his teeth. "I always wished to see you in combat," he managed. "How Faustian."

"You advocated this trip most strongly," Washington replied. "It is perhaps fitting you were shot."

Franklin laughed hysterically. "You're all heart, George. But I am curious. Was your defiance of the muggers an example of the caution you have been preaching?"

Washington glared at Franklin, then his wound. Blood no longer gushed, but it still flowed. Washington was not surprised. A tourniquet could alleviate flow on a limb wound, but it provided only modest help on the torso.

Washington ripped the shirt again, handed the rags to Jefferson, then lifted Franklin. "Place them on the rear of the wound."

Jefferson obeyed gingerly. The sight of the blood once again made him queasy, and it seemed he might vomit.

"For Providence's sake, Tom! I would rather have a popsy[97] at my side!" Washington snatched the rag from Jefferson, stuffed it onto the rear of the wound, placed another on the front, then tied a bandage tightly around them.

---

97 Popsy. Girl.

It was drenched almost immediately.

"The shot may have cleaved an artery," Washington said.

Grim glances. In the colonial world, this was a disheartening prognosis. On rare occasions, a skilled and fortuitous surgeon could tie an artery, but the standard treatment was amputation and cauterization.

"Even if I could remove the arm, you probably would not live," Washington said. "You are old and decrepit. I have seen robust young soldiers succumb to lesser wounds."

"In our time," Jefferson replied. "A futuristic physician might not need to remove the arm."

"Hopefully." Washington looked at Franklin. "Arm or no, there is little I or Tom can do for you. Without futuristic medical treatment, you will probably die."

"That is an assumption," Franklin said.

"Not a certainty," Washington conceded. "But certainly the most probable assumption."

A cyclical shrieking could be heard in the distance.

"Is a soprano being trampled?" Franklin joked.

"Cops," Jefferson said.

"If I obtain futuristic medical treatment, we will be forced to reveal our identities."

Washington sighed deeply. *After a lifetime spent on the stretch in service of America, I had hoped to retire to that tranquility which can only be achieved via anonymity.* "It is your life, Ben. The decision is yours to make." Washington knelt. "I pledge my life and my sacred honor to whatever verdict you render."

Franklin pursed his lips. "What would best serve America?"

"Certainly not your death," Jefferson said. "It is absurd to think our Puppeteer brought you here merely to expire."

"Perhaps, perhaps not. Another assumption. But here's the rub, regardless. It is time to face the question we have been avoiding. Why have we been brought to this future?"

"Uncertain," Washington answered.

"Unproven," Jefferson added.

"Perhaps not empirically," Franklin answered. "But I think we nonetheless know."

Washington sighed yet again. He and Jefferson both nodded.

"I think it is our destiny to reveal ourselves to futurity," Franklin said. "And to once again influence the cast of the American die."

As Jefferson thought of the income capitation and notes, he stood straighter and nodded with resolution.

"Yet I cannot escape the conclusion that initial impressions are indelible," Franklin continued. "If we revealed ourselves to futurity in our current state of ignorance, we would be forever viewed as decadent."

"You cannot die!" Jefferson whimpered.

"America is the paramount concern," Franklin chided. "Not a single American. I pledged my life to America past, and will gladly give it to America future if we determine this the most prudent course. Is this the most prudent course?"

"Of course not!" Jefferson said.

"Perhaps," Washington conceded.

"Only Ben can be President," Jefferson countered.

"Unless *The Constitution* is amended again," Washington replied.

The cyclical shrieking grew noticeably louder.

"I am lightheaded. I cannot think clearly." Franklin knew Washington made poor decisions under duress, and had limited intelligence, so he spoke to Jefferson. "Analysis?"

"You must live. All other concerns are secondar—"

"Analysis!" Franklin growled.

Jefferson smiled effeminately. "Leaving this region may be the act of a fugitive."

"We committed no crime," Washington replied.

"In our eyes," Jefferson countered. "Perhaps not futurity's. And even if futurity agrees we acted in defense, it is certainly a citizen's responsibility to give an accounting to magistrates. Early concerns about gaol or Bedlam now have renewed relevance. We have no provable identity. In this paper-obsessed futurity, this alone might result in our conviction or incarceration. If we reveal our true identity, we may be assumed ripe for Bedlam. Prolonged imprisonment would obviously prevent us from serving America."

"We must find a safe location and consider this question more thoroughly," Franklin decided. "I will live that long."

Franklin leaned on the world's bravest crutch and took another step. He felt Washington's muscles flex and lift, once again doing most of the work. The pain was dizzying, and to take his mind off it, Franklin sang.

"We have a bold commander, who fears not sword or gun, the second Alexander, his name is Washington . . ."

Jefferson smiled. The colonial favorite became popular just after Washington accepted command of the American Armies.

"His men are all collected, and ready for the fray,"

Except Tom, Washington thought.

"To fight they are directed, 'cause Tom is cowardlay . . ."

Washington laughed boisterously.

Jefferson looked away with irritation. "The verse I recall ended 'for North Americay'."

"I'm amending it," Franklin replied. "All tunes must adapt to the times."

Jefferson scowled.

"You don't want your deeds documented for posterity?" Franklin asked.

Washington laughed again, but quieted when a couple approached. Like other passersby, they noted the blood and brain flecks on his clothes. Franklin's wound was covered with a fleece, but the lower portion of the shirt was drenched crimson, and this also attracted attention.

Until Washington glared at the couple, anyway. They looked away immediately.

"We cannot hike the entire distance," Jefferson said, once the founders were alone again. "Magistrates may query its pilots, but a taxi seems our only option."

"If we don't vacate, magistrates will find us standing on this street." Mimicking a wench he had seen on television, Washington whistled at a passing taxi.

THE TRAMPLED SOPRANOS were in cars with rotating red and blue lights, and as these raced past the fleeing taxi, the pilot glanced at the founders in his rearview mirror. Washington glared back, and the pilot looked away quickly.

A game of cat and mouse ensued. Each time Washington looked away, the pilot examined the founders in his rearview mirror. When Washington's eyes darted toward the mirror, the pilot diverted his gaze.

Franklin disarmed the pilot with witty banter, and did everything in his power not to appear injured, but this helped little. The pilot was suspicious.

The founders soon exchanged nervous glances. The inability to discuss their predicament was maddening, so they did the next best thing, and outlined their options mentally.

Washington considered privateering the taxi. But they didn't know how to operate it. Bribe the pilot? Force him to chauffer? How far? Two towns away? Two states? D.C.?

No. The cab's absence would be noted. The pilot had telegraphed a commander who would be suspicious in ticks, not hours or days.

A different vehicle? Several vehicles?

No. Any pilot would be suspicious of Franklin's wounds, and contact magistrates after the journey, if not during. Traveling farther by taxi would merely lead the magistrates closer to their destination. Washington knew the only viable action was to murder and hide a pilot when they disembarked, but he rejected this course for moral reasons.

Jefferson wanted to ask the pilot if he knew a physician or had medical abilities, but this would confirm what he only suspected, albeit strongly. He nonetheless came close to inquiring at least a half dozen times. Fear of Washington stopped him initially. Later, images of gaol and Bedlam did.

Washington and Jefferson eventually found themselves peering at Franklin, hoping he had concocted some clever remedy. His glum expression was hardly comforting.

True to form, Washington made the cab drop them several blocks from their hotel. As Franklin exited, he gave Washington a warning glance, then stood before the pilot, flipped up his fleece and exposed his wound.

Washington's eyes darted warily. He kept the hand in his pocket on the gun and continued to watch the pilot.

Franklin gave a quick and truthful account of the mugging, omitting only the founders' identities. "I tell you this because I value truth," he concluded. "We are honest men. Honest men in peculiar circumstances." Franklin sighed. "Normally I would obey the law, but we are anonymous immigrants."

"Is that a clever way of saying illegal immigrants?"

"I am not clever." Franklin smirked morosely and let the depths of his fear and confusion pour out his eyes. "I can tell you only that we are immigrants. As for the descriptor? I am uncertain. We are uncertain. At present, there is much we don't understand."

Pilot glanced at Washington's hidden hand. "What do you want from me?"

"The same honesty I have offered."

"I can't lie to the cops."

"I would not ask you to lie to magistrates." Franklin smiled mischievously. "Perhaps a tiny fib."

Pilot glanced at Washington again, saw his lethal eyes, and returned his focus to Franklin immediately. "I got a family, man."

"My friend will not hurt you."

"I don't believe that."

Franklin smiled. "I respect your honesty."

"I give you my oath not to initiate conflict," Washington said.

Oh. Your oath. Now I feel safe. Yet as he looked back at Washington, Pilot believed him for some reason.

"I would be grateful if you would pass my narrative on to the magistrates," Franklin said.

Pilot seemed much more comfortable.

"In the morrow," Franklin added, as he held out a handful of blood-stained hundreds. "For altruistic reasons I am unable to illuminate, we cannot speak to the magistrates."

"Altruistic reasons, huh?" Pilot eyed the money lustily. "Those hundreds?"

Franklin nodded. "You are peering at Benjamins. Relate this story to the magistrates in its entirety, including the bribe. Tell them you wanted to make contact earlier, but were petrified of my companion."

That's no lie, Pilot thought.

"A single fib is necessary." Franklin broke the money into two piles. "As the magistrates will probably confiscate the bribe, understate its actual amount in your narrative."

Pilot laughed suddenly. He rifled through the hundreds and moved most into a larger pile. "I can see where you're coming from. You didn't do anything wrong, but the cops may not see it that way."

"A succinct summary." Franklin glanced at Washington, who stepped forward ominously. "My companion gave an oath, and now, so have you. If you violate yours, he will violate his."

"We don't want that," Pilot said.

"You may contact the magistrates anytime after the noon in the morrow. The later the better."

"Yeah," Pilot said, as he continued to stare at the money. "No problem."

Ironically, now that he held the money, Pilot was even more scared. He glanced at Washington, and pictured a second set of blood stains, namely his own, splattered across the money.

Pilot was both grateful and petrified when his radio crackled. He glanced at Washington as he answered it.

"Where you at?" the dispatcher asked. "Saskatchewan?"

"Traffic, man. Sorry. I'm not dickin' the dog or anything."

"Probably that shooting. Wasn't too far from you, actually. You see anything?"

"Nah. A couple police cars passed me, but I had no idea what for."

The dispatcher gave the location of the next fare. To prevent the tall, murderous man from "violating his oath," Pilot kept talking on the radio as he drove away.

Once the cab vanished, Jefferson said, "Franklin alia iacta est."

The First American nodded. "I hope you aren't angry. Consultation was impossible, and you agreed to support my decision."

"Your compromise is elegant," Washington replied. "You fulfilled our responsibilities as citizens while preserving our anonymity. Though I pity the French. No wonder they were almost bankrupt when you left!"

As Minister Plenipotentiary, Franklin convinced the French to give America loans far in excess of what they could afford. Shortly after the American Revolution, France was on the verge of insolvency, a major cause of her Revolution.

"I would have made a sorry diplomat were I not an acute judge of the human motive," Franklin said. "America's fate often hinged on this ability."

"You bet America's fate on this talent," Washington replied. "Would you also wager your own life?"

"I just did."

"DISCARD THE PISTOL," Franklin said, as he hobbled along, "in that slender, rectangular, road hole."

"We should keep it," Washington replied.

Franklin shook his head. "We must discard it. I believe it could link us to the miscreants."

"Are you certain?"

"No."

Washington thought for a long moment, made sure no one was watching, and then scuttled the weapon as Franklin instructed.

LIKE SOME DISTANT mountain being approached, the hotel grew larger gradually.

"I apologize," Franklin wheezed. "I am not my usual agile self."

"I am not sure which would be more conspicuous," Washington replied. "Hobbling forward like this, or carrying you."

"Don't be absurd, Atlas. Even your strength knows limits."

"I called you a continent, not a planet."

"I asked you to fight for North Americay, not lift it."

Washington swooped down and hoisted Franklin. "I've carried America before."

FRANKLIN WAS IN Washington's arms peering back at Jefferson, who walked as fast as he could, but still barely kept up. "If I'm Rocinante, George must be a Pegasus," the First American said.

"No Pegasus could fly bearing a burden this hefty," Washington groaned.

"I would make a joke about spurs, but I think you would drop me."

Washington spat and grimaced as they approached a gradual incline. "I may drop you regardless."

All three founders sighed deeply as Jefferson locked the hotel door, but the mood was nonetheless tense. The sense of security they'd felt two days ago when first sequestering themselves in a hotel room was absent.

Washington helped Franklin sit on the bed. He began to remove his bandages, but the First American pushed him away. "Parchment, George. And quill. For moral arithmetic. Let us decide our course while my thoughts are clearest."

Washington noted Franklin's pallor and obeyed.

"Choice 1 is a hospital," Franklin said. "Advantage: I obtain the best available medical treatment. Disadvantage: we are revealed to futurity."

"Choice 2: A rogue physician. Advantage: Futuristic medical treatment without revealing ourselves to futurity. Assuming the physician keeps quiet. Disadvantages: treatment may be inferior to a hospital's and we do not know a rogue physician. Locating and trusting one is a risk."

"The natural philosopher might know a physician or medical techniques," Jefferson said. "Or perhaps the soldier does. We could call physicians in the yellow phone cyclopedia and search for one that is pliable."

"All valid options," Franklin agreed. "Though risky ones. I am most intimate with the natural philosopher, and would choose him if this option were our disposition, but he suspects, has certainly done research, and would probably deduce my identity if we met again. I do not know the soldier well enough to trust him, and calling unknown physicians within minutes of a murder seems foolish."

"The natural philosopher might keep our identity confidential," Jefferson argued.

"Possible, but hardly certain. Choice 3: You and George remove my arm in this hotel room. Advantage: we remain anonymous, and I am trea—"

"Are you ripe for Bedlam?" Jefferson gasped.

"I pledged the whole of my body to America past, and will gladly give it a mere arm in futurity. Fear will not enter our moral algebra."

"Reason hopefully will," Jefferson said.

Franklin ignored the quip. "Choice 3: You and George remove my arm in this hotel room. Advantage: we remain anonymous, and I am treated and rendered fit for travel. Disadvantage: I could still expire, and lose an arm, which would make me extremely conspicuous. You can tie an artery, correct?"

Jefferson was appalled by Franklin's nonchalance. Washington admired a side of the First American he had never seen, and was pleased to find that, unlike Jefferson, he had mettle under fire.

"Stop fuddling like a wench, Tom! You can tie an artery?"

"In theory, yes, but surely you don't expect me to oper—"

"And George. You have seen enough amputations to perform one?"

"Yea. Though we lack a hatchet or cleaver."

"Surely a man of your strength can make do with a bodkin."

Washington nodded grimly. "Though the anguish would be incalculable."

"This is madness!" Jefferson howled. "We can't quack you when futurity's physicians are mere ticks away! Think of the hound surgery I described! By Providence I wish you'd seen it! Futurity's physicians probably have powers which border on the magical!"

"We must calmly enumerate all options," Franklin chided. "The moral algebra will decide."

Following Franklin's usual methodology when making a difficult decision, the founders continued listing options and documenting the pros and cons of each. They considered *all* possibilities, including abandoning Franklin at a hospital and seeking treatment in another town, but the fundamental dilemma remained unchanged; the actions that offered the greatest safety for Franklin were the riskiest for the party.

"My oath to see your will done stands," Washington reiterated, "but I agree with Tom. We should find futuristic treatment."

Franklin shook his head. "Our destiny is now lucid to me, George."

"That is blood loss speaking," Jefferson said, "not revelation."

"Was Tom this wenchly during your Presidency?" Franklin asked.

Washington nodded with chagrin.

"I was right then as I am now," Jefferson whined.

"You were right about television," Franklin replied. "As you so keenly observed, it gives some the ability to communicate with all. In such a medium, initial impressions would be most potent. Especially superficial ones."

"Even if I concede the point, it hardly seems significant enough to risk your life over."

"This point is paramount. You understand what is good for the people, but are less astute than I in discerning what moves the people. As you were never a commoner, you cannot think like one beyond a certain point. I think like a commoner because I am one."

"There is little common about you," Jefferson said. "Especially your sense right now."

"Imagine yourself as a commoner with minimal creativity and discernment," Franklin replied. "This television would exert a profound influence upon you. Imagine you first see your nation's founders, whom you idolize the way we did the ancients, on this television. They are in gaol or Bedlam, or even in an optimistic scenario, unimpugned, but befuddled by aspects of life which the thickest child can grasp. This would not be a written description, but a living image replayed repeatedly on the television and in your mind. An indelible initial impression that would taint all your future perceptions of these founders. You would forever view them as relics from an abstract and irrelevant past, and consider them unfit to lead."

Nausea filled Jefferson as he realized Franklin was right.

"Returning Gods might not be worshipped," Franklin concluded.

Jefferson wanted to ignore the First American's wishes and whisk him to a hospital, but George Washington was hardly a trivial obstacle. An oath from him was inviolate.

"I take it by your silence that you do not refute my supposition," Franklin said.

"My only argument is a dogmatic desire to see you live," Jefferson replied. "Lacking logic, I must voice it as a loving friend rather than a philosopher."

Franklin pursed his lips. Usually this trademark gesture conveyed mirth, but now there was something tragic in it. "There are no clever solutions to be had, I fear."

Washington nodded. "We must sacrifice something."

"My arm."

Jefferson closed his eyes and turned away.

"The natural philosopher mentioned a few discoveries which could save . . . my . . . lif—" Franklin's eyes lost focus, drifted, then closed.

Washington jumped forward immediately. "Ben!" He shook his friend. "Ben?"

Jefferson bent over, confirmed Franklin's breath, then placed his ear over his heart. "He is alive!"

"We must remove the arm immediately," Washington said. "He cannot afford to lose any more blood."

Colonial medicine was rife with quackery, but the theory of blood circulation had been advanced in 1616, and the founders knew why excessive blood loss was fatal.

Jefferson smiled sadly. "Ben would never complain. He must have been lightheaded or in excruciating pain for some time."

Washington began ripping sheets off the empty bed.

"What are you doing?"

"Surgeons in the television wore togas."

"We do not know why."

"But by mimicking them we may derive some advantage."

"This is absurd!" Jefferson said. "Take Ben to a hospital with me! We cannot let him die!"

Washington turned like a tornado and spoke through clenched dentures. "Ben exercised that liberty which I took the field to preserve. And I gave an oath." He stepped toward Jefferson aggressively, and bore down with an arctic glare. "Unless you wish to unleash my temper, make no further mention of a hospital. Desist your wenchly whimpering and help me operate."

Jefferson clearly wanted to retreat, but surprised Washington by standing his ground. Washington smiled, turned, and began slicing up the sheets. "We lack gunpowder. Find something to cauterize with."

Jefferson scoured the room. "This utilizes the electric fire rather than the conventional variety, and is constructed with futuristic materials, but otherwise it seems similar to irons we used to press clothes."

Washington nodded as he finished slicing the sheets. "Should I be starkers under this surgeon's toga?"

"I have no idea."

"You are the genius. What is your best guess?"

"Why would a surgeon wear a toga?" Jefferson muttered.

Silence.

"I have no idea," Jefferson whimpered.

"Your intellect eclipses mine. As does your natural philosophic intuition. Ben's life may hang in the balance. Starkers or no?"

"Starkers."

Franklin's eyes fluttered open. "Bacteria. The natural philosopher told me that most surgical deaths in our time were caused by bacteria." He began to say more, but then passed out again.

"Back-tear," Washington repeated. "Crying? Sweating? Back sweat? Blistering of the back caused problems perhaps? Or maybe backed-ear? Something that crawls in the ears? Some blockage of the ears?"

Jefferson shook his head. "It probably derives from Latin or Greek, like so many of futurity's words. Back-tear-e-uh. Backed-ear-ea. Backterea. Bakteria? Bakterion is Greek for staff. Bakteria would be the diminutive. A small staff?"

Washington tied a strip of sheet over his face and nose, as the surgeons on TV had, then walked toward the bathroom. "Deduce the implication while I change."

"This is more Franklin's purview," Jefferson said. "He excels at such deductions."

"Make it your purview." Washington closed the door.

While peering at Franklin, Jefferson once again thought of the absurdly advanced canine operation they had seen on television. He glanced at the bathroom, gulped hard, and began walking toward the telephone. "Small staff. Some new medical instrument, I would think."

Jefferson peered at the phone and read, "In case of emergency call 911." He picked up the receiver and hesitated.

"But what sort of instrument?" Jefferson dialed, and waited. The phone beeped loudly. He cringed and turned toward the bathroom. *Thank Providence cannon and musket fire have ruined George's hearing!*

"A staff supports one. Perhaps a surgical staff used to support something?" Jefferson obtained an outside line and began dialing. His fingers trembled. 9-1-2.

Jefferson cursed his clumsiness silently as he redialed. 9-1—

Washington opened the door, saw Jefferson using the phone, and leapt over the bed in a single bound. Jefferson wanted to drop the phone and run; he was able to stand his ground only by looking away from the fearsome form of Washington.

Jefferson pressed the "1" button again as Washington descended next to him. Washington snatched the receiver before his feet hit the ground. He landed, listened, heard it ringing, and hung up. Then he faced the Sage of Monticello.

Jefferson saw Washington look through him rather than at him, at a spot behind his head. Washington curled his hand into a C and his arm lashed out like a viper, smashing into Jefferson's larynx. The Sage of Monticello flailed with both arms as Washington's grip constricted his throat.

"Who were you telegraphing?"

Jefferson's eyes glared defiantly.

Washington smiled. Like so many others, he had made the mistake of underestimating Jefferson. Away from the battlefield, he had always possessed a measure of courage.

"Who were you calling?"

"Hospital," Jefferson managed.

"You. A Benedict." Washington shook his head.

"Com-pass-ion," Jefferson replied, in a raspy voice. "Not trea-son."

Washington thought of Lord Vader and the officer he had choked. Ben was right about television's powerful ability to instantaneously create lasting associations. "So much for the polis, I suppose?"

Jefferson said nothing.

"You hypocrite."

Silence again. Jefferson's eyes remained static. He seemed indifferent to the indictment.

"I can't have you scuttling us with subterfuge every time I turn my back. I require an oath."

"I can-not breaaathe."

Washington released his grip slightly. "Your oath."

Jefferson sputtered like an engine for several seconds, then said, "An oath extracted under duress is meaningless."

Washington retightened his grip. "Your oath!"

"You shall not have it."

"Then you shall not breathe."

Washington stared with a pitiless expression as Jefferson gradually turned pink. Jefferson always kept his word, and he knew he could rely on the oath. Assuming it could be extracted. Washington had assumed Jefferson would give in quickly, but as seconds passed and Jefferson's reddish hue gradually became purple, he grew concerned. If Ben died, and he killed Jefferson, he would be marooned in futurity without a genius. Yet the alternative, releasing Jefferson and enabling future treachery, was equally repugnant, for reasons of principle as much as practicality.

Jefferson observed Washington's petrified expression and smiled with triumph. He had only seen Washington scared a few times, but the same thought always struck him: George's face was ill-suited to expressions of fear.

Washington considered his dilemma, and decided to let principle override expedience. Jefferson would swear an oath or suffocate.

"Burton was wrong," Franklin said. "The sword bests the quill."

Washington dropped Jefferson, turned, and knelt.

Franklin smiled. "It's good to see that your and Tom's friendship is on the mend."

"Back-tear-e-uh," Washington blurted. "What is it?"

"The natural philosopher didn't tell me. I made a surgical remark in passing, and he mentioned bacteria."

"And you didn't think to ask?"

"Nay. Well, yea. But if I had pursued every avenue which confused me, I would have walked in circles rather than arriving at my distant destination of megascopic knowledge. And at the instant in question the natural philosopher was describing the Apollo Program. Surgery seemed trivial by comparison."

"Apollo Program?" Jefferson said.

"Bacteria," Washington growled. "The Gods can wait."

"Bakteria," Jefferson said. "Greek for small staff."

"A small staff? You'd have to ask George. Mine is large."

Jefferson wanted to laugh, but his eyes teared. "You cannot die."

"It is America that cannot die," Franklin countered.

Jefferson wiped his eyes.

"Is the irony not appreciable?" Franklin quipped.

"Nor appreciated," Jefferson said.

"You survived my death once," Franklin comforted. "You can do so again."

Washington summarized Jefferson's attempt to call the hospital, and his refusal to give an oath.

"Give your oath, Tom," Franklin said. "If I slip under the veil again, George will require your intellect. America will."

Jefferson closed his eyes for a long moment, then nodded.

"Good. Now were you two going to quibble all night, or could you spare some time to save my life?"

A COLONIAL PHYSICIAN might have had a larger array of surgical implements, and perhaps more space and some herbal medicines, but these were the only differences between the desk-top, knife-and-iron operation Washington was about to perform, and one that might have occurred in a cutting-edge 18th-century hospital.

While the iron heated, Jefferson tuned the television to ER and tried to connect to the internet to research bakteria. Like Franklin earlier, he was unable to log on. The First American attempted repeated troubleshooting, but was unsuccessful. "The problem may be the phone rather than our computer," he concluded.

"A uniquely futuristic frustration," Jefferson whined. "We have all futurity's knowledge at our beckon, but cannot conjure it!"

"Handsome fellow," Franklin said, "this ER's lead physician. But I would prefer baywenches."

"What fools are we," Jefferson whispered, as a swarm of toga-clad ER doctors treated a bleeding patient using futuristic implements. One hung a bag of fluid and drained it into the patient by inserting a flexible, clear catheter. "Access to this sorcery and we choose the quackery of our time. We might as well have been sent to the dark ages."

"I would prefer any program that denies Tom a chance to whimper," Washington said.

Franklin began channel surfing and stopped on a breaking newscast in a familiar alley. Police were shown mulling in the background while a reporter in the foreground said, "We just arrived on the scene, and present details are sketchy. No formal statement has been issued, but our sources tell us that two men were killed in what appears to be a robbery, and that at least one witness can identify the suspected assailants, who are still at large."

"The event was mere ticks ago," Franklin noted. "Yet already television has alerted local citizenry."

"We were wise not to contact strange physicians," Washington replied.

"Futurity's magistrates couldn't assume us the criminals?" Jefferson said.

Nervous, disheartened glances.

"I am beginning to doubt our ability to escape," Jefferson said. "If we are to be caught anyway, why not let one of futurity's physicians treat Ben?"

"I have eluded tighter nooses than this one," Washington said, "but the choice is still Ben's to make."

"Amputate," Franklin said without hesitation.

Washington did not want to disturb his bandages and increase blood loss until the moment of the operation, so Franklin was lying motionless on the desk. "I may die during the amputation," he said to Washington. "But it would bring me comfort to do so knowing something."

"What?"

"In the alley. You honestly weren't scared?"

"There is no shame in feeling fear. Succumbing to it is the only dishonor." Washington smiled with admiration. "I need not lecture you on the topic. Your bravery was a match for mine."

Jefferson watched Washington's glowing approbation with envy. This was the rare warmth he showed his favored few, Hamilton, Lafayette, Knox, and now Franklin. For the first time, Jefferson understood why he had not basked in it, and probably never would.

"What's the most afraid you've ever been?" Franklin asked Washington. "Monongahela? Monmouth? When you discovered Arnold's treachery?"

"I was never in graver danger than when breaking up the Forbes crossfire, but I was not frightened then. I was most afraid when appointed Commander in Chief of the American Armies. And you?"

"Now." Franklin laughed. "Every situation has an advantage to offer, though. If one is optimistic enough to find it."

"This situation?"

"I no longer notice the pain from my stone. And before long, the gout in my elbow will no longer be a burden." Franklin laughed again.

Washington flashed back and saw hardened veterans wailing like wenches as limbs were removed. He wanted to look away from Franklin, but knew this was the worst possible response, so maintained a steady gaze. He had been with enough injured men to know they wanted mental comfort as much as physical. Time and circumstance had not always permitted him to give that comfort to lesser men, but Benjamin Franklin, First American and fellow Apollo, would have it.

"The iron is ready," Jefferson said. "Would you like me to cauterize?"

Washington shook his head. "You may grow queasy. If depressed erratically or with insufficient force, the iron might become stuck in the wound or fail to close it." Washington gave Jefferson a threatening glance. "No wenchery.

Hand me the iron immediately. Once I remove the limb and the blood runs copious, seconds may be the difference."

As Washington approached Franklin he relived a post-combat infirmary where disheartened soldiers focused listless glances on the air where limbs had been.

Franklin glanced at his digital watch and the arm that bore it glumly. "Soon my chronometer won't be the only amputee."

Washington was about to remove a bandage when he crimped his knees together suddenly.

"Are you queasy?" Franklin asked.

"Certainly not," Washington replied. He tried to stand straighter to convey indignance, but his diarrhea forced him to slouch again immediately. "It is this futuristic food."

Franklin laughed. "You have the discipline to charge a point-blank pistoleer, but not pinch back a load?"

Washington quelled a curt response because he knew the levity helped Franklin. He scowled, then scurried to the bathroom to blow his ballast.

"I am sorry, Ben," Jefferson said.

"I can live without an arm. And who knows? Maybe futurity can grow it back like a plant."

"Have you any requests if . . ."

Franklin pursed his lips. His eyes bled sadness. "For my own personal ease, I should have died years ago, and though those years have been spent in excruciating pain, I am pleased that I have lived them, since they have brought me to see our present situation."

"No will or codicil?"

Jefferson was not joking, but Franklin laughed. "I leave you and George my satchel. And if . . . I can think of no greater gift for my last night than to see our Zeus hurl lightning."

"Our contributions were with the quill and powers of persuasion," Jefferson said. "We both realized America was baptized in bloodshed, and were enlightened enough not to be glib about other men's sacrifices on the field, but . . ."

"Understanding a principle theoretically is one thing," Franklin agreed. "Observing it empirically is another."

Jefferson nodded. "It is chilling to realize that we owe America's existence to thousands of acts like tonight's."

"I was never arrogant about my accomplishments," Franklin said. "But after seeing George today, I cannot help feeling that they are comparatively insignificant."

"I concur."

Sober silence and a simultaneous thought among two men. Hamilton, Madison, Adams. And of course, themselves. All America's great patriots had acknowledged Washington as their superior, the one indispensable figure in the revolution. For Jefferson and Franklin, never had the reason been clearer.

On the toilet with his toga around his ankles, the eavesdropping Washington smiled. He felt no humility, no need to pretentiously disagree. His sacrifice had been greater, and it was fitting that Franklin, Jefferson, and all Americans acknowledge it. Nothing less was just.

"I had always regarded the Indian Prophecy as savage superstition," Jefferson continued.

"I was at least skeptical," Franklin agreed. "But after seeing George taunt death so superciliously only a fool could doubt."

Washington once again smiled. This amazement was typical of those who saw him in battle. In 1770, while he and his physician Dr. Craik were exploring the Ohio Country, an Indian chief who had tried to kill him at Monongahela traveled a great distance to pay homage. To savages, the mounted redcoats that had charged into the Monongahela forest were essentially circus targets, but Chief Kiashuta remembered the regal Washington as the most conspicuous. Several Indians fired at him, but when numerous direct shots missed, his astonished enemies realized he was being protected by the Great Spirit and could never die in battle. On another occasion when an artillery shell landed mere yards from Washington but left him unscathed, Craik related the Indian Prophecy to his officers and pointed to the heavens. Thereafter, the tale took on a life of its own.

Washington finished, wiped, and exited the bathroom without washing his hands. He "cleaned" the knife off on his Toga, approached Franklin, and immediately began undressing him.

"I thought the site of me starkers was oppugnant to you," the First American joked.

"Not as oppugnant as this wound."

The entire right side of Franklin's shirt was drenched, and it stuck to his skin as Washington tried to pull it off.

"As if dipped in cochineal," Franklin muttered. "If I pass, and doing so is expedient, abandon my corpse. Maim it, if need be. To prevent futurity from determining my identity."

Washington nodded.

"Your oath, George."

"You have it." Washington began cutting the shirt.

"I am bleeding on the desk. It is probably costly to replace. We must conserve our funds."

"Damn the desk! Cloths, Tom. One wet, several dry."

Jefferson obeyed and Washington wiped the blood from Franklin. He used two belts to make a better tourniquet, then inspected the wound. In the dark alley it had been difficult to see, but the absurdly bright electric candles allowed a day-like view.

Washington noted that the entry was unusually small. He was used to the caves created by musket shots, which were essentially tiny cannonballs. He pressed his hand into the back of the wound, expecting the shrapnel-laden chasm an exiting musket shot would leave.

There was only a tiny hole!

Franklin saw Washington's brow furrow, and his did likewise. "George?"

"It looks more like a bayonet wound," Washington muttered. "If I did not know the cause of the injury, I would guess you had been run through, not shot."

"Is this good or bad?"

"The penetration is unusually narrow. Encouragingly narrow."

Franklin gritted his teeth as Washington poked his finger into the wound and searched for shrapnel. This process continued for several seconds.

Franklin clenched his eyes closed. "How long must you finger roger?"

"I am sorry. I am an inexperienced fisher of wounds."

Washington satisfied himself that there was no shrapnel, then ceased penetration and wiped his hands on his toga. "The shots did seem unusually fast. Yes. Futurity would probably have more potent gunpowder." A frown. "Yet your wound is nonetheless counterintuitive. How could futurity's pistols be less lethal than ours?"

Franklin laughed. "For anyone but you they probably would have been more lethal. Perhaps the ability to fire multiple shots necessitates sacrifices like smaller shells."

Washington's face shrugged. "We may not have to amputate. I am no physician, but I did not feel the copious flow which would seem characteristic of a breached artery. Sword wounds such as this are known to bleed, but as long as they do not grow septic, they heal admirably once cauterized."

"Thank Providence!" Franklin sighed deep, long, and loud. Only at this moment did Washington and Jefferson realize how stoic he had been.

Washington placed his wallet in Franklin's mouth, then held up the iron. "Better than losing an arm, but the anguish will still be intense. Are you ready?"

Franklin nodded.

"Hold his arms, Tom. We wouldn't want him to reach up reflexively and burn himself."

Jefferson held the limbs like a woman might a dead mouse.

"Hold them!" Washington growled.

Jefferson obeyed. As George Washington pressed the hot iron into the front of his wound, Benjamin Franklin whimpered like a wench.

Tension bled from the founders once the cauterization was complete, but a nauseating burnt-pork smell persisted. "I could never be a cannibal," Franklin joked.

"You would feed an Army," Washington replied.

"More details from the scene of a viscous slaying downtown," a television reporter interrupted.

The founders watched nervously. Police had identified the victims. Names would remain confidential, but one was a multiple felon, the other an ex-professional athlete. A witness observed the gangland-style execution, during which one surviving, obese suspect had been shot. Wallets found at the scene with IDs removed reinforced police suspicions that the crime represented some criminal activity run amuck. Sketches would be posted within the hour, but in the meantime, citizens should be on the lookout for any suspicious individuals, a tall one in particular. This individual was strong enough to overcome a pro football player, and had demonstrated a willingness to kill without hesitation or seeming remorse. He should be regarded as armed and dangerous, and an individual who made a sighting should contact the police rather than confronting him themselves.

"I am not armed," Washington complained.

"Thankfully, I am," Franklin replied.

The founders' nervous glances were interrupted by the distant sound of shrieking sopranos. They were growing louder.

Washington glanced around nervously. He thought of Jefferson's call, and found himself staring at the phone. "Suppose an injured telegrapher died."

Jefferson nodded. "Smoke leads one to a fire. Futurity may have a way to determine the origin of the telegraph."

"And magistrates investigating a crime might consult those who could determine call origins," Franklin said.

Washington rose and began packing their bags hastily.

"Leaving the hotel might lead to our discovery," Jefferson said.

"Magistrates might check hotels," Franklin countered.

The sopranos shrieked louder. They were affrighteningly close.

"We're leaving. Now." Washington was not done packing, and had only the money and some spare clothes in his rucksack, but he nonetheless tossed it into the air, slid one arm in, then ducked slightly as the pack fell and inserted the other.

Franklin threw several hundred dollars on the desk and scribbled a hasty note that said, "For Damages". Jefferson was shoving books into his rucksack.

"Grab the grooming implements," Washington said, as he heaved his shoes on. "And the mobile electric candle."

"I cannot live without books," Jefferson replied.

"I cannot live through a chase," Franklin said.

Washington bent and lifted Franklin with deceptive ease, then strode toward the door. "No dawdling," he said to Jefferson, as he disappeared around the corner.

Jefferson ripped its plug from the wall, shoved the laptop atop the books, then followed. Clumsily trying to thread his arms through the pack straps while chasing Washington, he resembled a drunk giraffe. "You need my intellect, George."

"I have Ben's. If you fall behind, I leave you. If you do anything to intentionally alert magistrates of our presence, you die."

Jefferson wondered if this was merely a motivational tactic, but doubted it. Washington never made idle threats. Jefferson wished he had the physical prowess to oppose Washington, but did not, so he gritted his teeth and remained silent.

Washington ran almost a block when he heard multiple, distant squelches that reminded him of the stopping Watt wagon on Rushmore. He looked around. They were still in the city. Every window seemed a nosy eye, every light an enemy conspirator. But thankfully, there were no people. Had they been scared inside by the television warning?

Washington ran another block, then saw a gully of trees behind a small conclave of closed shops. Unaware where he was going or what lay ahead, he trudged into the dark stretch of forest.

Ambient light from the city had aided Washington initially, but now he trekked blind. As he stepped into another divot, careened sideways, then recovered his balance, he resisted the urge to shout in frustration. "I wish the moon were fuller," he gasped.

Franklin was too petrified to speak. Washington was practically jogging, and shadows that were incoming trees became visible only at the last instant. He barely avoided most and Franklin was nauseated by images of his outstretched feet smashing into one, ripping him from Washington's grasp and hurling him to the ground. Such a fall might be fatal.

"How can you sprint hoisting our Continent?" Jefferson gasped.

Washington thought of Star Wars' whiney, gold-armored See-Three-Pee-Oh. "How can you not sprint propelling only yourself?"

"I pray the magistrates have no hounds," Franklin said.

"After all the hunts I've been on, it would not be an unjust end." Washington spat. "Even in the Revolution, I never felt this much the fox."

"How far shall we go, George?" Franklin asked.

"As far as we can."

WASHINGTON'S CHEST HEAVED and he now trotted. Jefferson's occasional comments were closer than they had been, but still yards behind.

"Where shall we go, George?" Franklin asked.

Washington's silence was as bleak as the night.

WASHINGTON WAS DESCENDING a steep hill when he heard Jefferson's distraught scream. It reminded him of someone jumping off a waterfall. He stopped, turned, and saw Jefferson tumbling like a doll rolled down a roof. The Sage of Monticello accelerated and became impossible to see. Thumps and grunts as he hit the ground repeatedly, a sickening crack, then a scream and groan.

"Damn you Tom!" Washington hissed, as he put Franklin down. "Couldn't you injure yourself quietly?"

As he searched for Jefferson, Washington wished for Alexander Hamilton. Genius be damned! They were still in the woods, both literally and metaphorically, and he needed someone he didn't have to babysit.

Washington expected to find Jefferson lying against some unbroken tree with a severed bone, but sighed with relief when he found the opposite. "Are you hurt?"

"Sprains," Jefferson said, as he rubbed his wrists, ankles, and back. "But nothing seems fractured."

"If something is broken, you deserve it. You made the telegraph which forced us to flee."

"I can continue moving."

"Admirable, but we have each been spared once tonight. It is best not to taunt Providence."

Washington began walking away.

"I have fallen and I cannot rise," Jefferson said.

"I thought you could continue moving."

"Once I rise."

Washington helped Jefferson up, then turned his back on him and returned to Franklin.

THERE WAS NO CAMP to pitch, so the founders lay in the most level clearing they could find. Franklin was given all the extra clothes, which he used as makeshift blankets.

Sleeping under the stars was relaxing to Washington. Camping conjured memories of the freer surveying days of his youth, when he'd spent months at a stretch in remote wilderness. Jefferson and Franklin were both in agony, and shared none of Washington's joy, but they did not complain.

"You and I are like the television Survivors George despises," Franklin said to Jefferson.

Tom is, Washington thought.

"How goes the relaxing retirement, George?"

Washington smiled at Franklin and shook his head.

"I know how you feel, my friend," Franklin said.

Washington knew this was true. After his tenure as Pennsylvania's Minister to Britain, Franklin returned to America expecting a respite. Before his foot touched soil he learned of Lexington and Concord, and within a day he was elected to the Continental Congress.

Jefferson also nodded. When he returned from a five-year tenure as American Minister to France, Washington immediately offered him the post of Secretary of State.

"At least I have escaped my correspondence," Washington said.

"I wish I'd escaped that bullet," Franklin replied.

"And I that tree," Jefferson added.

"I hope we can manage one last escape in the morrow," Washington said.

Stern nods. Though despite their precarious predicament, the mood was tolerable. All three men had survived greater dangers, and thinking about past trials made futurity's present ones more bearable.

Their usual roaming, tangent-laden conversations did not arise because the founders were exhausted. Franklin was especially spent and slept almost immediately, leaving Washington and Jefferson alone amidst a confrontational silence.

"I am sorry," Jefferson finally said.

For your cowardice in the alley? For being the Benedict? For falling and injuring yourself?

"I am sorry."

It sounds more pathetic each time you utter it, Washington thought. Yet he remained silent for a reason that had nothing to do with kindness. The moon had broken through the clouds, illuminating Franklin's face, which seemed deathly pale. *I need your penetrating intellect. Damn your brilliance!*

"I am sorry," Jefferson said yet again.

"I know. Don't fret. We shall not speak of the matter until after the bus ride."

"Is that still our plan?" Jefferson asked.

"For now. What else can we do?"

"Surely the magistrates will be combing transit regions."

"What else can we do?" Washington repeated.

"Shall we post guards?" Jefferson asked.

You didn't want to play soldier in the alley. "The magistrates will either find us or they won't. What could we do if they locate us?"

Jefferson shrugged and peered up at the stars. "All the way to futurity to sleep like primitives."

Washington smiled. "Providence never ceases to humble. Especially with irony. I would have envisioned us the toast of futurity. Yet here we lie, fugitives."

Jefferson nodded curtly, and tried to quell his fear. "Suppose a bus is not viable?"

"As I stated, I have no idea."

"Ben's natural philosopher?"

"Might have helped us before we were fugitives. Such types are seldom swashbucklers."

"Unless . . ."

Washington nodded. "Once again, ironic. Perversely ironic. But yes. Hopefully."

Stutters of tactical conversation filled the remainder of the night. Before they finally drifted off, Washington and Jefferson glanced at Franklin, and hoped their second night in futurity would not be the First American's last.

The founders rose with the sun, even Franklin, who seemed healthier, though still weak. Washington checked the First American's wound immediately, and frowned. The surrounding veins seemed varicose, and the flesh was a sickly, swollen pink.

"Septic," Washington muttered, "but at least the cauterization held, and it did not bleed."

This was a small consolation, and Franklin knew it. In the colonial world, there was no way to treat septic wounds. A small percentage of cases cleared themselves, but death or amputation were the usual cures.

"We must still find a futuristic physician," Jefferson said. "In a few days, Ben may once again face amputation."

No one argued this assessment, least of all Franklin, who made stoic jokes that Jefferson found heart-wrenching.

Washington demanded silence while he surveyed the perimeter for magistrates. He found nothing, but the sense of déjà vu was nonetheless disconcerting. This was the same routine the founders had engaged in immediately after arriving in futurity, and they had the sense that for all their struggles thus far, they had accomplished little and were essentially back where they started.

While he urinated against a distant tree, Jefferson said, "I had an odd dream last night."

"As did I," Washington replied.

"It wasn't exactly a dream," Jefferson said. "It was more of a th—"

"Don't say another word!" Franklin interrupted.

"Why not?"

"Experimental accuracy. Have we parchment or quills?"

"Yes," Jefferson answered. "I procured them with the books."

While Jefferson distributed writing utensils, Franklin said, "I too had a dream. Humor me. Draw your dream, so we can compare without our narratives influencing each other."

All three dreams were the same. There was no scenery, imagery, people, or anything else tangible, but a thought had been seeded so strongly in each mind that it seemed like a premonition. Each founding father had somehow been told that they could return to the past if they journeyed to Mount Rushmore that day at sunset. They would be returned to their original times at the exact moment they'd left.

Stupefaction at the mass consciousness was pronounced. Franklin recounted his radio signal conversation with Paul, in which he had asked why a human body that sensed television transmissions could not see a picture. In addition to a time transport device, had some future civilization extrapolated television, telephone, and radio technologies and created a telemens that allowed mind transmission?

Sustained culture shock had desensitized the founding fathers to a certain degree, and their incredulity faded quickly. They didn't waste too much time speculating how telemens might be physically possible, but instead concentrated on what to do if the dream was to be believed.

"Are we being monitored by our Puppeteer?" Franklin wondered. "Is it moral? Riddled by guilt? Averse to stranding us in the future against our will? Helping us to escape?"

"Interesting," Jefferson said. "The Puppeteer effecting a rescue."

"Or a trap. Perhaps we have eluded the magistrates and this is a ruse to reveal us to the public." Washington pictured television camera crews sprinting from the forest moments after they returned to Rushmore.

"Wouldn't someone who can manipulate time and transmit dreams have more sophisticated methods of making our presence known?" Jefferson said. "Why not transport us to an assembly of Congress instead of Rushmore?"

"It is possible the Puppeteer also wants us to learn about the world before becoming known," Franklin speculated. "And as stated, if it is moral, granting us freedom of choice would also be important."

"Home," Jefferson said. "We can go home!"

"To a death we now have foreknowledge of," Franklin countered. "If we return we will pass within a few years."

"We can utilize foreknowledge to alter these outcomes," Jefferson said. "George can avoid the ride that made him sick, for example."

"A treacherous path," Washington warned. "Altering behavior ex post facto. One could easily become obsessed. And wouldn't altered behavior change future events, negating foreknowledge?"

"We will probably live longer here regardless," Franklin said. "Who knows how long the inventive physicians and natural philosophers of this future may be able to prolong our lives?"

"This didn't seem to concern you last night," Jefferson replied.

"Nay. That is, no. But we will have access to futurity's medicine eventually. I expired painfully, suffering for almost a decade from gout and stone which this future can cure within a fortnight. With these ailments and my bullet wound cured, I might live another decade or more. And what of you, George? You are healthier than I, and two decades younger. You could live a score or two more."

"Years of extra life in most any time would compel me to choose it," Washington said. "But in a luxurious American future I want to explore? The decision isn't a decision."

Franklin nodded. "Even if my life was shortened and there was no compelling need for my talents, I would still stay here. The second I returned I would long for the luxuries of this world. And I would forever regret forsaking a chance to absorb such an enormous stockpile of knowledge. To have so many curiosities satisfied."

"I am grateful for the opportunity to return," Jefferson said. "But I too wish to stay. Monticello is here, and even were it not, I can build something greater with modern inventions. In the past I left, most of the people I loved are long dead, and those that remain are not a preponderance when weighed against other factors already mentioned. If I returned I too would forever regret enlightenment forsaken, though that is not my primary rationale."

"Maybe he has acted through the Puppeteer, or perhaps he has intervened overtly. It makes little difference. Like Ben, I believe Providence has brought us here for some weighty purpose that involves the American destiny. In our past, none of us accomplish anything else of significance before dying. What if America needed us, and we abandoned her by returning home?"

"That is highly hypothetical," Washington said.

"I realize that," Jefferson said. "But just suppose?"

Washington stood with finality. "We shall stay then."

Franklin looked at his watch and smiled. "But we must also leave."

"Where?" Jefferson asked.

"The bus station?" Franklin replied.

"There are surely magistrates there. Why not call the natural philosopher, tell him the truth, and ask his assistance?" Jefferson said.

"He would never help us once he realized we are the fugitives the magistrates seek."

"If you told him the *whole* truth, he might ferry us to a distant city or bus station in his Watt wagon."

"He might betray us," Franklin replied. "Inadvertently rather than maliciously, I suspect. Like most natural philosophers, he seems to derive joy from gleaning and sharing knowledge. He would burst trying to contain such a secret."

"If he revealed the truth he would be assumed ripe for Bedlam as surely as we," Jefferson countered.

Round and round the conversation went. Finally, Washington said, "Neither solution is ideal. We must choose the least of the ills."

Franklin thought a moment, then said, "The natural philosopher." He fished for his phone, opened it, and dialed, but there was no ring. "My phone is not functioning. Are yours?"

Washington and Jefferson checked, and found the same problem.

"The natural philosopher said the phones might not work in remote regions," Franklin said.

"How remote?" Washington asked. "Might movement help?"

Washington walked a quarter mile in each direction with all three phones, but they still did not work.

"We are trapped in another self-referencing conundrum," Franklin surmised. "We need to call the natural philosopher to find out why our phones cannot call."

The founders sat and soul searched. Every option was considered, no matter how absurd. Camping in the wilderness for an extended period, trying to hike to another town or bus station, hitchhiking, even the previously rejected option of privateering a vehicle and pilot. Franklin's health, the party's lack of mobility, searching magistrates, and the general conviction that their risk would increase the longer they stayed in the vicinity of Rushmore caused them to reject these measures. Eventually, the trio reached a sullen conclusion: they had to exercise their lone remaining option.

Washington was carrying Franklin back through the forest. He had no idea where the bus station was, and didn't know how to get to it. It didn't matter. They would find it somehow, and then confront the last obstacle preventing escape to anonymity.

Jefferson and Franklin seemed less comfortable than Washington with the sense of impending conflict. At their core they were thinkers, and their instinctual reaction was to search for some way to cajole or reason their way out.

Philosophers can outthink themselves, Washington thought. The approach of an unavoidable battle was nothing new to him. Sometimes you just had to stare into the guns and charge. Washington was a man of action who drew comfort from the fact that for ill or well, their situation would soon be resolved.

Still, one concern troubled him. Criminals were one thing, but if the situation took an unforeseen turn, would he kill American magistrates?

When the Greyhound sign became visible, the founders stopped and cleaned themselves up. A cloth was placed on Franklin's wound to avoid a conspicuous stain in case it bled.

As they once again resumed walking, Franklin checked his phone and realized they had reception. He was about to dial when he noted a tall, slender tower that was little more than a metal frame. "Could magistrates have the ability to monitor all telegraphs as they did Tom's?"

"You are the natural philosopher," Washington said. "You tell us. Could using the phone result in our capture?"

Franklin looked at the air like it was alive. "Could they not survey using signals? Determine a range like an engineer aiming artillery? Yes. Yes. And as the waves move quickly, and computers could do the ciphering, the process would be most expedient."

A surveyor and soldier, Washington saw the plausibility of what Franklin was saying almost immediately. "On to the station then."

"Founding Fathers Involved in Robbery!" the newspaper headline screamed. Below it were police sketches of Franklin and Washington, the digital photos the Rushmore family had taken, and colonial portraits. Though the sketches were rough, and the photos grainy, the resemblance was unmistakable.

"I knew we shouldn't have stood for the camera obscura portrait," Washington hissed.

Jefferson had inserted change, but the metal newspaper enclosure would not open for some reason. Washington shook the enclosure repeatedly. Still no luck. He looked around to make sure no one was watching, then kicked it so hard the glass rattled. "I wish I had a musket!" he cursed.

"Easy, George," Franklin said. "It's not a deserter."

Franklin studied the device and determined that a coin was stuck just inside the slot. When he pressed an additional coin in especially hard and fast, there was a pronounced jingling and the door opened easily.

Each founder grabbed a paper, and began reading feverishly as they walked away.

"Did we pay for one paper, or three?" Jefferson asked.

No one had sufficient change, so Washington turned around and began to shove a five dollar bill in the slot.

"I wouldn't do that, George," Franklin chided. "I think you could ruin the—"

Washington's murderous glare silenced Franklin. Normally he would have made some quip, but he was tired from his ordeals, and he sensed that Washington's temper was plotting an escape.

The founders devoured the article quickly. The police were still looking for a trio with a tall, athletic killer and a short, fat individual who had been injured. Most witnesses had concentrated on these two suspects, and a description of the third was proving elusive. The witness to the shooting had not been able to make him out because he had cowered against a shadowy wall that cloaked his features.

The most conclusive description was of the most dangerous individual, a man who bore a startling resemblance to George Washington. The shot individual purportedly resembled Ben Franklin. The third individual might resemble Jefferson, but this supposition was much more speculative. Only three groups of witnesses made the Jefferson comparison; most reported being drawn to "Washington's" stature and "Franklin's" wit, while somehow overlooking the third individual.

The story assembled an impressive array of testimony: the family who had contacted police at Rushmore, individuals who had approached them in bars, hotel clerks, strangers they had passed on streets. Everyone but the Samaritan seemed to have called the police once an initial report of a crime involving founding father lookalikes was broadcast.

The founders exchanged nervous glances while they read, but no one spoke because there was nothing to be said. They all felt more exposed, and nervous, but the article did not alter the realities of their situation. Not strategically, anyway. The tactical outlook was another matter.

"I WOULD FEEL less conspicuous starkers," Franklin whispered, as another family walked past.

Jefferson nodded. "Ironic, though. Or perhaps fortuitous. Everyone seems to be talking about the crime, but no one seems to notice us."

Franklin chuckled. "I knew a rogue who swore that the best place to commit crime was in plain view."

On they walked, and for once, Washington was the problem rather than the solution. As it always did, his regal stature attracted attention.

"Keep the paper above your head as you walk, George," Franklin said. "Your eyes would give you away in an instant. And for Providence's sake, stop strutting like a king!"

Washington did his best, but hiding his innate stature was like swimming in sand. The founders' progress nonetheless continued, and slowly, step by step, second by second, lingering look by lingering look, they approached their mecca.

"I STILL WISH we had disguises," Jefferson said, as the founders prepared to split up.

"Speaking of disguises, watch for magistrates dressed as commoners," Washington warned. "Especially on the bus."

The founders reviewed the times, places, phones numbers and e-mail addresses they would use to contact each other if their plan failed.

"How ironic," Franklin mused. "Tom's cowardice may prove to be our saving grace."

Washington scowled, but kept quiet.

"Let us swear an oath," Jefferson concluded. "Each to help the other. To rescue the other, if need be."

Franklin shook his head. "I will abandon you if it best serves America, and I expect you to do the same to me."

THOMAS JEFFERSON ENTERED the Rapid City bus station and approached the ticket counter. Spacious and bright, with clear glass doors and tall potted plants, it seemed more like a mall than a terminal.

And there were no magistrates.

Yet.

Jefferson waited for an individual in front of him to conclude a purchase, then stepped up and said, "Four tickets to New York."

The attendant typed quickly. "Hm." More typing. "Hmmm." Even more typing. "Strange. They're never full this time of the week. Or the year, for that matter. But it looks like you're out of luck."

"Scores of tickets were available last night," Jefferson said.

"That may be, but Greyhound operates on a first-come-first-served basis, not a reservation basis. I'm terribly sorry." The teller noted the old man's distraught expression. "Maybe this is a computer error. It does seem strange. Just a second."

Jefferson thanked her and waited patiently while she made several phone calls. He wondered if she had recognized him, and was perhaps calling the magistrates, but was surprisingly unafraid. Cops were surely mere ticks away, and even if he were younger and could flee, where could he possibly go?

"Real strange," the teller said as she hung up. "A single party purchased every ticket to New York."

"When?"

"They didn't say."

"What party?"

"Even if I knew that, I couldn't reveal it. Such information is confidential."

Jefferson was beginning to think the clerk was lying and had alerted magistrates. Might they approach stealthily this time, without the shrieking sopranos?

"When will transportation be obtainable?"

"That's the other weird thing. Whoever bought all those tickets did so for several days. There isn't a ticket available to New York until the morning of September 10th. But that wouldn't put you in New York until the 12th."

Jefferson's heart sank. "So no seats on this morning's bus are available?"

"There are plenty of seats on the bus out of here. It's the connections to New York that are full."

Jefferson resisted the urge to sigh. He purchased four tickets to an intermediate location, then exited the bus station.

Officer Carl Stratford exited his cruiser and was about to approach the Greyhound station when he noted a familiar form entering it. "Paul! Is that you?"

An ever-so-discernable slouching of the shoulders. The figure stopped, turned, and smiled. "Hey, Stratty. How goes it?"

Paul approached quickly. *Too quickly*, Stratford thought.

"Why you here?" Paul asked. "That thing in the papers?"

Stratford smiled smoothly. "Crazy, isn't it? Just when you thought the world couldn't get any wackier."

Stratford was a pitbull of an old soldier. High and tight crewcut, broomstick posture, trousers creased so stiffly they could give you a paper cut. Paul usually didn't notice Stratty's lean muscularity, or his athletic strut, but today it was his foremost observation.

"Media's gonna cannibalize this one," Stratford continued. "CNN already called this morning. Their correspondents are on the way. The rest of the jackals can't be far behind."

"It's not that big a story, is it?" Paul said.

"When we catch them it might be."

"Yeah, probably," Paul agreed.

"Somethin' wrong?"

"Nah. Just thinkin'. Wonderin'. What's gonna happen to 'em?"

"If we can take them alive, they're going to do some time."

If you take them alive? "How much time?"

"I ain't the DA, but Christ. They fled the scene of a multiple homicide. It's not like they'll skate with probation."

"But the paper said they were probably mugged. That would mean they acted in self defense."

"If they were mugged and acting in self defense, why'd they flee?"

Paul smiled ever-so-slightly.

"Something amusing?"

"You're right. This situation is crazy. What if they honestly didn't do anything wrong?"

"Then they probably wouldn't have fled. Look. Juries can understand defending yourself. And normally, when a couple multiple felons get slabbed, it's no sweat off anyone's nad-o-rewskies. But this was execution-style."

"You saw the scene?"

Stratty looked over. "Yeah. It looks like someone let the fucking Predator loose in that alley. I'm telling you, it won't matter what you tell a jury; they see those crime-scene photos, they'll have a hard time believing it was purely self defense. Hell, I have a hard time believing it."

"But what if they didn't do anything wrong?"

"Maybe they did, maybe they didn't. I wasn't there, so I don't know, but that isn't the point. I'm telling you what I think will happen, not what should happen."

Paul stopped, and stared at Stratford. "Why is it so many Americans think like you? Accept what's going to happen instead of demanding what should?"

"I retire in four years with full benefits, Paul. You're young and idealistic now, and I can respect that, but when you get to be my age you'll see."

"Well maybe America could use someone old and idealistic."

"I could use a third nut, but it hasn't sprouted." Stratty smiled at Paul's indicting stare. "It's not like I'm on the take. I'm not gonna look the other way if I see a real crime, but America's fucked, and I'm not going to change it. Why jump in front of a bus when it's going to keep rolling regardless?"

Paul hoped someone else was jumping on a bus while he delayed Stratty. "So three men who probably didn't do anything wrong could end up doing time."

"Yeah. Maybe."

"This doesn't bother you?"

"If I let everything that's wrong with America bother me I'd be in an asylum. Your father would agree. And I hate to sound like a hallmark card, but he's proud of you. Almost cries when he talks about that internship with Lawrence Livermore."

"SAIC, technically. And it's far from certain. Jobs like this are the nerd equivalent of trying to play in the NBA."

Stratty laughed. "If there's anyone smarter than you I'm afraid to meet them."

Paul wondered what Stratty would think of Mr. "Steele."

"Maybe one day you'll get to build UFOs after all," Stratty said.

"Don't tell them that when they come for the background check."

"You were always going to do something special," Stratty said. "Me and your Dad knew that even when you was little."

Paul shrugged.

"He's glad you're getting out of this town. Glad you didn't ruin your life like he did his."

"He said that?" Paul asked.

"Yeah. He said that. Last month while we were fishin'."

"What happened?"

"We caught a couple steelhead."

"Ha, ha."

"You know what happened."

"That's not an answer."

"'Nam fucked him up. That's what happened."

"It didn't fuck you up."

Stratty smiled sadly. "Yeah it did."

"My Dad never tells me about that stuff."

"If I had kids, I wouldn't tell them either."

"I deserve to know. At least, I want to know. How can I understand him if I don't know?"

"Be glad you don't know. Chain yourself in that ivory tower, kid."

The radio clipped to Stratty's shoulder crackled. The dispatcher wanted to know if the station was clear. Stratty told him he was about to inspect and would report back momentarily.

"I doubt I'm going to find anything inside," Stratty said. "But just in case, you'd better wait here."

"It'd be kinda cool to go in, if you don't mind."

"I do mind. Wait here. And if anything happens, run all the way to Livermore."

Stratford searched the bus station warily. Though large, it was devoid of effective hiding places, and practically empty. The only people Stratford saw didn't fit the bill. He felt the initial adrenaline surge that accompanied any entry dissipate, but didn't relax. He sure as hell wasn't ending up like the felons in the alley.

Three perps dumb enough to try and board a bus, Stratty postulated. *How could they think we wouldn't search it? Only a retard would think that, which is why they aren't and won't be here.*

Unless . . .

Unless what?

Unless this is their only option.

Why would this be their only option?

No IDs? Criminal records? Illegal immigrants? Canucks perhaps? They had no car.

Suppose I were them. Three men, two with sketches in the paper, one with some sort of professional hand-to-hand training, perhaps a soldier. What would I do?

I would split up. Have one take a train, another a bus, another a plane, and either separate permanently or rendezvous at some distant point.

But one perp was injured, perhaps too severely to travel alone, so splitting up might not be possible. One might stay with the injured individual, the other go alone. Or perhaps the injured perp is dead. The remaining two would probably split up; if I'm the unidentified perp, the last thing I'd want to do is travel with the conspicuous bad ass.

Stratty looked around again, and took another instant to finish churning the permutations. He was a man who considered all the possibilities, even the improbable, for he knew these were often the ones that killed you. He therefore revisited his initial, improbable supposition; suppose the trio had to stay together for some reason and was attempting flight on the bus.

I would board the bus quickly at the last minute. I wouldn't loiter where officers could scrutinize me at their leisure. But anything too last minute would be conspicuous. I would have the individual whose face was not in the paper purchase tickets. I would split the party up and have each individual board separately, like three strangers. And I would be in disguise.

In what order would I board? Who would sit where? Those would depend. Are we friends, or distant acquaintances who can abandon each other without remorse?

Something was eluding Stratford, but he couldn't put his finger on it. He searched the bus station perimeter, found nothing, radioed in, and then approached the teller.

"You seen anything suspicious?"

"No. Why?"

"You kidding?"

"Kidding?"

"You haven't heard about the homicides?"

"Homicides?"

Frustration followed. The teller hadn't heard about the robbery, and when she realized how deadly serious Stratty was, she told him bluntly that she'd gotten drunk and high the night before, and had been banging her boyfriend while watching porn until the moment she left for work.

Stratty nodded grimly. A typical, ignoramus American indifferent to everything but their own narrow reality. One who was hung over and struggling through the day, barely cognizant of what was transpiring. Elvis could have bought a bus ticket without worry.

"The guy I'm looking for might have looked like Jefferson," Stratty said.

"Jefferson?"

"Yeah. Jefferson. You know, Thomas Jefferson?"

"I know who he is, but I mean not what he like looks like."

Christ, Stratty thought. *How ignorant do you have to be to work thirty-two miles from Rushmore and not know what Thomas Jefferson looks like?* Paul's idealistic comments came to mind for some reason.

Stratty showed the teller police sketches, digital photographs, and portraits, and asked her to describe every person she'd seen that morning. There were only a few dozen, and none seemed exact matches, but they were a few older, taller individuals. Only one had purchased more than a single ticket, four to be precise.

The clerk gave few descriptive details, save "he was tall and kind." Real helpful.

But four tickets. A coincidence? Or a sophomoric attempt to mask the group's number?

Stratty wanted to sit down, but he remembered the cadavers in the alley and stood with his back to a wall, hand on his holster.

Of course they weren't here.

He was just being foolish.

But for a man who was simply being foolish, Officer Carl Stratford suddenly felt awfully nervous.

As HE WONDERED about Franklin, Paul peered inside the terminal and saw Stratford standing motionless against a wall. He knew Stratty would probably berate him if he entered, and felt fear as he thought of the murders, but a primal curiosity dispelled all sense of restraint. Paul entered the terminal and approached.

"I told you to wait outside!" Stratford barked.

"I have to drain the weasel."

"Make it fast."

As Stratford watched Paul head to the bathroom, something still nagged at him. Paul was acting strange, but this was unrelated.

The perps. Focus on the perps. I can catch them on the bus, or while boarding it, but this might result in a hostage situation.

The injured perp.

Some ungraspable realization tickled at Stratford. A frustrating, teasing tickle.

The injured perp.

His two companions could hide some distance away and approach the bus quickly, at the last moment, but if he was less mobile, he would be closer. Wouldn't he? Wouldn't he hide close, and then attempt to discreetly board the bus?

Yes, Stratford thought, as he looked around alertly, suddenly seeing the situation with greater clarity. *He definitely would.*

MAYBE STEELE isn't here, Paul thought, as he approached the bathroom. *Maybe he already got away. Maybe they were just actors who look like the founders. Maybe I'm a jackass for thinking time travel might be possib—*

Steele walked out of the bathroom.

He was walking out the bathroom!

Paul mustered maximum discipline and resisted the urge to gape. As Steele came closer, his features crystallized. The moles. The skin creases. The Droopy-Dog eyes. The slightly larger bag below the left eye.

Paul had spent hours studying portraits of Franklin, and with each step he saw some new detail that was *exactly* like a painting. Too much exactness for even a look alike.

Hundreds of Franklin's comments once again flooded through Paul, and he reconciled them with historical descriptions of the First American's personality. Matches. All matches.

Though the most convincing argument was Franklin's expression. A frustrated yet amused pursing of the lips. The countenance of a man who was beaten, and knew it, but hadn't lost his perspective and could still laugh. With a simple smile and a twinkling of his eye, Benjamin Franklin admitted his identity.

A thousand questions pulsed through Paul. So many that, ironically, counterintuitively, he had trouble formulating even one.

Paul wanted to groan with frustration as he kept walking and entered the bathroom. Euphoria and nausea wracked him. Ben Franklin was actually in the future! Holy shit! Holy freakin' shit!

Paul's knees buckled like some newborn calf's.

Ben Franklin was in the future!

Frustration began to penetrate surprise. *Ben Franklin is only a few yards away, but I can't talk to him without giving away his identity!* Paul wanted to scream like Charlie Brown whiffing a kick. "Fuck!" He pulled at his hair, then let out a wail of a chuckle. "Fu-uh-uck!"

Paul placed his ear on the bathroom door. He would wait long enough to make it seem like he'd pissed, then exit, and . . . and . . . and what?

Franklin sat on the toilet watching his watch.

At last it said 9:55.

Unfortunately it said 9:55.

He rose wearily. Painfully. Never had he felt so tattered. He opened the stall door, then watched himself in the mirror and practiced walking without a limp.

It was imperative that he appear healthy.

Though he had never braved battle like Washington, risking his life was nothing new to Franklin. When he sailed to Europe to serve as Minister to France, braving seas controlled by the indomitable British Navy, he faced hanging for treason if captured. His death would have been the equivalent of a battalion to Britain, and while Minister in France, he survived machinations by Crown spies. These latter dangers were eerily reminiscent of his current predicament to the First American.

Franklin sighed deeply, opened the bathroom door, stepped out, and saw the natural philosopher approaching. When Paul's eyes narrowed, then slowly grew larger, Franklin knew he had been identified. He pursed his lips mischievously, relaxed his gait, and was about to speak when he saw Paul stiffen and crane only his eyes.

Franklin could not see a magistrate, but knew there was one. Mimicking Paul, he swung his eyes but not his body, and located the cop on the far wall. Benjamin Franklin willed away pain and fear, stood as straight as he could, and approached the far exit that led to the bus.

Stratford saw Paul pause ever-so-suddenly as someone exited the bathroom. He couldn't make out the figure, but Paul's movements became more mechanical, more forced.

Suspicious, Stratford obeyed his instincts and approached the bathroom. Paul entered, and the figure that had exited approached the terminal doors with strides that were slow but true.

Stratford slowed, growing less suspicious.

Until the man's knee locked, and he limped momentarily, like a glitch in a video.

Stratford's feet pounded the floor slabs as he approached. He drew and raised his Gloch. "Stop and turn around, sir!"

Franklin obeyed, and smiled. "Yes, magistrate?"

Is he the only one? Stratford thought nervously. *Where's the tall one? The killer. At the airport? Christ. Anywhere but here.*

"Raise your hands, sir."

Franklin obeyed again.

"I don't want to hurt you, sir. But if you lower those arms or move, I won't miss. Do you understand?"

"Yes, magistrate."

Stratford watched Franklin while he performed a slow, circular sweep. As he completed it, Paul stepped out of the bathroom. "Hello, Professor Steele," he said to Franklin.

Franklin smiled as if everything were perfectly normal. "Hello, Paul. I'm glad to see you recognized me."

"You know him," Stratford said.

"Yeah. I know him."

"It wasn't a question."

"He's my American history professor."

Stratford's face tensed. On a whole lotta levels, this didn't jibe. The founding father lookalikes had been seen costumed near Rushmore, were described as somewhat clueless vagrants, and had told people they were actors or advertisers.

Stratford glanced at his best-friend's son. Paul never lied. Paul had never lied. Why would Paul lie?

George Washington entered the bus station through the same door the natural philosopher and magistrate did, and crept toward their rear like a ninja ghost. The natural philosopher was to the magistrate's left, so Washington approached from the right. If the magistrate heard him and turned left, the natural philosopher would impede his movement, and if he turned right Washington would sprint forward and hopefully grab his gun before he could shoot.

Washington held his knife cupped upward against his forearm to conceal it. Concealing himself was more difficult. The tip-toeing-tiger posture that made silent movement possible was conspicuous. A single chance glance by the teller or some entering citizen would end his gambit, but for now the terminus was empty and the teller was vegetating at her desk rather than vigilantly manning the window.

What am I going to do? Washington wondered, as he inched closer. *Take him hostage? No, he communicates with radio, like the taxi pilot. If he did not check in, magistrates would arrive shortly.*

Kill him? No. He is probably an honest underling trying to uphold laws and enforce a constitution. Of course, the same might be said about many of the redcoats I dispatched.

Washington wanted to sigh. As of yet, they had done nothing immoral. Their persecution for the alley murders was a misunderstanding that could eventually be rectified, but if he murdered a magistrate, they would truly be fugitives. Magistrates would probably crusade for criminals who killed one of their own, and show no mercy.

As George Washington took another step forward, he adopted the same mindset.

STRATFORD KNEW HE NEEDED to call for backup. The Predator might be lurking, and to arrest him in a crowded area, they needed overwhelming force that would deter any insanity. Other officers at airports and the train station checked in, reporting no signs of the suspects, but Stratford's hand hesitated near his radio.

Paul had lied.

Steele wasn't his history Professor, but he sure as hell knew him.

"Raise your shirt, sir," Stratford said.

"No need," Franklin replied. "I am the man you seek."

"One of the men I seek. Where are the others?"

Franklin smiled. He was careful not to divert his eyes toward the approaching form of Washington. "I will come quietly, but I am no Benedict."

No Benedict? "How do you know him, Paul?" Stratford asked.

"He's my history professor."

"Bullshit. How do you know him?"

"You wouldn't believe me if I told you."

"I don't believe what you've already told me."

Franklin looked at Paul and said, "Aren't you going to ask me why I'm here, magistrate? Or who I am?"

Paul stared at Franklin.

Benjamin Franklin!

Benjamin freakin' Franklin!

And was that cold-eyed dude he'd seen at the hotel actually Washington? Could the third member of their party be Jefferson?

Were the founding fathers in the present?

The founding fathers were in the present?

As Stratty reached for his radio, Paul trembled.

The founding fathers were in the present, and if Stratty arrested them, they would be incarcerated.

They can't have been brought here simply to be arrested, Paul thought. He flashed through the modern American history he knew. JFK's assassination. Vietnam. Watergate. Iran-Contra. Savings & Loan bailouts. Clinton's scandalrama. Dozens of other disheartening transgressions occurred. Paul knew that if he wanted to list them all in less than an hour he'd need that fast-talking fellow from the old Fed-Ex commercials. American politicians no longer even bothered with pretenses of honesty.

Like many scientists, Paul was a pacifist, but he wanted to punish the scoundrels who defiled America with impunity, perhaps even hurt them. How and why had the United States forsaken Franklins, Washingtons, and Jeffersons for Nixons, Bushes, and Clintons?

Paul had no idea, but as he thought about skyrocketing corruption, he felt consuming despondence. How did you restore American political integrity? Free energy seemed simpler.

Yet here he was, feet from the only man, and perhaps the only men, on Earth that probably had solutions and a realistic chance of implementing them.

As Paul stared into Benjamin Franklin's sagely eyes, he felt certain the founders had been brought to the future for a purpose. And that purpose sure as hell wasn't five to fifty for manslaughter.

You came here to help Franklin, didn't you?

I came here to see who he was.

You know who he is now, but that wasn't the only reason you came here.

Was it?

Paul thought of Lawrence Livermore and pictured himself building electrogravitic flying saucers, a dream he had pursued relentlessly since seeing a UFO as a young boy. His throat chalked suddenly and he hesitated. He recalled *The Declaration of Independence*, in which the founders had pledged their lives, fortunes, and sacred honor to preserve freedom and create America. Where were modern politicians willing to make this same commitment?

Our politicians are a shadowy reflection of the electorate, Paul thought, with growing discomfort. *America's leaders are drawn from its citizens, and few leaders have character because few citizens do.*

As Stratty reached for his radio, Paul imagined Washington locking George Bush Sr. in a BCCI vault to suffocate, Jefferson castrating Clinton by clapping Lewinsky's jaw shut, Franklin as a Godzilla who razed special-interest, corporate skyscrapers. He saw himself in jail at worst, and at best failing the background check all his dream jobs required.

Paul trembled as he stared at Benjamin Franklin, a man who had never hesitated to sacrifice everything for America. He hated himself for being seduced by uncertainty, obfuscation, and most of all fear.

I couldn't live with myself, Paul thought suddenly. *God will strike me down if I allow Ben Franklin to spend his last few years tossing salads and taking it up the ass.*

I must demonstrate character. If America is ever to be improved, peons like me must be prepared to sacrifice. I gripe about corruption, but what have I ever done to fight it? I must pledge my life, fortune, and sacred honor, so that our founders once again can.

But how?

As Washington continued to approach the magistrate, his unease grew. Were he, Franklin, and Jefferson truly destined to lead America again? Ascribing the Puppeteer more trivial motivations still seemed ludicrous, but . . .

And was it truly necessary to remain anonymous until they deciphered futurity? They might never do so completely.

Washington pondered his last question's nuances, but derived few insights, much less an answer. He had always relied on the counsel of geniuses when making weighty prognostications, and his limited education and vision angered him suddenly. Franklin and Jefferson could illuminate the tunnels of the future with their intellects, but he saw only flickers of factors.

Franklin was mere yards away, facing one of futurity's odd, square pistols with a bemused grin. Ironic to have the First American so close, yet unable to offer counsel! But he had already offered it, hadn't he?

Ben believed temporary anonymity was paramount, and was prepared to sacrifice his arm or life to preserve it. Washington gritted his dentures. *Am I supposed to murder a magistrate in defense of the same theoretical?*

Washington's step faltered momentarily. He tried to tell himself that one life was trivial when balanced against the preservation of the republic. Even the life of a martyr.

Washington approached an outward facing interior corner, and hid behind it while maintaining a casual facade. Once he stepped past this oasis, he was approaching the magistrate through the central, wide open portion of the terminal and alia iacta est.

Through the terminal exit opposite the one he had entered, the one that would lead to the bus, Washington glimpsed the distant form of Jefferson. Tom seemed to be squinting. Watching Ben's confrontation perhaps?

Alone, Jefferson might be able to board the bus and escape, but Washington felt that if he approached it, they would both be caught.

I could survive alone in the woods until the magistrates stop searching, then rendezvous with Tom. Together we might free Ben. But perhaps Tom would board the bus, something unforeseen would happen, and I would never see him again.

This seemed like more than an obscure possibility to Washington. Together the founders corroborated each other, alone they were more apt to be viewed as isolated lunatics. And if separated permanently, they were far less useful to America. Jefferson's hypocrisies would make him oppugnant to factions of futurity; alone, he could probably never be elected. Washington knew he was not smart enough by himself. The only one who could lead solo was the only one who could not escape their current predicament . . .

Yet alone, even Franklin would be hampered. Washington knew attempting the Presidency with a retinue of unknown advisors, all potential sycophants, would be impossible. The most skilled leader needed a few trusted old friends, even one of Franklin's intelligence and talent.

Peering down the dim tunnel of prognostication, Washington saw one flickering factor illuminate suddenly. Unity, the main strength of America, the paramount admonition he had always tried to preach, had to remain their axiom. Futurity was too daunting for any one man, infinitely more daunting than any casual contemplator might have supposed. The Puppeteer had transported a trio for a reason. Washington's gut told him that only a synthesis of Franklin's natural philosophic, Jefferson's political, and his military expertise would decipher the future completely. Learning to live in modern society was difficult, but becoming wise enough to govern it would be infinitely more onerous.

As Washington eyed his prey, he confronted a more fundamental problem: any attack on the magistrate would alert witnesses who would contact more magistrates.

He still had not made a decision, still hadn't even formulated a viable option, but it was now or never, for in moments, Franklin would be arrested.

George Washington took a deep breath, flipped his knife downward, then began his final approach to the magistrate.

PAUL GULPED HARD and said, "I was the third person in the alley, Stratty. I'm an accomplice. Jenny Benway saw Steele and I at Rushmore together. I do—"

"Not another word." Stratford slouched slightly. "Shit, kid. Shit."

Stratford wasn't sure about the college professor BS, but the rest of the admission had the ring of truth. Paul's anxious questions about how much time the perps would do now made a lot more sense. As did his nervousness. And the four tickets the perp purchased explained his presence at the bus station at 9:00 AM on a Friday. What the hell had Paul gotten himself into?

Officer Carl Stratford considered his options. Like most cops, he regularly abused his station to help people he knew. On nickel and dime stuff, anyway. Homicide was a whole different creature. Abetting a murderer wasn't like letting a drunk friend careen his way home. He could easily do hard time, and at the very least he would permanently be barred from all law enforcement and security work nationwide. And of course there was his precious pension.

"Please don't send me to jail, Stratty. I'll go to jail if you turn me in."

"I don't need a schematic."

"It was self defense. No bullshit."

"You say another word, I'll mash you. No bullshit."

Franklin saw the magistrate's eyes narrow, and was reminded of Washington, who was now only a few yards away. The First American was careful not to glance at Washington and give him away, but masking his shock and fear was more difficult. Was George actually going to murder a magistrate? Indecision wracked Washington's face, yet with each step he seemed to grow colder and gain resolve.

Stratty sighed deeply while he weighed the scales. The life of his best friend's son, one with a supernova future. Two career criminals who probably got what they deserved.

"You there, Stratty?" a radio voice said with concern.

Behind Stratford, George Washington raised his knife and prepared for a throat cut. He was about to slash, but stopped suddenly. Killing the magistrate was dishonorable. He lowered his knife, then backed away slowly.

Officer Carl Stratford stared straight at Benjamin Franklin, depressed his radio and said, "All clear. I say again, all clear. Over?"

"Roger that," the radio replied.

"Any luck elsewhere?" Stratford asked.

"Negative."

Stratford talked on the radio a bit longer. The moment he concluded, Franklin said, "Thank you."

"I'm helping him, not you," Stratford growled.

I was talking to him, not you. Franklin pursed his lips and smiled at Paul, conveying irony, relief, and most of all gratitude.

Paul felt pride, and a transcendental moral contentment. "There's so much I wanted to ask you!"

"There is much I would like to tell you." *And futurity.*

Stratford glared at Franklin and pointed at the bus with his gun. Franklin nodded, turned, and began limping toward it.

"Tell your Predator friend I'll be watching the bus," Stratford whispered. "You disturb the peace, you'll rest in peace."

Franklin nodded.

"I didn't see a thing," Stratford said to Paul, as he turned with tunnel vision and made a beeline for the door. "Neither did you."

"You have to go back and let me say goodbye to him!" Paul begged. "You made him leave before I could say anything!"

"And hopefully before anyone saw anything."

"Just five minutes. Please!"

"No way."

Paul clasped his hands as if praying. "Just one question. Please!"

"Do you realize what I just did for you?"

And America. "Yeah." Paul looked Stratford in the eyes. "Thanks."

"We get caught, the shit'll seem like quicksand. You wanna thank me, don't press our fuckin' luck any further."

"Sorry, Stratty. Sorry."

They entered the squad car. "Stop apologizing and tell me *exactly* what happened."

"You won't believe me."

"I'd better believe you."

WHILE THE BUS DRIVER loaded baggage, the founders sat on a nearby bench contemplating their past, the events of the last few days, and most of all their future.

People came and went like thoughts. Walking, talking, laughing, fretting, some merely being.

People.

People living, most of all choosing! To walk, talk, laugh, fret, or merely be.

"Everyone we've seen is free," Franklin shook Washington and laughed. "They are all free!"

Washington nodded. His smile conveyed deep satisfaction.

"The notes. The capitation." Jefferson's voice lacked the vehemence it usually contained when discussing such topics. "Though I have strong ethical and philosophical objections to these woes, the preponderance of this future impresses me. The lot of every American seems improved."

"By advancements in natural philosophy as well as the expansion of freedom," Franklin said.

Washington nodded. "Though I too have concerns, one cannot deny this future's grandeur. Much of what we hoped has come to pass."

"And much of what we feared most," Jefferson replied.

"This duality makes it extremely difficult to discern the state of the republic," Washington said.

Jefferson nodded. "We return like foreigners, and, like them, require a considerable residence here to become Americanized. It may be months or even years before we can formulate truly accurate and objective assessments."

Franklin peered at his surroundings with an overwhelmed expression, as if he were trying to gulp the whole of futurity in a glance, and choking on it. "Have we kept our republic?"

Uncertain silence.

"While we seek that elusive answer, mere survival presents many obstacles," Washington said.

Nods and grim glances. Though free from the immediate threat of incarceration, the founders felt no safer. An unknown futurity still lurked, one that remained truly daunting. A mere trip to a pub had turned into a fiasco, yet they were now journeying across the continent.

Like shooting Lewis and Clark in the shoulder and sending them westward with only a knapsack, Jefferson thought.

"We need false identities, papers, and portrait cards," Franklin said. "For the long term, income. As the professions we knew are almost certainly obsolete, we will probably have to learn new ones. We need to obtain a Watt wagon and learn to drive it. We must choose a place to settle, and secure housing. A Mason Lodge should be located, if they still exist. Monticello and Mount Vernon should be visited, as well as Philadelphia and New York. We must identify and confront our Puppeteer. Time transport must be researched, and some plausible technical explanation for our presence formulated. I must have this EWSL performed. We must visit physicians and aggressively seek out health enhancements that may prolong our lifespan. We must fly, roger, visit a post office, roger, tour France, roger, complete our surveys of natural philosophy and history . . ."

"And after all these things are accomplished?" Washington asked. "What then?"

"Did I mention rogering?"

Jefferson chuckled. "You mean when does Ben run for President?"

Franklin pursed his lips, but said nothing.

"No steadfast denial?" Washington asked.

"Besting death is a cathartic experience which has made me more comfortable with my destiny. If that is my destiny." Franklin pursed his lips as he gazed at the road east. "We are but three gnats in a swarm. Still, great affairs sometimes take their rise from small circumstances."

Another ponderous silence.

It was interrupted by a lumbering plane making a gradual upward ascent. Too large and loud to be a bird, it was nonetheless a somewhat indistinct fleck. "I must obtain a closer view of these airplanes," Franklin gasped.

Like the First American, Washington and Jefferson were awed, but also somewhat disheartened, for seeing the plane made them realize how much easier and faster transport east might have been.

"How could we see such wonders and ever live comfortably in our past?" Franklin said, as the plane slipped from view. "When we spoke of returning to it, our words sounded strange, almost foreign to me. We haven't been here long, but I already consider this future my home."

"America is our home," Jefferson said. "No matter what the time."

"I always wanted a son," Washington said. "To spend the twilight of my life watching him make his way in the world."

"Perhaps your wish has been granted," Jefferson replied.

"You are The Father of our Country," Franklin said. "Yours is a greater posterity than any son, or even a score of them."

"It is our posterity," Washington said, "not mine. Ours, and all of America's, and all of mankind's."

The bus opened its doors, and passengers began to board. Franklin rose enthusiastically. "Onward! To Washington's D.C.!"

TO BE CONTINUED . . .

Tempus Fugit

Bibliography

Ambler, Charles Henry. *George Washington and the West.* New York: Russell & Russell, 1971.

Aristotle. *The Complete Works of Aristotle.* Jonathan Barnes. Princeton: Princeton University Press, 1984.

Bailyn, Bernard. *The Debate on The Constitution: Federalist and Antifederalist Speeches, Articles, and Letters During the Struggle over Ratification, Parts1 & 2.* New York: Library of America, 1993.

———. *The Ideological Origins of the American Revolution.* Birmingham: Palladium Press, 2001.

———. *Origins of American Politics.* New York: Knopf, 1968.

Becker, Carl Lotus. *The Declaration of Independence: A Study in the History of Political Ideas.* New York: Knopf, 1942.

Bernstein, Barton. *Towards a New Past: Dissenting Essays in American History.* London: Chatto & Windus, 1970.

Billias, George Athan. *George Washington's Generals.* New York: William Morrow, 1964.

Black, Eric. *Our Constitution: The Myth That Binds Us.* Boulder: Westview Press, 1988.

Bowen, Catherine Drinker. *The Most Dangerous Man in America: Scenes from the Life of Benjamin Franklin.* Boston: Little Brown, 1974.

Brands, H. W. *The First American: The Life and Times of Benjamin Franklin.* New York: Doubleday, 2000.

rant, Irving. *The Fourth President: A Life of James Madison.* Indianapolis: Bobbs Merrill, 1970.

rodie, Fawn McKay. *Thomas Jefferson: An Intimate History.* New York: Norton, 1974.

rown, David Scott. *Thomas Jefferson: A Biographical Companion.* Santa Barbara: ABC-CLIO, 1998.

ırstein, Andrew. *The Inner Jefferson: Portrait f a Grieving Optimist.* Charlottesville: Uniersity Press of Virginia, 1996.

ry, John Bagnell. *A History of Greece to the eath of Alexander the Great.* London: Macillan, 1975.

ppon, Lester J. *The Adams–Jefferson Letters: e Complete Correspondence Between Thomas ferson and Abigail and John Adams.* Chapel ill: University of North Carolina Press, 1988.

Chernow, Ron. *Alexander Hamilton.* New York: Penguin Press, 2004.

Cicero, Marcus Tullius. *Cicero, Selected Works.* New York: W.J. Black, 1948.

Cleland, Hugh. *George Washington in the Ohio Valley.* Pittsburgh: University of Pittsburgh Press, 1955.

Collier, Christopher. *Decision in Philadelphia: The Constitutional Convention of 1787.* New York: Random House, 1986.

Corbin, John. *The Unknown Washington: Biographic Origins of the Republic.* Freeport: Books for Libraries Press, 1972.

Cunningham, Noble E. *In Pursuit of Reason: The Life of Thomas Jefferson.* Baton Rouge: Louisiana State University Press, 1987.

Dahl, Robert Alan. *How Democratic Is the American Constitution?* New Haven: Yale University Press, 2003.

Davis, Burke. *George Washington and the American Revolution.* New York: Random House, 1975.

Durham, Jennifer L. *Benjamin Franklin: A Biographical Companion.* Santa Barbara: ABC-CLIO, 2002.

Earle, Alice Morse. *Child Life in Colonial Days.* Bowie: Heritage Classic, 1997.

———. *Home Life in Colonial Days.* Stockbridge: Berkshire, 1992.

Ellis, Joseph J. *American Sphinx: The Character of Thomas Jefferson.* New York: Alfred A. Knopf, 1997.

———. *Founding Brothers: The Revolutionary Generation.* New York: Alfred A. Knopf, 2000.

———. *His Excellency: George Washington.* New York: Alfred A. Knopf, 2004.

Encyclopedia Britannica 2003. Chicago: Encyclopedia Britannica, 2003.

Fitzpatrick, John Clement. *George Washington Himself: A Common-Sense Biography Written from his Manuscripts.* Westport: Greenwood Press, 1975.

———. *The George Washington Scandals.* Alexander: 1929.

Flaumenhaft, Harvey. *The Effective Republic: Administration and Constitution in the Thought of Alexander Hamilton.* Durham: Duke University Press, 1992.

Flexner, James Thomas. *George Washington, Vols. 1–4.* Boston: Little, Brown, 1965–1972.

Ford, Paul Leicester. *The True George Washington.* Port Washington: Kennikat Press, 1970.

Franklin, Benjamin. *Benjamin Franklin: Writings, Vols. 1 & 2.* Ed. J.A. Leo Lemay. New York, Library of America, 1997–2002.

———. *Benjamin Franklin's Autobiography: An Authoritative Text, Backgrounds, Criticism.* Ed. J.A. Leo Lemay and P.M. Zall. New York: Norton, 1986.

———. *Fart Proudly: Writings of Benjamin Franklin You Never Read in School.* Ed. Carl Japikse. Columbus, Ohio: Enthea Press, 2003.

———. *The Ingenious Dr. Franklin: Selected Scientific Letters of Benjamin Franklin.* Ed. Nathan Goodman. Philadelphia: University of Philadelphia Press, 1931.

———. *The Papers of Benjamin Franklin.* Ed. Leonard W. Labaree. New Haven: Yale University Press, 2003.

———. *Poor Richard: The Almanacks for the Years 1733–1758.* New York: Paddington Press, 1976.

———. *The Way to Wealth: The Preface to Poor Richard's Almanack for the Year 1758 Written Under the Name of Richard Saunders.* New York: Random House, 1930.

———. *The Writings of Benjamin Franklin.* Ed. Albert Henry Smyth New York: Haskell House, 1970.

Freeman, Douglas Southall, John Alexander Carroll, and Mary Wells Ashworth. *George Washington, A Biography, Vols. 1–7.* New York: Scribners, 1948–1957.

Frisch, Hartvig. *Cicero's Fight for the Republic.* Kobenhavn: Gyldendal, 1946.

Frothingham, Thomas Goddard. *Washington, Commander in Chief.* New York: Houghton Mifflin, 1930.

Gibbon, Edward. *The Decline and Fall of the Roman Empire.* New York: Modern Library, 1983.

Grizzard, Frank E. *George Washington: A Biographical Companion.* Santa Barbara: ABC-CLIO, 2002.

Hall, Manly Palmer. *The Lost Keys of Freemasonry.* Richmond: Macoy Pub. and Masonic Supply Co., 1976.

———. *The Secret Destiny of America.* New York: Philosophical Library, 1950.

Hamilton, Alexander. *Alexander Hamilton: Writings.* Ed. Joanne B Freeman. New York: Library of America, 2001.

Hammond, Nicholas Geoffrey Lempriere. *A History of Greece to 322 B.C.* New York: Oxford University Press, 1986.

Hawke, David Freeman. *Everyday Life in Early America.* New York: Harper & Row, 1988.

———. *A Transaction of Free Men: The Birth and Course of The Declaration of Independence.* New York: Scribner, 1964.

Haworth, Paul Leland. *George Washington, Country Gentleman.* Indianapolis: Bobbs-Merril, 1925.

Hibbert, Christopher. *Redcoats and Rebels: The American Revolution through British Eyes.* New York: Norton, 1990.

Higginbotham, Don. *George Washington and the American Military Tradition.* Athens: University of Georgia Press, 1985.

———. *George Washington Reconsidered.* Charlottesville: University Press of Virginia, 2001.

Hirschfeld, Fritz. *George Washington and Slavery: A Documentary Portrayal.* Columbia: University of Missouri Press, 1997.

Humphreys, David. *David Humphreys' Life of General Washington: With George Washington's "Remarks".* Athens: University of Georgia Press, 1991.

Jefferson, Thomas. *The Life and Morals of Jesus of Nazareth, Extracted Textually from the Gospels in Greek, Latin, French, and English by Thomas Jefferson.* Washington: Govt. Print. Off, 1904.

———. *The Papers of Thomas Jefferson.* Ed. Julian P. Boyd. Princeton: Princeton University Press, 2004.

———. *Thomas Jefferson: Writings.* Ed. Merrill D. Peterson. New York: Library of America, 1984.

———. *The Works of Thomas Jefferson.* Ed. Paul Leicester Ford. New York: Putnam, 1905.

———. *The Writings of Thomas Jefferson.* Washington D.C.: Thomas Jefferson Memorial Association of the United States, 1905.

Ketcham, Ralph. *The Anti-Federalist Papers and The Constitutional Convention Debates.* New York: New American Library, 1986.

———. *James Madison: A Biography.* Newton: American Political Biography Press, 2003

Lacey, Walter K. *Cicero and the End of the Roman Republic.* New York: Barnes & Noble, 1978.

Larkin, Jack. *The Reshaping of Everyday Life, 1790–1840.* New York: Harper & Row, 1988.

Lederer, Richard M. *Colonial American English, A Glossary: Words and Phrases Found in Colonial Writing, Now Archaic, Obscure, Obsolete, or Whose Meanings Have Changed.* Essex: Verbatim Books, 1985.

Levy, Leonard. *Original Intent and the Framer's Constitution*. Chicago: Ivan R. Dee, 2000.

Lewis, Thomas A. *For King and Country: George Washington, The Early Years*. New York: J. Wiley, 1995.

Little, Shelby. *George Washington*. New York: Minton, Balch & Co., 1929.

Locke, John. *Two Treatises of Government and A Letter Concerning Toleration*. Ed. Ian Shapiro. New Haven: Yale University Press, 2003.

Loewen, James W. *Lies My Teacher Told Me: Everything Your American History Textbook Got Wrong*. New York: Simon & Schuster, 1996.

Longmore, Paul K. *The Invention of George Washington*. Charlottesville: University Press of Virginia, 1999

Lopez, Claude Anne. *The Private Franklin: The Man and His Family*. New York: Norton, 1975.

Madison, James. *James Madison: Writings*. Ed. Jack N. Rakove. New York: Library of America, 1999.

———. *The Journal of the Debates in the Convention Which Framed The Constitution of the United States of America, May–September 1787, As Recorded by James Madison*. Ed. Gaillard Hunt and James Brown Scott. Union: Lawbook Exchange, 1999.

———, and Thomas Jefferson. *The Republic of Letters: The Correspondence Between Thomas Jefferson and James Madison*. Ed. James Morton Smith. New York: Norton, 1995.

Maier, Pauline. *From Resistance to Revolution: Colonial Radicals and the Development of American Opposition to Britain, 1765–1776*. New York: Vintage Books, 1974.

Malone, Dumas. *Jefferson and His Time, Vols. 1–6*. Boston: Little, Brown, 1948–1981.

Mapp, Alf Johnson. *Thomas Jefferson: A Strange Case of Mistaken Identity*. New York: Madison Books, 1987.

———. *Thomas Jefferson: Passionate Pilgrim*. Lanham: Madison Books, 1991.

Mayer, David N. *The Constitutional Thought of Thomas Jefferson*. Charlottesville: University Press of Virginia, 1994.

Mayo, Henry B. *Introduction to Democratic Theory*. New York: Oxford University Press, 1985.

McDonald, Forest. *The Presidency of George Washington*. New York: Norton, 1975.

McGaw, Judith A. *Early American Technology: Making and Doing Things from the Colonial Era to 1850*. Chapel Hill: University of North Carolina Press, 1994.

Microsoft Encarta Encyclopedia Standard, 2004. Redmond: Microsoft, 2004.

Mitchell, Broadus. *Alexander Hamilton*. New York: Oxford University Press, 1976.

Montesquieu, Charles. *The Spirit of the Laws*. Amherst: Prometheus Books, 2002.

Moore, Charles. *The Family Life of George Washington*. New York: Houghton Mifflin, 1926.

Morgan, Edmund Sears. *Benjamin Franklin*. New Haven: Yale University Press, 2003.

———. *The Birth of the Republic, 1763–89*. Chicago: University of Chicago Press, 1977.

———. *The Genius of George Washington*. New York: Norton, 1980.

———. *Inventing the People: The Rise of Popular Sovereignty in England and America*. New York: Norton, 1988.

Mount Rushmore National Memorial Brochure. Washington D.C.: United States Government Printing Office, 2002.

Ovason, David. *The Secret Architecture of Our Nation's Capitol: The Masons and the Building of Washington D.C.* New York: Harper Collins, 2000.

Oxford Thesaurus of English. New York: Oxford University Press, 2004.

Paine, Thomas. *Common Sense, Rights of Man, and Other Essential Writings of Thomas Paine*. New York: Signet Classic, 2003.

Peterson, Merrill D. *Thomas Jefferson and the New Nation*. Norwalk: Easton, 1987.

Phelps, Glenn A. *George Washington and American Constitutionalism*. Lawrence: University Press of Kansas, 1993.

Phillips, Kevin P. *Wealth and Democracy: A Political History of the American Rich*. New York: Broadway Books, 2002.

Plato. *Plato: Complete Works*. Ed. John M. Cooper and D.S. Hutchinson. Indianapolis: Hackett, 1997.

Randall, Henry Stephens. *The Life of Thomas Jefferson*. Freeport: Books for Libraries, 1970.

Randall, Willard Sterne. *George Washington: A Life*. New York: Henry Holt & Co., 1997

———. *Little Revenge: Benjamin Franklin and His Son*. Boston: Little, Brown, 1984.

Reuter, Frank Theodore. *Trials and Triumphs: George Washington's Foreign Policy*. Fort Worth: Texas Christian University Press, 1983.

Rhodehamel, John. *The American Revolution: Writings from the War of Independence*. New York: Library of America, 2001.

Ritter, Halsted Lockwood. *Washington as a Business Man*. New York: Sears, 1931.

Roberts, John Morris. *Ancient History: From the First Civilizations to the Renaissance*. New York: Oxford University Press, 2004.

———. *The New History of the World*. New York: Oxford University Press, 2003.

Rothbard, Murray Newton. *A History of Money and Banking in the United States*. Auburn: Ludwig Von Mises Institute, 2002.

———. *The Panic of 1819: Reactions and Policies*. New York: Columbia University Press, 1962.

———, and Leonard P. Liggio. *Conceived in Liberty, Vols. 1–4*. New Rochelle: Arlington House, 1975–1992.

Sachse, Julius Friedrich. *Benjamin Franklin as a Free Mason*. Philadelphia: New Era Printing Co, 1906.

———. *Franklin's Account with the "Lodge of Masons" 1731–1737, As Found Upon the Pages of His Daily Journal*. Philadelphia: Lippincott Press, 1899.

Schachner, Nathan. *Alexander Hamilton*. New York: T. Yoseloff, 1957.

Smith, Page. *John Adams*. Norwalk: Easton Press, 1988.

Smith, Richard Norton. *Patriarch: George Washington and the New American Nation*. Boston: Houghton Mifflin, 1993.

Stearns, Peter N. *The Encyclopedia of World History: Ancient, Medieval, and Modern, Chronologically Arranged, 6th Edition*. Boston: Houghton Mifflin, 2001.

Stein, Susan R. *The Worlds of Thomas Jefferson at Monticello*. New York: H.N. Abrams and the Thomas Jefferson Memorial Foundation, 1993.

Stetson, Charles Wyllys. *Washington and His Neighbors*. Richmond: Garrett and Massie, 1956.

Tacitus, Cornelius. *The Complete Works of Tacitus*. Ed. John Alfred Church and William Jackson Brodribb. New York: The Modern Library, 1942.

Taylor, Dale. *The Writer's Guide to Everyday Life in Colonial America*. Cincinnati: Writer's Digest Books, 1997.

Thacher, James, M.D. *Eyewitness to the American Revolution: The Battles and Generals As Seen by an Army Surgeon*. Longmeadow: Longmeadow Promotional, 1994.

Thomas Jefferson Digital Archive. Charlottesville: University of Virginia, 2005.

Tocqueville, Alexis de. *Democracy in America*. New York: Library of America, 2004.

Tunis, Edwin. *Colonial Living*. Baltimore: Johns Hopkins University Press, 1999.

Van Doren, Carl. *Benjamin Franklin*. Westport: Greenwood Press, 1973.

———. *Secret History of the American Revolution: An Account of the Conspiracies of Benedict Arnold and Numerous Others, Drawn from the Secret Service Papers of the British Headquarters in North America, Now for the First Time Examined and Made Public*. Clifton: A. M. Kelley, 1973.

Wall, Charles Cecil. *George Washington, Citizen-Soldier*. Mount Vernon: Mount Vernon Ladies' Association, 1988.

Wanniski, Jude. *The Way the World Works*. New York: Simon and Schuster, 1983.

Washington, George. *The Diaries of George Washington, 1748–1799, Vols 1–4*. New York: Houghton Mifflin, 1971.

———. *George Washington: Writings*. Ed. John H. Rhodehamel. New York: Library of America, 1997.

———. *The Papers of George Washington, Colonial Series*. Ed. W.W. Abbot. Charlottesville: University Press of Virginia, 1995.

———. *The Papers of George Washington, Revolutionary War Series*. Ed. Philander D. Chase. Charlottesville: University Press of Virginia, 2004.

———. *The Papers of George Washington, Confederation Series*. Ed. W.W. Abbot. Charlottesville: University Press of Virginia, 1997.

———. *The Papers of George Washington, Presidential Series*. Ed. Dorothy Twohig. Charlottesville: University Press of Virginia, 2005.

———. *The Writings of George Washington from the Original Manuscript Sources, 1745–1799*. Ed. John Clement Fitzpatrick. Washington D.C.: United States George Washington Bicentennial Commission, 1972.

Webster's Third International Dictionary of the English Language, Unabridged. Springfield: Merriam-Webster, 2002.

Wills, Garry. *Explaining America: The Federalist*. New York: Penguin Books, 2001.

———. *A Necessary Evil: A History of American Distrust of Government*. New York: Simon & Schuster, 1999.

Wood, Gordon S. *The Creation of the American Republic, 1776–1787*. Chapel Hill: University of North Carolina Press, 1998.

World Book Encyclopedia. Chicago: World Book, 2005.

Wright, Esmond. *Franklin of Philadelphia*. Cambridge: Belknap Press, 1986.

Zinn, Howard. *A People's History of the United States: 1492 to Present*. New York: New Press, 1997.